ON COASTS OF ETERNITY

On Coasts of Eternity
Jack Hodgins' Fictional Universe

Edited by

J.R. (Tim) Struthers

oolichan books
Lantzville, British Columbia
1996

Copyright © 1996 by J.R. (Tim) Struthers and the authors

No part of this publication may be reproduced, stored in a retrieval system, or transmitted, in any form or by any means, without prior permission of the publisher or, in the case of photocopying or other reprographic copying, a licence from CANCOPY (Canadian Copyright Licensing Agency), 6 Adelaide Street East, Suite 900, Toronto, Ontario, M5C 1H6.

Oolichan Books would like to thank E.J. Hughes, Pat Salmon, and the Dominion Gallery for permission to reproduce the cover painting "The West Coast Near Bamfield, BC, II" (oil on canvas, 1981, Dominion Gallery, Montreal) by E.J. Hughes.

Oolichan Books gratefully acknowledges the support received for its publishing program from the Canada Council's Block Grants program, the British Columbia Ministry of Small Business, Tourism and Culture, and the Department of Canadian Heritage.

Canadian Cataloguing in Publication Data

Main entry under title:

On coasts of eternity

Includes bibliographical references.
ISBN 0-88982-156-9

1. Hodgins, Jack, 1938- —Criticism and interpretation. I. Struthers, J.R. Tim, 1950-
PS8565.O3Z82 1996   C813'.54   C96-910279-8
PR9199.3.H54Z82 1996

Published by
Oolichan Books
P.O. Box 10
Lantzville, B.C.
Canada V0R 2H0

Printed on acid-free paper

Printed in Canada by
Best Book Manufacturers

For

Art Fidler and Doug Daymond

and other inspiring teachers like them

Contents

9   Introduction: What Lies Between the Spaces
       W.H. New

17   The Elements of Fiction: An Interview with Jack Hodgins (1977)
       Jack David

23   Hodgins at Last Collected
       Margaret Laurence

27   Jack Hodgins and the Island Mind
       David L. Jeffrey

38   A Writer's Reservoir: Jack Hodgins' Literary Manuscripts
       Lorna Knight

49   Jack Hodgins and the Resurrection of the World
       William Butt

66   Visionary Realism: Jack Hodgins, *Spit Delaney's Island*, and the Redemptive Imagination
       J.R. (Tim) Struthers

87   The Design of the Story: *The Invention of the World*
     Louis K. MacKendrick

108 Life on the Brink of Eternity: *The Resurrection of Joseph Bourne*
     Lawrence Mathews

128 A Crazy Glory: Jack Hodgins' Secular Allegory
     W.J. Keith

153 Visions and Revisions: An Interview with Jack Hodgins (1981)
     J.R. (Tim) Struthers

162 Fiction as Invasion: *The Barclay Family Theatre*
     Ann Mandel

170 Creatures of Clay: *The Barclay Family Theatre*
     Wayne Grady

178 More Shenanigans: An Interview with Jack Hodgins (1990)
     J.R. (Tim) Struthers

190 Hodgins' Houses of Words: *The Honorary Patron*
     and *Innocent Cities*
     JoAnn McCaig

216 The Stuff of Literature and the Stuff of Life:
     An Interview with Jack Hodgins (1995)
     J.R. (Tim) Struthers

236 A Checklist of Works by Jack Hodgins
     J.R. (Tim) Struthers

Introduction:
What Lies Between the Spaces

W.H. New

The first Jack Hodgins story I can recall reading was an untitled novel, which, if I remember accurately, was collectively and temporarily christened "Blackberry Wine". I know I thought the writing magnificent. At nineteen or twenty, having just discovered Empson, I found it dark with textures of Empsonian ambiguity and rich with echoes of Faulkner. Hodgins' talent already showed. What I failed to distinguish at the time was that the novel was richly *Faulknerian*, not just an echo of the American writer; it was a talented apprentice writer's able imitation, an exercise, which he himself considered practice, put aside, and grew beyond.

We are fortunate that he did, though by Canadian norms in the 1960s it was a long apprenticeship. Hodgins published occasional short stories, articles, and in the 1970s three anthologies; but several novels he wrote were all turned down—including an ebulliently comic one about a garbage collector, which was a sprightly promise of the stylistic and imaginative extravagance by which he was later to become known. Publishers were polite, but they refused to publish. The public, they thought, was not ready. In retrospect it is possible to interpret these rejections as signs of editorial timidity or regional conservatism, although neither reason need necessarily be accurate. Certainly (in the nationalist 1960s) fiction took on some standard patterns in Canada—there was the socially realistic portrait of the struggles of an ethnic minority, the elliptical experiment in literary form, and the confessional account of adolescent discovery—and these were patterns into which Hodgins' stories did not fit. Equally certainly, the world that Hodgins portrayed—apparently a domain of West Coast eccentrics—was unfamiliar in central Canada; perhaps also, from that perspective, it seemed peripheral.

The "central" issues of the nation at the time concerned the Centennial celebrations, the "Quiet Revolution" in Quebec, and the separateness of Canada from the United States' involvement in Viet Nam. In part by reflecting these interests, the publishing industry thrived. But Hodgins' work did not directly address the issue of national survival; perhaps like many others of his generation, he accepted his Canadianism as something he started with. At once he looked at life more locally, finding characters and stories around him, and more widely, finding that they allowed him to comment on the human condition at large. In a way, the island he lived on had more in common with the "island" of Quebec than continental Ontario did, and his characters had something of the same imaginative dimensions as those of Jacques Ferron and Roch Carrier. But this was not a widely shared appreciation. Hodgins remained unpublished.

Yet the publishers' rejections, instead of proving dispiriting, had the effect of making him more than ever faithful to his own perception of human experience. He read widely—moving from Faulkner, William Styron, Juan Ramon Jiménez, and Reynolds Price to Patrick White, Rudy Wiebe, Alice Munro, John Fowles, Margaret Laurence, and John Gardner—and he contrived to find time on weekends and in summer holidays to keep writing. As he continued to write, a borrowed idiom died away in his work, and what emerged was a voice clearly recognizable as his own. By the late 1970s, then, with three books appearing in rapid succession—the short story collection *Spit Delaney's Island* (1976), the novel *The Invention of the World* (1977), and the Governor General's Award-winning novel, *The Resurrection of Joseph Bourne* (1979)—Hodgins seemed to burst upon the literary scene in full bloom. This was an experienced writer, writing something "different", not an imitative apprentice. Journalists trumpeted the arrival of a major talent. Interviewers asked where he'd been. Readers sat back and enjoyed.

"Where he'd been", of course, was where he lived: Vancouver Island. He was born there on October 3, 1938, the son of a family that had been logging on the north end of the island for two generations; he grew up and went to school in Merville, near Courtenay; and then in 1956 he headed to Vancouver, to the University of British Columbia, for a stimulating course in creative writing from Earle Birney, and for the five-year course in teacher training, majoring in English and mathematics. At the end of that time, he married Dianne Child, also a teacher; they moved to Wellington, a village just north of Nanaimo. Hodgins taught, until 1979, at Nanaimo Senior Secondary School; and whatever time he had to spare, he used to write and to build a home for himself and his family. Over the next few years, though they lived in the same house, boundaries shifted and their address changed from Wellington, to Lantzville, to Nanaimo. The lot on Rutherford Road was closely wooded in arbutus, fir, and pine, with a glimpse of a view east across the Strait of Georgia to the mainland.

The setting speaks something of the man, for one recognizes in his life the need for privacy: for the kind of separateness that derives from independence, the kind that preserves the powers of observation, the kind that the imagination bridges to the rest of the world. But "privacy" does not mean "reclusion". After his books began to appear, he accepted positions as writer-in-residence at various Canadian universities, and he travelled to Ireland, Japan, Austria, Finland, and Australia (winning the Canada-Australia Literary Prize in 1985). Out of these ventures grew such stories as "The Lepers' Squint" and "The Sumo Revisions", collected in *The Barclay Family Theatre* (1981), and the novels *The Honorary Patron* (1987) and *Innocent Cities* (1990). Another trip to Australia led to the comic travel narrative *Over 40 in Broken Hill* (1992). And more was still to come. After two years teaching at the University of Ottawa (1981-83), he returned to the West Coast, moving to Victoria in 1984. He now teaches, half-time, in the Writing Department at the University of Victoria, where his work led to the publication of *A Passion for Narrative: A Guide for Writing Fiction* (1993).

It is not insignificant that both the lifestyle and the travels constitute celebrations of islands, but it is important to note that they do so without sacrificing the values of human community or human connection. "I'm fascinated", Hodgins says in a 1979 interview with Geoff Hancock, "with the space that separates people, that keeps them from overlapping. But while I'm interested in what makes people on this side of the water different from people in other places, I'm much more concerned with finding out what makes people the same anywhere" (35). His fiction emerges from his own landscape, but it does not thereby become "autobiographical". Nor does it insistently chart islands out of human behaviour; it tries instead to explore the inner territories of human experience, and in stories about the exaggerated lives of ordinary people, it deliberately blurs the edges of what it finds.

Just as his work does not define a region, region does not define his work. Setting is important in his stories, but as *setting* and as *metaphor*, not as the main subject; his aim in writing is not to record what it looks like to live in a place, but what it feels like. The emphasis shifts from the place to the people whose lives are partly shaped by place. People matter more than external place does—matter more even than "story" does—and central to his view of people is the moral dimension which he sees their lives to possess. Hence he accepts, as one of the tasks of an author, the challenge of giving formal shape to such meaning. In a 1978 interview with Gordon Morash, after observing that myth is "the history of dreams", Hodgins adds that writers whom he finds significant—Gardner, Fowles, contemporary South American novelists like García Márquez, Borges, and Vargas Llosa (as opposed to many "game-playing" North American writers)—have recognized "a moral responsibility the novelist has: that by creating fiction they're creating myth, and myths are what people live and die by" (17-18). That is, anything with such an impact on people must address the evils that constrain their lives, and must explain, if it can, the powers of good to serve them. It is an attitude that allows for satire, for idiosyncrasy, for puzzles and monumental marvels; and it allows for people's failure. But not for cynicism. Because people matter, and because even unlikeable people warrant some measure of understanding.

It is a view that the author's literary technique prevents from becoming sentimentalized, and perhaps for this reason critics have recurrently tried to demonstrate how the technique works. Statements like the one Hodgins made about myth—or his suggestion that he writes about character and the "mystery" behind character (Hancock 38), or his declaration that "every story is an experiment in magic" ("Experiment" 238)—invite critics to put labels on his fiction: such as "magic realism", a term borrowed from the visual arts and the South American literary tradition (Hancock 56-57). Labels, of course, tend to define any fiction unduly, to classify and enclose the kind of experience that of its nature defies classification and containment. At best they are tentative descriptions, attempts to come to terms with the kaleidoscopic literary form the author has adopted; but the order they suggest is really illusory. Hence for me here to call Hodgins' novels "anatomies" is to risk another distortion of his accomplishment. (As David L. Jeffrey observes in the essay collected in this volume, nobody owns "the real story".) But Hodgins' stories do have about them something of the literary "anatomy" form: they contain at heart an idea of good and evil, and they express it in a theme-and-variations pattern, with dialogues, catalogues, a digressive narrative, highly stylized characters, and a gently satiric but basically positive view of human society.

My point in making the observation is to reinforce a view that is recorded in various ways in the essays which follow: that Hodgins' work belongs to a very old tradition in storytelling, though it offers a highly contemporary instance of it. It does not spring whole from Faulkner or García Márquez. Hence it constitutes in its own right—by its own method, as it were—a reflection on the nature and force of tradition, particularly in a new world, particularly on a frontier edge where the environment, as Hodgins says, is *not* hostile, and where it is still possible, "if we desire, to strike off entirely on our own into private landscapes" ("Deeper" 1). That phrase "if we desire" is important. It leaves human experience in some measure still under human control and it underscores the author's repeated revelation of the comic possibilities of life. There is some point in stressing here, too, that his characters are created out of the realities of experience, and are exaggerated by the comic imagination, not invented through idle and irrational speculation. "Legends seem to grow quite naturally in Fanny Bay", begins one of his accounts ("Bus Griffiths" 37). Indeed they do. To meet his characters is to recognize people we already know (the "Island eccentrics" who are also us, as Margaret Laurence avers in the review collected in this volume), and to be forced on further acquaintance to admit that miracles and madnesses happen every day.

Like the notions of regionalism, private and local mythologies, literary context, moral commitment, and the textures of style, the distinction, in Hodgins' terms (Hancock 47), between "creation" (the *valid* activity of the imagination) and "invention" (the counterfeiting powers which it also possesses in abundance) constitutes a recurrent theme in the following discussions. But there are many differences among the essays as well, and they speak best for themselves.

W.J. Keith's essay engages with the sprightliness of Hodgins' work; it examines the connection between myth and the parody of myth-making, out of which Hodgins contrives an energetic world. It is at once a world of fantastic possibility and a world of artificial borders, over and through which the characters are repeatedly trying to see. Ann Mandel addresses the cultural politics of the stories in *The Barclay Family Theatre*—for example, those set in Ottawa, Ireland, and Japan. William Butt emphasizes the inevitability of the spaces and edges that occupy the world and that so concern the author. Referring to "The Lepers' Squint", Butt also shows how "walls" help artists to write, to preserve their separateness from their own work; and he stresses the religious and creative impulse that is involved in the constant construction (or "resurrection") of civilization. Commenting on *The Barclay Family Theatre*, Wayne Grady observes how the comic surfaces of Hodgins' art always hide a greater "truth" about humankind which it is the function of art to "reveal". J.R. (Tim) Struthers, too, affirms the redemptive capacities of Hodgins' art, with particular reference to two stories in *Spit Delaney's Island*. And JoAnn McCaig stresses the resistant, residual optimism of *The Honorary Patron* and *Innocent Cities*.

Hodgins himself defends the plain truth of what he writes, but other commentators emphasize the imaginative elements of his fiction. Louis K. MacKendrick writes of the "fabular soul" that animates the society of *The Invention of the World*; commenting on the balance Hodgins achieves between myth and mimetic realism, between the designed world of fantasy, the fluidity of personality, and the direction of history, MacKendrick shows how the shape of the novel and the actions of the characters in it constitute a coherent view of life. Referring to *The Resurrection of Joseph Bourne*, Lawrence Mathews also stresses the structural and philosophical balances of Hodgins' work: in it, light and darkness, the holy city and the earthly city, are both available to mankind; the word "bourne" means both "boundary" and "light". (The word was consciously chosen for its ambiguity, as a manuscript annotation, quoted by Lorna Knight, makes clear; one might add that it echoes the words "born" and "burn"—both river and fire—as well.) The way we live our lives, that is, can provide metaphors for expressions of eternity. How to understand this? As Hodgins declares (Hancock 47), and as Butt reiterates, everything is a metaphor for that which lies beyond it; the task with life, as with a work of art, is to seek not just shape but also significance.

As if the evidence of technical practice supplied by *A Passion for Narrative* were not enough, the Hodgins papers at the National Library of Canada further demonstrate the careful process of transformation—of planning and rewriting—that goes into the design of the writer's work.

Lorna Knight refers to the newspaper clippings and other found materials that turned slowly and painstakingly into *The Resurrection of Joseph Bourne*, for example, and to the author's notes to himself, in the midst of writing, about image and pattern, colour and plot. Writing about *The Honorary Patron* and *Innocent Cities*, moreover, JoAnn McCaig looks at the finished novels, demonstrating how the organization of lines and circles and language codes shapes effect, hence interpretation, hence "meaning". Family anecdote, utopian aspiration, historical event, personal allusion: all become the stuff of a Hodgins narrative, not just written *as* fiction, but written *into* it, so that the sources of a finished story might end up being uncertain, even to the writer. The relevance of story, nevertheless, becomes as clear as revelation to readers, even beyond the edge of island locales, for in the act of reading language they are asked to wrestle with language and they end up shaping the world anew.

These essays thus stress the moral centre of Hodgins' work, and the degree to which the morality of myth is embodied in the comic passages and the satiric form. They call our attention to the power of the imagination, the strength of compassion, and the author's willingness (and ability) to write entertainingly of such serious concerns. Indicating Hodgins' range, they offer an interim report on a writer still in midcareer. They therefore serve most of all to invite us back into Hodgins' stories, where the probable recurrently gives way to the possible: where a man's passion for a steam locomotive proves stronger than any other attachment; where a mythical Irish giant leads a religious group to Canada, only to find that a false idea of colonizing Eden cannot match the daily creative norms of the island frontier; where a fat woman founds a town, a shell of a woman rules it, and a sensuous woman redeems it; where a boy leaves home, only to find that family icons never lose their power to enchant; where distant realities are rewritten as "margins" in the language of the expanding Victorian Empire—and all that lies between. Hodgins' stories reveal an entire society, where life is fundamentally something to enjoy despite its spaces and its illusions. And perhaps the lies that fiction tells speak truths.

Works Cited

Hancock, Geoff. "An Interview with Jack Hodgins". *Canadian Fiction Magazine* 32-33 (1979-80): 33-63.

Hodgins, Jack. *The Barclay Family Theatre*. Toronto: Macmillan of Canada, 1981.

———. "Bus Griffiths: A Legend All Unknowing; Logger, Fisherman, Cartoonist, Painter and Writer—He Creates the World He Loves Best in His Works". *Westworld* July-Aug. 1980: 37-38, 41, 42-43, 44, 46.

———. "An Experiment in Magic". *Transitions II: Short Fiction; A Source Book of Canadian Literature*. Ed. Edward Peck. Foreword by Geoff Hancock. Vancouver: CommCept, 1978. 237-39.

———. *The Honorary Patron*. Toronto: McClelland & Stewart, 1987.

———. *Innocent Cities*. Toronto: McClelland & Stewart, 1990.

———. "Introduction: Deeper into the Forest". *The Frontier Experience*. Ed. Jack Hodgins. Themes in Canadian Literature. Toronto: Macmillan of Canada, 1975. 1-2.

———. *The Invention of the World*. Toronto: Macmillan of Canada, 1977.

———. *The Macken Charm*. Toronto: McClelland & Stewart, 1995.

———. *Over 40 in Broken Hill: Unusual Encounters in the Australian Outback*. Toronto: McClelland & Stewart, 1992.

———. *A Passion for Narrative: A Guide for Writing Fiction*. Toronto: McClelland & Stewart, 1993.

———. *The Resurrection of Joseph Bourne; or, A Word or Two on Those Port Annie Miracles*. Toronto: Macmillan of Canada, 1979.

———. *Spit Delaney's Island: Selected Stories*. Toronto: Macmillan of Canada, 1976.

Morash, Gordon. "Jack Hodgins: An Interview". *Pacific Northwest Review of Books* July-Aug. 1978: 16-18.

The Elements of Fiction:
An Interview with Jack Hodgins (1977)

Jack David

JD: To start off, a general question. How did you get started writing—where and when were your first short stories published?

JH: I started to write once I learned how to read. The first novel I wrote, I was so young that I had to get the baby-sitter to type it for me and I illustrated it with a beautiful redhead and a loaded pistol—I think it was a murder mystery. But I was just a little kid.

There has never been a time that I can remember when I didn't write. I kept it a secret of course, because I was ashamed of it. To let somebody else find out outside my family would have been like declaring to the whole world that I wanted to be a ballet dancer. And in a logging community you can imagine the response there would be to that.

So I've always written. And during my twenties wrote while I was building a house; while I was starting a family; while I was beginning a career as a teacher; in every spare minute I could get. And got very—got nowhere with it. You know, I had piles and piles of rejection slips like

---

First published in *Essays on Canadian Writing* 11 (1978). Reproduced, with revisions, by permission of Jack David and Jack Hodgins.

everyone else. When I was getting towards the end of my twenties, I felt that either I might as well quit and say this was just a childhood dream that didn't come true, or else I'd better darn well find out how to write. So I deliberately set about re-reading with a writer's eyes all of the people I admired to see how they did it. And read dozens and dozens of books on creative writing, and went through them gathering together every possible way of developing a character that anybody ever mentioned, and made a list. And after that I used every one of these techniques and sold that story. And I thought, well, I guess this is not completely wrong. I mean I've never done that since, but it proved to me that it's a good thing I had the humility to decide I'd better learn instead of just continuing to daydream. So I was twenty-nine when I sold my first short story—to an American magazine. I even sold one to an Australian magazine before the rejection slips stopped coming back from Canadian magazines. It wasn't until I'd had maybe twenty short stories published in magazines that a collection was accepted for publication.

JD: What do you do in the summer?

JH: Write.

JD: You said you wrote the first draft of *The Invention of the World* one winter, and the second draft the next winter.

JH: Let me explain the situation I seem to find myself in. I'm a high school teacher and I have been successful, lately, in getting a leave of absence in each year for one semester, which means five months off. So these five months and two months of summer holiday are seven months of writing for me. In the case of *The Invention of the World*, it was the summer to go to Ireland, and the fall and winter to write the first draft. Last year it was summer and fall working on the new book. I'm writing whenever I can.

JD: Symbolism. Teachers usually try to get students to read a lot of things into authors' books. Do you think that some of this is just what teachers themselves see in the books?

JH: Oh, no doubt that happens. But I'd like to think there is something that starts that off. You know, there will be clues in a story that make a teacher or a student or any reader start a sort of chain reaction of associated thoughts. I can't remember ever writing a story and thinking from the very beginning I am going to use such and such a symbol in it, but by the time I've got to the end of the first draft I'm aware that there are certain things I'm preoccupied with. There are certain images that recur and I start to think, well, maybe this story has implications beyond the lives of the people in it, in which case I will take advantage of the symbolic things that point in another direction. But they have to grow out of the story, they can't be imposed on it. I have to discover them myself. Usually it's by accident.

JD: In "Three Women of the Country" you refer to *The Tempest* frequently. There's reference to Caliban, and there's reference to Miranda and Prospero.

JH: Yes, there are several references there.

JD: They're there, and I had trouble convincing the class that they were there, that I wasn't making it up.

JH: Well, you weren't making it up, as you're probably happy to hear. *The Tempest* is my favourite Shakespearean play. The imagery of *The Tempest* is some of my favourite imagery and the theme of *The Tempest* comes closer to my heart than, I think, any play I've ever read, or seen. And so it seemed natural to borrow some of the images from it. The whole island mythology—how can someone who lives on Vancouver Island not respond to a play about a mythological island? It's talking about us. And I guess I'm arrogant enough to think that my island can become a sort of mythical island too and maybe stand for people everywhere. So it was quite deliberate.

JD: In "Separating" and "The Trench Dwellers" and "Three Women of the Country", you show people to be dull and backward, and partners appear to be mismatched. Is this your impression of the people on Vancouver Island, or is this your general attitude?

JH: [laughter] That is a loaded question! Even to answer it, is to accept the premise. No.

First, I don't consider my characters to be dull and backward. I'm one of them. I'm not an outsider looking at them and laughing at them and saying, oh, ho, ho, look at these funny people who live on this funny island. They're not funny to me at all, except where they share the same feelings that I have. When I laugh at them, I'm laughing at us, all of us. Especially at myself. I don't consider them dull. I find them fascinating. And that's the only reason I can write about them, because I want to find out what's behind the surface, to discover the mysteries that are hidden in all of them, no matter how dull they may seem on the surface. And as far as the mismatching goes, there's nothing deliberate about that either, except that it's more fun, I suppose, to write about people where there are tensions. To write about a beautiful, happy marriage would be a wonderful thing to do, but you would be doing a different thing altogether. It would be a story about the marriage, rather than the individual. You can tell more about a person, or a character rather, by showing him in contrast, rather than by showing him in a team situation.

JD: Why was Stella called Stella?

JH: I'm sorry if you're looking for some symbolic reason. It just seemed the right name for her. Perhaps association with women who are actually called Stella, who seem to be— Well, Stella is a *bony* word, you know, with the t and the l's. It's a bony person's name. So that's the only reason. I think.

JD: What about Phemie then? What about her last name being Porter, the same as the other family?

JH: There's no connection between the two last names—except maybe subconsciously—although the name Phemie, or Euphemia, was quite deliberate. I did want a name that had something to do with the ethereal, the poetic. Porter of course is the person who carries things and she is the woman who kind of carries Spit through this rough time. So that name— Naming is very, very important to me. I can't get my hands on a character until I know the character's name, and it has to be just exactly the right name. Once I've got it, there's no way I can change a character's name unless my editor twists my arm, and that can only happen at the last moment when it doesn't matter to me anymore because the book, or story, is already alive. But while I'm writing it, I can't change the person's name.

JD: The same thing for place names? Like Cut Off?

JH: Quite deliberate, yes. This originates partly from an uneasiness about using real place names. When you live on an island and you're writing about an island, it's a pretty small community and to say that such and such a person lived in Nanaimo or Courtenay or Cumberland is limiting yourself. Everybody on that island knows that there is no hotel on that corner in Nanaimo where you put a hotel, so I will either avoid the name altogether or else make up a new one.

I usually avoid the name for the place where the main people live, and just use a name for the outlying districts. I don't think too often people think of their home as having a name. I think it's just "home".

JD: About point of view—in "Spit Delaney's Island" and "Separating" you change who is doing the speaking. Is that deliberate and why did you do it?

JH: There are some situations where you feel—where you just feel that this is the right way to do it. I actually started to write the second story in the third person, and it didn't feel right. I kept having to force myself to write it. And whenever I find myself feeling that way, that it's, you know, that it's an effort to sit down and write the next page of the story, I think there's something wrong. If it's an effort for me to write it, how can I expect anybody to want to read it? So I backed off and said in order to keep my own interest alive, I'm going to have to come at it from a completely different angle—something I haven't done before.

First person point of view is not usually the one I'm most comfortable with. So this time I'm going to use the first person point of view. Let me see if I know Spit well enough to tell it from inside him. And as soon as I started that, I realized it was the right thing for me to do. Because it came. I didn't have to create that story. I just had to listen to it.

JD: And in "Three Women of the Country" who is speaking is not always clear. We see things through Mrs. Wright's mind; we see her impressions of things; and we see other things which appear to be—well, when she's called a mop, for example, or when her hair is described as a nest, we weren't sure that she thought of these things, that she saw herself that way. There are two levels of narration going on.

JH: Yes, there are two levels of narration. In fact there are more than that because I've got the three points of view all contradicting each other. It becomes a complicated thing. And if I had thought about it ahead of time, I probably would never have been able to write the story. But the point of view in each of the separate sections is the limited omniscient; that is, I'm looking down like a god, and I know everything that Mrs. Wright thinks in part one, but I don't know what anybody else is thinking. So I've got Mrs. Wright's thoughts, and I've got the omniscient narrator's thoughts, but I don't have anybody else's. Then I switch over to Charlene in the second part, and I no longer know what Mrs. Wright thinks, but the reader remembers, I hope. So that I've got all these various layers complicating the web of the points of view.

JD: We had a discussion about what we thought happened to Mrs. Starbuck's son. What do you think happened?

JH: I got a phone call one evening, a few months back, from a woman who lives in Nanaimo, and she said, "Sir, you're the Mr. Hodgkins or Hodgson or whoever that wrote that book?"
"Yes."
"I enjoyed it, but could you tell me what happened to that boy at the end of the story? Is he still running free on the Island or has somebody taken him in and looked after him?"
And I said, "I'm sorry, Madam, I don't know."
Then there was this long silence and I could hear her thinking, "You stupid idiot, if you don't know, who does?"
But let me tell you, even though I don't know, and I really don't, I wouldn't be the slightest bit surprised to turn the corner some day and find him running down the road towards me. Because that kind of thing has happened to me before.

Hodgins at Last Collected

Margaret Laurence

In the early days of the *Journal of Canadian Fiction*, there was a column at the back of the publication which now strikes me as having been slightly peculiar. Somebody, each issue, would be sent the proofs and would do a critical commentary. After readers had perused the issue, they could turn to the back to be told what to think of it. Well, sensibly, the custom was soon dropped. I, as one of the *Journal*'s board members, agreed to do this assessment for, I think, the second issue, in which there was a story called "Three Women of the Country". It was by a young writer I had never heard about before. His name was Jack Hodgins, and he was from British Columbia. I wrote in my commentary that this was a fantastic story and that we would certainly be hearing more of this writer. Since then, I have read some of Hodgins' stories in such publications as *The Canadian Fiction Magazine*, *Capilano Review*, and *Wascana Review*. Although he has had stories published in various places, his work has remained much better known in B.C. than in the rest of the country. From time to time I wondered when on earth this state of affairs would

First published in *The Globe and Mail* [Toronto] 8 May 1976. Reproduced by permission of Jocelyn Laurence.

be altered, and when a collection of his stories would appear. It is, of course, well known that many publishers (despite the obvious proof to the contrary provided by Oberon's highly successful collections) feel about as welcoming towards a volume of stories as they would to a sudden attack of paper-eating termites in their warehouses. Now it is good to be able to report that a Hodgins collection has at last appeared. And a remarkable one it is.

In "Separating", we are shown Spit Delaney, whose wife is about to leave him. He lives in an ex-gas-station on the Island (Spit's Island, is, of course, Vancouver Island as well as the inner one) and he has worked for many years in the local paper mill, running his beloved Old Number One, a steam locomotive. When the mill phases out the steam engine, it also phases out Spit's life. His marriage with Stella has been fine; they have two nearly grownup kids. But when his meaning in life is questioned, Spit has to reassess himself and his entire view of life. He's not a verbal man. He takes his wife and kids on a world tour, with his life's savings, but he also takes a cassette tape of Old Number One, roaring and groaning, and plays it in unlikely places. Stella and the kids are embarrassed and outraged. Finally, when they are in Ireland, Stella throws the tape recorder onto the street. They return to the Island, but the good marriage is no more—and perhaps never was.

In "Three Women of the Country", the principal characters are Milly Wright, who is strong, self-righteous, and snoopy; Charlene Porter, who is very young and who has been brought up to believe that evil cannot exist; and Edna Starbuck, whose husband died some while back and who has been farming the land as though she were a man. The interaction among these women, and the revelation that Edna Starbuck's anguish has been the fact that she bore a brain-damaged child who has been, for fourteen years, hidden away from the world, on her husband's insistence—all this is dealt with subtly and with great dramatic power.

"The Trench Dwellers", dealing with family relationships and hassles, is good for its sense of place and of smothering community, but comes off less well, I think, than most of these stories, as does "At the Foot of the Hill, Birdie's School", which deals in a bizarre and almost surrealistic way with a young man who comes down from a mountain where he has lived in total isolation in an ex-commune with the Old Man, and who now wants to learn corruption and (perhaps) death. For my taste, Hodgins is best when he gives us characterizations of those Island eccentrics who are, of course, us as well. "Birdie's School" reminds me a bit of Flannery O'Connor, but without O'Connor's assurance. The symbolism seems somewhat heavy and forced.

In "The Religion of the Country", an expatriate Irishman runs a bookshop on the Island, goes back to Ireland to check on his old mother's decline, and is horrified that she, a Protestant, finally becomes a Catholic in a Catholic land, and is looked after by kindly Sisters of the faith. He goes back to the Island and enters the real estate business—they have both taken on the religion of the country. Told thus baldly, the story may seem facile, but it isn't. On the contrary, the characterizations are strong and complex and, as with all of Hodgins' work, there is a large element of ironic humour amid the sometimes grotesque events.

"By the River" is a touching and finally quite chilling story, about a young woman who goes to meet her husband at the train—they have chosen to live in an isolated area of B.C., and they haven't had much luck. We get the story from Crystal's view, nearly all the way through. Only at the end do we learn that her husband won't be on the train, for he is dead. In "Other People's Troubles", Lenore Miles, very strong within herself, goes out to listen to the anguish of other people, in a B.C. lumber community where forest fire and accidents are constant threats. She takes her young son, Duke, along with her on one such trip, and he learns a lot about human pain, enough, in fact, to make him the supportive force when his father is dreadfully damaged by a falling log and when his mother, who has been the pillar of strength, herself now needs strength.

"After the Season" takes place in an Island tourist camp, a small one run by Hallie and Morgan, who are not married and who, indeed, barely speak to one another during the season, when they play the strict roles of employer and employee. After the season, however, they spend the winter together in Morgan's shack, after a ritual mating ceremony in which they both pretend this has never happened before. This courtship serves their sense of propriety. The arrival of a stranger, who is stranded on their beach and in no hurry to leave, disrupts all this and brings evil into their lives, like the snake into Eden. Shame comes to Hallie, and anger to Morgan, even though both suspect that the stranger-intellectual ought not to have this power of corrupting their sense of themselves and each other. I don't wish to give away the ending. Suffice it to say that this is a strange and moving story of primeval things.

The title story, placed at the end, brings us back to Spit Delaney, a first-person narrative which succeeds extremely well, Spit being a man who has many questioning thoughts, and who cannot communicate them. He meets, in an odd way, Phemie Porter, who is a weird-looking woman poet, a person who perceives him truly. In talking with Phemie, and in trying (in his almost inchoate way) to communicate with her, Spit discovers that his ex-wife, Stella, has done something so terrible he can hardly believe it. He has not played the cassette of Old Number One since Stella broke his tape recorder in Ireland. Now he borrows a tape recorder and begins to play the cassette for Phemie, only to discover that Stella has taped over the locomotive sounds with messages (and yes, some of them are even justified) to Spit. Old Number One's voice is gone forever. Phemie tries to tell him that the real voices are forever in the head. But it's not all that simple. Spit can only accept her comfort and wisdom at his own distance.

These stories, at their best, contain an impressive ability to convey individual human beings in all their uniqueness and nuttiness, and an ability to convey a sense of place—that Island which is both a vivid geographical place and an island of the spirit.

Work Cited

Hodgins, Jack. *Spit Delaney's Island: Selected Stories*. Toronto: Macmillan of Canada, 1976.

Jack Hodgins and the Island Mind

David L. Jeffrey

Because the centre of Hodgins' geographical world is his native community, and because the grotesque extravagance of his characters might seem plausible only in such a place, one could extend the tempting analogy with Faulkner or Flannery O'Connor and simply categorize him as a gifted regional writer. Indeed, he is, as W.J. Keith has noted, "a regional writer in the most profound sense of that term: he transforms his local backyard into an image of the whole created universe" (31). But, like other Canadian writers of his generation (Blais, Wiebe, Kroetsch, Carrier), Hodgins is, in fact, also a subcultural writer. The distinction is not so subtle as it might seem. The regional writer's work is imbued with particular landscape, manners, colloquial speech, and local tradition. Such a writer makes a microcosm from the local world and so translates it to the world at large. The subcultural writer adds to these features his community's prepossessing sense of contest with the outside

---

First published in *Book Forum* 4 (1978). Rpt. (revised and expanded) as "Jack Hodgins (1938-)". *Canadian Writers and Their Works*. Ed. Robert Lecker, Jack David, and Ellen Quigley. Fiction Ser. Vol. 10. Toronto: ECW, 1989. Reproduced by permission of ECW Press.

world and strives to articulate the community members' desire for peculiar magic or, as Maggie, the adolescent heroine of *The Invention of the World* puts it, their essential "difference". "'Different from what?'" asks Wade, her quasi-cousin, recalcitrant companion, and, years later, last husband. "'Different from *them*. Different from me'", she replies. "'Different'" (146/186). The regional factor is inescapably a material element of his expression, but motive in the subcultural writer is often shaped by the wider struggle around him for differentiation. In Hodgins' writing, the drive for differentiation is less to divide Vancouver Island itself from the rest of the province or the country than to distinguish its rural community values from urban values. He resists domination by any pattern of consensus and expresses discomfort with critical judgement that insists upon universal conformity to categories of so-called normal reality even as it purports to champion freedom of expression for the autonomous ego.

If Hodgins is more interesting and accessible than some subcultural writers working out of the Canadian mosaic, it is partly because the subcultural proclamation to which Vancouver Island offers so extravagant a paradigm naturally occasions in his work a species of historical cartoon by which a much wider contemporary psychosis may be vividly dramatized. The island to which Hodgins invites us on his mythic ferry boat is not so much a state of nature or civilization as it is a modern and especially North American state of mind. Here is a kind of reserve of lost causes, misty nostalgia for a tarnished and compromised Europe, thoroughly mixed up with innumerable backyard versions of the original American dream, and set in a place where history has been condensed and motives and patterns made more visible (and usually far more interesting) by the force of particular extremes. What Hodgins writes about is the Island Mind itself, its bizarre dreams, its truncated perspectives on the world, its frenetic ambivalence about history, its flight from the world—above all its unending pursuit of the private mythology—but what he mirrors is the frustrated questioning of a whole frontier-less continent now increasingly turned in upon itself and unable to discern where mythology stops and reality begins. "*Where is the dividing line?*" asks Spit Delaney, the "separated" man, suddenly forced to experience his separateness, but not necessarily its meaning (7/14).

The form of Spit's question may not be unlike questions in the mind of many of Hodgins' early readers. But it is surely a question regularly formalized in some of Hodgins' own favourite works of fiction and philosophy. In fact, one begins to understand here why reading Conrad's *Lord Jim* is an annual ritual for him. In its disturbing preoccupation with the possibility of an alternative and untestable reality which counters the apparently real, and in its profound exploration of the island of the mind, the concerns of *Lord Jim* are not so far apart from the *a posteriori* questions of *Spit Delaney's Island*. But in Spit's questions it is not a Conradian or Aristotelian sequence that we read. The questioning is Socratic:

> *Where is the dividing line?*
> ....
> "Between what and what?"
> ....
> *Between what is and what isn't.* (7-8/14)

And in the opening story of this book, it is actually the deserting wife Stella, who, as her name suggests, is the approximate Platonist. When Spit, mournfully referring to the loss of his steam locomotive, calls it a "'real'" thing, she retorts dismissively: "'The only things you can say that about ... are the things that people can't touch, or wreck. Truth is like that, I imagine, if there is such a thing'" (20/28). The condemnation of Spit's mother-in-law is more extreme: "'All a mirage!' she shrieked, and looked frightened by her own words" (20/29). For Spit, as for the reader, Stella's words are provocative, but not an answer. Reality seems at least somewhat contingent upon what we can touch, taste, hear, feel, and see with our ordinary eyes. We stand on the last beach with Spit Delaney in unanswered confusion: "There was no magic here. No traffic, no transformations" (17/25). For the real division is within, the boundary reached, not the real border at all. Separation occurs as often as not because one is standing on the line itself, unable to cross over to anything that will give meaning back to our history or that will interpret life. Like other characters in an apocalyptic age, Hodgins' personalities look for a conclusion they can believe in, some dream which could put time and the world back together. Unable to find such a form outside themselves, many of them—each in their own peculiar way—are driven to invent a universe in the private world, an island, an island within an island, an island in the mind.

Hodgins endeavours not to permit himself such a retreat. The problem for his characters is locating personal reality in the larger context;

for the author, it is not in the singularity of the self, but in the mutuality of personal perspectives that the theme and issue of his work are sketched. The line between reality and mythology is, he argues, impossible to determine from within a solipsism. If we could construct it in a more complete and yet practical way, as that same line between Self and Other, then, he suggests, certain real frontiers might be recognized and, perhaps, mutually crossed. Among other things, Hodgins here delineates his own basic authorial stance as that of a reader among readers.

Writing out of an isolationist subculture to an audience for whom isolation is powerfully attractive, Hodgins' perspective on this attraction can seem as superficially sympathetic as the Paul Simon and Art Garfunkel lyrics his ferry worker and historian Becker sings in *The Invention of the World*: "I'd rather be a sparrow than a snail" (ix/7). But his characterization is as ironically critical, however Chaucerian and gentle, as that other Paul Simon lyric: "I am a rock, I am an island". The invention of the world is, for Hodgins, a psychological fact of contemporary life to which Vancouver Island offers an unblushing advertisement. But such invention can be blatant evasion too—can contain a terrible lie.

Readers of *Spit Delaney's Island* laugh easily with Hodgins at the astonishing hilarity afforded by the spectacle of ordinary mortals in pursuit of a perfect cosmos, but readers also have to confront moments of sharp discomfort, vivid dramatizations of the personal agony Hodgins portrays as bred by evasion, failure, and a disturbing lack of communal vision. One of his observer-characters, in a barely tolerant and casual condescension, exclaims of a neighbour woman careening towards her in panicked distress: "My God. . . . If you could only see yourself" (25/35). Hodgins' world is peopled with moderns who see little of what they look at, outside or in. For Hodgins himself, accurate vision can only be achieved by first getting what is inside out, whether in the pursuit of self-knowledge or merely in the achievement of perspective on a work of art in progress. Commenting on the writing of "Three Women of the Country" from *Spit Delaney's Island,* he illustrates something of the process and, perhaps, the final balance of vision he strives to achieve:

> It was not until I had nearly finished writing the story that I began to see what it was about—or one of the things it was about. I seemed to be having a look at three people with different concepts of reality: one who believed in only what is seen; one who believed in only what is not seen; and one who had no notion at all of what she be-

lieved (except that she appeared to be the slave of other people's will). I'm glad I didn't know from the beginning what I was up to or I might have had a difficult time keeping the three women from becoming types or symbols. It is important for me that the theme of a story finds its own way out, that it be an unselfconscious part of every word in the story without dictating its direction. I would prefer to put my energies into the job of making the characters seem alive, since all stories—whatever their individual themes—have the same purpose: to explore what it is like to be a human being and alive in this world. ("Experiment" 238)

In Hodgins' stories, initiation from adolescent into adult life is not, for example, the cliché of sexual initiation, but rather an initiation into interpersonal reality, into another's point of view. Even life's losers, like Mrs. Bested, the motel keeper in the story "Spit Delaney's Island", however blatantly unattractive, often have a truth to tell. Usually, in fact, it is in the lives of such persons that the necessary truths turn up. The critique of Spit's misproportioned affection for "real" things—material realities, especially his beloved steam locomotive—is in that instance best afforded by the unpleasant commentary of his departing wife Stella. In the same vein, Hodgins' implicit critique of the false realism of documentary narrative (cf. Becker, the failed professor with his tape recorder in *The Invention of the World*) or of any pretended omniscient perspective (cf. the *Je regarde autour de moi* of Mrs. Wright, the newspaper correspondent from Cut Off, in "Three Women of the Country"), while not extreme, is nonetheless firm.

Hodgins' short stories have a way of anticipating the reader's prejudices: often we are driven to a dismissive cynicism when we encounter characters who are advocates for that at which they themselves have failed; it can invite an easy and self-congratulatory reflex (as in "The Trench Dwellers"). Hodgins, in everything from his avoidance of omniscient narrative overview to his Chaucerian respect for the flotsam and jetsam of creation, does not expect truth to come down from some academic mountain; nor does he like to offer us prophetic characters as "absolute" voices in his stories. In this way, his sense of the real shows not merely the continuing impact of his early intensive reading of Plato, but, beginning in the early 1960s, the impact of reading Mary Baker Eddy and other writers working in a basically neo-Platonic religious tradition. That is to say if his structure of ideas is not Aristotelian, it is not pure Plato either. If he usually avoids the precise formulation of his Mr. Porter in "Three Women of the Country" that "every human being is a spiritually perfect idea" (44/57), or of Webster Traherne's Old Man in "At the Foot of the Hill, Birdie's School" that "time was meaningless and God was All" (137/164), he regularly translates the general precept, protesting that to realize the self one must first love creation, love others. Otherwise, the trip to Eden (or Vancouver Island) is not likely ever to be quite the voyage of discovery the wishful pilgrim has in mind.

Two of Hodgins' stories, mirror images to each other, make this central point dramatically, one in a comic, the other in a tragic vein. The first is "At the Foot of the Hill, Birdie's School", an account of a boy's emergence from a natural, nearly Edenic mountain isolation to pursue his bookish fantasy of a cowboy-outlaw-hero existence. The characterization is flawless, the central encounter with reality a masterpiece of the writer's craft. In it, Webster Traherne (cf. Stephen Vincent Benét's "The Devil and Daniel Webster") comes upon a West Coast free school, into which he is dragged by a suspiciously maternal and whore-of-Babylonish proprietress (Birdie) and then cast upon the further tender mercies of the devilish Mr. McIntosh, who teaches a class in "love". (Webster is evidently his first student.) The first lesson in love embodies its own analysis:

> Mr. McIntosh pulled a cluster of grapes out of a paper bag, ripped a handful free and tossed just one at Webster. "If I loved even so much as that one single grape," he said, "I would also have to love God. And then where would I be?" Webster ate the grape and held out his hand for more.
>
> "I didn't come all the way down out of the mountains for fresh fruit," he said. "You'll have to try a little harder than that."
>
> So Mr. McIntosh waited until Webster was asleep on his narrow cot in the back-corner room and hung a hand-painted sign on the wall beside him. Sometime in the night Webster awoke and lit a match to get a decent look at the big white patch on the wall. It said:
>
> WARNING
> If you express even the tiniest bit of love
> you will be a part of him. . . . BEWARE
>
> Webster blew out the match and turned away. (145/172-73)

The mirroring story to this comes as one axis of the x-shaped plot in *The Invention of the World*. In this novel, the other axis is a contemporary story, a quixotic romance between a kind of logging-camp Mamma named Maggie and Wade, a jaded tourist-trapper who has built his castle out of glass bottles. The comparison tale with "At the Foot of the Hill, Birdie's School", however, is the novel's counter-stroke, the mythic history of Donal Keneally and his captive Revelations Colony of Truth. It relates to the history of Vancouver Island in the manner of some of Hodgins' early stories, in this case calling up the actual, yet fantastic history of Brother Twelve, a crackpot religious colonist who claimed to be waiting out the end of the world with his band of self-willed slaves on Valdes Island, killing or copulating among his subjects as he chose. Local history is alluded to specifically, then adapted, so that the mythic roots of Vancouver Island are traced back to an Irish grotesque who is rumoured to have been fathered on an idiot girl by a great black bull. The Taurus-Europa myth here provides a correlative for the comparably bizarre actual history. The offspring, Keneally, prodigious in all respects, comes to Vancouver Island, conquers everyone from loggers to the wife of the mayor of Victoria, leaves the city in a shambles, and then goes back to Ireland to hypnotize his whole former village into following him to the promised land. On his way, he swindles them out of money and personal integrity alike, and through their subjection builds his own island kingdom, the "Revelations Colony of Truth". He becomes, in so doing, a larger Mr. McIntosh, a manically successful *Übermensch* who preaches that the only reality is material and that the only god is the man who can master it, namely himself. He becomes, accordingly, a "god-man", an incarnation of material egocentrism so perverse as to horrify.

Yet it is Hodgins' point that between the manic egocentrism of Donal Keneally or Mr. McIntosh and the very much more plausible egocentrism of his more mundane characters—even Spit Delaney—there is only the thinnest and most confusing of distinctions, that between manipulative self-advocacy and unacknowledged selfish reflex. In the carefully x-shaped plot of *The Invention of the World* both types of character create island history; each pursues a private mythology and each is a manifestation of the island mind. All face, therefore, the same peril, and the same need for crossing the "dividing line", for making choices which involve ultimate and communal values.

In this context one sees in Hodgins, as in Flannery O'Connor, for example, or in Rudy Wiebe, a writer of evident religious concerns. Yet part of the appeal of his books is that they pursue religious questions without being "religious". There is no sense of any doctrinaire perspective: there are touches of Christian Science, Alan Watts, and a kind of old-fashioned Christian humanism, but Hodgins, inasmuch as he is concerned with spiritual issues, would be Chaucerian not Presbyterian, catholic not Catholic.

Hodgins shows us a subculture that cannot do without religious phenomena, whether of the sort presented by Brother Twelve, or, as Keneally's last wife puts it, "'some sort of magic'" (244/321), whether it be an electronic gadget, the Second Coming, a world government that would solve everything, science, medicine, or sensitivity therapy—whatever faith or antifaith structure might be imagined. What animates all of these options for Hodgins' characters is that they offer some sense of personal control, some semblance of defence against confusing and insecure times. Among his books, *The Invention of the World* particularly bears the stamp of literature written for an apocalyptic age and culture, one which is afraid that the end might well come upon it before there can be any real sense of personal conclusion. It records, therefore, the yearning for a sense of story with conclusive personal meaning, and the elaboration of defences around that meaning. It records also the contemporary desire to flee history, the script already written, and to become fully the author of one's own mythology, to escape creation for invention. But the book says more: that not even islanders escape history and that no individual really writes his own script. Becker, Hodgins' note-taking Marlow, tells the reader:

> Trust me or not, believe what you want, by now the story exists without us in air. I am not its creator, nor is any one man; I did not invent it, only gathered its shreds and fragments together from the half-aware conversations of people around me, from the tales and hints and gossip and whispered threats and elaborate curses that float in the air like dust. Listen. (69/93)

Nobody ever really invents a successful private mythology, says Hodgins, and nobody owns the story—not even his own story—all temptation and fantasy to the contrary. The community is not only the subject of the novel, its "hero", but even, in a sense, its author.

What is the real story? Where was it written? Where can it be read? Hodgins prods his readers with these questions at every step. Becker, the tape-recording documentary narrator, whose control on the diversity of stories is more complete, explicitly disclaims possession. Yet he offers hints concerning the relationship between story and life, creation and creativity. Picking up a Bible, Becker reflects on Creation:

> A strange story, he said, if you'd read it. It has two beginnings. The first, a single chapter, would have us all made in the image of God, perfect spiritual creatures. Then someone else came along, started it all over again, and had us all made out of clay. The rest of the story shows a lot of people trying to get back to that first beginning, back before the mist and the clay. You get all the way up to nearly the end of the book before you meet the man who knows how to manage it.
>
> Magic? she'd asked him, but he shook his head. Well, magic is what people want, she said.... (244/320-21)

Later, flying in over the Strait of Georgia, Becker, whose own reality is in note taking more than anything, reflects on the possibility that there might be a more convincing reality:

> *Maggie happier. Words only nibble at reality, don't really touch it, can't really burn through to it. Symbols not much better. If words won't do, and symbols fail, maybe only the instinct; some kind of spiritual sense, can come close. All we can trust. Maybe all our lives that instinct is in us, trying to translate the fake material world we seem to experience back into pre-Eden truth, but we learn early not to listen. Instead, we accept the swindle, eat it whole.*
>
> *Learned strange lesson in Canadian history from a Cork man on a street in Skibbereen.* "If Wolfe hadn't defeated Montcalm," *he said, and touched two fingers on my forearm.* "If Wolfe hadn't defeated Montcalm and brought the open Bible to the land, your country by now would have become as corrupt as South America." (319-20/413-14)

But the documentary realism of Becker's notebook imagination suddenly carries him back to his academic's desire for a more definitive, controllable world: "*Back to editing Lily's tapes tomorrow*" (320/414), he concludes his text, evading the implications of his own reflections.

Becker, unlike the reader, is of course unable to see himself as a kind of Charon who ferries men over the forgetfulness of the Strait of Georgia to an island which can be hell as quickly as paradise, and it is consistent that in his documentary mentality he does not develop many of his own thoughts; indeed, he is ultimately not even particularly attractive as a character. But like homely character after homely character in Hodgins' fiction, he often grasps the truth of a moment with unsuspected clarity. It is Becker whose structuring analysis completes that part of the history—the lives of Wade, with his one-horse apocalypse, and Maggie, with her erratic and undefined energy—which could not, in living actuality, be consummated. By his challenge, he forces them to choose against invention and for creation (316/409). And so the story comes to the only kind of conclusion which Hodgins will postulate, a point of "overlapping", to apply his own term (Hancock 35), where the dividing line melts away and personal reality, such as it is, is shared almost sacramentally.

The line between possession and affection must surely be the most difficult divide of them all. And, as in its more subtle incarnation, the difference between definition and identification, it is here that Hodgins brings us to his basic boundary, the whole wobbly line between mythology and life, between invention and creation. *The Invention of the World*, from "The Eden Swindle" through "Pilgrimage" to "Second Growth", is a book about the real nature of our original malady, fleeing under the distant trees, hoping to make somewhere our own private garden. For Hodgins, the story of our present island is not therefore a chronicle of mere concupiscence, but rather a tale of our rejection of creation in favour of seeming to author our own invention.

A Note On The Texts

Page references to the original hardcover editions of *Spit Delaney's Island* and *The Invention of the World*, published by Macmillan of Canada, and to the New Canadian Library paperback editions of these works, published by McClelland & Stewart, are provided following the quotations.

Works Cited

Benét, Stephen Vincent. "The Devil and Daniel Webster". *The Best Short Stories of the Modern Age*. Ed. Douglas Angus. Rev. ed. New York: Fawcett Premier Books, 1974. 202-16.

Conrad, Joseph. *Lord Jim*. 1900. Ed. Robert Kimbrough. 3rd ed. Norton Critical Editions. New York: W.W. Norton, 1988.

Hancock, Geoff. "An Interview with Jack Hodgins". *Canadian Fiction Magazine* 32-33 (1979-80): 33-63.

Hodgins, Jack. "An Experiment in Magic". *Transitions II: Short Fiction; A Source Book of Canadian Literature*. Ed. Edward Peck. Foreword by Geoff Hancock. Vancouver: CommCept, 1978. 237-39.

———. *The Invention of the World*. Toronto: Macmillan of Canada, 1977. Afterword by George McWhirter. The New Canadian Library. Toronto: McClelland & Stewart, 1994.

———. *Spit Delaney's Island: Selected Stories*. Toronto: Macmillan of Canada, 1976. Rpt. as *Spit Delaney's Island*. Afterword by Robert Bringhurst. The New Canadian Library. Toronto: McClelland & Stewart, 1992.

Keith, W.J. "Jack Hodgins's Island World". Rev. of *The Barclay Family Theatre*, by Jack Hodgins. *The Canadian Forum* Sept.-Oct. 1981: 30-31.

A Writer's Reservoir:
Jack Hodgins' Literary Manuscripts

Lorna Knight

Looking through criticism about the fiction of Jack Hodgins, a reader can't help but be struck by the recurrence of terms like mythic realism, mythologizing, and magic. Hodgins' thematic concerns, structural virtuosity, and allegorical implications have intrigued critics and reviewers since the publication of his first book, *Spit Delaney's Island*, in 1976. Hodgins is a writer, these critics agree, whose ideas must be taken seriously. But who is Jack Hodgins? Apart from biographical dictionaries and interviews, a writer's papers often help the curious find out. However, the literary papers of Jack Hodgins, housed at the National Library of Canada, are fascinating in terms of how much they both reveal and conceal. Selected and sorted by Hodgins himself, these papers reflect a deliberate self-construction of Hodgins the creator and reflect his intense passion for narrative.[1]

When the literary papers of contemporary writers are acquired by an archival institution, writers include just about everything that could be of interest to future scholars and readers. Correspondence, diaries, and memorabilia all supplement manuscripts of written works and bring a personal dimension to a writer's papers, the kind of primary evidence which makes literary biographers hum. Although restrictions on access may delay revelation about personal lives, there is an understanding or assumption that personal and professional selves are intricately and irrevocably connected and that knowing something of both may be a prerequisite to understanding a writer's work.

Not so with the papers of Jack Hodgins. When the National Library of Canada acquired a first accession of Hodgins' papers, correspondence between Hodgins and Curator Claude Le Moine, dated April 23, 1984, reveals Hodgins' decision not to include personal materials: "Now that everything is sealed in boxes I've become nervous about the fact that I didn't read through every single page in search of comments or doodles or marginal notes that could prove embarrassing!" His initial offer to include professional correspondence is tacitly withdrawn and a story based on his own life—"The Piano Lesson"—which Hodgins mentions in a letter to Gordon Lish of *Esquire*, dated September 8, 1977, is mysteriously absent from the first accession: "I feel a bit uneasy about sending the piano story, partly because it's so new I haven't been able to view it objectively, partly because it's about my first attempt at autobiographical fiction and I find it hard to see if it's working".

In editing his own papers before their arrival at the National Library, Hodgins was creating a persona of himself as writer. It was as though Hodgins were making of himself a fictional character not unlike those who occupy central positions within his fictional universe; Hodgins' papers could be read as fiction, like his novels and short stories. He might well have provided a curious researcher with the disclaimer which appears, more or less unchanged, at the beginning of virtually every work of fiction: "These papers are a work of fiction; its characters and situations are imaginary. The people, the events, and to a certain extent even the places should be taken as imaginary". Only the imagination is real.

If not a great deal about Jack Hodgins' personal life, what will a researcher find? A smart-aleck response would be: Don't waste your time. Go read Hodgins' thoughts on creative writing in *A Passion for Narrative: A Guide for Writing Fiction* instead. Certainly, a diligent researcher will find abundant proof that Hodgins practises what he preaches; examples of the elements of fiction which he discusses in *A Passion for Narrative*—setting, character, plot, structure, point of view and voice, metaphors, symbols, and allusions, literary resonances, and revisions—abound in his papers. Close examination of the genesis of any of his works of fiction shows just how carefully and thoroughly Hodgins creates and how serious he is about his craft. From original idea, through research, initial drafts, revisions, to final manuscript, Hodgins has scrupulously saved the documentation of his creative process. Almost startling is the degree to which Hodgins reveals his own aims as a writer, his hopes from his readers, and his faith in the role of artists to make a difference. To demonstrate Hodgins at work, I have arbitrarily chosen his second novel, *The Resurrection of Joseph Bourne; or, A Word or Two on Those Port Annie Miracles*, published in 1979.

The reader, attempting to situate *The Resurrection of Joseph Bourne* within Hodgins' writing career, might be surprised to discover—from an undated note by Hodgins written in all probability in 1976—just how many projects Hodgins has on the go at once (see *Figure 1*). Since Hodgins seldom dates his manuscripts or notes, it is not possible for an archivist or researcher to be certain the reconstructed order of manuscripts is entirely accurate. However, using internal evidence, it is possible to trace the progress of Hodgins' writing, which, not surprisingly, includes consideration of all of the elements of fiction outlined in *A Passion for Narrative*. Given the wealth of primary materials documenting his creative process, a few selected examples will serve as parts which illuminate a rich and fascinating whole.

"I think of my writer's reservoir—all memory and imagination and hoarded experience—as a kind of private aquarium whose thick waters teem with a wondrous population of unusual creatures, all constantly in motion", Hodgins remarks in *A Passion for Narrative* (30). Then he lists a dozen possibilities:

- memories of personal experiences
- aspects of people recalled or encountered
- anecdotes told by friends and acquaintances
- overheard contests of wills
- stories and novels read and admired
- snatches of dialogue
- haunting images recalled
- places that continue to fascinate
- archetypal figures that haunt
- feared anticipated scenarios
- dreams
- events read about in newspapers and magazines. (*Passion* 30)

For *The Resurrection of Joseph Bourne*, materials from the reservoir are numerous.

```
WRITING JOBS FOR 1976    (JAN - JULY)
```

SPIT DELANEY'S ISLAND

response from Wooden Nickel ✓
Doreen? ✓
proofread galleys ✓
promotional work
    Mike Mann ✓
    ads ✓
    see Courtenay ✓
    Winnipeg ✓
    etc Toronto ✓
        Hamilton ✓

BOURNE

collect notes for new novel ✓
plan to visit Port Alice again ✓
interview Peter McCue often ✓
work on "chorus" chapters ✓
    1 ✓
    2 ✓
    3
    4 ✓
    5
start writing ✓

READINGS

my writing class × ✓
visit Dave A's class ✓
Winnipeg reading ✓
hint about Mal. C.?
any other invitations CANADA DAY ✓

Letters

Nigerian novelist
South American novelist
Irish story writer

THE EDEN SWINDLE

get back from Dave A ✓
add recent changes to it ✓
consider Dave's suggestions ✓
revisions, retyping ✓
send Macmillan ✓
type sections and send to mags
revisions to Ms ✓

NEXT STORY COLLECTION

Go Save Larry...revise and publish ✓
The Leper's Squint...type and pub.
More than Conquerors...pub and rev.
new later story about Hallie
house auction story (see old nvel)
story salvage from Passing
experiment new very short stories
        (3?)
Great Blue Heron...improve?

THE WEST COAST EXPERIENCE

final additions ✓
proofread galleys ✓

OTHER

begin a play based on "After
            the Season"
try a half-hour radio play
×submit Ireland article to
    Monitor again in February
submit mountain article
try couple mood pieces for Forum
                page

Figure 1

Credit: Literary Manuscript Collection, National Library of Canada

When I sorted Hodgins' papers for the National Library of Canada, I came across an unpublished story "Go Save Larry or The Road to Port Alice". From Hodgins' notes to himself about "Go Save Larry", the connection between the flawed story and the ending to Hodgins' work-in-progress seems obvious. Responding to his own rhetorical question "What do I have here, in the first draft?" Hodgins writes: "a story about a man who journeys to the edge of the world to save a friend and gets an astonishing look at himself, a story about the danger of stereotyping people, and the surprises people can be, even to ourselves, the use of place (the road to Port Alice) as both setting and symbol, a sense that this is in fact a spiritual journey" [n.d.]. Among the story's "possible weaknesses" Hodgins notes: "too many references to the edge of the world (reader not stupid) and climax a bit melodramatic, must be understated, more subtle—it's awful!" [n.d.] Evidently, Hodgins had an ending to a story, the length of which was, as yet, uncertain; it would be through exploring how Larry (called Larry Bowman in the novel) got saved that *The Resurrection of Joseph Bourne* would be written.

Setting, for Hodgins, is of the utmost importance: "As a fiction writer, you are obliged to pay attention to place, I think, and to its effect upon its inhabitants, and to the metaphors it offers" (*Passion* 76). Evidence of Hodgins' early research for *Bourne* reveals two trips to Port Alice, the flavour of which provided the basis for the fictional Port Annie. Among his files can be found a package of information about Port Alice provided by the municipality and newspapers saved from Hodgins' visits there. Research about Jamaica in the form of a brochure, *General Facts: Jamaica*, lends credibility to one of the novel's sub-plots. In addition, innumerable clippings about logging, about destruction of the wilderness of North Vancouver Island, collected since the early 1970s, an article from *The Christian Science Monitor*, dated November 14, 1974 and titled "Eddie Brooks: Modern-Day Paul Bunyan", among others, document the factual research essential to a Hodgins story.

Early in the process of writing, Hodgins takes time to select and delineate character; choosing the right name is as important as finding what Hodgins calls "the unique spark—whether mannerism or habit of speech or personality quirk—" (*Passion* 102) that becomes a pivot around which accumulating experiences and reactions that make up the story revolve. Clearly, character is directly related to the kind of narrative Hodgins writes. He supports a notion of Frank O'Connor's which suggests that novels are about people who fit into society and short stories are about people who don't (*Passion* 152). Hodgins' expectations about the scope and length of this novel evolved with his main character; during early stages of writing, as he discovers that his main character is Bourne, so the scope of his work grows from novella to novel. Hodgins records his elation: "Sideroad Willy Bourne", he writes, "IS MAIN CHARACTER OF NOVEL" [n.d.].

Immediately, Hodgins begins to work out the symbolic possibilities of the character and his name in a list:

>Bourne—limit, boundary
>Borne—burden
>Born—birth
>Reborn—resurrection
>Borne—carried
>Bourn—a stream
>Bourne—a goal, destination
>His tension must be the greatest
>His goal must be the strongest
>His character must be the most thoroughly explained
>His consciousness must be the strongest
>His person must evoke the greatest empathy from readers
>HIS PERSONALITY MUST DOMINATE THE BOOK. [n.d.]

Hodgins concludes: "a God-figure at the very edge of the world!!!" [n.d.]

Plot and thematic concerns are inseparable in the evolutionary creative process. Hodgins chooses his themes—love first and possession second—then weaves the threads of his various plots and works at structuring all the parts into a whole. Again, once the themes have evolved from the writing, Hodgins works at reinforcing them as his undated list of synonyms for possession suggests (see *Figure 2*).

Plot, Hodgins admits, is the hardest element to talk about: "The truth is, of all the aspects of fiction writing, it is in discussing plot that I feel the least confidence. If written or spoken about with too much authority, plot begins to look like a formula or a blueprint" (*Passion* 128). Initially, Hodgins writes a plot outline from which a more complicated set of plots evolves.

>The story of two men, one a runaway country singer searching for new meaning to his life, the other a welfare recipient fighting to hold

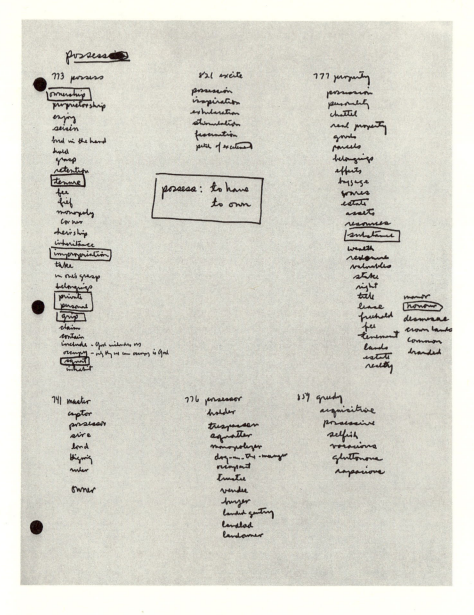

Figure 2

Credit: Literary Manuscript Collection, National Library of Canada

onto his place in the world, both drawn to the very edge of the world where they must look into hell before coming back; and of two women, one a crusty old mother of eight who considers marriage only when her man's promotion makes it socially desirable, the other a beautiful outsider whose search for healing brings healing to the lives of all she meets; and it is the story of two villages, one perched on the edge of the world braced against almost inevitable disaster, the other snuggled into a fertile valley in the shadow of a mountain, both about to be devoured by the greed of the land developers and real estate agents whose movement up the length of the island is steady and destructive as a creeping leprosy. [n.d.]

Close readings of numerous drafts and revisions for each of the three sections of *Bourne* would help a researcher trace the evolution and imposition of design, a structure which is, when Hodgins is at his most successful, virtually seamless.

Perhaps of greatest interest are the metaphors, symbols, and allusions, the literary resonances, and the revisions since these are the elements which occupy Hodgins on the home stretch. From the first draft, he advises: "Assume there is a secret story hidden within the story you thought you were writing, then search for its clues, think what the clues might mean; have enough respect for both the material and the process to believe there's more going on here than you have consciously done" (*Passion* 39). Using Hodgins' extensive notes to himself, it is possible for a researcher to trace how Hodgins adds symbolic emphasis, reinforces ideas, and works to delight and teach his readers something about how he views his fictional universe. It is clear, for example, from his earliest notes for *Bourne* that resurrection and healing, the edge of the world, bounds and boundaries, and the end of the world are all integral to the plot and climax of the novel and were implicit from the outset: five motifs in particular—rain, edges, apocalypse, transcendence, and healing—all merit extensive note-taking and list-making. To add magic to his climactic scene, Hodgins focusses on the rain, light, and colour: "Rain is falling from a high, white sky, as if from no cloud at all but from a ceiling of light—a surface to the ocean—a strange brilliant unnatural light over everything throughout (emphasize colours)" [n.d.].

A random unidentified quotation—"'For the artist, especially, it is necessary to live on the edge, to peer into impossible geographies, and to risk falling away'" [n.d.]—lays bare some of what Hodgins hopes to convey about the role of the writer, himself, in the creative process. It is apparent that Hodgins, at least the Hodgins of *Bourne*, needs to state and even overstate the edges for himself. His ambition is remarkable. On another undated sheaf he admonishes himself to

> Consider:
> the novel is set on the *edge of the world*   BRINK
> it climaxes in a calamitous *landslide*   DISASTER
> it deals with the *need to create myth and legend* while *doing exactly that at the same time*   MYTH
> it needs to be a *fat* novel   EPIC
> it deals, symbolically, with a universal religious theme   ALLEGORY
> it is set in *two* villages, one of birth, one of death   TWO SETTINGS
> it is comic, ironic, passionate, compassionate in tone   COLOURFUL
> it has a series of "chorus" chapters where we listen in on beer parlour conversations creating myths   CHORUS. [n.d.]

Finally, Hodgins is concerned with intertextuality: "The sense that a story is related to other stories can give added depth and richness to the reading experience.... An implied relationship with other stories can seem to support the truth suggested by a new narrative by giving it authority. And of course, the writer is attempting to find that place in the reader's consciousness where myth already exists, to set free the ghosts and archetypes that stalk about and haunt" (*Passion* 217). Parallels with *Piers Plowman* are made explicit in numerous notes to himself and a careful reading of others would uncover many more. Yet, he is aware of the dangers of reliance on those writers he admires. "NOTE: this time I MUST avoid being influenced by other books and by other authors' styles... and also, must avoid changing the type of novel it is.... *I must trust myself this time*" [n.d.].

Uncertain of his success, before the manuscript is finished, Hodgins sends it to two trusted readers with a series of questions.

> Some things I'd like to hear about: "symbolism" ever too thick or too obvious? tone consistent? theme—whatever it is—seem clear? too clear? characters consistent? complete? onstage enough? too often? used to full potential? anyone you can't *see*? any opportunities I missed in Part 3? any places where you cringe? where I've gone too far? places where I've taken risks and failed? a need anywhere for more specific

scene details? can you always tell whose voice you're hearing? does the voice ever bother you? does the spell of the wave *last* for 425 pages? does ending *end* the novel well? any places where your attention wanders? where it should be speeded up? [n.d.]

Fortunately, the readers' detailed replies are included in the papers; they concur that his third section wants subtlety, that he must work to make his symbolic characters, especially Bourne, show less strain in their symbolism. Rewriting again, Hodgins carefully checks off those suggestions he has incorporated into his final revision and then submits the manuscript to his publisher.

Even then, Hodgins is full of doubt, insistent on the novel's unfinished state and the weaknesses he hopes one day to correct: "Do not write this until talents are ready! Do not publish this until it is perfect!" [n.d.] Inevitably, the manuscript is accepted and typesetting begins; four years in the writing with innumerable rewrites and five complete drafts, *The Resurrection of Joseph Bourne* takes on a life of its own. From his readers and critics, attention to what Hodgins most treasures is what delights him most: "The only stories that give me sufficient pleasure that I can bear to send them out into the world for other eyes to see are those that, when I read them, make me wonder where on earth they came from" (*Passion* 268). Hodgins describes his creative process in this way: "Sometimes I am playing with fire, sometimes with magic, sometimes merely with little black figures on a page. Always, always, though, I am indulging in the marvellous business of constructing a *story*, of building a structure out of words, of spinning out a yarn, of listening to the heavy breathing from that other world" (*Passion* 269). A researcher in Jack Hodgins' papers will perhaps come as close as possible to discovering how Hodgins the writer does it and perhaps we shouldn't ask for more.

Note

[1] Interested researchers should contact the Literary Manuscript Collection at the National Library of Canada for a detailed finding aid to Jack Hodgins' papers.

Works Cited

Hodgins, Jack. Jack Hodgins Fonds 1984-4. Literary Manuscript Collection, National Lib. of Canada, Ottawa.

——. Letter to Claude Le Moine. 23 Apr. 1984. "Hodgins, Jack", Administrative File, Literary Manuscript Collection, National Lib. of Canada, Ottawa.

——. *A Passion for Narrative: A Guide for Writing Fiction.* Toronto: McClelland & Stewart, 1993.

——. *The Resurrection of Joseph Bourne; or, A Word or Two on Those Port Annie Miracles.* Toronto: Macmillan of Canada, 1979.

——. *Spit Delaney's Island: Selected Stories.* Toronto: Macmillan of Canada, 1976.

Jeffrey, David L. "Jack Hodgins (1938-)". *Canadian Writers Since 1960: Second Series.* Ed. W.H. New. *Dictionary of Literary Biography.* Vol. 60. Detroit: Gale Research, 1987. 122-30.

Knight, Lorna. *Jack Hodgins Fonds 1984-4: Finding Aid.* Ottawa: National Lib. of Canada, 1985.

O'Brien, Peter. "Jack Hodgins". *So To Speak: Interviews with Contemporary Canadian Writers.* Ed. Peter O'Brien. Montreal: Véhicule, 1987. 194-228.

Twigg, Alan. "Western Horizon: Jack Hodgins". *For Openers: Conversations with 24 Canadian Writers.* Madeira Park, BC: Harbour, 1981. 185-95.

Jack Hodgins and the Resurrection of the World

William Butt

"All stories", Jack Hodgins tells us, "—whatever their individual themes—have the same purpose: to explore what it is like to be a human being and alive in this world" ("Experiment" 238). This essay explores what that is like according to the first two novels by Hodgins, *The Invention of the World* and *The Resurrection of Joseph Bourne*. The essay is a tour of Hodgins' fictional world, the sort of tour where you come back sometimes to places you've visited already, but bringing to them knowledge which you've picked up in the meantime, so that you see them with different eyes and insights.

Prominent in this what you might call thematic geography of Hodgins' world are the notions that it is an extremely physical world—which means one of forms and shapes with spaces in between them, and also of people's bodies and personalities with spaces in between *them*; that the world therefore can be limiting, it can threaten and mislead; that there are ways to overcome the fears and spaces, by joining one person's self to another; that when people manage to do so they are divine as well as human, both at once. That summary covers a lot of ground, true; but Hodgins is the sort of writer who takes you through that large and contradictory territory from various starting places, with points made as clear as they need be, and letting you enjoy yourself immensely along the way.

To begin with, Hodgins' is a physical world, packed with energy, gross, raucous, intractable. The wedding feast at the end of *Invention* is food and stomachs, haunches, chain saws, happy brawling. In *Resurrection*, as Slim Potts tells us, people mostly work, eat, worry about their kids, make love, sleep, fish, hunt, hike, drink (86). There are good and bad *necessary* consequences of this world being physical, and there are also good and bad *potential* consequences.

To be in the physical world is to have shape and edges. Shape and edges are what separate one thing or person from another.[1] Edges define the shape, make each be what it is and not something else. Edges are stopping-places. Vancouver Island is "Fin del Mundo" (*Resurrection* 64-65) and "The Ragged Green Edge of the World" (in the title of Part One of *Resurrection*); a bourne is also an edge. The edges to a person are physical—shape of body, curve of skull—and at the same time they are mental: each person is his/her special and distinct personality—whether or not they know it, or like it.

While the shape and edges to personality are inevitable, they are also necessary for life as we know it. "Build your fences strong and high and you'll never have trouble with your neighbours" (*Invention* 114) is the death-bed advice of one of Keneally's immigrants. Maggie Kyle has the same sentiment when she spends the early part of *Invention* shutting out Danny Holland because he threatens, in all innocence, to violate and absorb her personality. When the world out there beyond our edges is bigger than any one of us, then it may be frightening: it can gobble. Julius Champney spends a life as town planner drawing tidy boundaries, and then fearing the sea: "he'd never trust a body of water whose edges were capable of creeping up on you like that" (12). Keneally cleaves to the same control which the bounds of self appear to grant. "A man shouldn't put his faith into anything else but himself" (197), he tells Dairmud Evans. Your self is your single most precious possession—which the world beyond your edges may try to wash away.

And therefore people build protective banks around their selves, against the world. In *Resurrection*, when Fat Annie loses her husband, she walls herself upstairs in the Kick-and-Kill Hotel. When Raimey the seabird leaves Port Annie, Larry Bowman locks himself in the library. Like Fat Annie, he feels that a part of himself has gone with the one he loves. Wade Powers in *Invention* sits glum and snail-like in the shell of a rented car while Maggie and Becker bound out to explore the Irish mists. Lily Hayworth shuns Becker's recorder, afraid of what the world remembered could unchain:

"Leave things alone, it's safer. I don't want to remember Keneally at all" . . . Lily Hayworth didn't need to be told that the lives of real people around you were dangerous, once opened, because there was nothing as simple as covers or dust jackets to keep them in check, to stop them from going wild, and interfering in the business of others. (243-44)

Reciprocally, Keneally fears Lily: "he wanted to be the one to control how much I saw, how deep I saw into him" (262), says Lily. In *Resurrection*, Mr. Manku, ears beneath his bathing cap's barrier, discovers too late the riot his public launching causes. Why does he promptly wall himself in his basement? Mr. Manku knows: "simply his own silly fear" (193)—fear of what is around everyone, crowding, mocking our limits, and (so it seems at times) uncontrollable.

Fear comes to the Irish villagers of *Invention* when the mists surround them. Then they are ripe for Keneally, ready to let Keneally's commune and his promises and personality be their buffer against the world. Keneally's bamboozling, his sleights-of-hand, are designed only to distract them from the fear created by limits. Magic, says Lily, "comes from the shock of discovering the limits which are put on us by this sack of bones we call ourselves" (244). On the one hand Fat Annie, Larry Bowman, Wade Powers, et al., garrisoned within their solitudes; on the other the communal colonists of the House of Revelations: the two groups show opposite strategies toward the same fear-inspired end.

Other characters also flee like the colonists into community—fleeing from the notion that the physical world encourages, the notion of single separated selves versus the world out there. They grope after bonds, an audience, a feeling of connection to others across the spaces. This is what Jenny Chambers tries to do, flaunting a new fur coat through the streets of Port Annie and later planning her wedding—bridesmaids, showers, white gown, and all: "I never wanted a wedding, I . . . I only wanted the fuss" (*Resurrection* 220). The example of Jenny reminds us how often clothes are part of a performance which frightened people put on to win others' notice: Greg Wong as Fat Annie; Jacob Weins as Fartenburg or Captain Vancouver; Larry Bowman dressed in mid-70s macho; or Donal Keneally as a Southern gentleman. "They'll do anything that comes into their stupid heads to get attention, anything at all," says Mr. Guthrie, "and I know what I'm talking about" (*Invention* 214). Jeremy Fell even *owns* a clothing store, and appropriately enough craves attention worse than the others. "They would recognize that Jeremy Fell had turned out to be their saviour", his fantasy runs. "They would make a hero out of him" (*Resurrection* 107). Costumes in Hodgins are metaphor. While costumes shout out pleading for attention, they really are walls which shut their wearers deep in their fear-ridden selves, as deeply as Keneally at his life's end shuts himself in earth.

There are ways other than costumes and communes to let a person get away from separateness. In Port Annie, the hotel coffee shop, post office, Kick-and-Kill bar-room, community centre, Bourne's radio show, Fat Annie Festival, and newspaper all exist, like the House of Revelations in *Invention*, to make connections between people: because people by themselves are not enough.

Is there anything wrong with this urge to community? Yes—when what prods community into being is fear, a sense of weakness and individual insufficiency. In that case what you have is false community, a parody of the real thing. Parodies, such as costumes, are rife in Hodgins' novels, that is in the physical world they portray. Parody is in the titles: *The Invention of the World*, "The Eden Swindle", David Malouf's *An Imaginary Life* (source of an epigraph to *Resurrection*). When the world is full of separated shapes and personalities, and each personality has its own limited point of observation, then things can appear to be what they are not. Necessarily, as Horseman says, people "spend their lives being satisfied with reasonable facsimiles" (*Invention* 160): Keneally's God-machine, Wade Powers' "historic" fort; Damon West's real estate utopia; the trailer/church that Weins makes a tourist booth; Fat Annie's dead aquarium, which parodies the living ocean. It isn't surprising that Lily Hayworth wonders, "*how do I know that what I see is true? and if people started telling me lies, would I be smart enough to see through them?*" (*Invention* 271)

Illusory, that physical world out there; and hard, and dangerous. Earthquakes; tidal waves; fires; English landlords; bulldozers; murder in the Hed commune; Nell's murder in the woods; slaughtered goats on a stony island: physical forces and instruments of pain. Corpses: sometimes, like Jeremy Fell, physically alive—but a corpse nonetheless. Everything living sometime dies. "'Fat Annie has always meant the same to everyone. Flesh'" (*Resurrection* 200). "The old death-whore herself" (29), Bourne calls her. Flesh is death. The buzzard looming over him looms over everyone.

And yet: you can't even read past Hodgins' titles without realizing that there is more to his world than victims, death, and isolation.

Resurrection. Invention—which means creation as well as counterfeit.[2] These are books very much alive; in the telling they *rejoice* in description of physical phenomena. Loggers' games; racing, crashing cars; a town's festoons; and jewels of kelp and seashells. Food and drink, like the legendary menus at Wade and Maggie's wedding or the soup served at The Paper House after the Port Annie disaster—a soup which is "more like a bouquet of flowers" (*Resurrection* 264). And lots and lots of joyous unrestrained sex. Keneally with his wives and other women in Canada and Ireland; Maggie with her glorious body and four children; Raimey with that awesome swivel to her hips; Angela Turner with her Peruvian sailor; Dieter and Fat Annie and

> the exuberance of the love affair those two carried on.... Fat Annie's great jubilant whoops clapped thunder-like across the bay, kept everyone awake.... There wasn't a man in the camp who didn't dream every night of wallowing in that enormous tub of love.... (*Resurrection* 66-67)

Certainly this is not Fat Annie in her death-whore incarnation, and the difference is central to the nature of Hodgins' world. Then we have to look again at the problem of the relation between self and physical world. The point is not only that the physical world is good or bad, attractive or dangerous, one or the other. At different times, from differing perspectives, it can be either. But what really matters is how humans respond to that world. The two Fat Annies represent the two possibilities.

A spectrum of Hodgins' characters lies between these poles. In the two novels, where ocean is metaphor for life, the poles of responses are: Raimey and Larry Bowman and Jenny Chambers, all strong swimmers at their moments—versus Julius Champney huddled paranoid as he watches the creeping tide. The mistaken way of response to life is also Amelia Barnstone's disgust in the library where Larry's hand rests on Angela's pregnant belly: "'Honestly I could spit'" (*Resurrection* 177). The mistaken way is also that of Wade Powers, who shuns work—i.e., shuns involvement. The other pole is that of appetite, the way for example of Danny Holland, "always grinning, always flushed up and waiting for the next laugh, his eyes unlike the others' always busy" (*Invention* 47). The energy and the zest of the Danny Hollands and the Preserved Crabbes is physical energy, nothing more or less. It makes the novels a vivid delight to readers, who respond as the audience within the books responds—for example, Larry Bowman who watches Preserved Crabbe and thinks, "Imagine having that scar on his scalp as a badge! Imagine being so confident over a woman that he'd risk his life, steal someone else's wife, get into a fight" (*Resurrection* 46).

These are people who, by the sheer physical strength of their bodies and selves, draw a crowd like the field of force about a magnet; and that crowd and that strength spread back out into the world around them like concentric waves expanding. "I felt like there was a giant beside me", Cyrus Durrand says of Keneally; "I got the feeling he took up a lot more space even than his big body seemed to" (*Invention* 205).

Taking up space beyond yourself suggests houses, and we notice how houses have a special importance in Hodgins' fiction. People live in houses, and also *through* them. Their architectural style, their interior design, the view out from them (Is it of ocean or forest or sky? And how *far* can you see?) have a lot to tell about the people who inhabit them. The House of Revelations and its surrounding cabins; the shack of Maggie Kyle's childhood where she bumps her head on the floor joists; Wade Powers' ersatz fort; Damon West's abortive blueprint for Cathay Towers in *Resurrection*: examples are numerous. It comes as no surprise to hear that in real life Jack Hodgins once wanted to be an architect, and built his own house (Hancock 33). One of his most important stories, "More Than Conquerors", is controlled largely by a house which is both setting and symbol. Three families live on three levels of an A-frame, and in each case home has to do with state of mind. Buildings are extensions of ourselves—media, as McLuhan defines them—a way of covering the spaces out there around us; they're a form of performance, a way to draw in an audience of guests.

Those people in the surrounding crowd—the audiences—are all-important. The people at Wade and Maggie's wedding: "A wedding, for them, was a show, better than a movie, more exciting than any play" (*Invention* 342). Those Port Annie people who follow Preserved Crabbe's post-card odyssey, visiting the post office to read the mail Crabbe has sent to his brother. The conclusion this phenomenon of the audience points to is that a person is the sum of his or her own self *plus* all of the effects that self has on the world as perceived from every existing point of view. For every person there is a scrapbook, like Becker's on Keneally, waiting to be gathered.

And after they watch—people being what they are—they tell stories. In Hodgins' fictional world as in our everyday one, story is an irresistible impulse, a pleasure both to tellers and to listeners. The legends of Fat Annie and Port Annie's founding; the seabird Raimey's story which every radio in town tunes into; Keneally's immigrants' tales of the new land and its "Irish" leader:

> "May I die if it isn't so. Sir Sean A. McDermott, I heard all about him. The whole country worships the ground that he walks on and damned if he wasn't born in Macroom. . . . They called him Honest Sean for refusing to cut down a cherry tree no matter how much the English bastards tried to force him. . . . Cherry trees as far as your eye can see, my girl, and every one of them wild as a Dublin hoor. . . . " (*Invention* 112-13)

What stories do is put ideas and perceptions outside us, palpable in the spaces between us, there to be grasped and shared by teller and listener. Telling is giving back into the world some of what through our minds and senses the world has given us. By minds and senses altered, no doubt (Sir Sean and the cherry tree), but there is no other way, for people are the only story-telling devices this world has produced. Giving back is what finally Becker does, Becker who for so long "opened only to pull in, it seemed, never to let anything out" (*Invention* 317). In the end he releases Keneally's story. "*His story has returned to the air where I found it,*" Becker says, "*it will never belong to me, for all my gathering and hoarding*" (339).

Although story can grow from our fear and ignorance (Amelia Barnstone's tale to the mayor, of lust in the library, when she "proceeded to fill the mayor in on all her suspicions, sticking mostly to what she'd seen, but elaborating just a little with what she'd guessed" [*Resurrection* 177]), story can grow too from intense and attentive focus on our world. And when it does—as in that same Amelia's epic poem at the Fat Annie Festival—then story-telling is more than just self-expression, it's a bond from self to self:

> The story according to Mrs. Barnstone stumbled ahead from laugh to laugh, through guffaws and cheers, past hollered-back comments and outbursts of friendly back-slapping, finding its way past sudden interruptions by people who felt they could improve a line by rewriting it for her and people who felt they could improve a line by acting it out for her. Only Jacob Weins in all that crowd had ceased to listen to the poem. (243)

Such story-telling is only one specific kind of performance, as the quotation demonstrates, with everyone brought into the act. As in the two kinds of stories by Mrs. Barnstone, a huge difference lies between the acts put on by Keneally as a Southern gentleman or with his God-machine, and the spontaneous and shared Festival performances. The difference is between, first, people desperately insufficient in themselves, craving others' notice to prop up their own teetering sense of self, and, second, people with a sturdy sense of their lives and talents, and with a yen to make life—theirs *and* others'—larger by display. The difference between sharing with and begging from, the difference between a community and an aggregate of solitudes.

The argument brings us back again to the matter of edges. We saw how in people as in things, by the nature of the physical world, edges are inevitable; how they limit and can therefore frighten us; how in fear people may retreat within selves or within herds; and yet how people with firm edges, unique and vivid selves, are the ones whose performances are the main stuff of these novels. Limits are a hardship, a forced isolation; and yet, twist the prism of life a few degrees and we see that limits make possible the state from which our visions rise. We *need* those boundaries. In the same way, a painting has an edge that shapes and contains. In her early confused and dependent state, Lily Hayworth paints but "couldn't stay within the lines to save her life" (*Invention* 42); likewise, Virginia Kerr finds her painting going all wrong when Wade Powers intrudes unfeelingly upon her. "'When I look at the damn thing I can't see it any more, I see what *you* see.' She began to cry" (162).

"The Lepers' Squint" is what Hodgins calls this solid frame of reference in one of his most successful short stories, in which a writer affirms the necessity of walls. Narrow our view may be, a slit we squint through, but if seen with love and from a solid base in self, what each of us sees through our own single window can not be invalidated merely by the fact that it is not seen identically by others. Julius Champney sneers at the young man with the shell-less snail which may or may not be a slug; but the young man has the proper answer. "'Stupid old goat!' he shouted. 'For all your sourness you can't spoil it for anyone else'" (*Invention* 236). All the jeering of the Chamber-Potts kids and the brawl they cause can't diminish the nobility of the motive for Mr. Manku's learning to swim: "A place didn't become your home, he believed, until you'd claimed it—by committing at least one act of tremendous courage" (*Resurrection* 51). And jeering can't take away the richness of his project's consummation:

the day finally came when it happened.... Everyone clapped, congratulated one another. And Mr. Manku did it over and over again until he was absolutely certain that he would always be able to do it, then came up out of the pool laughing and crying and forgetting all about the dignity of a great actor. (105-06)

Also in *Resurrection* is the instance of Dirty Della of Squatters' Flats. Initially she has no boundaries whatever; "for money she could turn herself into anything you wanted" (196). But after a talk with the resurrected Bourne, suddenly—boundaries with a vengeance: she locks her door on the bewildered bikers. Then, a few days later, a compromise: "What she meant by compromise . . . was only one gentleman caller at a time after this. And only if they treated her like a real lady" (198). Della's career, in a way, tells the whole story so far. In the physical world we are all alone behind our walls—"single all our lives" (*Invention* 16), says Madmother Thomas; we want to let others enter; but we each must have doors whose openings and closings we each alone control.

Relations therefore between individuals are a matter of continuing and controlled discovery, as Larry Bowman knows:

> There, though he knew he was risking everything, could ruin it all for ever, he told her all about the shame of having been in love with a woman once who'd laughed in his face. . . .
> "Do you hear me laughing?" she said. . . .
> So he didn't bother to tell her about the magazine ice-cube images he studied every day. . . . Why push his luck? (*Resurrection* 202)

Larry may never tell his lover all, holding to his human privilege to maintain walls of his choosing. Morris Wall (whose name suggests the theme) recalls for Becker the tale of his brother and Nell Keneally, but leaves out the more lurid and intimate details. "I think some things are just too private", he explains. "I am his brother after all, was his brother, and he's got a right to expect I wouldn't go telling everything" (*Invention* 186). Morris acts humanely, responsibly. The difference is huge between Morris Wall's decision and the erection of barriers by, say, Fat Annie after her mock-funeral. The difference is between those who control their walls, and those who are controlled *by* them.

"*Possessing Me*" (*Resurrection* 91) is the title of a book of Bourne's poems; it is also each person's job. Hodgins' novels show us people who have accomplished it. Maggie Kyle at her wedding: "A woman like that wasn't given", the taxi driver says; "she gave or she didn't give but she couldn't be given" (*Invention* 341). Joseph Bourne, resurrected, has the same self-assurance, a faith in the strength of what he is which even the pushy, bumptious mayor can not touch. "'What luck,'" says Bourne, twinkling, and referring ambiguously to the giant cactus and to the mayor, "'to be welcomed back from the grave by one of the natural wonders of the world!'" (*Resurrection* 143).

So it is that people rejoice in walls and in the capacity to erect and to remove them with true freedom. Times of bonding, when community is formed between two people or among more than two, are precious only and precisely because bonding starts with, and is of, unique and separate shapes. The people in Maggie Kyle's home are unique and separate, to put it mildly; and yet, Maggie feels, she "could never find another group so sure to make her feel that this was the way for things to be. . . . This was what she wanted for herself, she said, a solid base from which to rise" (*Invention* 46).

A base from which to rise: that's what the physical world can be for those with a firm sense of self and with appetite and respect for the world around them. A pattern of ascent is strong in these two novels. From what, to what, and how? In *Resurrection*, ascent starts (for Bourne and therefore for them all) with Raimey and what she embodies. Ascent starts from joy at the possibilities for beauty in the physical world. "Such calves", Larry Bowman exclaims, "and had you ever seen such delicious insteps?" (2) But as Raimey intimates later with the librarian naked and sexually erect before her, "a knight was more than his sword" (127): there must immediately be *more* than just physical appetite. A human is not just sword or sheath, but a body entire, and a personality which subsumes it. As well, reverence for the wholeness and uniqueness of another cannot be without a similar knowledge of and reverence for yourself. Initially incapable of this, Larry hides in mediaeval fantasies where he might be the warrior which his surname suggests; and Maggie Kyle flees from the loggers' games and from Danny Holland.

Ascent, then, does *not* leave behind the boundaries of self and physical sense. It *includes* them. Maggie Kyle's "extra instinct" for ascent is "like a sweet tooth, or a passion for pickles" (*Invention* 293). The simile of food is fundamental. Similarly, Bourne wants people to sink their roots into something solid and lasting; "'like what?'" Larry Bowman asks, and Bourne's hand emerged with an apple, which he held up by the stem and examined. "Like those good old invisible things that can't be stolen or disappear." He polished the apple on the front of a sweater. "What our grandparents used to call the things of soul." And bit. (*Resurrection* 228)

Madmother Thomas achieves her quest for her cliff-top birthplace by falling down a hole while urinating in the woods. Rescued people of Port Annie in The Paper House after the disaster share communion to the sound of slurped soup. Apples and souls, soup and sanctity, piss and pickles and ascent: for the whole man, the rising man, there is distinction but no division between them.[3]

Examples abound. Becker on a bumpy airplane ride scribbles in his diary, "*Aeroplane inadequate symbol for transcendence. On the contrary, it makes you more aware than usual of your bones, and flesh*" (*Invention* 319); but bumpy airplanes are Hodgins' idea of adequate symbol, if they aren't Becker's. When Becker and her fellow pilgrims stand on that Irish hilltop, a bottle, thrown from a carload of drunken joy-riders, smashes against the tallest stone. "'My God, look'", Maggie says, "'Look at them go down, look how high we've come'" (316). Like a one-note coda, the smashing bottle recalls the happy drunks and crashing cars at the novel's opening. The point is, Maggie and her friends haven't left that world behind. It has come with them, they've included it.[4] But now they see it from a higher perspective, which means that they see *through* it. In Hodgins' fiction, all the pleasurable things of this world—ocean; trees; yes, even a humble booze bottle—are loved, not for what they are, but for what they *mean*. That is, everything is metaphor for what lies past it.[5]

Bourne, reborn (his name suggesting the pun), full of confidence in himself and his powers as poet and healer, moves out into Port Annie renovating buildings and lives, heeding the warning from 1 John which Mayor Weins has pasted over with a portrait of the death-whore Fat Annie: "'For he that loveth not his brother abideth in death'" (*Resurrection* 210). To echo Maggie, how high he has come. Abiding in death is Bourne's state at the novel's beginning, down on the flats with the buzzard overhead. It is Mrs. Landyke's state, brooding obsessively at the tomb of her husband. It is Keneally all alone digging his own grave. Abiding in death is the state of anyone turned from the joys of the world and the other humans in it, like Jeremy Fell's wife Cyn (/sin: another of Hodgins' rich puns)—"a dry hot discontented woman, who offered him only one part of herself, grudgingly, once a week like Sunday chicken" (*Resurrection* 53).

Exactly opposite in his risen state, Bourne "simply recognized no alternative to life" (*Resurrection* 262). "This man was more than just alive, he was nearly bursting" (142). When Bourne spreads out, touching and renovating lives, those lives bond together. That state of bonding is what God makes possible—or perhaps it's what God *is*. As Mr. Manku says of Port Annie's people,

> "And of course they live in God, my children, as you have been taught at home."
> "Babaji?" one of the children said.
> Mr. Manku nodded, "Eko Ankar, God is One." (195)

To be part of that God is to perceive with His love: "'Isn't love of any kind an attempt to see what God must see—with *His* perfect vision?'" (229), Bourne wonders. To be part of that God is what all are seeking, even those who don't know it, even sour Julius Champney who can't stop himself from asking the young man on the bench: "'Tell me, Mr. Corbett,' he said, 'Do you . . . do you believe in a God of any kind?'" (*Invention* 233)

In his wedding speech, Wade Powers has a quotation: "'What was good shall be good, with, for evil, so much good more: On the earth the broken arcs; in heaven, a perfect round'" (*Invention* 351).[6] Humans, all of us, are single broken arcs. Seeing with God's vision is seeing each and all of us as a perfect round, that symbol of divine perfection which so obsessed Keneally (who didn't at all understand how to go about achieving it). Lily Hayworth's Bible tells the same story. It has two beginnings:

> The first, a single chapter, would have us all made in the image of God, perfect spiritual creatures. Then someone else came along, started it all over again, and had us all made out of clay. The rest of the story shows a lot of people trying to get back to that first beginning, back before the mist and the clay. You get all the way up to nearly the end of the book before you meet the man who knows how to manage it. (*Invention* 244)

That man, of course, would be Christ. "Our real roots grow upward" (*Resurrection* 142), Bourne says, and his logic suggests that when we keep our grasp on the things of earth *and* grow up to God, then we're stretched to giants. Or to *a* giant. The third part of *Resurrection* is subtitled "The New Man": not just Bourne or any other single individual, but the whole community united after the holocaust into one figure: like Christ, or like William Blake's giant Albion, or like Wade Powers, high on that hilltop in Ireland, at one of his and Maggie's most loving moments:

> Deliberately, Wade put his foot, his shoe, in the middle of her opened-out map, covering whole counties. She stared at it, at the shoe. . . . For a moment she wanted to touch it, to put her face down, to feel the childlike shape of it in her hands. She was tempted to brush the mud away, with her fingertips.
> "I'm sorry," she said. . . .
> "What are you saying? Maggie? . . . " He looked worried. His hand touched her shoulder, fell away, then came back to rest there. "I can't follow you, Maggie. There's too much, you have too much feeling in you for me to follow, you've always had." (*Invention* 315)

A couple in love, or a town in communion, are not monolithic but separate interdependent cells or organs within a body, love flowing between or among them like blood.

Each embrace is a hugging of broken arcs. Jems the Cripple hugged by Keneally in the narrative of Edward Guthrie; stripper Jennie sobbing on the jacket of fat Mr. Manku: unpromising specimens, perhaps, unless we perceive (by means of love, as Bourne says God perceives) the love by which those embraces are inspired. Then their clasping appears as a sacred circle—like rainbows seen from airplanes, as Wade Powers reminds us in his wedding speech. "In the end it comes down to just the two of us, Jems" (*Invention* 213), Keneally is reported to have said while embracing the cripple who from love and loyalty had lied at the inquest to save his leader's life. It does come down to love: of self, so that self is not a prison but a foundation from which to rise; and love of this populated world of things and living creatures and its gaudy, tumultuous gamut of humans.

An embrace concludes each novel: the great big wedding of Maggie and Wade; and the gathering of survivors in The Paper House on the flats. The more who are gathered together in communion, the closer the approximation to the God who is One. (Julius Champney is haunted by that woman on the airplane, "The woman whose husband built apartments right to the top" [*Invention* 228], who wanted to see every country in the world and who momentarily achieved her goddess state on her flight to the last one.) No one mentions God in the concluding scene of either novel; but we don't need the name to make it true that love of self and love of this populated world lead to, or make, or *are* love of God.

In The Paper House, people have been busy "turning garbage into some kind of notepaper" (*Resurrection* 153). Garbage (the world's broken arcs—the Hill Gins or for that matter any of us in unresurrected form) is transformed there into tools of communication, communion, wholeness. Jenny Chambers' dance in that House is a strip act, physical in its reference and yet a stripping away of all those accoutrements of the physical world, the ones which Bourne says you have to see through in order to see with love: her dead Slim, her love of clothes ("cocoon of stylish pretensions" [269]), loneliness, humiliation. She is stripping for everyone, and so unites them, expressing and defining the links of love and sharing among them. Again, Wade Powers' recollected line: "'What was good shall be good, with, for evil, so much good more'" (*Invention* 351). Evil in whatever form will always be a part of this physical world of separation; but the world "couldn't break that link which ran from soul to soul" (*Resurrection* 270). Evil—another name for the forces that fragment—only inspires the dances of bravery and love which forge links the stronger: so much good more.

Links grow in many forms. Attractive personalities, public performances, marriages, gifts, rescues, the coffee shop, the Kick-and-Kill, and so on are aspects of the same impulse. One link grows from art. Becker with his notebook, "caretaker-god" (*Invention* xii), joins past and present, links the sundry points of view of his sources, and attempts to synthesize a vision entire of Keneally and his colony. He fails, in a way, just as Jenny Chambers fails to shed that final garment. Because in this world—bucking bronco, world of clay and mists and fragments—such failure must be. None of us sees whole; only God does. Yet the ending of each book—each with its artist, Becker and Jenny—points beyond clay and time:

> *And if,* as Becker will tell you, with borrowed words, pulling you closer, rolling his eyes in the direction of the House, *if they're not dead nor gone they're alive there still.* (*Invention* 354)

> Let these others carry on if they wanted to, like a clumsy chorus line of salvaged bones, but she wasn't going to break her neck to complete the dance. She'd rather it hung in the air unfinished. After all, as some of them knew, the things that aren't seen never end. (*Resurrection* 271)

Art is one of those acts in which people try to see with God's eyes; and we notice that Hodgins' books manage this not only in plot and theme and characterization, but also in style, the way the author moves so fluidly from authorial voice to the voice of a character.[7] Any of many examples will suffice:

> Even the sight of that Peruvian freighter slipping past his [Bourne's] window in the rain raised up no other response but a chilly trembling in his bones, a vision of that deep sunless ocean it was heading for, of the endless desolate Pacific waiting to swallow it.
>
> Of course others, seeing the freighter, had other reactions. A big black piece of junk was what Eva McCarthy thought, standing tiptoe with her tiny hands in a sink full of dishes, and thank goodness that seabird had gone at last. It made you mad to think these two-bit cheapies could sail in out of nowhere, turn the whole place up on its end, and then leave without even telling anybody why they'd come in the first place. But at least now she'd gone and maybe life would regain its sanity. (*Resurrection* 20-21)

Individual voices are subsumed within the novel's whole, discrete but not apart: the style reflects the task of human lives.

Similarly, Bourne's poetry holds different meanings for different readers—sex to Larry Bowman, love to Angela, communication to Cartwright the journalist—and all are correct. For Bourne's poetry, like Hodgins' fiction, is about linkage. "It won't mean anything by itself" (*Invention* 250), Lily Hayworth says of her story. Nor will any story. Bourne's and Lily's and Becker's and Hodgins' stories, like Jenny Chambers' dancing, matter most in the way they link the members of their audience, as each artist interprets his or her unique vision and shares its experience with the listeners or readers or watchers who in turn interpret it according to the unique gifts of each. The artists and the audience of art join as workers at the hallowed job of constructing a civilization—invention of our world, which is also the coming-in of God. So long as we remain at the task, our world is revived—resurrected—at each moment. Wise, alive, and sacred, like all great art, Jack Hodgins' novels and stories encourage us to get to work.

Notes

[1] Hodgins himself talks about this matter in an interview by Geoff Hancock: "I'm fascinated with the space that separates people, that keeps them from overlapping" (35).

[2] In the interview by Hancock, Hodgins seems to use "invention" to suggest "counterfeit" only (47). But when in doubt, always trust the art, not the artist.

[3] See J.R. (Tim) Struthers' summation in "Fantasy in a Mythless Age", a review of *The Invention of the World*: "Hodgins' characters ... discover and embrace the eternal in the temporal, the sacred in the profane, the visionary in the ordinary, the spiritual in the human" (145).

[4] Robert Lecker, in "Haunted by a Glut of Ghosts: Jack Hodgins' *The Invention of the World*", tells us that this episode of the breaking bottle is designed to show that the "achievement" of the pilgrimage is none at all (102). Obviously, I disagree thoroughly.

[5] Hodgins, in the interview by Hancock, makes the point about metaphor explicit: "What you and I call the ocean is to me only a metaphor. All those trees, for instance, are metaphors; the reality lies beyond them. The act of writing to me is an attempt to shine a light on that ocean and those trees so bright that we can see right through them to the reality that is constant" (47).

[6] Lecker in "Haunted by a Glut of Ghosts" (104-05) and Struthers in "Fantasy in a Mythless Age" (145-46) both comment on Hodgins' use of this quotation, which is from Browning's "Abt Vogler"—slightly misquoted. For a fuller discussion, see Laurence Steven's article "Jack Hodgins' *The Invention of the World* & Robert Browning's 'Abt Vogler'".

[7] The grace and beauty of this style of Hodgins' has been noticed by others: W.J. Keith, in a review of *The Resurrection of Joseph Bourne* (107); and J.R. (Tim) Struthers, in "The Mind of the Artist: The Soul of the Place", a review of *Spit Delaney's Island*, where he calls this style "oblique discourse", borrowing the term from Ronald Bates (94).

Works Cited

Hancock, Geoff. "An Interview with Jack Hodgins". *Canadian Fiction Magazine* 32-33 (1979-80): 33-63.

Hodgins, Jack. "An Experiment in Magic". *Transitions II: Short Fiction; A Source Book of Canadian Literature*. Ed. Edward Peck. Foreword by Geoff Hancock. Vancouver: CommCept, 1978. 237-39.

———. *The Invention of the World*. Toronto: Macmillan of Canada, 1977.

———. "The Lepers' Squint". *The Story So Far 5*. Ed. Douglas Barbour. Toronto: Coach House, 1978. 49-65. Rpt. (revised) in *The Barclay Family Theatre*. By Jack Hodgins. Toronto: Macmillan of Canada, 1981. 160-80.

———. "More Than Conquerors". *Journal of Canadian Fiction* 16 (1976): 49-88. Rpt. (revised) in *The Barclay Family Theatre*. By Jack Hodgins. Toronto: Macmillan of Canada, 1981. 101-59.

———. *The Resurrection of Joseph Bourne; or, A Word or Two on Those Port Annie Miracles*. Toronto: Macmillan of Canada, 1979.

Keith, W.J. Rev. of *The Resurrection of Joseph Bourne*, by Jack Hodgins. *The Fiddlehead* 124 (1980): 105-07.

Lecker, Robert. "Haunted by a Glut of Ghosts: Jack Hodgins' *The Invention of the World*". *Essays on Canadian Writing* 20 (1980-81): 86-105.

Steven, Laurence. "Jack Hodgins' *The Invention of the World* & Robert Browning's 'Abt Vogler'". *Canadian Literature* 99 (1983): 21-30.

Struthers, J.R. (Tim). "Fantasy in a Mythless Age". Rev. of *The Invention of the World*, by Jack Hodgins. *Essays on Canadian Writing* 9 (1977-78): 142-46.

———. "The Mind of the Artist: The Soul of the Place". Rev. of *Spit Delaney's Island: Selected Stories*, by Jack Hodgins. *Essays on Canadian Writing* 5 (1976): 93-95.

Visionary Realism:

Jack Hodgins, *Spit Delaney's Island*, and the Redemptive Imagination

J.R. (Tim) Struthers

The poet constructs wholes or configurations; these become in their turn part of the one great poem that all the poets in history have helped to construct, that is, the mythological universe which is a model for the world man wants to live in, as distinct from the world that is there.
 —Northrop Frye, "The Rhythms of Time" (166)

Language from this point of view becomes a single gigantic metaphor, the uniting of consciousness with what it is conscious of . . . , the transfiguring of consciousness as it merges with articulated meaning.
 —Northrop Frye, "The Expanding World of Metaphor" (115)

When we are at the point of taking in a vision of time and space of the kind that myth and metaphor offer us, we are ready to meet the conception of a mythical and metaphorical creation that was there from the beginning, but is there again, reborn as soon as we look at it with fresh eyes.
 —Northrop Frye, "The Mythical Approach to Creation" (254)

I

To live on Canada's western frontier is to find oneself, in the words of the poem "Emily Carr" by Wilfred Watson, "on coasts of eternity" (Klinck and Watters 385). One of Carr's paintings, "Wood Interior", is reproduced on the dust jacket of Macmillan of Canada's original hardcover issue of Jack Hodgins' first book, the highly memorable story collection *Spit Delaney's Island*. The image appears again on the front of the first softcover issue of the collection, published by Macmillan of Canada in its Laurentian Library series. Another of Carr's paintings, "In the Forest", is reproduced on the front of the New Canadian Library edition of *Spit Delaney's Island*, published by McClelland & Stewart with an Afterword by British Columbia poet Robert Bringhurst. Such gestures pay tribute to Emily Carr, the visionary artist who did much to shape—as other predecessors of Jack Hodgins such as Ethel Wilson, Howard O'Hagan, and Roderick Haig-Brown also did much to shape—the way we imagine and therefore see and finally comprehend the world of British Columbia. Perhaps we may say of Hodgins and these figures what Michael Ondaatje says about a not dissimilar group of his predecessors in an Afterword to Howard O'Hagan's novel *Tay John*: "Any reader or writer likes to find his [or her] own literary touchstones.... These works enter us not as part of a curriculum but as the markings on a personal map to which we know, subconsciously, we belong.... Seen together they are, in a way, a tradition" (231-32).

Examining the case of artist and writer Emily Carr with a view to identifying points of connection between herself and Jack Hodgins, we discover how she became dissatisfied, part way through her career, with the art of surface representation and so began, under the influence of West Coast Native art, to reach into an interior landscape. As she explained in "Fresh Seeing", to the Native eye "All nature seethed with the supernatural. Everything, even the commonest inanimate objects—mats, dishes, etcetera—possessed a spirit" (20). Consequently, in developing her own art, Carr sought "to grasp the spirit of the thing itself rather than its surface appearance, the reality, the 'I am' of the thing, the thing that means 'you'" (11). The strong focus and the rich resonance of Carr's words and images would seem to suggest much of Hodgins' purpose and achievement as well. Indeed, her paintings "Wood Interior" and "In the Forest" powerfully convey the inward and upward striving—the moral and spiritual force—that is central to Hodgins' fiction.

Looking at these paintings by Emily Carr, the viewer is pulled into an illumined wilderness that forms a kind of natural cathedral. Similarly, the reader of Hodgins' fiction is caught up in and animated by a reality that is larger than the artist, larger than art, larger than our collective experience and understanding: the all-encompassing, all-defining Divine Word. The wilderness of trees depicted in these paintings represents—to use the title of the selection from Carr's journals that Hodgins included in one of his anthologies—"An Artist's Tabernacle". And, as Carr reflected in these journals, "If you face it calmly, claiming relationship, standing honestly before the trees, recognizing one Creator of you and them, one life pulsing through all, one mystery engulfing all, then you can say with the Psalmist who looked for a place to build a tabernacle to the Lord, I 'found it in the hills and in the fields of the wood'" (83). With the same commitment and awareness and humility, Jack Hodgins locates the soul of individual places and of the world at large. With the same vision, he reveals the soul of individual people and of humanity.

Like the works of Emily Carr and other frontier and west coast writers described in the introductions to Hodgins' anthologies *The Frontier Experience* and *The West Coast Experience*, Hodgins' fiction mythologizes and de-mythologizes, illuminates and probes, the sometimes beautiful and sometimes threatening landscapes or seascapes of his favourite setting, his native region. *Spit Delaney's Island* vividly depicts the lovely though rugged physical environment of the lumbering, agricultural, and recreational districts of Vancouver Island—primarily the area along the east coast of the Island overlooking the Strait of Georgia. Yet the stories in this collection also re-create the human experiences of flight and discovery that take place there. As an artist, Hodgins considers that "What you and I call the ocean, is to me only a metaphor. All those trees, for instance, are metaphors; the reality lies beyond them. The act of writing to me is an attempt to shine a light on that ocean and those trees so bright that we can see right through them to the reality that is constant" (Hancock, "Interview" 47). Hodgins perceives his native region as a setting or a stage for human and ultimately divine actions: as a world or a cosmos in which marvellously tragicomic characters struggle, fall, suffer, learn to love, laugh, rise again, and—as William Faulkner, the writer whom Hodgins has admired most, stated twice in his "Address upon Receiving the Nobel Prize for Literature"—"prevail" (724).

It is these profound human experiences—along with human longings for an ideal world and the metaphoric significance of islands discussed by David L. Jeffrey in his essay "Jack Hodgins and the Island Mind" (71-73)—that Hodgins emphasizes in his introduction to the photographs by Menno Fieguth in *Vancouver Island and the Gulf Islands*. As we quickly perceive, the statements that Hodgins makes in his introduction suggest a good deal about his own interests and concerns. Hodgins says of Fieguth:

> His eye, which seems to seek out life in all its forms for celebration, has found plenty of evidence that these islands are home to people as well as to trees and wild animals. Even in the thickest corners of wilderness there are signs that people have been coming here for a long time, and for special reasons. Small settlements and peculiar ruins encourage us to see the history of these islands as the history of utopian colonies, most of which have failed to realize their original dream. From all over the world people have come, often in small groups, and once here have proceeded to make even smaller islands for themselves by creating exclusive societies dedicated to the pursuit of idealistic visions. (n. pag.)

Here and elsewhere, Hodgins is concerned not so much with the outer reality of his chosen region as with the inner reality of its inhabitants, the struggles and aspirations that constitute their moral and spiritual being.

Throughout his work, Hodgins demonstrates the importance of looking for what he calls "The Reality that exists beyond this imitation reality that we are too often contented with" (Hancock, "Interview" 47). If the characters in *Spit Delaney's Island* are to reach this goal, what they require is not some fanciful or imaginary dream but rather a complete imaginative re-awakening. Significantly, because most of them live in thinly populated areas and on an island, the characters in these stories are isolated geographically from almost the whole of mankind. Still more significantly, however, they find themselves isolated emotionally and spiritually from one another. In most cases, the men and women in these stories are separated from each other not by accidents of fortune but by failures belonging within the realm of personal choice and responsibility. Having lost touch with their own humanity, or with the reality of the spirit, these characters fail to offer the love and hope and vision necessary to sustain fulfilling relationships with other people. Caught in mazes that they have themselves largely constructed, these men and women find themselves pressed consciously or unconsciously by fundamental questions about the nature of reality and the nature of humanity, about how to fulfil their own identities, about how to determine truth and value.

Such questions supply the two framing stories about Spit Delaney—and the stories arranged between them—with much of their force and unity. As we proceed through the opening story, we participate with Spit Delaney as he contemplates the seemingly unanswerable, yet all-important question *"Where is the dividing line?"* (7/14) However, questions about the nature of reality and the nature of humanity preoccupy various characters in the collection. Implicit in their struggle is the notion that the mind of man can be the instrument not only for asking these questions but also for providing some answers. By the time we finish the closing story, we recognize that the creative imagination—once revitalized—can be our instrument for imitating the Divine Act of Creation, for participating in Divine Knowledge, and for emulating Divine Love. As Samuel Taylor Coleridge argued in *Biographia Literaria*, "The primary IMAGINATION I hold to be the living Power and prime Agent of all human Perception, and as a repetition in the finite mind of the eternal act of creation in the infinite I AM" (1: 202). In Hodgins' fiction, the creative imagination, the faculty that thinks in metaphor, represents a means of finding the ultimate reality that we discover to be immanent, at least in potential, in ourselves.[1]

Typically for Hodgins, the search for answers to questions about the nature of reality and the nature of humanity, about personal identity, about how to ascertain truth and value—questions that concern him, his characters, and ourselves—involves not only the shining of a light but also entry into a fictional underworld, a world of symbol and metaphor, dream and fantasy, legend and romance, spirit and myth. In "Something Plus in a Work of Art", Emily Carr commented that the great early West Coast Native artists appeared to be "striving to capture the spirit of the totem and hold it there" (37); Hodgins' stories have a similar purpose and effect. "At the Foot of the Hill, Birdie's School" possesses something of the logic of a dream, reverie, or hallucination—as does "By the River". The story of Hallie Crane and Morgan in "After the Season" is a contemporary version of the myth of Proserpina, who is carried off annually into hell by Pluto, king of the underworld. "At the Foot of the Hill, Birdie's School", "By the River", and the two Spit Delaney stories reach back into the legends and myths of Hodgins' own region. He uses, for example, the story of the three McLean brothers and Alex Hare, who were hanged for murder in 1881,[2] as well as Native myths about Coyote and the hungry river monster, about the Sea-Wolf, and about Kanikiluk emerging from the ocean and changing a man into a fish. These local legends and myths serve as a mysterious context that informs, deepens, and adds extra life to the surfaces of the stories.

The overall structure of *Spit Delaney's Island*, therefore, involves a progression from the beginning to the end. The direction that this progression takes, however, involves a darkening of Hodgins' vision before it brightens, a figurative descent, in the middle stories of the book, to a kind of hell on earth before the possibility of ascending to some sort of earthly paradise can be affirmed. The structure or pattern of the collection as a whole may be seen as replicating the essential story of Ovid's *Metamorphoses* followed by the counter-story to Ovid, as Northrop Frye outlines these complimentary movements in his essay "The Expanding World of Metaphor": a pattern of breakdown or disintegration followed by union or transfiguration (112-13, 115). This pattern is reminiscent of the progression from loss to recovery that Frye describes in *The Secular Scripture: A Study of the Structure of Romance*. But even more importantly for understanding Hodgins, the structure or pattern that shapes the collection as a whole is clearly based on Old and New Testament allegories of fall and redemption, death and resurrection.

As William Faulkner said about the resurrection myth in his novel *A Fable*, "I simply used an old story which had been proved in our western culture to be a good one that people could understand and believe, in order to tell something that I was trying to tell" (Meriwether and Millgate 99-100). Certainly this pattern has been of great importance to Hodgins' work from the outset. And certainly it is fundamental to the two companion stories about Spit Delaney that open and close his first book. The twin movements of breakdown and union, disintegration and transfiguration, loss and recovery, fall and redemption, and death and resurrection appear in miniature in "Separating", the opening story of the collection. The second part of the pattern, however, emerges more strongly in the closing story of the collection, "Spit Delaney's Island", which literally and figuratively completes the first Spit Delaney story. Together, these two stories provide not only a frame for the entire collection, but also a focus: a circumference and a centre.[3]

Here, in the form of twin short stories, is a remarkable illustration of a phenomenon that Northrop Frye in his essay "Preface to an Uncollected Anthology" observed of certain lyric poems. To alter only slightly the remarks that Frye made there: All good short story writers have a certain structure of imagery as typical of them as their handwriting, held together by certain recurring metaphors, and sooner or later they will produce one or more stories that seem to be at the centre of that structure. These stories are in the formal sense the writers' mythical stories, and they are for the critic the imaginative keys to the writers' work. The writers themselves often recognize such a story by making it the title story of a collection. These stories are not necessarily the writers' best stories, but they often are, and in a Canadian short story writer they display those distinctive themes we have been looking for which reveal the writers' reaction to their natural and social environment. Nobody but a genuine short story writer ever produces such a story, and they cannot be faked or imitated or voluntarily constructed. Such stories enrich not only our experience of short stories but our cultural knowledge as well, and as time goes on they become increasingly the only form of knowledge that does not date and continues to hold its interest for future generations. (See *The Bush Garden* 181-82 or *Reflections on the Canadian Literary Imagination* 63-64.)

Like exquisite and compelling lyric poems, Hodgins' two Spit Delaney stories exhibit, and invite us to participate in creating, the kind of renewal of vision that is possible if we are willing to work hard enough, imaginatively, at our individual forges to produce it. Together, "Separating" and "Spit Delaney's Island" offer that overwhelming and redemptive knowledge which, when fully comprehended and rightly verbalized, as Frye explains in his essay "The Search for Acceptable Words", locates "its center everywhere and its circumference nowhere" (*Spiritus Mundi* 26).

II

At one dumbfounding moment in the opening story, "Separating", while Spit Delaney is inattentively soaking up sun with his family at a beach on the west coast of Vancouver Island, the doors of perception abruptly and mysteriously open—calling into question his notion of reality, his attitudes and values, and ultimately his basic identity and purpose. As

Margaret Laurence noted in her review of the collection, Spit's "meaning in life is questioned" (38). Up to this point, Spit has been living according to the assumptions of a materialist, giving importance to so-called external things. He has failed to perceive, in the words of William Blake's *Jerusalem*, that

> ...in your own Bosom you bear your Heaven
> And Earth & all you behold: tho' it appears Without, it is Within,
> In your Imagination, of which this World of Mortality is but a Shadow.
> (Plate 71, ll. 17-19, *The Poetry and Prose of William Blake* 223)

Spit's oceanside experience initially causes him, by a Blakean kind of logic, to lose everything that has seemed real and valuable to him: Old Number One, the steam locomotive that he operated in the paper mill for twenty years until the company sold it to the National Museum in Ottawa; the respect of his children; and finally his wife, Stella. But eventually Spit passes from a state of loss to a state of recovery, from a state of self-delusion to a state of self-discovery.

"*Where is the dividing line?*" (7/14), Spit wonders while lying on the beach in the opening story. The question involves, as Marian Strachan has pointed out, "The definition of reality and illusion" (46) or, as David L. Jeffrey has observed, the recognition of "where mythology stops and reality begins" (72). A little later Spit thinks of a related question: "*And what does it take to see it?*" (10/17) But for Jack Hodgins, as for Native storytellers and artists of the West Coast, the intersection of the supernatural and the natural, the "'traffic back and forth between sea and land'" (8/15), is more significant than the divisions with which Spit Delaney is temporarily obsessed. Even more important to Hodgins are the connections that human beings sometimes achieve, like the insight into one another that the poet Phemie Porter and Spit Delaney share fleetingly in the closing story.

In the opening story, however, Spit Delaney's compulsion to find answers to the troubling questions about reality and perception leads him on a fruitless tour with his family through parts of Africa and Europe, including such spots as an ancient pyramid in Egypt, Anne Hathaway's Cottage in Stratford, England, and an area of countryside in the extreme south-west of Ireland. While Spit visits each of these places, his anxiety and the memory of Old Number One, which he loved more than he loved any human being, grow so overwhelming that he is driven to the edge of madness and plays full-blast a tape-recording of the locomotive's sounds until "Old Number One came alive again, throbbed through him, swelled to become the whole world" (15/23). Spit's disturbing and embarrassing actions so deeply alienate his family that his children quit speaking to him for some time and his wife, as soon as they arrive home on the plane, announces her desire for a separation.

    The trauma of the Delaneys' separation—reinforced, perhaps, for the reader, by Hodgins' reference to the cottage where Anne Hathaway lived apart from Shakespeare—leaves Spit without the sense of identity that being married conferred on him, as if an arm or both of his legs have been amputated. "I am a wifeless man" (5/12), Spit remarks to a youth, or rather thinks to himself, in "Separating", as the youth heads off after hitching a ride in a pickup truck with his St. Bernard. Moments earlier, their eyes met briefly as Spit sat on a big rock close to the highway junction and watched with fascination the hitch-hikers lined up "across the front of his place like a lot of shabby refugees" (4/10). The image of Spit sitting on his rock and watching the hitch-hikers at the juncture of his life when Stella is preparing to leave him is one that Hodgins returns to later in the story, following an extended flashback portraying the rapid disintegration of Spit's world and his sense of identity. The rock may symbolize Spit's previous confidence in external forms of security. "'Everybody said we had a good marriage'", Spit complains shortly before Stella finally departs. "'Spit and Stella, solid as rocks'" (20/29). Like the landform called a "spit", which is almost surrounded by water and is therefore nearly an island, the rock may also represent Spit's self-constructed insularity.

    What troubles Spit about the hitch-hikers is their indifference to their journeying, to the people who might pick them up, and to one another. Spit can remember how differently he used to hitch-hike:

> he tried to have a pleading look on his face whenever he was out on the road. A look that said Please pick me up I may die if I don't get where I'm going on time. And made obscene gestures at every driver that passed him by. Sometimes hollered insults. (22/30)

The potential for feeling that led Spit to show his hopefulness and his disappointment in this fashion remains alive in him, as Phemie helps him to recognize in "Spit Delaney's Island"; yet his wife and various other characters cannot see his full potential—or have lost sight of it. As we are told at the very beginning of "Separating", "People driving by don't notice Spit Delaney" (3/9).

Because Spit, too, has gradually been losing contact with other human beings and with the humanity inside himself, his separation from Stella may be seen as confirming a state of isolation that has been developing for many years. But late in "Separating", once his marriage with Stella has clearly reached its end and he finds himself stripped of everything that mattered to him, Spit begins to rediscover his vitality. First, he becomes intensely aware of "the things that are happening here and now" and attempts to hold onto their essences: "The sound of Stella's shoes shifting in gravel. The scent of the pines, leaking pitch. The hot smell of sun on the rusted pole. . . . The feel of the small pebbles under his boots" (22/31). Yet as Phemie instructs Spit in "Spit Delaney's Island", "'There is no truth in things, . . . except as they bring out the truth in a person'" (194/229). Slowly, Spit's consciousness opens further and begins to partake of the full range of vision, of fellow feeling coupled with imagination, that he will enter into deeply, though still not entirely, by the end of the title story when he responds to the poem that Phemie has written for him.

At the end of the opening story, Spit sees himself riding west to the ocean in the pickup with the youth and his St. Bernard, laughing, singing perhaps, touching the boy and patting the dog goodbye, and finally,

> Sees himself at the water's edge on his long bony legs like someone who's just grown them, unsteady,
> shouting.
> Shouting into the blind heavy roar.
> *Okay!*
> *Okay you son of a bitch!*
> *I'm stripped now, okay, now where is that god-damned line?*
> (23/32-33)

Like Job crying out defiantly to God, like the naked King Lear raging against the storm, like Cuchulain fighting the waves at the close of W.B. Yeats's tragedy *On Baile's Strand*, or like the people eaten on the beach by the monstrous Sea-Wolf in the Native myth that Stella repeats to Spit earlier in "Separating"—though on a level more like that of Willy Loman in Arthur Miller's *Death of a Salesman*—Spit Delaney still angrily confronts an apparently uncomprehending, unfeeling, and chaotic universe that he still mistakenly believes to be responsible for bringing him low. Yet potentially, Spit's spiritual nakedness at the end of "Separating" suggests not the "poor, bare, forked animal" of Lear's speech to the disguised Edgar (*King Lear* 3.4.105-06) but rather an anti-heroic version of what Milton described as the "naked Majesty" of Adam and Eve, in whose "looks Divine / The image of thir glorious Maker shone" (*Paradise Lost* 4.291-92).

By the conclusion of the first story, Spit Delaney—unlike the many lost and deluded souls who come to Vancouver Island searching for a possible utopia—has achieved, however shaky he may appear to be on his newly grown limbs, a state of imaginative preparedness that will enable him to participate in the redemptive activity that could transform the Island, at least for himself, into a new Eden. As Kenneth Muir, echoing the words of Jesus in The Gospel According to St. Matthew, said of Lear, Spit "loses the world and gains his soul" (lv).[4] By the conclusion of the final story, Spit learns to look inward instead of raging outwardly, accepts responsibility for his own well-being, and begins to act on the basis of his rediscovered humanity. Under the guidance of Phemie Porter, Spit saves his soul and, one suspects, may, like Job, regain a form of paradise here in this world.

III

In "Spit Delaney's Island", the closing story of the collection, we find Spit Delaney living "On the edge of the village, right on the beach" (171/202), by the water's edge. Like the opening story, "Separating", this story reverberates with metaphors of edges or dividing lines.[5] Spit experiences a recurring nightmare of being transformed into a fish by the powerful Kanikiluk of Native myth and being left to flop around on the sand, "beached, neither in ocean or land" (181/214), with the sun drying him out, killing him. The undifferentiated state in which Spit finds himself in his nightmare symbolizes his undifferentiated state—neither married, nor single—in his waking life. Spit's frustration with this state explains the urgency with which he continues to look for an answer to the question "*Where is the dividing line?*" (7/14) In Spit's view, as soon as he can find an answer and differentiate "*Between what is and what isn't*" (8/14), he can begin to place himself and to discover his new identity. The answer to this question, however, may be that there is no real answer, or, rather, that there is no fixed answer.

In the opening story, the metaphor of the dividing line is reintroduced just after Stella announces her wish for a separation and Spit flees for the west coast. Here Spit talks at the water's edge with a naked young man who is presumably both a false Adam and a false prophet. The youth tells Spit about a crack running "'all the way around the outside edge of this ocean'" that is squirting up lava and "'Pushing the continents farther and farther apart'" (18/26-27). The youth alludes to the description of God's Creation of a firmament dividing the waters (Genesis 1.6-8), and seems to interpret the phenomenon of continental drift as signifying the coming of the Apocalypse. This crack or seam separating the continents becomes a metaphor for the separation between Spit and Stella. This particular metaphor is then recalled in the closing story through Spit's nightmare when, after being transformed into a fish, he swims out into the Pacific looking for the crack. But the seam eludes his search, just as the meaning of his separation and the meaning of existence have eluded his comprehension.

At one point in the closing story, Spit invites Stella out for dinner to celebrate their first anniversary as "a Separated Couple" (176/208). Spit hurts Stella's feelings, their attempt at some sort of reconciliation fails, and he learns for certain that their relationship is finished. The scene at the restaurant, however, represents not only an end but also a beginning: here Spit first encounters the poet Phemie Porter, whose name suggests an ethereal carrier (David, "Interview" 144) and who serves as Spit's spiritual guide as he undertakes a gradual and unself-conscious process of self-inquiry during the remainder of the closing story. Judging Phemie initially by her hideous appearance, Spit jokes about her, further irritating Stella, who suddenly leaves the restaurant. As Spit follows past Phemie, she astounds him by grabbing his pants above the knee, exclaiming "'Aren't you a find'" (183/216), then advising "'Some day you'll learn to walk'" (184/217), as if by some psychic power she knew about the nightmare in which Spit became a fish and was left flopping around on the beach, the nightmare which Spit had just been thinking of telling to Stella.

The dead seal that Spit finds the following day is symbolic of the lifeless state that he is passing through, and is analogous to the image of Spit as a dying fish in his nightmare. A little later while Spit is walking, appropriately, along the edge of the water, he meets Phemie, also appropriately, at the foot of a large totem pole, a symbol of immense spiritual power. Looking at the children playing in the tide pools, Phemie entreats Spit, "'Let these fish splash around in the water. People are meant to climb mountains. Take me inland, Mr. Man, take me up into the hills!'" (187/220) Climbing mountains, a motif used in each of the last three stories of the collection—"At the Foot of the Hill, Birdie's School", "After the Season", and "Spit Delaney's Island"—emerges clearly in the final story as a symbol of what Phemie says her father described as "'going into yourself'" (189/223), a symbol of the search for a form of transcendence within the human soul.

As Spit drives Phemie and her "'portable prick'" (186/219), Reef, up the mountain, they reach a second-hand store called the Wooden Nickel. The name seems half-joking, half-serious. It suggests false currency—thereby reminding us that the entire material world is only an imitation—but it also suggests something collectable, a rarity. The store contains a whole inventory of authentic goods—partly junk, partly of great value—from Vancouver Island and is a place of great spiritual importance to Spit and Phemie. Here at the Wooden Nickel, when some American tourists insult Phemie, Spit feels enraged and reaches out emotionally to her as she had reached out physically and psychically to him at the restaurant. Phemie senses this compassion and understands its importance. As she explains to Spit while they sit together on the verandah of the Wooden Nickel with her hand holding on to his arm, "'For just a split second we touched, we overlapped'" (197/233).

Like Spit and Stella, or Phemie's own parents, Phemie is separated from her husband—spiritually, as well as geographically, because he lacks the vision that she possesses. Phemie, Spit learns, has been travelling coast to coast in preparation for her next book of poems—not in search of scenery, she says, but in search of humanity: "'It's evidence I want, of the humanity that's hiding in man'" (188/222). When Spit asks why she wants to continue her search up into the mountains if there are few or no human beings residing there, Phemie replies, "'There'll be me.... I'm in search of my own too, especially. What better place to find it?'" (188/222) As Spit and Phemie talk on the verandah of the Wooden Nickel, she encourages him by pointing out that he does not need the tape-recording of Old Number One that Stella erased. "'You've already got everything in you that you need'" (197/233), Phemie says.

Phemie has begun to tap the source of love deep in Spit's heart, something that Stella—despite the accuracy of her long catalogue of Spit's problems—did not accomplish. Phemie has uncovered in Spit what she earlier called "'the humanity that's hiding in man'" (188/222), making a sort of rebirth possible for him. For the time being, Spit remains afraid to follow Phemie farther up into the mountains. He still doubts his capability, still lacks some confidence, but not nearly as thoroughly as before. He does know, although his friends Marsten and Mrs. Bested are unable to see it, that he has started to change. He is getting ready to proceed farther along the road past the Wooden Nickel, to proceed farther with the journey of self-inquiry symbolized by mountain-climbing: "I just may go up yet," Spit thinks, "to see for myself" (199/235).

Like Spit Delaney, the reader of *Spit Delaney's Island* is introduced to a fresh way of seeing, one which defines and makes articulate the spirit of Spit Delaney's Island. Jack Hodgins, to borrow a general definition of regional fiction that W.J. Keith puts forward in *Regions of the Imagination: The Development of British Rural Fiction,* has succeeded "in creating an imaginative world which is unique in that it establishes its own 'reality' . . . but taking its origin from a recognizable stretch of countryside" (10). Or as Keith observes in *An Independent Stance: Essays on English-Canadian Criticism and Fiction* about Hodgins' individual accomplishment, "He creates (not invents) a world which is (like Thomas Hardy's Wessex and William Faulkner's Yoknapatawpha and Margaret Laurence's Manawaka) both a mirror image of a particular part of the earth's surface and a looking-glass land (there is at least a hint, surely, of Lewis Carroll in his work)—an imaginative space, a world with its own laws and logic" (276). The mode of writing that Hodgins employs can perhaps be characterized by Michael Ondaatje's term "mythic realism" (265), which Ondaatje uses to describe Howard O'Hagan's novel *Tay John* as well as works by Ethel Wilson, Sheila Watson, and Elizabeth Smart—works that Ondaatje calls "private and eternal, gnarled and graceful, regional and mythical" (272). Yet I would prefer to characterize Hodgins' writing by the term W.B. Yeats uses to describe the poetry of William Blake: "visionary realism" (Grant 54). In applying the term "visionary realism" to Hodgins' fiction, I mean to suggest how the geographical and psychological realism of these stories, the detailed sense of place and character, takes on the more poetic elements of symbol and metaphor, dream and fantasy, legend and romance—and ultimately takes on something of the more spiritual qualities of myth, sacred parable, and allegory.

This sense of parable is conveyed most strongly in "Spit Delaney's Island" when Phemie Porter discovers an old oak chest of drawers at the Wooden Nickel which the proprietor has begun to strip down in order to find its "'real value'" (193/227). The old chest of drawers which Phemie sees at the Wooden Nickel reminds her of the chest of drawers that a little fat cabinet maker named Eloff Nurmi built for her when she was a child. The cabinet maker (whose profession recalls Jesus's occupation as a carpenter) told Phemie that the chest contained a hidden compartment:

> "It was the invisible soul of the chest," he said, where I could keep things that belonged just to me. But I never found it myself, and I was afraid to admit it to him, so I learned to store everything important in my own mind, and later in poems, and gradually began to suspect this was what he intended." (193/228)

This parable radiates in various directions; it contains numerous echoes and implications.[6] By introducing it, Hodgins emphasizes the theme of vision that he explores in the many references to sight and blindness throughout the collection. "'Vision is a thing of the heart'", says Mrs. Bested near the beginning of "Spit Delaney's Island"; "'A person could be blind as a bat and have vision clear as glass'" (172/204). Thus Phemie, whose "eyeballs were great scarred knobs, diseased probably and discoloured too, nearly yellow", although "they were not hard, or cruel" (184/217), has a second sight that allows her to see more deeply into Spit than anyone else can. Later, Spit wonders "if you could get your eyeballs scarred from what you've *seen*" (187/221).

Through Phemie Porter, Hodgins stresses the visionary and redemptive power of the creative imagination, which for Hodgins is fuelled by human love and feeling. The imagination of an artist can manifest "'the invisible soul'" (193/228) of a thing or a place or a person—as Phemie's poem about Spit, "The Man Without Legs", testifies. Spit remarks that if he had known initially that Phemie was a poet he would have had nothing to do with her. By the end, however, Spit acknowledges that sometimes when he reads her poem,

> it starts to make a kind of sense to me, if I don't try too hard. . . . She's in there somewhere looking at me clearer than anyone's ever seen me before. If I could understand, if I could get inside those words with her, I think I'd be able to know what it was she saw

when she looked at me, what it was that made her believe I could manage, that I could survive and go on. (199/235)

Phemie remains in the poem, in Spit's newly awakened imagination, and in the reader's imagination as a spiritual guide, as a leader of a secret army planning "to set the island afloat and liberate us all from something" (199/235). Like the writing of visionary poets such as Samuel Taylor Coleridge or William Blake or W.B. Yeats or Dylan Thomas (whose poem "Fern Hill" is alluded to in "At the Foot of the Hill, Birdie's School"[7]) or Wilfred Watson or Margaret Avison or Don McKay[8] or Robert Bringhurst, and like Alice Munro's extraordinary short stories,[9] the two stories that circumscribe Hodgins' *Spit Delaney's Island*—and the other stories resounding within—offer a memorable celebration of the powers of the creative imagination to reshape and to redeem the world.

A Note On The Texts

Page references to the original hardcover edition of *Spit Delaney's Island*, published by Macmillan of Canada, and to the New Canadian Library paperback edition of this work, published by McClelland & Stewart, are provided following the quotations.

Notes

I would like to thank Jack David and Robert Lecker, co-editors of *Essays on Canadian Writing*, for encouraging my early interest in Jack Hodgins. I would also like to thank Stan Dragland and Doug Daymond for their comments at different points in the writing of this essay.

[1] For my understanding of the workings and the importance of the redemptive imagination in nineteenth- and twentieth-century Romantic literature, I am indebted to Ross Woodman's essays "Imagination as the Theme of *The Prelude*" and "The Death and Resurrection of Milton According to the Gospel of Blake", along with M.H. Abrams' study *Natural Supernaturalism: Tradition and Revolution in Romantic Literature* (117-22 et passim). For further insight into the continued significance of Romanticism in twentieth-century art and thought, I am

indebted to Hugh Hood's essays "Sober Colouring: The Ontology of Super-Realism" and "The Persistence of Romanticism".

[2] For an account of the McLean gang, see Mary Balf's entry on "McLEAN, ALLAN".

[3] For Hodgins' own perspective on the Spit Delaney stories, see "Breathing from Some Other World: Notes on Writing the Spit Delaney Stories".

[4] To cite the words of Jesus that Muir is echoing, "For whosoever will save his life shall lose it: and whosoever will lose his life for my sake shall find it. For what is a man profited, if he shall gain the whole world, and lose his own soul? or what shall a man exchange for his soul? For the Son of man shall come in the glory of his Father with his angels; and then he shall reward every man according to his works" (Matthew 16.25-27).

[5] British Columbia fiction writer Keath Fraser offers his own particular and splendid associations for the metaphor of lines in his brief essay "Nazca".

[6] Hodgins' description of the old oak chest of drawers with its secret compartment which Phemie can never find—leading her to store everything important in her imagination and later in poems—connects in my mind with the central image or metaphor of Margaret Atwood's early short story "Testament Found in a Bureau Drawer". It also reminds me of the description of the old washstand containing a drawer in which the narrator of Alice Munro's early short story "The Peace of Utrecht" finds pages from an old loose-leaf notebook on which is recorded in her own handwriting the emblematically suggestive statement that "The Peace of Utrecht, 1713, brought an end to the War of the Spanish Succession" (*Dance of the Happy Shades* 201). The original hardcover issue of *Spit Delaney's Island* bore three endorsements on the back cover, including one by Alice Munro, one by Margaret Laurence, and one by Margaret Atwood. Munro said: "Jack Hodgins' stories do one of the best things fiction can do—they reveal the extra dimension of the real place, they light up the crazy necessities of real life". Laurence said: "Jack Hodgins writes with a saving humour and with an extraordinary grasp of idiom. His fiction is revealing and—yes—chilling. But chilling in the sense that tragedy is—it does not turn us away from life or away from one another". And Atwood said: "*Spit Delaney's Island* is an eerie collection of stories, with the density of earth but some of the fifth dimensional quality of science fiction. Jack Hodgins is obviously a new writer worth watching".

[7] In "At the Foot of the Hill, Birdie's School", Hodgins writes, "Yet time, a poet told him from the dusty back pages of a fat collection, would take him by his shadow-hand and lead him up out of childhood to the dark swallow-thronged loft of mysteries and manhood" (138/164). The final stanza of Thomas' poem "Fern Hill" begins, "Nothing I cared, in the lamb white days, that time would take me / Up to the swallow thronged loft by the shadow of my hand . . . ". In "Dylan Thomas' Cosmology", Don McKay remarks that for Thomas, "When man's vision is broad enough to perceive in his own birth and death the pervasive rhythm of life, he is able to redeem his world without transcending time and space" (v).

[8] Don McKay's essay "Baler Twine: Thoughts on Ravens, Home, and Nature Poetry" represents a brilliant commentary on the limitations and the possibilities of contemporary criticism.

[9] I am thinking specifically of the celebration of the imagination that is found in the final scene of the title story—and the closing story—of Alice Munro's *Dance of the Happy Shades* (her first collection, as *Spit Delaney's Island* is Jack Hodgins' first collection): the piano recital at Miss Marsalles' house featuring the extraordinary performance by the long-legged, plaintive-looking, nearly white-haired, somehow freakish, and ungraceful (but manifestly grace-filled) girl from Greenhill School: "What she plays is not familiar. It is something fragile, courtly and gay, that carries with it the freedom of a great unemotional happiness. . . . The music is in the room and then it is gone and naturally enough no one knows what to say. For the moment she is finished it is plain that she is just the same as before, a girl from Greenhill School. Yet the music was not imaginary. . . . 'The Dance of the Happy Shades,' says Miss Marsalles. *Danse des ombres heureuses*, she says, which leaves nobody any the wiser" (222-23).

Works Cited

Abrams, M.H. *Natural Supernaturalism: Tradition and Revolution in Romantic Literature*. New York: W.W. Norton, 1971.

Atwood, Margaret. "Testament Found in a Bureau Drawer". *Prism international* 5.2 (1965): 59-65.

Avison, Margaret. "The Dumbfounding". *The Dumbfounding*. New York: W.W. Norton, 1966. 58-59.

Balf, Mary. "McLEAN, ALLAN". *Dictionary of Canadian Biography*. Gen. ed. Francess G. Halpenny. Vol. 11. Toronto: U of Toronto P, 1982. 568-69.

Blake, William. *The Poetry and Prose of William Blake*. Ed. David V. Erdman. Commentary by Harold Bloom. Rev. ed. Garden City, NY: Doubleday, 1970.

Bringhurst, Robert. "Afterword". *Spit Delaney's Island*. By Jack Hodgins. The New Canadian Library. Toronto: McClelland & Stewart, 1992. 237-42.

Carr, Emily. "An Artist's Tabernacle". *The Frontier Experience*. Ed. Jack Hodgins. Themes in Canadian Literature. Toronto: Macmillan of Canada, 1975. 74-81, 83.

——. "Fresh Seeing". *Fresh Seeing: Two Addresses*. By Emily Carr. Toronto: Clarke, Irwin, 1972. 7-21.

——. "Something Plus in a Work of Art". *Fresh Seeing: Two Addresses*. By Emily Carr. Toronto: Clarke, Irwin, 1972. 27-38.

Coleridge, Samuel Taylor. *Biographia Literaria*. Ed. J. Shawcross. 2 vols. London: Oxford UP, 1907.

David, Jack. "An Interview with Jack Hodgins". *Essays on Canadian Writing* 11 (1978): 142-46.

Faulkner, William. "Address upon Receiving the Nobel Prize for Literature". *The Portable Faulkner*. Ed. Malcolm Cowley. Rev. ed. New York: Viking, 1967. 723-24.

——. *A Fable*. New York: Random House, 1954.

Fraser, Keath. "Nazca: *Notes on Fiction*". *Event* 18.1 (1989): 28-29. Rpt. as "Nazca". *How Stories Mean*. Ed. John Metcalf and J.R. (Tim) Struthers. Critical Directions 3. Erin, ON: Porcupine's Quill, 1993. 273-74.

Frye, Northrop. "The Expanding World of Metaphor". *Myth and Metaphor: Selected Essays, 1974-1988*. By Northrop Frye. Ed. Robert D. Denham. Charlottesville: UP of Virginia, 1990. 108-23.

——. "The Imaginative and the Imaginary". *Fables of Identity: Studies in Poetic Mythology*. New York: Harcourt, Brace & World, 1963. 151-67.

——. "The Mythical Approach to Creation". *Myth and Metaphor: Selected Essays, 1974-1988*. By Northrop Frye. Ed. Robert D. Denham. Charlottesville: UP of Virginia, 1990. 238-54.

——. "Preface to an Uncollected Anthology". *The Bush Garden: Essays on the Canadian Imagination*. 1971. Introd. Linda Hutcheon.

Concord, ON: House of Anansi, 1995. 165-82. Rpt. in *Reflections on the Canadian Literary Imagination*. By Northrop Frye. Ed. Branko Gorjup. Afterword by Agostino Lombardo. *Studi e Ricerche* 39. Rome: Bulzoni Editore, 1991. 49-64.

——. "The Rhythms of Time". *Myth and Metaphor: Selected Essays, 1974-1988*. By Northrop Frye. Ed. Robert D. Denham. Charlottesville: UP of Virginia, 1990. 157-67.

——. "The Search for Acceptable Words". *Spiritus Mundi: Essays on Myth, Literature, and Society*. Bloomington: Indiana UP, 1976. 3-26.

——. *The Secular Scripture: A Study of the Structure of Romance*. Cambridge, MA: Harvard UP, 1976.

Grant, Damian. *Realism*. The Critical Idiom. London: Methuen, 1974.

Hancock, Geoff. "An Interview with Jack Hodgins". *Canadian Fiction Magazine* 32-33 (1979-80): 33-63.

Hodgins, Jack. "Breathing from Some Other World: Notes on Writing the Spit Delaney Stories". *How Stories Mean*. Ed. John Metcalf and J.R. (Tim) Struthers. Critical Directions 3. Erin, ON: Porcupine's Quill, 1993. 202-12. Rpt. (revised) as "Breathing from Some Other World: The Story of a Story". *A Passion for Narrative: A Guide for Writing Fiction*. By Jack Hodgins. Toronto: McClelland & Stewart, 1993. 255-69.

——. "Introduction". *Vancouver Island and the Gulf Islands*. By Menno Fieguth. Toronto: Oxford UP, 1981, n. pag.

——. "Introduction". *The West Coast Experience*. Ed. Jack Hodgins. Themes in Canadian Literature. Toronto: Macmillan of Canada, 1976. 1-2.

——. "Introduction: Deeper into the Forest". *The Frontier Experience*. Ed. Jack Hodgins. Themes in Canadian Literature. Toronto: Macmillan of Canada, 1975. 1-2.

——. *Spit Delaney's Island: Selected Stories*. Toronto: Macmillan of Canada, 1976. Laurentian Library 58. Toronto: Macmillan of Canada, 1977. Rpt. as *Spit Delaney's Island*. Afterword by Robert Bringhurst. The New Canadian Library. Toronto: McClelland & Stewart, 1992.

Hood, Hugh. "The Persistence of Romanticism". *Unsupported Assertions*. Concord, ON: House of Anansi, 1991. 60-69.

——. "Sober Colouring: The Ontology of Super-Realism". *Canadian Literature* 49 (1971): 28-34. Rpt. (revised) as "The Ontology of Super-Realism" in *The Governor's Bridge is Closed*. By Hugh Hood. Ottawa: Oberon, 1973. 8-20.

Jeffrey, David L. "Jack Hodgins and the Island Mind". *Canada Emergent: Literature/Art*. Ed. James Carley. [*Book Forum* 4 (1978):] 70-78.

Keith, W.J. "Introduction". *Regions of the Imagination: The Development of British Rural Fiction*. Toronto: U of Toronto P, 1988. 3-20.
——. "On the Edge of Something Else: Jack Hodgins's Island World". *An Independent Stance: Essays on English-Canadian Criticism and Fiction*. Critical Directions 2. Erin, ON: Porcupine's Quill, 1991. 267-77.
Laurence, Margaret. "Hodgins at Last Collected". Rev. of *Spit Delaney's Island: Selected Stories*, by Jack Hodgins. *The Globe and Mail* [Toronto] 8 May 1976, sec. Entertainment-Travel: 38.
McKay, Don. "Baler Twine: Thoughts on Ravens, Home, and Nature Poetry". *Studies in Canadian Literature/Études en littérature canadienne* 18.1 (1993): 128-38.
——. "Dylan Thomas' Cosmology". M.A. Thesis Western Ontario 1966.
Meriwether, James B. and Michael Millgate, eds. *Lion in the Garden: Interviews with William Faulkner 1926-1962*. New York: Random House, 1968.
Miller, Arthur. *Death of a Salesman: Certain Private Conversations in Two Acts and a Requiem*. 1949. Compass Books ed. New York: Viking, 1958.
Milton, John. *Paradise Lost. Complete Poems and Major Prose*. By John Milton. Ed. Merritt Y. Hughes. New York: Odyssey, 1957. 173-469.
Muir, Kenneth, ed. *King Lear*. By William Shakespeare. The Arden Shakespeare. London: Methuen, 1966.
Munro, Alice. *Dance of the Happy Shades*. Toronto: Ryerson, 1968.
Ondaatje, Michael. "Afterword". *Tay John*. By Howard O'Hagan. The New Canadian Library. Toronto: McClelland & Stewart, 1989. 265-72.
Strachan, Marian. "Magic Island Captured in Its Captives' Tales". Rev. of *Spit Delaney's Island: Selected Stories*, by Jack Hodgins. *The Gazette* [Montreal] 5 June 1976, sec. 4: 46.
Thomas, Dylan. "Fern Hill". *Collected Poems: 1934-1952*. London: J.M. Dent, 1952. 159-61.
Watson, Wilfred. "Emily Carr". *Canadian Anthology*. Ed. Carl F. Klinck and Reginald E. Watters. Rev. ed. Toronto: W.J. Gage, 1966. 385.
Woodman, Ross. "The Death and Resurrection of Milton According to the Gospel of Blake". *English Studies in Canada* 3 (1977): 416-32.
——. "Imagination as the Theme of *The Prelude*". *English Studies in Canada* 1 (1975): 406-18.
Yeats, W.B. *On Baile's Strand. The Collected Plays of W.B. Yeats*. [2nd ed.] London: Macmillan, 1952. 245-78.

The Design of the Story:

The Invention of the World

Louis K. MacKendrick

I

The title of Jack Hodgins' first novel, *The Invention of the World*, provokes some literary generalizations. Much contemporary criticism of prose fiction recognizes the reflexive or "metafictional" nature of particular narratives—that is, the manner in which they purposely highlight the devices of their own composition—and identifies the conventions or techniques there displayed. Again, each novel "world" can be appreciated as a literary creation asserting the inherent logic of its own imagined place and style. The idea of many fictions as proposing self-contained worlds is hardly novel, though criticism often responds to such inventions by pretending their reality and exploring them for plausibility or even for their approximate representation of life. They are treated as variations of factual, referential phenomena, and are only in passing considered, if at all, as the products of purely literary devisings, as artefactual. As Roger Fowler says of "naïve realism" in *Linguistics and the Novel*,

> Even though we may empathize with the fates and fortunes of the people in fiction, they are not "real", and the novel is in no sense

simply a transparent, undistorted, picture of a palpable reality. The content can only be experienced as *represented* content, and representation (thus, our experience) is controlled by the techniques of language. (71)

A critical approach which sees fiction as invention is comparatively unambiguous. It is in this light that Hodgins' novel was patented as ISBN 0-7705-1518-5 in 1977: it creates an autonomous order—indeed, *The Tempest*, with its mythical island, is his "favourite Shakespearean play" (David 143)—within a predominantly literary scheme. Its world, which may look very much like one that did or might exist on Vancouver Island, is often presented through an accentuation of its narrative practices.

The novelist John Barth has spoken of the substitute worlds of some fiction, not mentioning his own *The Sot-Weed Factor* and *Giles Goat-Boy* as notable instances.

> If you are a novelist of a certain type of temperament, then what you really want to do is reinvent the world. God wasn't too bad a novelist, except he was a Realist. . . . But a certain kind of sensibility can be made very uncomfortable by the recognition of the *arbitrariness* of physical facts and the inability to accept their *finality*. . . . And it seems to me that this emotion, which is a kind of metaphysical emotion, goes almost to the heart of what art is, at least some kinds of art, and this impulse to imagine alternatives to the world can become a driving impulse for writers. . . . So that really what you want to do is reinvent philosophy and the rest—make up your own whole history of the world. (Enck 8)

One technique of fiction which satisfies this impulse has been called "magic realism", a relatively straightforward notion which often implies an attendant distinctiveness of expression. In "Magical Realism in Spanish American Fiction", Angel Flores has described the mode as a conflation of the romantic or fantastic and the realistic, as a "transformation of the common and the everyday into the awesome and the unreal" (190). Furthermore, Flores notes, "time exists in a kind of timeless fluidity and the unreal happens as part of reality" (191)—the aesthetic reality, it is understood. Geoff Hancock cites "juxtapositions of unlikely objects and events" ("Magic Realism" 9), and elsewhere states that

"Magic realists place their extraordinary feats and mysterious characters in an ordinary place, and the magic occurs from the sparks generated between the possibilities of language and the limitations of physical nature" ("Future" 5). The language act suggested here is reinforced by Robert Rawdon Wilson, who considers "another aspect of magical realism: the theory (amounting to invariant conviction) that literature creates an alternative universe of words, autonomous, integral and non-referential, that stands over and against the world of actual experience and can replace it" (46).[1]

What distinguishes magic realism from other forms of fiction would seem to be some degree of "fabulation". As described by Robert Scholes, the technique asserts "the authority of the shaper, the fabulator behind the fable" (10). Such narratives, Scholes finds, are "less realistic and more artistic", and manifest "an extraordinary delight in design" (12). Modern fabulation, he adds, "tends away from the representation of reality but returns toward actual human life by way of ethically controlled fantasy" (11). The writer, then, is perceived as a story-teller, even as a "fabulous artificer"—Stephen Dedalus' phrase about his mythical artist-figure in Joyce's *Portrait* (189)—who often uses a style which foregoes objectivity about its materials and itself.

Magic realism disrupts "realistic" time, place, action, and character, to the end of creating an independent literary reality. Its wonders and narrative freedoms may suddenly invert the ordinary but not, as in fantasy, for the duration of the fiction. Magic realism raises enigmas about orders and degrees of fictional actualization and expression, the World made fit for Art. Its fabrications and rhetorical impulses are invariably estimated within the realist tradition, whose conventions are challenged but not completely disengaged. The prime model of magic realism is Gabriel García Márquez's *One Hundred Years of Solitude*, a leisurely chronicle of the possible and the improbable in the imaginary South American town of Macondo. His influence is clear in such passages from *The Invention of the World* as an old lady's being bullied in her dreams by a baby's late mother, or the glow that emanates from the principals of a wedding-reception embrace. García Márquez has also had a powerful effect on Robert Kroetsch's *What the Crow Said*, where the inventions of prose and the unexpectedly irrealistic are comically combined, and most emphatically on Hodgins' second novel, *The Resurrection of Joseph Bourne*, a book of "miracles". In all such instances, realism and the fantastic become, in effect, a compound mode.[2]

Geoff Hancock has claimed much for *The Invention of the World*:

> All the devices of magic realism are turned loose. Language is telescoped and compressed. Literary works are Chinese-boxed inside the literary work. Characters split off into doubles. Various fictional layers are confused with reality, and the relationship of the reader with the main characters constantly shifts. Hyperbole and humour is given a fast spin and takes off [sic]. Unreliable narrators stalk the pages. ("Future" 5)

Despite the generosity of this summary, Hodgins' novel can be seen as a working through and assessment of the practices of realism. He has declared that "I'm not playing games with words. Important as rhythm, language, vocabulary and all those other things are when I'm writing, I'm not playing games" (Hancock, "Interview" 48); his realist orientation—"Mostly I'm interested in writing about human beings" (Twigg 13) is towards depth and distinction of character in particular: "the spoken word to me is very important. I feel compelled to get the way people talk exactly right in my fiction" (Hancock, "Interview" 36). Given Hodgins' exactitude of ear and eye, and his gift for distinctively realistic dialogue and portraiture, it should also be noted that he exhibits an equally sure touch in picturing the environments of Vancouver Island and Ireland, local colour both human and natural. He has an accomplished way with the description and evocation of place, and is an acute observer of particular life. It is, invariably, the realist perspective which judges the success of Hodgins' novel, despite clear evidence of his less mimetic intentions.

Yet *The Invention of the World* does invite reading beyond realism. In an interview with Geoff Hancock, Hodgins has said, "To me myth is closer to reality than history. While history is a collection of the facts, myth is the soul that surrounds those facts" (62). The suggestion of the higher realities of myth is prosaically confirmed through Strabo Becker, Hodgins' choric character in *The Invention of the World*: "'Myth,' he said, 'like all the past, real or imaginary, must be acknowledged'" (314/ 406-07).[3] In an introduction to *The West Coast Experience*, Hodgins has remarked how his place prompts the crossing of many frontiers:

> Certainly it is possible to get the impression that B.C. writers are like a lot of Adams gone mad in Eden, naming everything in sight. But it

must be remembered that this is, in a literary sense, unexplored territory; writers are making maps. And it must not be ignored that very few of the contemporary writers in British Columbia are content simply to record the landscape, or even just to celebrate it. (1)

His reality, in fiction, is beyond frontiers, like the contemporary Irish in the novel who, Becker believes, seem *"eager to be ushered as hastily as possible into another world"* (320/414). Similarly, Hodgins has spoken of

> The Reality that exists beyond this imitation reality that we are too often contented with. The created rather than the invented world. I didn't call my novel *The Invention of the World* because it is an arresting title. It is a story about counterfeits. (Hancock, "Interview" 47)[4]

The Invention of the World is "about" a great deal; I will suggest only part of its compass of idea and structure. For example, its concern with different views of reality and with self-possession can serve as an introduction to the careful relationship and frequent repetition of its dominant motifs. This foundation of reiterated metaphors and simple statements of theme in turn leads naturally to an informal engagement with the narrative's structure and with several of its prominent verbal strategies.

One perspective on reality is the apparent exactitude of history and the collative efforts of Strabo Becker, a reality which includes the scrapbook of clippings and often contradictory interviews gathered by Becker for the purpose of chronicling the life of Donal Brendan Keneally. The historical Strabo, a Greek geographer who lived ca. 64 BC to 23 AD—see the novel's many allusions to maps—was likewise a compiler, noted for his interpolations of historical curiosities in his work and for his love of legend.[5] In this way Hodgins alerts us to the ultimate difficulty of documentation and of ascertaining unmediated "fact". Even the novel's prologue plays with the idea of real versus composed, of physical environment and the debris of history set over against the creation of an artistic design. Becker's authorities are merely oral and hearsay; he is an orderer and gatherer who attempts to structure opinion rather than to establish its relative truth. He is less disciplined than Julius Champney, ex-town planner and self-convinced failure, who says, "'You can't pretend there is any history on this island, this is still the frontier'" (54/77). Nonetheless, Keneally's graveward digging—along with much of his feudal thinking—was modelled on an Irish historical past. It is not the authority of history, however, that Hodgins wishes to establish but rather the reality of personality.

Another perspective on reality is implied by Virginia Kerr's abstract painting, which troubles the indolent Wade Powers; his expectation of an exact representation or imitation of the real in her art is fantastically answered in Horseman, his physical double. His Fort, too, attempts to duplicate a historical reality; and, as a copy or counterfeit, like many illusions in the novel, it enjoys a local success. The distinction between Virginia's impression of reality and Wade's facsimile is as metaphysical as it is practical. Yet Wade becomes guiltily uneasy about his materialist motives when his image says of the money-making replica and its visitors, "'If you've offered it to them with love, if you're giving them this because it's the closest you can come to the real thing, and if the real thing is something you want them to have, then you're not really cheating them at all'" (160/202). Part of Hodgins' plan, however, includes such disruptions of the given:

> One of the things I sometimes do in a story is set somebody up who thinks he knows what life is all about. Then I pull the rug out from under his feet to find out how he functions when I challenge his values. In a way that's a way of challenging a reader's concept of reality too. (Hancock, "Interview" 49)

During Maggie Kyle's Irish pilgrimage Becker frequently suggests the notion of reaching beyond the literal: "'Are there laws that say a map has to conform to reality?'" (289/375) Maps are a motif in *The Invention of the World*; as distinct from Becker's figurative meaning, they usually signify a version of actuality not susceptible to variant interpretation. This quality does not describe the late Keneally, according to Becker: "'As long as he was out there, unreckoned with, unlabelled, he was a fascination and a threat. You couldn't be sure how much reality to grant him'" (306/396). Along the same lines, Maggie's journey to the remains of Carrigdhoun is reminiscent of the Year of the Mist: "To be wrapped in this mist would be like living in the cold, damp, frightening world of fantasy all your life, you'd never really be sure that anything was real" (300/389). Lily Hayworth is an undeluded advocate of the actual and of Hodgins' particular Reality, even in anticipating Becker: "Maybe our natural life goes on without us while we slap on layer after layer of what we think is life but is only pretence" (261/341). Becker appreciates the endurance of world beneath man's impositions, though it is left to the pilot of Maggie's flight home to stress the persistence of natural forms: "'That's what real is, that's what true is, it can be hid but it can't be changed'" (322/417). This is the reality which is "the C Major of this life", the return to "the common chord" which resolves both Browning's "Abt Vogler" (cited by Lily Hayworth) and Maggie's increasingly fantastic post-nuptials. But Hodgins fastens true Reality on Becker as an artist: "all the way through the novel he is dropping hints to the other characters that there is another way for them to perceive things. Not necessarily the story of Donal Keneally, but their own realities" (Hancock, "Interview" 59).

Much of *The Invention of the World* is similarly concerned with authentic selves, or the imagined fulfilled personality which first moves Maggie to forsake her "bush" roots and inadvertently to become the haven for other people and their kinds of incompletion, for her so-called "'Casualties'" (289/375). Danny Holland constantly reminds her of her apparently futile attempt to transcend indignity and a directionless past, while her sense of self-importance is eroded by the sour Cora Manson and, in that past, even by hens which treated her as of no consequence. Maggie epitomizes a quest for something too ambitiously and inhumanly spiritual: she wishes to be "able to understand all there was to understand about the universe and be all that she was capable of being" (293/380). This yearning is implied even in the transfiguration going on in her weight-loss group. However, she is often too other-minded; Becker oracularly cautions her, "'When you begin to disbelieve in Keneally you can begin to believe in yourself'" (314/407).

The aphoristic Madmother Thomas recognizes that "'Even those of us who walk the aisle, we're still single all our lives, you can only be one person at a time'" (16-17/32). Wade Powers, the perennial losing contestant at the Loggers' Sports, encounters his sage double, who tells him of his imprisoned self, and subsequently Wade begins to complete his aimless and evasive individuality; on the other hand, Keneally himself when young had conjured himself into oppositely-charactered and unreconciled twins. In the interests of singularity Becker pursues that illusionist's seemingly protean identity, but it is Lily's memory of living with a legend past its prime and sinking into mortality that directly addresses the problem of self-possession and truth of being. It is a personal concern which she confesses to Becker's recorder: "I lie here and start thinking about myself from the outside and the inside at the same time and I can't stand it, it makes me want to get out of here and be someone else" (260/340). She often remarks on the difference between Keneally's legendary attributes and the pitiful compulsions of the elderly reality. She is literate, reflective, and practical, telling of make-believe and persistently introducing an earth-bound note of irony. She, at least, is familiar with affirmative selfhood, just as the novel, to be brief, argues strongly against the diffusion of personality and for the integration of the individual.

Such a cursory identification of the ideas of reality and self-possession in *The Invention of the World* does not begin to intimate the range of interrelated subsidiary motifs which complement them. Inevitably, too, these themes work towards an ultimately structural weave in the fiction, and their clarity is paralleled by the forthrightness of Hodgins' ideas and the emphasis on such spokesmen as Strabo Becker and Lily Hayworth. This cohesion is not artless but the outcome of an even more programmatic original design, as Hodgins has explained:

> I was aware of seven different levels [on which] the story could be read. I was aware of a single theme that controlled the imagery on every page and tied all these "layers" together. I had drawn strange charts and diagrams and written volumes of what could be considered literary criticism of the as-yet invisible novel—and yet, in the page-by-page writing of the novel, all of that had to be pushed aside in favour of the story teller's *instincts* and *intuitions*. (Hancock, "Interview" 50)

Becker, for instance, sings that he'd rather be a sparrow than a snail, an overseer's view which personalizes his wish to control and to re-create the debris of history and chaos: "Becker wants to be God" (x/8). It is the controller's view which Maggie actually gets of Vancouver Island on her return from Ireland; it is also the one she imagined as a child: "All she could think about was getting out of there, getting up into the mountains where she could see the whole island and pick out the right kind of life for herself" (292/379). This "view" is close to the idea of purely physical control which underscores Keneally's enterprise, as Carrigdhoun had learned of its vulnerability to outside control by bailiffs and by Keneally himself. As is characteristic of the novel, connections between human actions and philosophical implications radiate and reverberate.

The concept of control is further associated with that of determinism. As Maggie reflects, "amen to anything you could think of so long as it stopped the inevitable" (7/20). Her decision to leave the bush was made in order to break a deterministic social pattern. Similarly, Wade Powers resists conventional norms and the behaviour expected by a work-centered society. Julius Champney, however, is secure only with the unvarying formulae and predictability of maps and grids. Records, geometry, ceremony, legend, conditioning: each imposes a pattern or order on intractable natural and human matter. As a complementary example of Hodgins' incidental metaphoric structure, the metaphysically inclined Lily Hayworth refers in passing to the sucking nothingness of black holes in space and the losing of control to "a lightless rupture" (280/364) like Keneally himself—who in the end, not unlike Rumpelstiltskin, digs his own fatally attractive black hole. As David L. Jeffrey has observed of *The Invention of the World*, "It records . . . the contemporary desire to flee history, the script already written, and to become fully the author of one's own mythology, to escape creation for invention" (76).

A related idea-complex is that of the hoax, illusion, forms of magic, fairy tales, and make-believe. "The Eden Swindle", Keneally's colonizing ambition, describes his use of magic and pretence as much as it suggests Wade's fake Fort and his smug existence. Keneally is a splendid charlatan whose Eden is a sham based on gullibility, fear, and the urge to believe; his colony and the Fort are invented worlds for which there are willing conscripts. Lily's musings on life with Keneally continually stress deceit and flummery, rhetorical flourish and sagging reality, the counterfeit become flesh. It is Becker who characteristically provides a verdict, on deception in general and language itself in particular:

> *Words only nibble at reality, don't really touch it, can't really burn through to it. Symbols not much better. If words won't do, and symbols fail, maybe only the instinct, some kind of spiritual sense, can come close. All we can trust. Maybe all our lives that instinct is in us, trying to translate the fake material world we seem to experience back into pre-Eden truth, but we learn early not to listen. Instead, we accept the swindle, eat it whole.* (319-20/413)

Here again is Reality; here is another indication of how Hodgins' themes meld.

The novel is also packed with casualties and cripples of many conditions, the disabled and the eccentric, the compulsive, or the obsessed. To these characters we may add the breed of spoilers, whose need is to disrupt and to sour. Prominent here are Danny Holland, the spirit of misrule, Cora Manson, a martyr to uncharitable notions chiefly regarding herself, and Julius Champney, whose faith is failure. On another level of thematic insistence, it is difficult to avoid the many allusions to the centre or the circle, epitomized by Keneally's circular Revelations Colony with its central wellhead which is as much a metaphorical as a literal figure. Becker's search is for "the tale which exists somewhere at the centre of his gathered hoard" (xi/10). It is her personal centre which Maggie guards so firmly, and which she also wants to find: the perfect form at the centre of the revelation of truth. Lily Hayworth, however, characteristically denies the notion of symmetry as well as the traditional symbol of perfection—"Nothing in my experience had run to circles" (247/324)—though ironically she quotes Browning's "Abt Vogler", inexactly,[6] over Keneally's excavation: *"On earth the broken arcs, in heaven the perfect rounds"* (283/367). The associations here are multiple: Maggie's spiritual aspirations, Lily's own earthy humanity, and Keneally's ultimate failure.

Hodgins' weave also includes many references to the ideal, Edenic restoration, new kinds of life, and the unspoiled land which all of the novel's maps cannot show. For those who wish to set up their own independent worlds, the story invariably favours ones of the spirit, and it is such an emphasis—either in tangible example or in rhetorical proposal—which brings *The Invention of the World* close to allegory and parable. Maggie's trailer park, Wade's Fort, and Keneally's kingdom are created worlds which are placed in a more realistic perspective by one of Becker's interviewees: "So many pioneers to this island seem to have had some tribal instinct to create even smaller islands once they got here, separate isolated communities all over the place and all of them failures" (196/254). Hodgins has said of such "romantic idealists" that "They have been defeated, not because their dreams weren't worth going after, but because they brought with them their old values" (Hancock, "Interview" 49). Yet some dreams succeed, like that of the young semi-pioneering squatters in Maggie's old home who rejoice in the life she has fled. Their promise is echoed when Maggie and Wade are called "the new man and the new woman" (354/455), to whom the Eden of the fulfilled life has explicitly come.

II

Any closer examination of these or associated motifs in *The Invention of the World* would only confirm the frequency of their iteration and their mutual correspondences. Above all, their clarity sets them in high relief within the fiction and helps them serve a structural function without abrogating their thematic duties. Yet an insistence on the repeating nature of the motifs leads to reflections on the novel's formal designs, in which Hodgins would seem to take the fabulator's delight. As he has said, "At university I majored in mathematics. I like things to have shapes. I love patterns" (Hancock, "Interview" 58).

One obvious pattern is the focus on Donal Brendan Keneally in the novel's alternating narrative divisions—"The Eden Swindle", "Scrapbook", and "The Wolves of Lycaon". The other sections, excluding a prefatory passage on Becker and a finale at Maggie's wedding, are concerned with Maggie, Wade, Julius, and Maggie's "Pilgrimage". There are contrasts and parallels between the successive parts, in terms of character, incident, mood, and theme, as well as significant internal structural considerations and incidental echoes from elsewhere in the story.

The first purely narrative division, "Maggie", features a host of nagging details and the threat of an unruly Danny Holland; it also includes a central chapter of flashback on Maggie's earlier existence which was similarly spoiled by a violent intruder. The counterpointed ideas of second growth and transcendence begin to become noticeable: "She had schemes, she had plans for the unspeakable, she had decided that the only appropriate direction for her life from now on was *up*, she intended to rise somehow until she could see right down into the centre of things" (13/27). The "battle" between Danny and the Zulu is repeated in the conflict of bush and town guests at novel's end; images of renewal—"Keneally and his crazy colony were erased when she set a match to the furniture; the flames reminded her of a slash fire, burning off the nuisance debris to make room for newer growth" (43/63)—are repeated often in "Pilgrimage", and are epitomized in Maggie's marriage.

The first Keneally section, "The Eden Swindle", is anticipated in the person of Danny Holland, a contemporary but reduced version of the one-time roaring boy from Carrigdhoun. When Julius asks Maggie of her "bush" connection, "'What is the nature of his power over you?'" (54/77), we are again reminded of the extravagant character of the man-messiah. Hodgins has pointed out the distinction between Maggie and Keneally:

> They had to be opposites in every way that I could think of....
> Keneally's story is a downhill slide, inevitable from the moment it
> begins. He moves from the top of a mountain to a hole in the ground.
> Hers begins under a cabin, a shack, and rises gradually through the
> whole novel. (Hancock, "Interview" 59, 60)

"The Eden Swindle", in its light-hearted treatment of features associated with the provenance and feats of legendary or mythic heroes, mixes miraculous and profane, vision and mountebankery. Keneally's dedicatory performance at the Revelations Colony of Truth, when he promises his own transformation into spirit, is a facetious complement of Maggie's own similar urge. She, too, is a colonizer, while Nell Keneally's role as a comforter and healer is a real prefiguration of Maggie's importance to her casualties.

Keneally's early life, compounding substance and illusion, has a forceful heroic cast which is immediately countered in Wade Powers' lackadaisical existence; nevertheless, like that earlier trickster, Wade has also perpetrated an illusion: his Fort, an invention not unlike Keneally's God-machine. He, too, reigns in a private self-accommodating world; he, too, has an exact duplicate. Hodgins' structural design here is uncomplicated, but his distinction between the seemingly grand past and a casual present is more subtly implied.

With Becker's "Scrapbook" the narrative continues to pursue a now more accessible mystery personality, just as Wade has been attempting to locate his Horseman physically and metaphysically. The erosion of legend and Keneally's engagement with the ordinary world are matched by a Canadian society less susceptible to blarney: "When story people become flesh people we can't bear the evidence" (202/265). The underlying note of falsification and the descent from aspiration carry over to the following section, "Julius", with its emphasis on looking, failure, and untruth. Most central, however, is the misanthropic Julius' imagination, "free to play with the skeleton elements of history" (223/296) as did "The Eden Swindle". In remembering a murder and trial he reminds us, by association, of the unrecorded demise of Nell Keneally and, later, of Jimmy Jimmy's slaughter. In Champney's attempt to ascertain fact and order by having consulted documents we recall the content and implications of Becker's sources. The young man whom Julius meets might be a mirror of his failure and cynicism about law and truth.

"The Wolves of Lycaon", the third narrative division devoted to the memory of Keneally, meditates on the humanizing of a legend; its facts are no longer quasi-epical or merely hearsay and speculative as they were in "The Eden Swindle" and "Scrapbook". The principal structural motif here is descent—of the rumoured into the visible, of an alleged hero towards an inverse apotheosis underground, like his mother swallowed up by earth. The Lycaon story, offered by Lily Hayworth as a cryptic clue to her recollections of Keneally, represents an appropriate mythic model since it deals with a challenge to divine knowledge and with rudenesses offered to a god. Ironically, Keneally dies on Easter Sunday, the day of resurrection and transcendence. "Pilgrimage" reverses the direction: Maggie experiences an epiphany atop a mountain in a chapter filled with intimations of ascent, while Keneally becomes blown ashes. Her Irish journey is paralleled by her consequent pilgrimage to the place of her own past, Hed, simply to learn that she will accept her self-imposed responsibilities without pretending otherwise. The temporarily fallen Madmother Thomas is a final parody of Keneally as mystic excavator: "'it'll take more than a hole to finish me off, I'll be out of here in no time at all'" (333/430).

"Second Growth" is, as Hodgins has remarked, "a mock epic", balancing the "mock myth" of "The Eden Swindle" (Hancock, "Interview" 63). Both narrative sections parody the conventions peculiar to a literary type, a relaxation of received forms which complements the collapse of the Keneally mystique and the idea of legend itself. Both "myth" and "epic" are fanciful and exaggerated narrations, with a lightness of tone which characterizes much of the novel and which leavens the presentation of its undeniable seriousness through a comic perspective. In "Second Growth" the story of the living and whole replaces that of the crazed messiah; Becker, no longer compulsive, admits his own illusion of control and says of Keneally, "*His story has returned to the air where I found it, it will never belong to me, for all my gathering and hoarding*" (339/437). As the novel began with a prospective marriage, it concludes with an accomplished one. Maggie's reception, however, assumes some bizarre shapes; Becker, disappointed of one legend, begins a new one, and perhaps becomes an unreliable witness. The mock-heroic feast and list of gifts recall the hyperbole of Keneally's early life, and we may question Becker's ingenuous assurance that his is "*the true story of what happened when they finally admitted it*" (339/437). The reception has its own fantastic dimensions: there are touches of epic and grotesque;

and, even with the normalcy of middle C, Wade and Maggie are finally translated, in a parody of traditional mythic ascension. Though the comic treatment seems at variance with the earnestness of Becker's usual pronouncements, it suits Hodgins' serious motives: *The Invention of the World* has resisted strictly objective narrative throughout in examining contemporary figuration of what seemed so acceptable, so simple, in the past.

The craft of Hodgins' structural and literary designs in this novel is often incorporated in an apparently unaffected expression that does not entirely conceal some studied skills. The narrative persona, for instance, is not above literary jokes; he suggests older stories of gods visiting mortals when he says of the former Hattie Scully, "In some of the books Maggie had read, a person as strange as Madmother Thomas would have ridden in for just a short while and then disappeared, like a sign of some truth that had managed to escape you" (15/30). This explicitness about traditional literary agency, about the sage or guide, is extended into Becker's own telling of the Keneally saga, an often unawed chronicle of the marvellous features common to heroes' early lives. The Keneally legend is an amalgamation of familiar improbable features, and even their subject "had read the legends himself and remembered them well" (87/115). Hodgins' hero constructs a literal *deus ex machina* to sway potential recruits, and even his consort is possessed in aesthetic fashion of "not only beauty, either, but a calm and ethereal manner that novelists and maiden poets reserve for the sickly heroines destined for an early genteel death" (119/154). *Doppelgängers* appear literally and figuratively, while one area in Wade's Fort is, again in both senses, a prison of the self. Symbols are used unashamedly: maps; a snail without a shell; a virtually allegorical climb up a mountain, rewarded with the traditional visionary experience. Lily Hayworth makes several specific literary allusions,[7] and her Browning reference does further service; it is cited by Wade in praise of Maggie as well as for the reader's appreciation of earlier mentions of circles and the god's-eye view: "He didn't know what it meant, he said, but it had made him think of a rainbow, and that reminded him of a pilot who told him once that a rainbow, from up in the sky, was a full circle" (351/452).

A further literary level in *The Invention of the World* is its use of narrative voice. David L. Jeffrey has commented:

> That the novel should be focused not through the eyes of any single narrator, but through the several worlds of minor as well as major

characters (on stage and off stage), that it should be told in a plurality of voices and perspectives, is one of the novel's most important ideas. (71)

Hodgins does not create a wholly independent narrative persona, as distinct from Lily Hayworth's taped or silent reminiscences and Becker's re-creations of legend and wedding. Yet the narrator is less than objective and more than impersonally characterless. His voice begins the novel imperatively—"Follow" (ix/7), "Ride" (ix/7), "don't ask" (xi/10)—directing the reader's attention to Becker while often indulging in a familiar form of address to "you". The story-teller knows his people, sharing their moods and sporadically making small colloquial interpolations or confidences like "of course" and "after all". Becker is the teller told of at the outset, and thereafter the narrative shows varying degrees of informality and friendliness in the alternating, technically third-person sections "Maggie", "Wade", "Julius", and "Pilgrimage".

One technique Hodgins employs has been identified by J.R. (Tim) Struthers as "oblique discourse", after Ronald Bates's discussion of the same (also called "free indirect discourse") in Joyce (Struthers, "Mind" 94, 95). The style is one "through which the author objectively narrates in the third person but also achieves the immediate effect of first person narration through describing the events in the exact style appropriate to the consciousness of the individual at the centre of the story" (Struthers, "Mind" 94). Among the wealth of examples which illustrate this practice, consider the rendering of Maggie's reaction to Madmother Thomas:

> And yet she'd been glad enough to come back and park her old self on Maggie. Banging on the front door as if she'd just gone out for a minute and the wind had slammed it shut behind her. Impatient, after forty-two years. Angry. When Maggie had opened the door she thought it was some kind of joke, some kind of costume, people that old didn't just turn up on your front verandah uninvited and without an escort. (45/66)

The narrative advances, yet the tone and syntax dramatize Maggie's exasperation. The language is familiar, not what is expected in third-person narration—an extension of the unforced expression mentioned above. The style also lends itself to ambiguity about the exact voice in play, whether of narrator or immediate character—in the following case, Wade: "One of the problems with telling Maggie anything was that she sometimes missed the point, or pretended to, and burrowed straight for something you'd never thought of" (164/207). The question is academic, for the benefit is ease in story-telling—a word more appropriate when the concept of "narrator" seems too technically restrictive.

In commenting on Gabriel García Márquez, Robert Coover has pointed out "one dominant force: *the love of story*", and this is a significant consideration in related fictions whose narrative voice can also be described as "humorous, mock-omniscient, warm, exuberant, witty, very winsome" (381)—not unlike the one in question. Hodgins' tone is very oral in its nearer reaches, accessible, relaxed, and often neighbourly; it is one best suited to his admitted interest in "the *sense of community*" (Hancock, "Interview" 40) he finds in Latin-American novels.

Good humour and geniality generally mark the narrative of *The Invention of the World* and make it, and its principal teller's voice, so personable. He personalizes his story without going completely into oblique discourse:

> She'd been bush herself once, and there were people who said Maggie Kyle had the smell of pitch and the mountains on her yet for all her moving down to civilization, to the coast; but others claimed it was because she hadn't moved all the way in to town the way you'd expect a forest refugee to do, she'd settled into that sagging old house out north a ways, surrounded by second-growth fir. And a good thing, too, they said, until she learned to laugh like a lady instead of like a chokerman stomping on a snake. (6/19)

The regional expression and the intimacy of the unpretentious language make character and tale extraordinarily engaging. The voice has several distances from its material; it is more obviously formal when thematic points are highlighted, though even here it sounds as unaffected and as unself-conscious as elsewhere. The reader, or the narrative's general audience, is never far from consideration and inclusion, and even an objective look at an appraising Danny Holland is kinetically vivid:

> He chewed gum then with his mouth open a little, always grinning, always flushed up and waiting for the next laugh, his eyes unlike the others' always busy, always scouring up and down the street, casually running up legs, idly following a pair of shifting hips, flickering across store signs, estimating the value of parked cars, sliding up to identify a passing bird or plane. (47/69)

As a narrator himself, Becker shows a quality of wit which marks much of his story of Keneally as a child, as in the parodic education of the hero who learns both practical and conceptual wisdom from rocks under the tutelage of his armless and legless mentor.

> "Look up along the moor there, Donal," Quirke said. "Now count those rocks." Within minutes the boy had discovered the concept of infinity. Within hours he'd learned how to add stones together into fences, subtract them from the fields, divide them among the farmers, and multiply them with a hammer. He went on, then, to learn about shapes and sizes and angles and strength from them, and finally even discovered how to turn them to a profit, though this part of the lesson was the least successful of all and tended to be highly theoretical. (80/107)

Becker's arch account of Maggie's reception, furthermore, is rich in catalogues of personalities and allegorical presents, in broad jokes and slapstick, and in epic and rhetorical touches like the "So much food was consumed . . ." (346/445) sequence. He can also be whimsically sophisticated:

> The people of the town, rewarded now beyond their dreams, had no weapons handy so dramatic as chain saws, and had to resort to all they'd brought, their wits. They hurled insults, like hand grenades, which exploded in the air above the loggers' heads. They flung elaborate comparisons and dire predictions, they tossed innuendoes and shreds of gossip and unsavoury speculations about the manner of their opponents' births. They raised their prices, they cancelled appointments, they cut off supplies. (348-49/448-49)

While the perspective is that of "The Eden Swindle", the tall tale in latter-day form, Becker's voice and character are developed significantly beyond his initial introduction as a stumpy and incongruous pretender to omniscience. His awareness of literary form and conventions alone argues against taking him, and by extension his various comments, simplistically.

The same point may be made about the entire novel. In content and style *The Invention of the World* often shows a deliberate co-existence of the literal and the metaphorical, of the realistic and the fabulated. For example, a far from minor motif such as the journey—spiritual or sociological, transatlantic or up-island, on a manure-spreader or with a sentimental cabbie—recurs in solidly physical situations which become more deeply significant through that intentional figuration. The appeal is that of a story which speaks familiarly of flesh and spirit through a coherent literary form, a linguistic construct. This artifice convincingly manages the difficult feat of rendering a credible life and an authentic world through what is essentially an extended parable. Hodgins' particular talent is his ability to present engaging characters and apparently spontaneous, even impressionistic, narrative within a frame which underlies these freedoms and this facility with pattern, structure, and meaning. The illusion is intentional, the invention overt, and its fabular soul is exemplary.

A Note On The Texts

Page references to the original hardcover edition of *The Invention of the World*, published by Macmillan of Canada, and to the New Canadian Library paperback edition of this work, published by McClelland & Stewart, are provided following the quotations.

Notes

[1] For additional elaboration see Geoff Hancock, "Magic or Realism: The Marvellous in Canadian Fiction".

[2] In Stephen Slemon's "Magic Realism as Post-Colonial Discourse", *The Invention of the World* and *What the Crow Said* are seen as suspended between the codes of narrative realism and the fantastic, so illustrating the "double vision inherent in colonial history and language" (20) which is argued as characteristic of such cultures.

[3] For another perspective on myth see Robert Lecker's "Haunted by a Glut of Ghosts: Jack Hodgins' *The Invention of the World*", where the emphasis is on a seeming parody of conventional mythic assumptions and structures.

[4] A substantial consideration of magic, reality, and some distinctions of created and invented worlds in this novel is pursued in Cecilia Coulas Fink's "'If Words Won't Do, and Symbols Fail': Hodgins' Magic Reality".

[5] See, for example, the entry "Strabo" in *The New Encyclopaedia Britannica*.

[6] The Browning allusion, and its inexactness, was first noted by J.R. (Tim) Struthers in his review of *The Invention of the World*, "Fantasy in a Mythless Age" 145-46. For a full consideration of its relevance see Laurence Steven, "Jack Hodgins' *The Invention of the World* & Robert Browning's 'Abt Vogler'".

[7] The allusions include quotations from Milton's *Paradise Lost*, book 1, Burns's "To a Mouse", Browning's "Abt Vogler", and Shakespeare's *Macbeth*, act 5, scene 8.

[8] Ronald Bates, working from Stephen Ullmann's *Style in the French Novel*, describes this "reported speech masquerading as narrative" in "The Tradition of the Marketplace: Joyce's Nice Use of Diction" 208. It has also been dubbed "The Uncle Charles Principle" by Hugh Kenner in his *Joyce's Voices* 15-38. On free indirect style consult also Roger Fowler, *Linguistics and the Novel* 97-103 and W.J.M. Bronzwaer, *Tense in the Novel: An Investigation of Some Potentialities of Linguistic Criticism* 41-80.

Works Cited

Barth, John. *The Sot-Weed Factor*. 1960. New York: Grosset & Dunlap, 1966.

———. *Giles Goat-Boy; or, The Revised New Syllabus*. Garden City, NY: Doubleday, 1966.

Bates, Ronald. "The Tradition of the Marketplace: Joyce's Nice Use of Diction". *English Studies in Canada* 1 (1975): 203-16.

Bronzwaer, W.J.M. *Tense in the Novel: An Investigation of Some Potentialities of Linguistic Criticism*. Groningen, Neth.: Wolters-Noordhoff, 1970.

Browning, Robert. "Abt Vogler". *Robert Browning: The Poems*. Ed. John Pettigrew. Supplemented and Completed by Thomas J. Collins. Vol. 1. New Haven, CT: Yale UP, 1981. 777-81. 2 vols.

Burns, Robert. "To a Mouse". *Burns: Poems and Songs*. Ed. James Kinsley. London: Oxford UP, 1969. 101-02.

Coover, Robert. "The Master's Voice". *American Review: The Magazine of New Writing* 26 (1977): 361-88.

David, Jack. "An Interview with Jack Hodgins". *Essays on Canadian Writing* 11 (1978): 142-46.

Enck, John J. "John Barth: An Interview". *Wisconsin Studies in Contemporary Literature* 6 (1965): 3-14.

Fink, Cecilia Coulas. "'If Words Won't Do, and Symbols Fail': Hodgins' Magic Reality". *Journal of Canadian Studies* 20.2 (1985): 118-31.

Flores, Angel. "Magical Realism in Spanish American Fiction". *Hispania* 38 (1955): 187-92.

Fowler, Roger. *Linguistics and the Novel.* New Accents. London: Methuen, 1977.

García Márquez, Gabriel. *One Hundred Years of Solitude.* Trans. Gregory Rabassa. New York: Harper & Row, 1970.

Hancock, Geoff. "An Interview with Jack Hodgins". *Canadian Fiction Magazine* 32-33 (1979-80): 33-63.

——. "Magic or Realism: The Marvellous in Canadian Fiction". *Magic Realism and Canadian Literature: Essays and Stories.* Ed. Peter Hinchcliffe and Ed Jewinski. Waterloo, ON: U of Waterloo P, 1986. 30-48.

——. "Magic Realism". *Magic Realism: An Anthology.* Ed. Geoff Hancock. Toronto: Aya, 1980. 7-15.

——. "Magic Realism, or, the Future of Fiction". *Canadian Fiction Magazine* 24-25 (1977): 4-6.

Hodgins, Jack. "Introduction". *The West Coast Experience.* Ed. Jack Hodgins. Themes in Canadian Literature. Toronto: Macmillan of Canada, 1976. 1-2.

——. *The Invention of the World.* Toronto: Macmillan of Canada, 1977. Afterword by George McWhirter. The New Canadian Library. Toronto: McClelland & Stewart, 1994.

——. *The Resurrection of Joseph Bourne; or, A Word or Two on Those Port Annie Miracles.* Toronto: Macmillan of Canada, 1979.

Jeffrey, David L. "Jack Hodgins and the Island Mind". *Canada Emergent: Literature/Art.* Ed. James Carley. [*Book Forum* 4 (1978):] 70-78.

Joyce, James. *A Portrait of the Artist as a Young Man.* 1916. Harmondsworth, Eng.: Penguin, 1976.

Kenner, Hugh. *Joyce's Voices.* Berkeley: U of California P, 1978.

Kroetsch, Robert. *What the Crow Said.* Don Mills, ON: General, 1978.

Lecker, Robert. "Haunted by a Glut of Ghosts: Jack Hodgins' *The Invention of the World*". *Essays on Canadian Writing* 20 (1980-81): 86-105.

Milton, John. *Paradise Lost. Complete Poems and Major Prose.* By John Milton. Ed. Merritt Y. Hughes. New York: Odyssey, 1957. 173-469.

Scholes, Robert. *The Fabulators*. New York: Oxford UP, 1967.
Shakespeare, William. *Macbeth*. Ed. Alfred Harbage. *William Shakespeare: The Complete Works*. Gen. ed. Alfred Harbage. Baltimore, MD: Penguin, 1969. 1107-35.
———. *The Tempest*. Ed. Northrop Frye. *William Shakespeare: The Complete Works*. Gen. ed. Alfred Harbage. Baltimore, MD: Penguin, 1969. 1369-95.
Slemon, Stephen. "Magic Realism as Post-Colonial Discourse". *Canadian Literature* 116 (1988): 9-24.
"Strabo". *The New Encyclopaedia Britannica*. 15th ed. (1974).
Steven, Laurence. "Jack Hodgins' *The Invention of the World* & Robert Browning's 'Abt Vogler'". *Canadian Literature* 99 (1983): 21-30.
Struthers, J.R. (Tim). "Fantasy in a Mythless Age". Rev. of *The Invention of the World*, by Jack Hodgins. *Essays on Canadian Writing* 9 (1977-78): 142-46.
———. "The Mind of the Artist: The Soul of the Place". Rev. of *Spit Delaney's Island: Selected Stories*, by Jack Hodgins. *Essays on Canadian Writing* 5 (1976): 93-95.
Twigg, Alan. "The Invention of Hodgins' World". *Quill & Quire* Dec. 1979: 11, 13.
Ullmann, Stephen. *Style in the French Novel*. Cambridge, Eng.: Cambridge UP, 1957.
Wilson, Robert Rawdon. "On The Boundary of The Magic and The Real: Notes on Inter-American Fiction". *The Compass: A Provincial Review* 6 (1979): 37-53.

Life on the Brink of Eternity:

The Resurrection of Joseph Bourne

Lawrence Mathews

> ... death,
> The undiscovered country, from whose bourn
> No traveller returns...
> —William Shakespeare, *Hamlet*, 3.1.78-80

> Many a man can travel to the very bourne of Heaven...
> —John Keats, "To J. H. Reynolds", 3 Feb. 1818, *Letters* (1: 224)

I

These are the two most famous appearances of the word "bourne" in English literature, and it is necessary to read *The Resurrection of Joseph Bourne* with both in mind. The lines from *Hamlet* have the most obvious relevance to the novel's action, in which Joseph Bourne *does* return from the country of death, but the quotation from Keats is the more important for critical understanding of Jack Hodgins' work. Joseph Bourne, "an old sour cramp of a man terrified on the brink of eternity" (34), can make the journey himself, and can also show others how to get there. Such travel is not the prerogative of an élite; Larry Bowman and

Jenny Chambers, ordinariness personified, are able, like the Sancho of Keats's next sentence, to "invent a Journey heavenward as well as any body" (1: 224). And Jenny, in her jubilant novel-stopping strip-tease, is able to entice the whole community of Port Annie to join her.

Keats's letter is germane not simply because it includes the word "bourne" but also because it raises an issue which Hodgins' novel addresses in some detail. Keats objects to the Wordsworthian tendency to burden poetry with philosophical cargo: "but for the sake of a few fine imaginative or domestic passages, are we to be bullied into a certain Philosophy engendered in the whims of an Egotist. . . [?]" (1: 223) For Keats, the power and the value of poetry lie elsewhere: "We hate poetry that has a palpable design upon us—and if we do not agree, seems to put its hand in its breeches pocket. Poetry should be great & unobtrusive, a thing which enters into one's soul, and does not startle it or amaze it with itself but with its subject" (1: 224). We are told that Joseph Bourne's poetry works in this way—indeed, that his life works in this way. It is easy enough for a novelist to incorporate such assertions into his text. But a crucial question for the critic of *The Resurrection of Joseph Bourne* is whether the novel itself fulfils the requirements of Keats's prescription, since there are clear indications that its author wants it to do so.

Of central importance here is the discussion between Bourne and Larry Bowman on the topic of "poetry and the artist's role", in which Bourne considers the problem of the twentieth-century writer who wants to preserve what is valuable in Romantic tradition:

> The old metaphors for eternity didn't work any more, he said, peeling an orange. We know too much for that. Keats and Byron, if they were around today, would have to take another look at their urns and oceans. Works of art could be burned or smashed, oceans could be killed off by men, even that famous steadfast star could have burned itself out years ago. "If symbols don't work—and what else can a poet use?—then eternity can only be expressed by implication, by the way we live our lives." (226)

To our eyes, according to Bourne, even the Grecian urn has a palpable design upon us, its poetic force impaired by the fact that it is no longer a credible metaphor for eternity. If we do not already "agree" with Keats, even the Odes will refuse our handshake. But for Bourne—and, the implication is, for Hodgins—"'the way we live our lives'" can provide the material for a convincing metaphoric expression of eternity. Bourne does not explain further, but Hodgins could hardly be more direct in announcing how he wants his novel to be understood.

The phrase "'the way we live our lives'" is of course ambiguous. Mrs. Barnstone, the local poetaster, would interpret it literally. She includes in her epic every fact she can gather about the doings of the people of Port Annie, but she herself comes to see that this approach is inadequate: "She had the uncomfortable feeling that, though her masterpiece was recording all the action she could find, the real story was going on behind it somewhere, perhaps invisibly, or just out of range of her vision" (236). And when, in a panic inspired by the landslide, she begins "to get a glimpse of what her epic poem had entirely missed", she decides that "the faster she put it all behind her the better" (254).

Bourne's poetry, too, is about "'the way we live our lives'", but it captures a sense of that "real story" which eludes Mrs. Barnstone. Although we learn tantalizingly little about his epic-in-progress on Port Royal, we are given a detailed account of the effect of his collection of poems, *Possessing Me*, on four representative Port Annie readers. For Larry Bowman, this poetry has the unobtrusiveness that Keats praised:

> They all started talking about something a person could relax about, like a walk through an alder grove, then just when you were nodding yes you knew what he was talking about, he snuck up and hit you with something bizarre that went hand in hand with what you'd just agreed to. One of the poems told the librarian, just when he was nodding in recognition over a described boat journey up a coastal inlet, that a search for a home in this earth was pointless, life couldn't be nailed to a spot. Another suggested that the librarian himself (the poem spoke to him as "you") was really a windowpane! His sole purpose on earth, according to the poem, was to let through a light that shone from somewhere else. (91-92)

Unlike Mrs. Barnstone, Bourne is able to link the world of ordinary experience, in which one walks through an alder grove, with the action that goes on "behind it somewhere, perhaps invisibly" (236)—the "somewhere else" (92) of the windowpane poem. Unlike Keats and Byron, Bourne does not meditate on urns and oceans; it is the librarian himself through whom the light should shine.

It shines in different ways for different readers. For Larry Bowman, "there was no doubt about it, the whole book—every word—was about copulation. Pure and simple pornography" (93). For Jenny Chambers, "What every poem in that book was about was the terrible feeling of looking for a place where you belonged" (93). For Angela Turner, the book contains "'The most beautiful love poems I've ever read'" (94). For Charlie Reynolds, editor of the *Port Annie Crier*, "'This little baby is about communication!'" (94)

These responses articulate desires which are finally fulfilled. Various journeys—to use Keats's metaphor—are made to the "bourne of Heaven". Larry's sexual frustration is transformed into something higher as he eventually falls in love with Angela, who has already had her fill of casual sex (there has been a brief liaison with a Peruvian sailor), and whose reaction to Bourne's poetry reveals her need for the deeper commitment that Larry offers her. Jenny discovers, ultimately, that Port Annie is the place where she belongs—once it can be perceived as a community composed of "Neighbours somehow linked" (270). Charlie Reynolds, a minor character, is significant here as a representative of that community, whose collective—and, for the most part, unconscious—desire for "communication" is brought to fruition as Jenny dances for them in the aftermath of the disastrous yet liberating slide.

But Joseph Bourne himself is the key to the "real story" of the Port Annie miracles. His name points to his thematic significance. The *Oxford English Dictionary* defines "bourne" as "A boundary"; "A bound, a limit"; "The limit or terminus of a race, journey or course; the ultimate point aimed at, or to which anything tends; destination, goal". The two major meanings work together nicely for Hodgins' purpose, since for Bourne the goal *is* always to extend the limit of human experience. At one point he tells Jenny Chambers that "'Sometimes the only way we grow is by pushing against the limits that try to hold us back'" (222). One of the three epigraphs is from contemporary Australian writer David Malouf's novel *An Imaginary Life*: "What else should our lives be but a continual series of beginnings, of painful settings out into the unknown, pushing off from the edges of consciousness into the mystery of what we have not yet become, except in dreams . . . " (Malouf 135). Other characters make such voyages, but Bourne is the explorer *par excellence*, the man who, we learn in Part 1, is poised "on the brink of eternity" (34). Larry Bowman, musing on the possibility that Bourne is "a space-age equivalent of Sir Lancelot", suggests this parallel: "Instead of fighting dragons or slaying villains he challenged the limits of mortality" (199).

The concept of "'pushing against the limits that try to hold us back'" has, we discover, social and psychological implications: the town of Port Annie becomes a community in the full sense of the word; Larry Bowman and Jenny Chambers have individual identity quests to achieve. But these dimensions of the novel are given powerful metaphoric resonance by the poetic exuberance with which Hodgins presents Joseph Bourne and the two mysterious women associated with him—the beautiful Raimey and the sinister Fat Annie.

II

The Resurrection of Joseph Bourne occupies part of that largely undiscovered territory (largely undiscovered by Canadian novelists, anyway) beyond realism. Geoff Hancock has called Hodgins a "magic realist" ("Magic Realism" 9), and Hodgins has acknowledged his debt to a number of Latin American writers—Gabriel García Márquez, Jorge Amado, Mario Vargas Llosa, and others—who are often so labelled (Hancock, "Interview" 39); however, he denies that there is anything doctrinaire about his relation to them: "I can't say that I sit down and say, 'Now I'm a magic realist and I'm going to do it this way'" (Hancock, "Interview" 57). In fact, the ultimate sources of the extra-realistic elements in the novel are biblical. Hodgins has taken pains to evoke this context, especially in his presentation of Bourne, Raimey, and Fat Annie Fartenburg. "I'm writing allegories I suppose", he has said in his interview with Geoff Hancock (62). Reviewers—especially David L. Jeffrey and J.R. (Tim) Struthers—have stressed the importance of this dimension of the novel.

Bourne is associated with a number of biblical figures. He is "the Lazarus man" (54, 100), "Melchizedek if you please" (55), "'Joseph Somebody-else in the Bible . . . who never gave up no matter what happened'" (57), even "a risen Christ" (174). Like Lazarus only in his physical death and resurrection, Bourne resembles Melchizedek both in his immortality—"having neither beginning of days, nor end of life; but made like unto the Son of God" (Hebrews 7.3)—and in the quasi-priestly role he plays in the community; and like Melchizedek, he is (for all practical purposes) without father, mother, and descent. He is also like the Joseph of Genesis, a dreamer and an interpreter of dreams in his poetic vocation, and an exile in Port Annie, having repudiated the *persona* of internationally famous poet, with its attendant glamour.

The use of biblical reference does not imply that Hodgins is simply retelling the biblical narratives, however. The parallels between Bourne and Jesus are extensive, but they are not exact or systematic. Bourne, like Jesus, dies and is resurrected—but his death is neither sacrificial nor redemptive. Bourne, like Jesus, is both teacher and miracle-working healer—but Bourne's public life (in this sense) is confined to the period after his resurrection, and his teachings are not nearly as precise as those of Jesus. Like the Jesus of Revelation, Bourne inspires his followers to join in an apocalyptic struggle against the forces of evil—but Bourne, unlike Jesus, disappears at the height of the local Armageddon, and is not there to preside over the renewed community of Port Annie, analogue of the New Jerusalem. Despite the similarities between the two, the Bourne story is not a systematic retelling of the Christ myth. But the connotative power of Jesus and the other biblical figures is associated with Bourne; clearly he is meant to belong to their tradition of the larger-than-life.

Raimey's biblical roots are not quite so obvious, but their presence can be discerned as early as the first scene of the novel. She is a "seabird" who arrives in Port Annie "on the twenty-second day of constant rain" (1), the day on which the sun finally shows itself. Like Noah's dove, she finds land; the event signals both the end of a Flood and the beginning of a new covenant for Joseph Bourne himself and, later, for the whole community. Raimey is responsible for both Bourne's death and his resurrection, events which transform him from an "Old Man" to a "New Man" (to use significant phrases from the titles of Parts 2 and 3). Before his death, Bourne is plagued by a "huge generalized dread" (20). Resurrected, he has, in Paul's words, "put off the old man with his deeds" and "put on the new man, which is renewed in knowledge after the image of him that created him" (Colossians 3.9-10): "Restored, he'd become a restorer. Repaired and resurrected, it looked as if he'd set about repairing and resurrecting everything in sight" (156). Raimey is therefore analogous to the Holy Spirit, a point Bourne comes close to making when he tells the townspeople about her after his resurrection: "never had he met anyone so full of the strength of spirit, the vitality of life, the gentleness of love, the beauty of soul . . . and so on and so on, you could add all the other synonyms you could think of for God" (157).

Raimey's earthly (as opposed to spiritual) dimension does seem to have a non-biblical provenance, however. The notion that God can appear in the guise of a sexually attractive young woman is a stumbling-block for Bourne's audience—"'But when you think of God walking the earth you don't usually imagine such a cheeky rear-end'" (157). Hodgins' readers should not have so much difficulty with this association, especially if they have also read Jorge Amado's *Gabriela, Clove and Cinnamon*, whose title character's innocent sexuality shines radiantly in the context of the folly and moral corruption characteristic of the world in which she lives. Hodgins appears to be signalling this connection by his use of the word "cinnamon" to describe Raimey's skin (2, 126), and his use of Brazil as the setting for one of her past adventures (32). Ilheus, Brazil, the setting of Amado's novel, is, like Port Annie, an isolated seaport just beginning to be affected by progress, "a land of outsiders, of people who had come from elsewhere" (Amado 68). Much of the plot describes—with comic irony—the petty intrigue engaged in by various pillars of the community in their efforts to increase their power and wealth. Gabriela is a mulatto servant-girl whose spontaneity and lack of interest in material possessions win the reader's sympathy. But Amado's vision is darker than Hodgins'; there is no Bourne-figure in *Gabriela, Clove and Cinnamon*, and Gabriela herself has none of Raimey's spiritual significance. Raimey, however, may be understood as a sort of born-again Gabriela, a woman whose physical beauty is not to be identified with carnality but has become a metaphor for something higher.

Fat Annie Fartenburg's biblical origins are much more readily apparent than Raimey's. She is the "death-whore" (29) who is "God of This World" (145), a phrase which in its New Testament context (2 Corinthians 4.4) refers clearly to Satan. She plays darkness to Bourne's light. Their mysterious spiritual enmity is only hinted at in the early sections of the novel, but in Part 3 it is presented in starkly apocalyptic terms, spirit versus flesh, love versus lust, altruism versus selfishness.

What we have learned about Fat Annie up to that point is ominous enough. According to local legend she was originally an incarnation of Leviathan, "a gigantic blue whale" (65) which beached itself near the townsite and was magically transformed overnight into a human being. Her career in Port Annie—the town is named after her—is marked by commercial success (lumbering), a marriage which results in her becoming locally famous for her sexual exuberance (her "great jubilant whoops clapped thunder-like across the bay" [67]), and the death of both her husband and her lover under very ambiguous circumstances. Fat Annie reacts to these last events by slaughtering her lover's herd of goats and swallowing her husband's pulverized bones. Then she becomes a recluse, staying for twenty years in her room in the local hotel.

In Part 3 Hodgins contrasts Bourne's significance and Annie's in terms of the thematically central issues of the nature of community and romantic love. Bourne's concept of community is embodied by his actions. He performs miracles of healing (both physical and psychological), teaches children, performs simple acts of kindness, speaks about the value of love. Fat Annie, on the other hand, becomes the symbol of Mayor Weins's social vision, which is rooted in greed: "The Creator of this world made people greedy so they could get ahead, he told himself" (217). Nor are we allowed to retain any illusions about the value of her passion. Angela Turner explains to Larry Bowman that "'Fat Annie has always meant the same to everyone. Flesh'" (200). It is Larry and Angela, characters linked closely to Bourne, who exemplify authentic love.

But the struggle between Bourne and Annie is personal as well, as Larry explains to Angela later in the same conversation: "'The end of the world, he calls it, him and the old death-whore at the end of the world together, and only one of them—he says—with any hope of surviving'" (201). Bourne prevails. Annie dies and is not resurrected, while Bourne leaves town very much alive; "he must have intended to go on much as before" (248), Jenny Chambers observes. Annie's death-scene is grotesquely comic. Like Milton's Satan, she has lost her physical impressiveness, having become "A shrivelled parsnip head and tiny legs that didn't reach the floor" (244). When she dies, Larry is at first unable to recognize her corpse, thinking it may be a "bundle of rags", a "gnarled root", or a "wind-up toy" (246). Her defeat is total. The god of this world, Vancouver Island's equivalent of both the beast from the sea (Revelation 13) and the whore of Babylon (Revelation 17-18), has been overthrown. The earthly city to which she has given her name has fallen, buried in the slide. In the final pages of the novel, a new community begins to form, one which gives promise of incarnating Bourne's spirit.

III

Insofar as *The Resurrection of Joseph Bourne* is about society, it is a straightforward thesis novel: two visions of community are juxtaposed, and one is declared to be superior. At issue is the question of whether the future of the town is to be given over to commercial development, to "progress" in the crudest sense of the word. A small group of unambiguously evil characters (Mayor Weins, Jeremy Fell, Damon West) works to achieve this end; they are opposed by a much larger group of characters who instinctively resist the mayor's plan, and gradually discover within themselves the potential for real community, a potential tentatively realized after the landslide. The connection between this conflict and the spiritual struggle between Bourne and Fat Annie is made clear, too. Weins adopts Fat Annie as the civic symbol; Bourne's post-resurrection behaviour personifies the kind of community that seems to be taking shape in the closing scenes.

The tension between the two visions does not manifest itself until Part 2, when Weins tries to get support for a scheme which would exploit Bourne's fame as great poet and resurrected man to attract tourists to Port Annie. The mayor's simple greed is complemented by the more sinister cunning of Jeremy Fell, who runs the local clothing store but is secretly an agent of American real estate interests. He joins forces with Weins, in order to be able to manipulate him.

But other tendencies in Port Annie society also become evident in Part 2. We learn of Mr. Manku's desire to learn to swim because "A place didn't become your home, he believed, until you'd claimed it—by committing at least one act of tremendous courage" (51); we learn, too, of Jenny Chambers' desire to feel that Port Annie is "home"; we witness Papa Magnani's assertion that Bourne's presence should not be exploited commercially because "'he doesn't belong to us, he belongs to the world'" (78). When Weins imports a giant cactus from Arizona in order to "'prove this place is more than a watery jungle'" (111), its presence offends Jenny, who had been in favour of the scheme to make Bourne a tourist attraction. In her opinion, the cactus "'looks like it's giving us all the finger!'" (139) For Larry Bowman, "'It looks like an overgrown hatrack'" (140). The potential for disaffection with Weins's concept of the town's future has found a focus. The official unveiling of the cactus coincides with Bourne's return from self-imposed exile in Squatters' Flats. The struggle for the town's collective soul is ready to begin in earnest.

The social issue is defined clearly for the townspeople by the arrival of Damon West at the beginning of Part 3. West, the chairman and largest shareholder of Evergreen Realty Company, has plans for developing Squatters' Flats, a piece of land inhabited by hippies and other eccentrics, including Bourne. Traditionally, hatred of the squatters has been one of the few sentiments shared by all of the citizens of Port Annie; yet they are not enthusiastic about West's plans. At a town meeting, Slim Potts makes the case for retaining the status quo: "Some people need to know that every morning when they wake up their neighbours will be the same people they were yesterday, not strangers, the trees will all be in the same place, not bulldozed out of the way for a building, the sea the same as it always was, not filled in for a parking lot" (168).

Bourne comes to embody the view of community suggested by Slim's speech. In his role as volunteer teacher, he tells Mr. Manku that "'Tomorrow... we'll be learning all about families'" (195); in his role as Port Annie's holy man, he treats the whole town as an extended family. Weins, on the other hand, continues to preach the doctrines of material progress and self-interest. The message which he puts on his tourist poster (which features Fat Annie's face) is succinct:

> Grab your chance
> Don't think too small
> The future's coming
> With fortunes for all. (210)

The mayor staples these posters to the wall of a trailer which had once been used as a church, and is now to be the Port Annie tourist bureau; the posters cover gold-leaf messages from 1 John left behind by the congregation, one of which puns on Bourne's name: "'For whatsoever is born of God overcometh the world'" (1 John 5.4; Hodgins 213). Bourne's spirituality is not specifically Christian, but his vision of community is certainly congruent with John's.

Larry Bowman gets a sense of this vision after the landslide: "The town had gone, but he didn't feel that he'd lost a thing that mattered. No one had. The community still existed.... they'd been freed from something—don't ask him what—they'd been given a chance to find out what they were capable of being" (259). The "town"—this world—has disappeared; the "community" of Port Annie has been revealed—spiritual, born (Bourne?) of God. Weins, Fell, and West have failed. The people of Port Annie achieve, momentarily at least, the sense that they do constitute an extended family.

Bourne's vision triumphs. The townspeople escape the ravages of the slide by converging on Squatters' Flats, where they are received with charity by the people whom they have so long despised. With remarkable efficiency, the squatters organize themselves to provide food and shelter for the survivors. That evening, Jenny Chambers' strip-tease expresses publicly the newly found sense of family which all of the people of Port Annie now share:

> What were they watching? Was she shedding something for them as well? Their own contributions to the music's beat, the body movements, the frenzy of her need to free herself from that thing, all of it united them somehow. This old earth could throw you off its back like a bronco any time it wanted, but it couldn't break that link which ran from soul to soul. (270)

But only a few characters—Larry Bowman, Angela Turner, Jenny Chambers—know that "the things that aren't seen never end" (271), that what has happened to the community is directly linked to the spiritual warfare between Bourne and Fat Annie. In the case of most of the townspeople, Hodgins has been concerned only in a perfunctory way to show how "'eternity can . . . be expressed by implication, by the way we live our lives'" (226). It is not eternity that he slights (for the meaning of the characters' lives *sub specie aeternitatis* is obvious enough), but daily reality. The minor figures are—as John Mills has suggested—as simple as Jonsonian humours (39). It would be a mistake, though, to charge Hodgins with artistic failure here, since there is evidence that he has quite deliberately made these characters one-dimensional, mixing the conventions of realism and romance—partly no doubt for comic effect, but perhaps also in order to give the reader clear guidelines for evaluating the more complex experience of the main characters.

As in Dickens, a minor character's name may reveal the character's thematic significance. Weins suggests "venal" or corruptible, and perhaps "venial", forgivable. Damon West is close to "Demon of the West", an association reinforced by the reference to him as "The handsome devil" (241) in the opening lines of Mrs. Barnstone's epic, lines which parody the opening of *Paradise Lost*. Jeremy Fell's internal monologues are a series of jeremiads, and his fallenness is so evident as to make his surname almost redundant. The flirtatious, pathetic Rita Rentalla can perhaps be "rented"—she will drink with anyone who will buy beer for her—and is certainly "rent" in the sense of psychologically wounded or torn. Papa Magnani, on the other hand, is as magnanimous as his name implies.

Hodgins also tends to identify these characters, again and again, by referring to a particular personality trait, idiosyncrasy, or verbal tic. After a certain point we know that Rita Rentalla will not appear without some mention being made of her out-thrust hip (65). Mrs. Barnstone will not speak without saying "'Honestly, . . . I could spit'" (62) as preface or conclusion. Slim Potts is known for his collection of machines, Dirty Della and Linda Weins for their sexual appetites, Greg Wong for his motorcycle (and, later, his Fat Annie costume), Preserved Crabbe for his inexplicable passion for his ugly woman, Hill Gin for her apocalyptic rantings. We do not expect these characters to deepen or to change— Dirty Della is the only one who does, and that happens by means of Bourne's quasi-miraculous intervention. We tend to respond to them in terms of what they "represent", rather than as we would to characters portrayed as autonomous individuals.

Hodgins has presented most of the characters—Jeremy Fell is an exception—as ironically unaware of the larger significance of their actions. Thus Mayor Weins does not know that his effort to bring "progress" to Port Annie is part of a spiritual struggle between light and darkness; Fat Annie is to him no more than a convenient advertising device, but by the time he begins to put up the posters, the reader knows that she is the "death-whore" (29) whom Bourne must overcome. The residents of Squatters' Flats do not connect their spontaneous hospitality to the survivors of the slide with Fat Annie's death and Bourne's victory, nor are they making a conscious effort to follow Bourne's teachings. Both for them and for most of their guests, the final scene in which Jenny's dance binds them together is fortuitous, inexplicable. For the reader, it is not; nor is it so for Larry Bowman and Jenny Chambers, characters whom Hodgins has made more complex and, in terms of the canons of realism, more credible than their neighbours.

IV

One reviewer, Rupert Schieder, has used the phrase "seeker figures" (35) to describe Larry Bowman and Jenny Chambers. What each seeks is a sort of psychological resurrection. Bowman, hearing that Bourne has returned from the dead, recognizes his own parallel need: "Now that would be a true resurrection, Mr. Bourne! To wake up some morning and find that he'd been turned into a brute, a lady-killer, a man of terrific confidence" (47). Jenny does not think of her quest in such explicit terms, but in the final scene she rises, phoenix-like, from the pyre of discarded selves which have prevented her from discovering that Port Annie is "home" (or as close to home as one can get, this side of Bourne's eternity). In the dance she regains her original beauty and vitality—"Jenny, Flaming Jenny, was afire again"—and becomes the catalyst for the resurrection of the community's sense of itself: "as if she were charged with dancing life back into things, or into *them*" (270). Jenny loses her common-law husband; Larry gains a wife. Their stories reinforce each other, twin affirmations of the value of pursuing one's individual quest.

Larry Bowman performs no miracles, though, like Bourne's, his name is freighted with figurative meaning: Larry, Lawrence, laurel; Bowman, bow-man, Apollo. His most significant predecessor in this context is the Apollo of Keats's *Hyperion*, who, as the result of an encounter with the goddess Mnemosyne, awakes to a knowledge of his divinity. Larry Bowman awakes to a knowledge of his humanity, as a result of his encounter with Raimey.

In Part 1, Larry's most noticeable characteristics are his sexual frustration and his Walter Mittyish day-dreams of emulating Preserved Crabbe and becoming "romantic, heroic, a real man" (46). Overwhelmed by Raimey's beauty, he decides finally that "the time had come for him to make his move, show himself, stand up like a man and declare his feelings for that woman" (120) whose presence has had the power "to raise up something that he'd thought was dead in him, his manhood" (45). One day he follows her to a deserted spot on the shoreline, watches her swim in the nude, and then, "amazed at his own courage", finds himself joining her, "hardly able to believe that this was him, this was Larry Bowman, this was himself burst free at last of those clothes and that timidity and all the years of hiding" (127). His sexual desire remains unsatisfied, but, after a second meeting, he realizes that this is no longer so important: Raimey's smile is "not only woman-beautiful . . . but another kind of beautiful, too, that had nothing at all to do with being a desirable woman. This was some other quality . . . that had made her capable of raising up Bourne" (129-30). Her departure leaves him desolate, "driven back to his books, a shaken and heartbroken man" (147). Yet the possibility of a happiness based on something other than sexual satisfaction has been revealed to him, and he has been prepared for his relationship with Angela, which develops in Part 3.

Up to this point Larry's story parallels Apollo's. In Keats's *Hyperion*, Apollo is first presented as suffering from an unhappiness he can neither understand nor control. Then, wandering near the shore of *his* island, he comes upon the goddess Mnemosyne, who reveals his true (divine) nature to him—at which point, the fragmentary poem ends (*Hyperion* 3.28-136). Larry's experience is not a parody of Apollo's. Raimey is presented with the same sort of seriousness as Mnemosyne. At one point Raimey is described as "Pure goddess" (126), and later in the novel (in a passage quoted in Section II above) Bourne himself alludes to her possible divinity (157). Larry's discovery of the mysterious spiritual quality in her marks the beginning of his own rebirth.

Eventually he falls in love with Angela Turner, whose story is the obverse of his. A liaison with a Peruvian sailor (who has left her pregnant) has given her the knowledge that the value of sexual gratification is limited. When she hears of Bourne's resurrection, she undergoes an initiation by water which anticipates Larry's, impulsively swimming across the inlet and back, made jubilant by the insight that "not everything after all had to come to an ugly end" (44). It is she who is more aggressive in the early stages of her relationship with Larry, but he gradually becomes used to the idea that they are, indeed, meant for each other. At one point we are given a neat summary of his story: "When he'd been spending all those months fantasizing a sex life for himself he'd never dreamed that he would end up falling in love" (227). Before Larry's sea-change, Angela could have been no more to him than a subject for erotic day-dreaming. His transformation has, in its way, been as profound as Apollo's.

Unlike Larry, Jenny Chambers at the beginning of the novel already knows a great deal about sex and something about love. Introduced as "that ex-stripper with pink hair" (5) who chews gum with her mouth open, she seems even less promising than Larry as a candidate for transformation of any kind. Living with Slim Potts and his eight children, she finds herself leading the dull life that he had described to her, shortly after her arrival, as typical of the citizens of Port Annie: "'They work and eat and worry about their kids and make love with somebody if they're lucky, and sleep. Some fish. Some hunt. Others hike. Most drink'" (86). To have come to this is bitterly disappointing for her, since she had once enjoyed celebrity status, as the first stripper to perform at the local tavern: "She didn't have any trouble remembering what it was like the day she came here, a shapely sexy broad, believe it or not, and how they made her welcome for a while, and then reversed themselves and made her feel a stranger again, the very people she'd thought were friends" (83).

Her longing for community first becomes explicit when she reads *Possessing Me* and discovers that every poem is about "the terrible feeling of looking for a place where you belonged" (93). She tries to ingratiate herself with people who might make her feel accepted, but when buying a new wardrobe fails to achieve this result, and when Slim's dissatisfaction with their relationship becomes apparent, her sense of isolation is total. In a final desperate attempt to get attention and approval, she decides to marry Slim. This strategy seems to work: "Just as she'd hoped, it had brought her more friends than enough. Overnight. A bride was always the most popular girl in the town" (151).

When Bourne's shack burns down, she invites him to live at the Chambers-Potts house. His influence ultimately causes her to decide to cancel the wedding:

> And he was to blame, if he really wanted to know. If he hadn't moved into her house she might never have questioned what she was doing. But there he was, every day, a constant reminder of how good he was, how selfless, how dedicated to making other people happy. A model of generosity. And there she was, taking advantage of all those women to make herself more popular. . . . (220-21)

Larry's insight into Raimey's extra-womanly beauty has its parallel in Jenny's perception that honesty is more important than the comfort of social acceptance. And eventually, of course, Jenny *is* accepted, not as a spurious bride, but as someone who meets a real community need.

Slim's death in the landslide does not break her spirit. Her dance is partly a response to her personal grief, partly a response to the anonymous onlooker who tells her to "'Dance that bloody slide right off our backs'" (267). What she does is cathartic both for her and for her audience. We are told that "she had plenty to shed in this dance": her memory of Slim, her misguided desire to gain popularity, and her fear of Slim's "eight rotten brats" (269) for whom she is now responsible. For their part, the members of her audience forget that they are separate individuals, and become "Neighbours somehow linked" (270). Jenny is home.

As she moves purposefully through the "flickering dark" (270), the reader may speculate that her surname, too, may contain an allusion to Keats. We move through life, Keats writes, as through "a large Mansion of Many Apartments", from "the infant or thoughtless Chamber" to "the Chamber of Maiden-Thought", which, although initially delightful, becomes in time akin to the mental state in which Jenny finds herself when she struggles for acceptance, a sense "that the World is full of Misery and Heartbreak, Pain, Sickness and oppression—whereby This Chamber of Maiden Thought becomes gradually darken'd and at the same time on all sides of it many doors are set open—but all dark—all leading to dark passages" ("To J.H. Reynolds", 3 May 1818, *Letters* 1: 280, 281). For Keats, as for Jenny and Joseph Bourne, the appropriate course of action is to go beyond previously known limits, to "make discoveries, and shed a light in them" (1: 281). Jenny, "afire again" (270), finds that what Keats prophesied for his friend may become true for her: "Your third Chamber of Life shall be a lucky and a gentle one—stored with the wine of love—and the Bread of Friendship" (1: 282-83).

There is an audacity about Hodgins' handling of the stories of his "seeker figures". Few contemporary novelists would, under any circumstances, choose to write about the continuing validity of the ideals of romantic love and authentic community; fewer still would embody such a theme in a story whose characters are as unexceptional as Larry and Jenny, and whose setting is as unlikely as Port Annie. But (one suspects) in so doing, Hodgins is giving voice to the deeply-held beliefs of many in the wide audience his work should one day reach. Unlike the urns and oceans of Romantic poetry, such beliefs—whether we consider them to be banal or profound—cannot be "killed off by men" (226).

V

More complex and fully-rounded than the minor characters, Larry Bowman and Jenny Chambers are nevertheless not out of place in the Port Annie of Rita Rentalla and Jacob Weins. Yet Hodgins' theme demands that we take Larry and Jenny seriously, and we do. It is an index of his artistic achievement in *The Resurrection of Joseph Bourne* that their kinship with the minor characters is never in doubt. It is an index of his artistic ambition that he tackles the more complex problem of integrating Joseph Bourne into this world as well. Bourne, I have argued above, succeeds as metaphor; it is perhaps inevitable that he should fail to move or convince as a human being.

Consider the scene in which Jenny, mourning Slim's death, is aware that she is weeping in public, feels embarrassed, then decides to "put on a good show" (256). She at once expresses genuine grief and quite consciously acts the role of mourner for her unwelcome audience: "it was time they found out she was a passionate woman, not a cold fish like some other people she could mention!" (257) On the one hand, there is the sense that Hodgins is having good-natured fun with Jenny, as he does when, for example, he mocks Mrs. Barnstone's literary pretensions. On the other hand, though, Jenny's comic self-righteousness does not completely undercut the sincerity established earlier. There is no significant ironic distance between the reader and Jenny, as there is between the reader and Mrs. Barnstone. If most people would smile at Jenny's reaction, it is because hers is one which they themselves might experience. Many such illustrations could be given. Larry, aware that he is falling in love with Angela, and gradually giving himself to the experience, is nonetheless also "getting a little fed up with the loss of privacy" (175). Again, there is the comic presentation of the character's reaction, combined with a sense of the relative complexity of his inner experience (none of the minor characters would be concerned about privacy). Preserved Crabbe's passion is purely comic in a way that Larry's can never be; we know too much about the librarian's frustration, loneliness, and desire for love.

Further, in certain crucial scenes Larry and Jenny experience moments of visionary intensity, instant journeys to the bourne of Heaven, which separate their experience from that of their fellow townspeople in a definitive way—Larry in shedding his clothes to join Raimey in the water, Jenny in shedding hers to bind the community together with her fire. These scenes are presented absolutely without irony, in the tradition of the Wordsworthian spot of time. They are, perhaps, examples of the kind of experience Bourne records and re-creates in the poems of *Possessing Me*.

But Hodgins does not render Bourne's own experience in this way. In fact, in Parts 2 and 3, after the resurrection, we have no access at all to Bourne's inner life. We are distanced from him in the same way as we are distanced from the minor characters. Perhaps this point would not be worth commenting on if Larry and Jenny were not also major characters. Bourne must suffer by comparison with them in the sense that his humanity is not so fully realized as theirs, however much Hodgins claims for it. Reminders that "He was a human being too ... for all the marvels he performed" (248) are not enough. We *know* that Larry and Jenny are human because we know what they think and feel; Bourne, despite his poetic celebration of the windowpane, remains, in a sense, as opaque as Damon West, more opaque than Jacob Weins.

Hodgins seems to be doing his best to make Bourne the kind of figure about whom Larry Bowman meditates in this passage:

> Being a hero had strict requirements. A code of honour. A grand enormous soul. It required courage and strength and patience and love and sacrifice. And outside of the pages of those books, where had he ever seen such a thing? ... If Joseph Bourne was beginning to act as if he belonged in an allegory, or an ancient romance, it was only natural that Larry Bowman should look for some gimmick, some flaw, some ulterior motive. (199)

Of course it turns out that Larry's suspicions are never confirmed. The narrative reveals that there are no gimmicks or flaws, that Bourne has no ulterior motives. But neither is there much to suggest that he has "A grand enormous soul". What evidence there is—the good deeds, the miracles—is purely external, and Hodgins does not give us a reliable way of evaluating it. We are not allowed to be present at Bourne's resurrection, nor at any of the miracles he performs, scenes which might have been presented as visionary moments of the kind experienced by Larry in his encounter with Raimey and by Jenny in her dance. Bourne's one act of public courage—outfacing Jeremy Fell when the latter begins to bulldoze the squatters' shacks (232-34)—seems to have as much to do with Fell's cowardice as with Bourne's heroism: "If Bourne thought he was being heroic, Larry thought, he ought to know that what he looked like now was just a stubborn old man" (232).

Nor does Bourne's own testimony convince us that he possesses "A grand enormous soul". There is something glib and vague about his praise of "'those good old invisible things that can't be stolen or disappear... What our grandparents used to call the things of soul'" (228). We are being asked to take too much on trust when, commenting on the squatters' perversity, he says "'there's nothing left for me to do ... but love them, I guess'" (229). God, though referred to frequently, exists primarily as a comforting ecumenical source for Bourne's metaphysical blandness: "'Isn't love of any kind an attempt to see what God must see—with *His* perfect vision?'" (229) The reader who answers this question in the affirmative is, in the context of the novel, making a commitment to nothing precise. Perhaps the worst that can be said about Bourne's rhetoric is that it never gets specific enough to cause anyone to consider disagreeing with its implications. Certainly Bourne's "grand enormous soul" is never realized in Hodgins' language.

Despite Hodgins' apparent intention, then, it is not Bourne, but Larry Bowman and Jenny Chambers who move us most deeply. Bourne has a palpable design upon us. Larry and Jenny will shake hands with anyone; they enter our souls unobtrusively, and it is through them that Hodgins' subject gains its power to amaze. In their case, we are not asked to take anything on trust. The way they live their lives in all its flawed and confused immediacy is as fully available to us as Hodgins' art can make it. When we learn that Jenny has, figuratively, "plenty to shed" (269) in her dance, and that she goes on to do it successfully, we find the image convincing, because we know the depth of the experience which informs her actions. We know how desire and suffering have prepared her for this moment; we know the sense in which the striptease enacts her own resurrection. Similarly, when we watch her through Larry Bowman's eyes, and learn that "she danced unseeing, as if she were charged with dancing life back into things, or into *them*" (270), we are moved because we know that he is capable of making such a judgement; we know the sense in which Raimey has, in effect, already danced life back into *him*. Significantly, Bourne is not mentioned in the last three paragraphs. Instead, centre stage is given to Jenny and her audience, that "clumsy chorus line of salvaged bones" (271), who do as much as any characters in recent fiction to make visible "'those good old invisible things that can't be stolen or disappear'" (228), "the things that"—as we are reminded in the final sentence—"never end" (271).

Works Cited

Amado, Jorge. *Gabriela, Clove and Cinnamon*. Trans. James L. Taylor and William L. Grossman. New York: Alfred A. Knopf, 1962.

Hancock, Geoff. "An Interview with Jack Hodgins". *Canadian Fiction Magazine* 32-33 (1979-80): 33-63.

———. "Magic Realism". *Magic Realism: An Anthology*. Ed. Geoff Hancock. Toronto: Aya, 1980. 7-15.

Hodgins, Jack. *The Resurrection of Joseph Bourne; or, A Word or Two on Those Port Annie Miracles*. Toronto: Macmillan of Canada, 1979.

Jeffrey, David L. "A Crust for the Critics". Rev. of *The Resurrection of Joseph Bourne*, by Jack Hodgins. *Canadian Literature* 84 (1980): 74-78.

Keats, John. *Hyperion: A Fragment. Keats: Poetical Works*. Ed. H.W. Garrod. London: Oxford UP, 1956. 221-43.

———. *The Letters of John Keats 1814-1821*. Ed. Hyder Edward Rollins. 2 vols. Cambridge, MA: Harvard UP, 1958.

Malouf, David. *An Imaginary Life*. New York: George Braziller, 1978.

Mills, John. Rev. of *The Resurrection of Joseph Bourne*, by Jack Hodgins. *West Coast Review* 15.1 (1980): 38-40.

Milton, John. *Paradise Lost. Complete Poems and Major Prose*. By John Milton. Ed. Merritt Y. Hughes. New York: Odyssey, 1957. 173-469.

Schieder, Rupert. "Setting Out into the Unknown". Rev. of *The Resurrection of Joseph Bourne*, by Jack Hodgins. *The Canadian Forum* Dec.-Jan. 1979-80: 34-36.

Shakespeare, William. *Hamlet*. Ed. Willard Farnham. *William Shakespeare: The Complete Works*. Gen. ed. Alfred Harbage. Baltimore, MD: Penguin, 1969. 930-76.

Struthers, J.R. (Tim). "Thinking about Eternity". Rev. of *The Resurrection of Joseph Bourne*, by Jack Hodgins. *Essays on Canadian Writing* 20 (1980-81): 126-33.

A Crazy Glory:
Jack Hodgins' Secular Allegory

W.J. Keith

One of the stories in Jack Hodgins' first collection, *Spit Delaney's Island* (1976), is remarkable for its apparent (but, as we shall see, only apparent) generic incongruity so far as the rest of the book is concerned. While the other stories conform to a basic realism, frequently heightened to the extent of suggesting "magic realism", "At the Foot of the Hill, Birdie's School" can only be described as a kind of allegory. A young man by the name of Webster Treherne has been living in a now-disbanded commune in the hills with his father, "the Old Man", who "taught him that time was meaningless and God was All" (137). Descending to a town in the valley with the "one and certain goal" of joining the McLean gang, a historical group of outlaws in British Columbia active in the late 1870s, he enters a school run by Balk-Eyed Birdie where courses are offered in Truth, Love, and Life. But Birdie assures him: "'we don't teach you how to *find* those things, we teach you how to *lose* them'" (141). In

---

First published, in an earlier version, in W.J. Keith, *A Sense of Style: Studies in the Art of Fiction in English-Speaking Canada* (Toronto: ECW, 1989). Updated and enlarged by the author. Reproduced by permission of ECW Press.

the valley, Webster continually encounters a small boy who throws chunks of coal at him, and a group of girls who tempt and mock him; in his turn, though he shows clear signs of being too compassionate for a real criminal, he holds up a local storekeeper (with an unloaded gun). The man curses him by invoking the consumption that is killing his wife. Webster indeed falls sick, and appears to be dying; but at the end, when Birdie has gone for a doctor, Webster knows that "when she came back . . . he wouldn't be there" but would have returned "in his freedom" to the hills from whence he came (151).

Clearly, this story can only be understood if it is interpreted to reveal a hidden meaning. Webster Treherne is obviously a significant name, and Hodgins has observed: "I don't know a character until I know his or her name" (Hancock 74). Allan Pritchard has noted that the name brings together the two greatest English visionaries of the seventeenth century, one seeing corruption, the other goodness (35). His place of origin in the hills suggests a heaven or paradise, and his descent to the town either a Fall or a Christ-like incarnation. The town presumably represents the evil of the world in which Webster, despite his ambition to crime, can never ultimately remain. The syllabus at Birdie's school suggests an image of education in our world seen through a glass darkly, as well as an inversion of an ideal trivium like St. Paul's faith, hope, and charity. Throughout the story are scattered allusions to the apocalyptic poetry of Dylan Thomas, and the final paragraph in which Webster returns "in the pale April sunlight" (151), the time of resurrection as well as the cruellest month, suggests an ultimate divine comedy of redemption. The allegory here is tricky. At first Webster, with his ostensible aim "to pistol-whip Chinese, to shoot Indians right and left, stab policemen, murder strangers" (137), seems closer to Antichrist than to Jesus, but we are invited to consider the difficulty of goodness trying to acclimatize itself to a world of violence and evil. In order to inculcate Truth, Love, and Life, one must go through the way of their opposites. The hold-up of the shopkeeper, a crime in our world, may look different if we can see Webster (remember the ambiguous unloaded pistol) attempting to lure mankind away from material things while remaining within human (fallen) conventions. This is a dark, perhaps dangerous allegory without rigid elucidations, one in which individual elements within the story are open to a series of seemingly traditional but in fact radical and shifting symbolic meanings.

"At the Foot of the Hill, Birdie's School" is not, I think, a successful story within *Spit Delaney's Island*, whatever its (arguable) separate merits, since it breaks the tonal unity of the rest of the volume. Waldemar Zacharasiewicz has compared it to Flannery O'Connor's work and also detects within it "a Kafkaesque touch" (99); in addition, we may feel that it might have been managed more deftly by a consistently explicit modern allegorist like T.F. Powys. One wonders, indeed, why it was included in an otherwise carefully integrated collection. A possible explanation is that it alerts readers to the underlying levels of meaning that exist in the other stories and to the more general tendency towards allegory in Hodgins' approach to the art of story-telling ("I'm writing allegories I suppose", he admitted to Hancock [77]). In his most characteristic work, certainly, he has created for himself a form in which allegorical meanings are available, not always consistently or continually but intermittently and sometimes even to comic effect, beneath the surface of the literal story.

This is true, for example, of the two Spit Delaney stories that frame the book. The first, "Separating", alerts us even in its title to a more generalized significance. Separation is a theme that echoes throughout the story—Spit's separation from "Old Number One", the break-up of his marriage, the continuing image of the "long curving line of sand that separates island from sea and man from whale" (4), and the larger, more philosophical *"dividing line"* separating *"what is and what isn't"* (8). It also echoes throughout the volume—the "three women of the country" all separated from each other in the story of that title, the way the Strait of Georgia separates island from mainland in "The Trench Dwellers", the lonely deserted woman in "By the River". I am even tempted to extrapolate and suggest that Hodgins himself is here exploring the dividing line that separates what is and what is not possible in fiction. In addition, other words, notably "edge", "real", and "touch", recur in this story and become resonant concepts throughout Hodgins' work. We soon realize that, without in any way undervaluing his regional preoccupation, he is concerned to communicate something far more ambitious than a vivid portrait of the colourful and often idiosyncratic inhabitants of northern Vancouver Island.

When Spit is suddenly confronted with the profound—and ultimately dislocating—question that pops into his mind on the beach (*"Where is the dividing line?"* [7]), he necessarily embarks on a journey that is much more than the standard world-trip of the average tourist. (This sequence is present, I assume, to suggest that the answer to Spit's problem is not to be found among the things of this world.) When, at a moment of spiritual crisis, he goes to the shore and encounters "a naked youth coming up out of waves to greet him" (17), mythological as well as allegorical analogues become available. Finally, these images converge as he imagines himself going off with the hitch-hikers into an unknown but clearly different future, standing at the edge of the water, himself stripped metaphorically as the youth was physically (an image Hodgins considers again in a climactic scene in *The Honorary Patron*), and then addressing himself to God or, at any rate, to the unknown:

> *Okay you son of a bitch!*
> *I'm stripped now, okay, now where is that god-damned line?* (23)

In "Spit Delaney's Island", at the close of the book, Spit is led up from his symbolic seashore (he is now living in a motel where "tides slosh forward . . . almost to the cabin door" [171]) to an equally symbolic yet at the same time, of course, equally authentic British Columbian mountain. Phemie Porter, the grotesque but liberating poetess who takes him in tow, insists on referring to him as "'Mr. Man'" (184, 187), thus establishing him as, in part, an Everyman figure. She invites him to follow the pattern of her own father, to disappear into the mountains as a way of "going into yourself" and to come back as "a changed man" (189). Spit only gets part of the way up the symbolic ascent, and eventually turns back; nonetheless, he has obviously learned something from Phemie, and we sense at the close that he is less "'a man who is trapped by [his] own limits'" (194) than he was at the beginning. Here and elsewhere in the book the stories are embedded far more firmly in realistic conventions, yet like "At the Foot of the Hill, Birdie's School" they respond to interpretation as allegorical fables.

In "Three Women of the Country" the allegorical possibilities are signposted by the choice of names. Pritchard has already written of these, noting the apparent borrowing of the resonant place-name Cut Off from a late Ethel Wilson short story ("A Visit to the Frontier", where she too moves towards allegory), the allusions to *The Tempest*, and the connection with Melville's *Moby-Dick* through the name Starbuck, the last two of which, he says, put us in mind of other islands and other isolations (22). This is helpful. It needs to be pointed out, however, that other names in this story are less erudite and certainly less solemn in their implications. Mrs. Wright is appropriately named in view of her incorrigible self-righteousness (Hodgins has remarked how he likes to create a character who thinks he knows "what life is all about" and then to "pull the rug out from under his feet" [Hancock 64]); but she has already been married to a Mr. Left, and the joke warns that allusive interpretation can be carried too far. Is Hodgins here setting an Atwood-like satiric trap for excessively close readers? Certainly the Larkin triplets—Percy, Bysshe, and Shelley—strengthen this possibility, a possibility heightened by the fact that they spend much of their time skylarking around. Hodgins' mischievous humour sets a necessary brake on over-subtle connections and over-ingenious parallels. Within these limits, however, he does encourage us to consider his Vancouver Islanders in the light of previous literature (Canadian and otherwise) and to recognize that they belong not just to their all-important local place but to a world of larger patterns and universal meanings.

The same is true of the more specifically mythic references that underlie some of the stories. When, for example, in "Every Day of His Life" Big Glad Littlestone holds out an apple to Mr. Swingler, we register consciously what we would in any case have sensed implicitly: that a unique variation of the old pattern stretching back to Genesis is being played out in a very different Eden and in a very different key. The latter needs to be stressed; it is not enough to pick the Eve reference out of the myth-kitty. Big Glad is not tempting Swingler to sin—though she has already "fallen" in the popular sense since there is "'no sign of a father for that boy of hers'" (86)—and Swingler refuses the apple but takes her. The Eden myth is both used and altered, and in this instance, because the myth and its symbolic situation are so well known, Hodgins does not have to underline the connection. In "After the Season", however, since Classical allusion is no longer part of the common store, he has to point up his mythological reference. Hallie Crane, who runs a tourist cabaret in a remote fishing-camp during the summer and spends most of the winter in bed with Morgan the camp owner, is in conversation with Mr. Grey, an unwelcome stormbound visitor:

> She told him about this story she once read, an old-fashioned tale in some book somebody'd given to her when she was a little girl. This girl in the story, this Proser-something, was out running around in a place something like this, . . . and up out of that hole came old Pluto, the king of the underworld, riding in a chariot, and hauled her off against her will down into his deep horrible black place. (164)

This passage could also be a trap for a narrowly archetypal critic; the point is not so much an analogy between Proserpina's situation and Hallie's as a contrast between Hallie's version of the pattern and its high classical equivalent. Despite her claim that Morgan is "'pulling me down into his hell with him'" (165), she ultimately descends of her own free will, and refers in the last word of the story to "'us'" (169). Once again, the myth is invoked and then adapted. Hodgins' analogies are invariably flexible comparisons, never point-by-point correspondences. They serve to connect his highly localized stories with predominant and recurrent patterned sequences in the larger world. Such connectives indicate the guaranteed presence of the universal within the regional.

Hodgins seems, then, to be interested in an allegorical form that offers insight into a higher reality while remaining within a fundamentally comic mode. This balance receives its most brilliant treatment to date in *The Invention of the World* (1977), and, so far as this novel is concerned, Hodgins has been unequivocal about his intentions. The "different levels of the novel are allegorical", he told Alan Twigg; "the primary concern is the search for the return to the 'created' [as distinct from the 'invented'] world" (192). And to Geoff Hancock he was even more explicit:

> While I was writing *The Invention of the World*, ... I was aware of seven different levels that the story could be read on. I was aware of a single theme that controlled the imagery on every page and tied all these "layers" together. I had drawn strange charts and diagrams and written volumes of what could be considered literary criticism of the as-yet-invisible novel. (65)

This sounds daunting, as if Hodgins, like Hugh Hood, were inviting us to read him as a Dante or a Spenser, but he is really drawing our attention to the serious structure behind the comic surface of the book. He is insisting that comedy, and even farce, can be as profound as more obviously serious forms of literature, that the all-important tone determines how we read but must not blind us to the ultimate significance of what we are reading.

No one can read *The Invention of the World* attentively without becoming aware of the comic variations that are being played on traditional mythic patterns. Most obvious are those drawn from biblical sources (Genesis and the Eden story, Exodus, Revelation) and from Classical tradition (Jove and Europa, Becker as Charon, "The Wolves of

Lycaon"), but Hodgins also draws quite extensively on Celtic myth, from the *Táin Bó Cuailnge* onwards. Once again, however, he takes pains to avoid solemnity in these academic matters. While such patterns are seriously intended, and contain profound meanings, they are never exempt from playful parody. Nor are they invariably imported myths (though part of his point is the way human beings tote alien myths in their baggage). Moreover, he is fascinated with the problem of how myths are invented and take on power. In the following (highly concentrated) passage concerning the Irish immigrants' journey to Donal Keneally's colony, Ned O'Mahony fabricates a North American myth before our eyes:

> "They say the hero of the land we're sailing for had a fine hand at the harpsichord.... A fine big red-nosed Irishman named Sir Sean A. McDermott.... The whole country worships the ground that he walks on and damned if he wasn't born in Macroom.... 'Twas his father, pardon me, that was born in Macroom.... The man himself was spawned in a log cabin somewhere in the wilds. Did his lessons by the candle light. They called him Honest Sean for refusing to cut down a cherry tree no matter how much the English bastards tried to force him.... The boy came out of those wilds wearing a raccoon on his head and shooting up the redskins right and left.... He made a fine great hero out of himself for sure and marched himself straight as you please to the big white palace up in Ottawa where he crowned himself the king." (112-13)

Here we are present at the invention (*not* creation) of a mythic world in which Sir John A. Macdonald, George Washington, Abraham Lincoln, and Davy Crockett all combine into a counterfeit hero.

Hodgins may here be indulging in a parody of the mythic process but he is also making fun of his own practice as a novelist. He is continually developing his characters in such a way that they illustrate a particular pattern of behaviour, and so can be interpreted allegorically, and even take on roles that align them with myth. Madmother Thomas provides a conveniently clear example. She is introduced complete with manure-spreader and all her eccentricities at the loggers' sports early in the novel, but she is much more than a merely colourful and idiosyncratic supernumerary. Her allegorical function is in fact made clear from the start: "Madmother Thomas, like someone in an ancient book, was looking for the place where she'd been born" (15). We are also told that she turns up regularly in Maggie Kyle's life "two or three times a year" (14). In a flashback through which we witness their first encounter, she reveals herself as a sibyl-figure with the ironic habit of giving advice that is the opposite of her own practice: "'If you've any sense, child, you'll just stay put'" (18), she advises while she is herself continually on the move, and later tells the young Maggie: "'the where of a life don't matter at all, it's the how of your life that'll count'" (19). If on first acquaintance we see her on a literal level as a comic grotesque, we soon find reason to change our opinion. By the time we come to the section entitled "Pilgrimage", in which Maggie, Becker, and Wade go off to Ireland, we realize that they too are engaged in a quest for origins. So, in a curiously ambiguous way, is Keneally when he burrows down into the earth that originally spewed him up (a variation, incidentally, of the cyclical pattern of ascent and descent employed in Howard O'Hagan's *Tay John*). So is Becker by virtue of his role as historian, since an important aspect of history is the discovery of origins. To return to Madmother Thomas, it is clearly not accidental that, as soon as the three get back from Ireland, they return to Maggie's personal origins, discover the old woman in Maggie's shack, and find that she has abandoned her quest just as theirs is completed. Appropriately, since she is a survivor of Keneally's colony, she is taken back to Maggie's trailer park where she replaces the dead Lily and so provides an element of continuity within Maggie's new dispensation.

Madmother Thomas is a typical Hodgins character because, although her quest may be both futile and absurd, she is herself portrayed as, by turns, grotesque, amusing, pathetic, and sometimes even wise. She is a reminder, if such were needed, that Hodgins is a master of varying tones, and that it is always a mistake to assume that an initial response to a character or a situation can be more than provisional. For example, the final section of the novel, which Hodgins has described as "a mock epic" (Hancock 77), is a veritable literary roller-coaster of shifting responses. It begins with Becker assuring us that what follows is *"the true story of what happened"* (339), and this prepares us by a Hodginsian law of opposites for the outrageous climactic fantasy. The loggers' riot, "the best damn brawl the island had ever seen" (347), is at once an exaggerated presentation of British Columbian celebratory energy and a parody of the traditional epic games. The list of wedding presents (352-53) begins with standard items ("pillows and sheets"), proceeds through the menacingly unlikely ("a book of matches, a tin of peaches, a promise of peace") and the farcically impossible ("Twin grandchildren. American oil tankers. Bad television programmes"), and ends with the patently allegorical ("Beauty. Grace. Forgiveness") and the genuinely moving ("Passion. Retirement. Neglect. Loneliness. Love"). A little later, the arrival of Horseman initiates a shift to an almost mystical transformation in which "the bride and the groom" become "the new man and the new woman" (353-54) and are led out of the hall into a new dimension.

One would have thought that Hodgins' exuberance made an obvious point; here, however, we encounter a characteristic preference of Canadian critics for rigid categories and their reluctance to follow the clear tonal and stylistic indications provided. Thus Gaile McGregor goes to extraordinary lengths to force upon *The Invention of the World* a vision related to Kierkegaardian *Angst*. Despite Hodgins' own assurance that "the novel has a positive ending.... It's a story of triumph" (Hancock 70), she is determined to read it as presenting a world with "no redeeming promises to offer at all" (81), a world in which any "possibility of transcendence" is precluded (83). She argues that "Hodgins' Fall into the absurd world is non-reversible and non-transformable" (81), and, in more detail:

> In Hodgins' fictional universe, ... life is a closed system, a *box*, from which—as from the reception hall that stands as its symbolic correlative at the end of the novel—there is only one exit, under the aegis of the Horseman, death. It is possible (and only human), of course, to euphemize this finale, as Becker does, but the nursery rhyme echo evoked by his choice of closing words quite pointedly undercuts both the redemptive implications of the so-called House of Revelations, ... and the religious rhetoric that has historically provided man with a kind of consolation. (82-83)

Far from presenting "a closed system", Hodgins takes care to leave the precise details of his ending intriguingly and (from a literary viewpoint) appropriately vague. The stranger "*apparently* drove the new couple all the way back to their home at the House of Revelations" (my emphasis); "*if they're not dead nor gone they're alive there still*" (354). A certain flexibility of interpretation is possible here, within limits, but we can be sure that Maggie and Wade are translated, if at all, into a higher realm of experience, perhaps the world of eternity, but certainly not death or nothingness. McGregor significantly omits

Hodgins' reference to "the new man and the new woman" and neglects the fact that the section is entitled, positively, "Second Growth".

The assumption seems to be that any playful allusion to myth "undercuts" (McGregor's word) the original to which it refers. McGregor is not alone in this. In an essay on Hodgins' "burlesque", Susan Gingell Beckmann maintains that the "mythopoeic trappings" in *The Invention of the World* "are deliberately undercut by the burlesque" (123), and even Robert Lecker says much the same thing: "through parody and burlesque he undercuts the belief, expressed by Morag Gunn near the end of *The Diviners*, that 'The myths are my reality'" (86). This insistence on undercutting is currently fashionable: a similar argument has been made about Howard O'Hagan's use of myth (see Davidson and Fee). If a mythological pattern is altered, so the argument runs, then the author is thereby exposing the falsity of the original myth. But this does not follow. When O'Hagan has Father Rorty crucify himself on the school-marm tree in *Tay John*, this doesn't mean that the Crucifixion is an exploded myth but rather that human beings can follow Christ too literally and for varied motives. Rorty demonstrates, indeed, that crucifixion is a potent image continually applicable to human dilemmas. Denham's curt comment, "Priestly arrogance could go on farther" (219), represents one view, but another allegorical meaning, equally available in context, implies that Rorty undergoes an agony that symbolizes his betrayal by sexual desire. He thereby becomes an emblematic figure torn between flesh and spirit. Similarly, Tay John himself leads his tribe "into the wilderness" like Moses; like Moses, too, he is prevented from experiencing the Promised Land (which may not be attainable, least of all for Canadian Indians, in the modern world). This does not "undercut" Moses or Exodus or the concept of the Promised Land, but uses them for a new purpose. O'Hagan seems to me neutral in his employment of religious patterns for secular and literary ends. Hodgins, on the other hand, rearranges traditional myth in what can only be called an exhilarating way. The "Eden Swindle", Hodgins' "mock myth" (Hancock 77), is eventually redeemed by Maggie Kyle's community on the same site. A genuine "creation" is always available as an antidote to demonic "invention". Indeed, Hodgins' capacity to alter established myths, his ability to envisage new endings as well as new beginnings, represents a delivery from the tyranny of an inevitable repetition of a predestined Fate.

It would, of course, be possible to continue this examination of Hodgins' secular allegory by tracing it all through his later fiction. Indeed, *The Resurrection of Joseph Bourne* (1979) especially encourages this kind of approach, since there the allegorical allusions are not complicated, as they are in *The Invention of the World*, by intricate shifts of narrative and perspective. But the basic point should now be clear, and it will be more useful to proceed a little differently. Now that the fact of Hodgins' allegorical concerns has been documented, it is important to show how the otherwise austere effect of allegory is humanized by means of his congenial narrative voice.

As early as the opening page of *Spit Delaney's Island* we are made aware of the casual, relaxed quality of the narrator's prose: "People driving by don't notice Spit Delaney". The first sentence with its contracted verb sets the tone, and the paragraph ends with Spit muttering "that he'll be damned if he can figure out what it is that is happening to him" (3). A little later, we catch a glimpse of Spit's confidence before his world suddenly fell apart: "'This here's one bugger you don't catch with his eyes shut,' was his way of putting it" (5). The "way of putting it" is essential. As we proceed through the book, we encounter numerous individual ways of putting it, from Mrs. Wright's genteel rationalism in "Three Women of the Country" through Gerry Mack's staccato impatience in "The Trench Dwellers" ("*Macken this, Macken that.* Gerry Mack had had enough" [73]) and Mr. Swingler's laconic conversation in "Every Day of His Life" to the final story in which Spit returns as first-person narrator. Part of the almost Dickensian vitality in Hodgins' work derives from his ability to record faithfully and convincingly an abundance of distinctive speech-rhythms.

This gift is developed in *The Invention of the World*, where the verbal variety is an intrinsic part of the richness of the book. It is most obvious in the "Scrapbook" section, where a representative cross-section of local inhabitants talk briefly about their responses to the Keneally colony and are all clearly and immediately differentiated from each other. It is also evident in the confidently established idiolects of Becker and Julius and Lily Hayworth and Maggie and Wade Powers—and even in a minor character like Ned O'Mahony, whose story of "Sir Sean A. McDermott" I have already quoted. But this quality comes into its own in *The Resurrection of Joseph Bourne*. This novel differs from the rest of Hodgins' work because the central protagonist is really the community of Port Annie as a whole; it is made up of the stories—and the language—of an astonishingly large cast of characters. Hodgins has himself described it as a "concert of voices" and has observed how he was able to "float from person to person for reactions to certain events" (Twigg 193).

At this point he has also perfected the art (perhaps under the influence of Ethel Wilson, whose work he has praised [Hancock 54, 60]) of floating from authorial narrative into the words and rhythms of his characters. Here, for example, is Jenny Chambers:

> Three days later she was on the phone again, to Mabel (let Eva wait, the skinny traitor): two days in Nanaimo, it was like a dream, Mabel. She stayed in the Tally-ho, no less, with a view over the swimming pool and under a bridge and out to the harbour where there were sailboats; she hated to leave the room. But she did, because cripes, guess what—it didn't rain a drop the whole time she was there, she could hardly believe air could be so dry, she didn't even wear her fur, just carried it over her arm, and stores stores stores . . . (101-02)

It isn't merely the verisimilitude that impresses here, but Hodgins' capacity to make ordinary chitchat sound warmly human. Moreover, Jenny's accents and emphases are effortlessly absorbed into the omniscient narration.

But more is involved than a capacity for dramatic monologue. Hodgins is also adept at blending and contrasting voices. The scene where the squatters are preparing to resist eviction is an excellent example:

> Larry looked at Bourne and lowered his voice. "And you encourage them in this game? A lost cause like this?"
> The old man's hands were busy ransacking his pockets. "I don't encourage them, I don't discourage them. . . . I've told them to try sinking their roots into something a little more solid and lasting than a piece of earth, but nobody listens to me down here any better than they do in the town."
> Hill Gin grunted. "Babble, babble."
> "Solid and lasting like what?" Larry said.
> "Like what?" One hand emerged with an apple, which he held up by the stem and examined. "Like those good old invisible things that can't be stolen or disappear." He polished the apple on the front of a sweater. "What our grandparents used to call the things of soul." And bit.
> "Babble, babble," Hill Gin said. "People still have to live somewhere.

That old fool would have us floating off into space like ghosts."

Bourne accepted the rebuke with a nod. "So you see, Larry Bowman, there's nothing left for me to do but . . . what?"—his hands turned up in a gesture of mock helplessness—"but love them, I guess."

The old woman, recoiling, cracked her skull on the floor. "Crap."

Bourne laughed—and sank his teeth once more into the apple. (228-29)

The control of tone is masterly here. Bourne is offering an old-fashioned and potentially vulnerable positive. Stated baldly, it could easily be dismissed as weak and sentimental. But Hodgins inserts it in a beautifully modulated scene that moves gracefully and with aplomb between the practical, the idealistic, the earthy, the whimsical, the grotesque, the amusing, and even perhaps the sublime. The values of traditional Christian "love" (Bourne, we remember, has returned from the undiscovered country as a resurrected man) are upheld against secular, twentieth-century "crap". And they are upheld by a character who would seem closer to Beckett than to any traditional optimist. (Technically, I am reminded of the scene at the close of Dickens' *Hard Times* where the gin-sodden, lisping Mr. Sleary, proprietor of a shabby circus-ring, announces "that there ith a love in the world, not all Thelf-intereht after all" [222]; in both cases a serious moral positive is rendered acceptable by its subtle placing within a crisply humorous context.) Bourne's apple is not a symbolic/allegorical one like Big Glad Littlestone's in "Every Day of His Life", but its homely particularity is essential to the overall effect of the scene—which is dependent, once again, upon a skilfully managed artifice.

Voice—or, rather, voices—may be recognized as the key to Hodgins' art. "People have their own way of talking, everybody's different", says Lily Hayworth (*Invention* 251), and Hodgins demonstrates the truth of this in his fiction. Ironically, he found his own voice by discovering the diversity of other voices. As a beginning writer he had fallen under the stylistic influence of William Faulkner, and, as he was later to realize, "there's nothing worse than imitation Faulkner" (Hancock 54). He emerged from this unfortunate period when, as he told Twigg, he "started listening to the voices of people who live on Vancouver Island" (188-89). This proved to be a revelation. Not only did he discover that "people have different speech patterns, different favourite expressions and different rhythms of speech" (189), but—perhaps unwittingly, since he does not seem at this time to have ventured outside British Columbia—he incorporated into his work many of the distinctive phrases and usages of his region. Pritchard has noted a number of these, including "up-island people", "spat snoose", "gyppo logging camp", "fire season", "watching for sparks" (30). Numerous others could be added: "hightail", "pickup", "logged-off hillsides", "whanging up", "the little scrunch", "second growth", etc. Hodgins displays a remarkable capacity to combine these elements into a style that is indisputably his own. His "concert of voices" depends for its effectiveness on his distinction as a consummately skilful and versatile conductor.

But "style", here as elsewhere, is inseparable from a concern for art and artifice. Writing of *The Barclay Family Theatre* (1981), Waldemar Zacharasiewicz points out that the stories in this collection "deal more clearly with questions of the arts than does Hodgins' early work" (102). This is true, and the subsequent publication of *The Honorary Patron* and *Innocent Cities* underlines the point, though it is also true that the experience of reading *The Barclay Family Theatre* leads us to appreciate the extent to which the subject of art, especially within a context of philistine hostility, has been a constant preoccupation in his writings. As early as the opening story in *Spit Delaney's Island* we see Spit employing an artist to create a pictorial record of "Old Number One", and in the final story, while he is puzzled and outraged by Phemie Porter—"You can't trust people who write things on paper, they think they own all the world and people too" (187)—he is also clearly affected by her artistic life-style. We may also recall Mr. Swingler, the artist in "Every Day of His Life". But for the most part the emphasis falls, as in "The Religion of the Country", on "the logger and coalminer mentality of the island" (98), with Halligan the bookseller's admittedly snobbish preference for *Rigoletto* over the loggers' sports very much the exception. This is a society in which "'if they have any spare time you'd never catch them reading a book'" (99), where Spit's library is "a pile of dog-eared old paperbacks I'll never read" (171).

In *The Invention of the World* the arts are more prominent. Julius is a poet who liked "pushing words around on paper" (55), Wade's girlfriend Virginia Kerr is a serious painter who has her demonic counterpart in Lily Hayworth with her painting-by-numbers, while Becker, the historian who "wants to be God" (x), is seen throughout as an image of the artist. But philistinism is strong. When Wade quotes poetry in his wedding-speech, he prefaces his recitation with the assertion that he "hated the stuff" (351), and Julius sums up what is becoming a familiar view of the Island: "it leapt over civilization, . . . all the way from frontier town to Disneyland. You'll find pornography shops and slot machines and periodic festivals of idiocy, but you'll never find an art gallery" (233). In *The Resurrection of Joseph Bourne* the process is extended still further. Mayor Weins here represents the forces of philistinism: "By cultural centre, he explained, he meant a tourist-information bureau" (207). To Weins a church is just "a piece of real estate . . . unexploited" (210). What he calls "honest-to-goodness culture" means "Hollywood screen-writers and people who wrote television commercials" (216); he is looking for "the most tasteful rows of fast-food outlets and car-dealers and tourist attractions" (265). "'Who needs you, you uncooperative old goat'" (7), he says to the genuine poet Joseph Bourne. Mrs. Barnstone is Bourne's demonic counterpart as bad epic poet, but Jenny Chambers' strip-tease transforms miraculously into an authentic art-form as she is shown "dancing life back into things" (270).

In *The Barclay Family Theatre*, however, the concern with art is continual. Desmond is pushed by his mother towards the concert stages of Europe, but instead he becomes a novelist (in "The Lepers' Squint"); a disagreeable poet appears in "Invasions '79"; Eli Wainamoinen is a painter with vision in "More Than Conquerors"; the art of *kabuki* is both celebrated and parodied in "The Sumo Revisions". Of course, the philistine world is still conspicuous. Mr. Pernouski's dream is to convert the natural paradise of Vancouver Island into profitable lots for the Eden Realty Company. Unease about "matters of history and culture" (24) are expressed throughout. Cornelia Hardcastle learns to play the piano on a paper keyboard so that her mother "doesn't even have to miss an episode of *Ma Perkins*" (2); Sparkle Roote is named after a character in a comic strip (104); David Payne "had never pretended to understand what the business of art and artists was all about" (141); Jacob Weins deserts *kabuki* for *sumo*, while Conrad "made it sound as if reading a book was one sure sign of senility" (239). At least two of the imaginative Barclay sisters consider they inhabit a "hickish dump of a place" (282).

In *The Honorary Patron* (1987), Hodgins carries his preoccupation with the arts still further. Here an art critic is the main protagonist. That he is an Islander might suggest that the arts are now flourishing, but he left as a young man and has made his reputation in Europe. True, he is invited back for a hitherto unlikely "Pacific Coast Festival of the Arts" (25), but once again the forces of philistinism are supreme. The patrons are regarded as "'artsy-fartsy people'" (68, 215); a representative response to *Macbeth* is "'Thought those guys'd never stop talkin' and get on with it'" (65). And the Festival folds, despite Elizabeth's back-handed confidence "'that something so fine just couldn't fail—*not even here*'" (243; my emphasis). But the really popular activity is stock-car racing, and the narrator finds it easy enough to imagine the populace "hurrying towards a scene of promised violence—a public execution or a duel" (296). Here Hodgins has made the fact of philistinism, a complaint voiced directly or indirectly by many Canadian writers, a central subject within his fiction.

In both *The Honorary Patron* and *Innocent Cities* Hodgins explores new fictional possibilities. *The Honorary Patron* differs from his earlier books in having an elder protagonist who, though attracted to the vigour of the youth that he encounters, is generally passive, introspective, and retrospective. This novel sounds deeper and more threatening notes than we have heard in Hodgins before, but this should not blind us to the characteristic Hodginsian exuberance that remains prominent. On the one hand, we have Jeffrey Crane realizing that he had "made himself enough of a clown and a sad, sad fool to be taken at last for a genuine specimen of twentieth-century man" (263); on the other, we find him protesting against a world of relativity: "What else was the twentieth century about, if not an attempt to recover from Einstein's blow?" (24) By the end of the novel, a promising young local artist (whom Crane has, to his chagrin, neglected) displays a series of canvases in which "'the tunnel walls'" of subterranean Nanaimo (which are also the abysses beneath all our crumbling houses) are portrayed with "'the old guy's [i.e. Einstein's] face just sort of peeking out'" as if in search of something "'that would sort of balance out what he scared everybody with before'" (317). The phrasing is that of a youthful acquaintance, but it embodies a confidence from which Crane takes hope. Much earlier—in equally hesitant phraseology—Crane had offered his own decidedly traditionalist aesthetic: "'the fashion has been to acknowledge little more than excellence of form. Yet beauty, dignity, that sort of old-fashioned thing is what I've gone on looking for—amongst other things, of course'" (47).

So, one might add, has Hodgins. "'That sort of old-fashioned thing'" recalls Joseph Bourne's already quoted "'good old invisible things that can't be stolen or disappear'" (*Resurrection* 228). (The basic psychological pattern of Crane's life, indeed, will be seen to bear some notable resemblance to Bourne's.) All Hodgins' work seems based on the conviction that there is "lots of room for new ways of looking at things" (*Resurrection* 205). His strategy, ironically in view of what I have said about critical response to his mythologizing, is to "undercut" the now conventional view of a meaningless world with disturbing intimations of mystery and purpose. Hodgins doesn't ignore the disasters and fears of our world—these are represented by the cataclysmic landslide at the end of *The Resurrection of Joseph Bourne*, and the violence typified by Blackie Barnstone and his tribe in *The Honorary Patron*—but he refuses to acquiesce in a numbed helplessness. Jacob Weins ceases to be an absurd grotesque at the end of the former novel and urges the townspeople to "spring back to life from the ashes of disaster" (265). In the latter, Crane's experience on Vancouver Island is ultimately seen as a curious combination of the shaming and the liberating. He knows a little more about "how to live" his remaining years (272) at the end of the book than he did at the beginning. The fact of "growing old" naturally remains, but it is now recognized as a "giant comedy" (293); he learns from his sister about "'the great old joke that life is'" (73). Even the fatal accident at the stock-car races, involving Blackstone's terrorist son and recounted in the final sentences of the book, includes instinctively heroic self-sacrifice as well as violent absurdity.

Innocent Cities (1990) characteristically rings new changes on the Hodginsian preoccupations I have already discussed. At first, this book may seem a dramatic departure from his customary approach, since it is described on the original dust-jacket as "the ultimate Victorian novel". It is, to be sure, Victorian in various senses. A historical novel set during Queen Victoria's reign, most of its action takes place in Victoria, British Columbia, or in Ballarat in the colony of Victoria in Australia (these are the two supposedly innocent cities of the title); moreover, it offers a kind of breadth and amplitude that one associates with Victorian fiction. In addition, an Indian, Mary One-Eye, haunts the margins of the novel dressed as a kind of satiric parody of the aging queen. Yet the plot, with its focus on bigamous relationships and sexual intrigue (including a wife who suggests that a younger unmarried sister come over to satisfy her husband's sexual appetites), defies all that we have been brought up to recognize as Victorian propriety. Even here, however, Hodgins has an extra trick up his sleeve: the main lines of the sensational narrative are derived from reliable nineteenth-century sources as recorded in Terry Reksten's *"More English than the English": A Very Social History of Victoria* (103-07). In other words, this "ultimate Victorian novel" ends up by challenging—even destroying—our notions of what the word "Victorian" implies.

But this "ultimate Victorian novel" is by no means anachronistic in the world of the 1990s. In technique and execution *Innocent Cities* is as post-modern as its setting and atmosphere are conventionally Victorian. The plot may be traditionally complex, but it does not resolve itself in a neat or morally suitable way. As in Hodgins' other longer fictions, especially *The Resurrection of Joseph Bourne*, the book contains a number of separate narratives that are never integrated in any sanctioned Victorian manner. The ending, indeed, is a skilful exercise in suspension, and readers seeking structural connectives are likely to be disappointed; instead, the various sections are linked by means of tonal contrast, irony, and comic paradox.

Once again an allusive, allegorical reading is appropriate. James Hardcastle gambles throughout the book only to lose out at the end to accident and destiny—and one of the things he loses is language, a recurrent topic in this decidedly metafictional book. Kate, who deceives an elder sister whom she detests, is left living with her in a self-imposed prison of hatred, while the youngest sister, advocate of an early brand of feminism, ends up happily married, continuing with the support of her husband to lecture *"on the subject of female shackles"* (386). The verbal self-consciousness of the book is underlined in the story of the husband who, before remarrying, writes and continually revises his biography on his prematurely erected gravestone. A prominent and rather whimsical sub-plot involves early attempts at flight and subjects "post-colonialism" to a combination of sympathetic presentation and good-natured parody. A Chinese, Chu Lee, pilots the pioneering aircraft but only to find himself intercepted for attempted smuggling by the United States authorities, while the Indian Zachary Jack, the chief organizer of the project (who speaks fluent English with his employer friend but exaggerated pidgin when anyone else is within earshot) spends most of the novel living in a house of words, a shack decorated with English words inscribed on the wood wrecked from ships.

The paradoxes and hermeneutic possibilities are alike rich. As a whole, this is no monolithic Victorian fiction but rather a loose confederation of separate narratives that continually threaten to come apart at the seams. This sounds like a recipe for the elusive "Great Canadian Novel", but is better read as its parody, as an intellectually inventive satiric romp that makes fun of our contemporary hang-ups. A tale of two (not-so-innocent) cities becomes a tale of two ages—but one that, for all its metafictional artifice, never loses touch with the fallibly and endearingly human.

Here as elsewhere Hodgins sets his main characters in what might reasonably be called an absurdist plot, but he refuses to accept an absurdist philosophy. Thus *Innocent Cities* ends with the two great rivals in the book, Norah and Kate, "'trying to build some kind of new language between them, to build something out of silence that isn't death'" (391). It is difficult to write about this aspect of Hodgins' work without making it seem didactic and tiresomely uplifting, but within fiction that encompasses the horrendous and the hilarious, that combines the lusty with the tender, the flamboyantly grotesque with the humanly pathetic, this positive stance contributes to a sense of rich complexity. Hodgins' depiction of life seems not only more attractive but more accurate and more "real" than that of the post-modern cynicism which has become the convention of the supposed avant-garde. His distinction consists of an unfashionable but refreshing and sustaining enthusiasm for the miracle of life.

The publication of *The Macken Charm* (1995) constitutes both a new development and, following the example of Madmother Thomas, a return to origins; it therefore provides an appropriate concluding point for this survey. *Innocent Cities*, which in some respects could be seen as a foray on to the unstable post-modern terrain of Robert Kroetsch, was the furthest Hodgins could safely venture in that direction. With this new novel he turns back, like a contemporary composer rediscovering the joys and possibilities of tonality, to the tried-and-true, multifaceted blend of human comedy and "magic realism" that characterized his earlier work. Yet instead of using his original brand of secular allegory directly, Hodgins filters it through the canny exploration and mixing of fictional kinds that was so evident in *Innocent Cities*.

Ostensibly, Hodgins offers in *The Macken Charm* what most novelists present in their first or second books: a fictional account of their early years. To be sure, Hodgins had already drawn upon his personal experience and family history in a number of short stories in *Spit Delaney's Island* as well as in the containing framework of *The Barclay Family Theatre*. Moreover, I am in no way suggesting that "real-life" events happened as chronicled here or that he is merely retelling the story of his childhood. I would argue, however, that here for the first time Hodgins portrays, within secular allegory, what he has hinted at in interviews but as yet only obliquely treated in fiction: the growth of an imaginative, artistically-inclined child in a richly idiosyncratic yet closed and oppressively philistine community. Rusty Macken, at seventeen, is going through what for Hodgins can be seen as an intensely personal rendition of a universal crisis: he is about to leave both the context of his family and the extended family of the Island to face the outer world, which in this case means the University of British Columbia and all the mysteries and challenges of Vancouver and the mainland. Rusty both yearns for and fears this new and crucial period of his life. The Macken family, the only society he has hitherto known, is presented through his eyes with love but also with an objectivity that borders on impatience.

Rusty may be the narrator, but the most memorable character in the novel (characteristically, a literary allusion—in this case to Sterne's *Tristram Shandy*—is involved) is his Uncle Toby, the most exuberant and extreme in a family of uninhibited individualists. Rusty hero-worships Toby—"Uncle Toby had been my hero all my life. I'd wanted to *be* him once" (36)—but Rusty is himself the son of the most sensible of the Mackens, "probably the most reliable person in the district" (28), and feels a resultant split in his allegiances. He is also painfully aware that "to *be*" Toby Macken would count for little in the outer world; Glory, Toby's wife from the mainland, has remarked of her husband: "'He couldn't be Toby Macken over there, he was just another jerk that nobody noticed'" (212). Rusty, about to depart for the mainland, inevitably takes this to heart.

Rusty both is and is not a Macken. He is aware of strong creative impulses and knows that they are related to his Macken inheritance. Yet he also knows that the Mackens have no use for his particular form of creativity. Besides, the Macken exuberance can all too often turn into the destructive—as Toby admits, "'I want to burn things down'" (52)— and even the self-destructive. Toby's culminating act of excess, dancing "'On the top of the goddam Comox Glacier'" (264), is both a climax of ingenuity and an illustration of creativity wasted. For all Rusty's admiration, Toby and he are opposites—"'You're supposed to be the one with sense'" (94), Toby remarks, half admiringly, half critically. Rusty's life-objective is to channel the Macken creativity into disciplined artistic form.

The Macken Charm, then, is Hodgins' contribution to the *Bildungsroman* or novel of growth, but it is more than a *Bildungsroman*, a form that invariably risks descent into too-easy nostalgia. Hodgins is careful to qualify the "charm". Here the immediate occasion is all-important: although Rusty is the narrator and Toby the most memorable figure, the event that dominates the novel is the funeral of Glory, Toby's wife. Indeed, the novel could aptly be entitled *The Macken Wake*. While the book demands, like most of Hodgins' work, to be classified as comedy, a strong vein of the serious, even the potentially tragic, runs through it. There is, too, a palpable hint of the mystery story: only later in the narrative do we learn about the incidents that lead to Glory's death and about how she died. Moreover (and here the complexity of Hodgins' sense of structure becomes evident), we become aware only gradually of the subtly intricate relationship that links Rusty and Glory and so links two seemingly disparate elements in the plot.

In addition, though I almost hesitate to mention it since the form is currently so unfashionable in Canadian literary-critical circles, in *The Macken Charm* Hodgins unabashedly revives the tradition of the regional novel. Of course, he long ago staked out his literary proprietorship to northern Vancouver Island, but nowhere are the terrain and the human denizens of the area more consummately presented than here. The Mackens are more than a family; they are a people. Their locale—dominated by mountain range and glacier, embracing timber forest, stump lots, and debris-strewn foreshore—is recognized as a microcosmic human world. Also, as in many traditional examples of regional fiction, the form enables Hodgins to include a motley collection of Macken stories told and retold by the family with characteristic exuberance. Together, they form an anthology of the Mackens, the Island, the Hodgins world, and here they are integrated smoothly into the text by contrast with the rather artificial formal scheme of *The Barclay Family Theatre*. In this new book, it might be said, his gifts as short story writer and novelist are happily combined.

Yet, in insisting on the regional aspect of the book, I must not imply that Hodgins is reverting to a simpler narrative mode. Far from it. The regional novel is just one strand in a complex tapestry. In fact, although there is little of the mythic fantasy that proved so engaging in *The Invention of the World,* or of the self-conscious discursive play that was both exhilarating and vaguely disturbing in *Innocent Cities*, this novel is, in its own way, as artistically integrated and, arguably, even more deeply controlled. Indeed, one of the more recondite pleasures of the text for seasoned readers of Hodgins consists in our recognizing his considered ringing of changes on situations, themes, and images that he has explored before. The regional links with *Spit Delaney's Island* I have already indicated, though it is important to add that one of the stories,

"The Trench Dwellers", involves the Macken clan, is indeed about Rusty's younger brother, and can now be seen as a rehearsal for the more intricate concerns delineated here. Similarly, the world of loggers' sports, images of ascending the spar-tree, the tone of "good-natured excess" (9), all echo *The Invention of the World*. Perhaps more daringly, when Hodgins describes how Glory "descended upon them from another world" (10) at the time of the earthquake, we recall Raimey emerging Venus-like from the sea after the tidal wave in *The Resurrection of Joseph Bourne*. Rusty himself is an elaboration of Barclay Desmond in *The Barclay Family Theatre* (Rusty's mother, Frieda, appeared in "The Plague Children"), while the chirpy but ingrained philistinism of the whole Macken mentality evokes the cultural realities portrayed in *The Honorary Patron*.

But what are the links—if any—with *Innocent Cities*? The verbal hijinks of Logan Sumner's ever-expanding tombstone and Zachary Jack's symbolic house of (alien) words are replaced here by recurrent references to the content and the technique of popular cinema. For his own secret attempts at writing, Hodgins substitutes Rusty's youthful dreams about becoming a movie director, the one artistic endeavour acceptable, albeit with reservations, to the Macken clan. The names of Hollywood personalities pepper the text, and the youthful Rusty rather pathetically seeks evidence that a reasonable number of them were born in Canada—and predictably finds the tally for Vancouver Island ominously slim. The nearest he has come to his dream in practical terms is a video camera, stolen for him by his Uncle Toby, that is too seriously broken to repair. He is constantly pondering angles and perspectives, and asking "what if I made a movie of this?" (130), when in fact, Hodgins-like, he is making a novel of it. (The progression echoes that of Barclay Desmond from—in his case, reluctant—pianist in "The Concert Stages of Europe" to novelist in "The Lepers' Squint".) Still, like Hodgins himself, Rusty picks up some useful hints. His English teacher, Mr. Collins, sensibly advises him to "start with something closer to home" (133), and, even more crucially, he is forced back upon "imagination"—a word which, like "dance" and several others (including, of course, "crazy"), becomes a significant leitmotif within the novel.

But there is another aspect of *The Macken Charm*, less conspicuous within the text though unquestionably present, that merits attention because it is evident elsewhere in Hodgins' work. I refer to a spiritual dimension that hovers over the novel. For many readers, this will, at first mention, seem dubious. After all, we are specifically told that "church was the last place in the world [the Mackens] were likely to meet" (46) and we are also assured of their "disdain for religious matters" (88). Yet one of the more startling moments in the novel occurs during the funeral service, here predominantly a setting for broad comedy, when the officiating minister reveals that Glory had been "A visitor to [his] office along with her husband, where they talked over matters to do with the purpose of life and her own future" (91). This sounds unlikely, until we remember the acknowledged recognition between Toby and the minister after Toby has climbed the church steeple (78). As the Mackens note with unease, "If one member of the family had been secretly visiting the clergy, might there not be others?" (91).

There might indeed. The climax of the novel is the quixotic Macken-family gesture when they get together and not only make the improvements to Toby's shack that he had continually promised and never produced but also restore the adjoining family hotel that had burned down years before. It is a curious scene that persistently hints at spiritual meaning—secular allegory perhaps veering, as so often in Hodgins, towards its religious origin. To suggest that the Mackens are attempting to build Jerusalem in Vancouver Island's green and pleasant land might be extreme, but there are surely hints of the regaining of a lost paradise, even a recreation of lost time. And certainly the language takes on religious connotations. The hotel is *"resurrected* out of memory" (274; my emphasis), and Toby ultimately characterizes it as "'a goddam miracle'" (277). Even more indicative are earlier phrases in which the Mackens are seen as "'Fixing it up for Glory'" (238) and are described as "'Heathens hammering like crazy for the glory of God'" (249). Here we are forced, if we have not done so already, to ponder the implications of Glory's name—and we recall Hodgins' insistence on the importance of names. One could do worse, when attempting to sum up Hodgins' fictional achievement, than describe it as a crazy glory.

With this novel, Hodgins has returned with renewed vigour and confidence to an accessible form of novel that can be read with pleasure and profit on a wide range of levels, a form neither kowtowing to commercial conceptions of popular fiction nor hamstrung by pretentious academic theory. Hodgins is determinedly faithful to the continuity of fictional tradition. This is a novel that displays vitality, humour, pathos, warmth, surprise, suspense, as well as a satisfying impression of symmetry. It ends as Rusty imagines a concluding cinematic "helicopter shot" of his own, Spit Delaney's, and Jack Hodgins' island world:

> Rising higher, we would see down the curving coastline, fold after fold of soft blue peninsulas and furry slopes of trees and crawling grey waves, and of course the long dark ribbon of highway leading away from the hotel site, down through the creek-veined stumpy district of our childhoods and the little town beneath the enduring glacier, and down along the coastline leading south eventually to the steamship terminal and out into the world. (294)

It is the route that Rusty himself will take a few weeks later—but, as readers of this novel will note with pleasure, the Trench can be crossed in both directions, and the Island always beckons.

Works Cited

Beckmann, Susan [Gingell]. "Canadian Burlesque: Jack Hodgins' *The Invention of the World*". *Essays on Canadian Writing* 20 (1980-81): 106-25.

Davidson, Arnold E. "Silencing the Word in Howard O'Hagan's *Tay John*". *Canadian Literature* 110 (1986): 30-44.

Dickens, Charles. *Hard Times*. 1854. Ed. George Ford and Sylvère Monod. Norton Critical Editions. New York: W.W. Norton, 1966.

Fee, Margery. "Howard O'Hagan's *Tay John*: Making New World Myth". *Canadian Literature* 110 (1986): 8-27.

Hancock, Geoff. "Jack Hodgins". *Canadian Writers at Work: Interviews with Geoff Hancock*. Toronto: Oxford UP, 1987. 51-78.

Hodgins, Jack. *The Barclay Family Theatre*. Toronto: Macmillan of Canada, 1981.

——. *The Honorary Patron*. Toronto: McClelland & Stewart, 1987.

——. *Innocent Cities*. Toronto: McClelland & Stewart, 1990.

——. *The Invention of the World*. Toronto: Macmillan of Canada, 1977.

——. *The Macken Charm*. Toronto: McClelland & Stewart, 1995.

——. *The Resurrection of Joseph Bourne; or, A Word or Two on Those Port Annie Miracles*. Toronto: Macmillan of Canada, 1979.

——. *Spit Delaney's Island: Selected Stories*. Toronto: Macmillan of Canada, 1976.

Lecker, Robert. "Haunted by a Glut of Ghosts: Jack Hodgins' *The Invention of the World*". *Essays on Canadian Writing* 20 (1980-81): 86-105.

McGregor, Gaile. *The Wacousta Syndrome*. Toronto: U of Toronto P, 1985.

O'Hagan, Howard. *Tay John*. 1939. Afterword by Michael Ondaatje. The New Canadian Library. Toronto: McClelland & Stewart, 1989.

Pritchard, Allan. "Jack Hodgins's Island: A Big Enough Country". *University of Toronto Quarterly* 55 (1985): 21-44.

Reksten, Terry. *"More English than the English": A Very Social History of Victoria*. Victoria: Orca, 1986.

Twigg, Alan. "Western Horizon: Jack Hodgins". *For Openers: Conversations with 24 Canadian Writers*. Madeira Park, BC: Harbour, 1981. 185-95.

Wilson, Ethel. "A Visit to the Frontier". *Stories, Essays, and Letters*. Ed. David Stouck. Vancouver: U of British Columbia P, 1987. 45-55.

Zacharasiewicz, Waldemar. "The Development of Jack Hodgins' Narrative Art in his Short Fiction". *Encounters and Explorations: Canadian Writers and European Critics*. Ed. Frank K. Stanzel and Waldemar Zacharasiewicz. Würzburg: Königshausen, 1986. 94-109.

Visions and Revisions:

An Interview with Jack Hodgins (1981)

J.R. (Tim) Struthers

TS: I'd like to ask you about the form of *Spit Delaney's Island* and the form of *The Barclay Family Theatre*. Replying to a question of mine about the organization of *Spit Delaney's Island,* you noted in a letter that "The first two stories, it seemed to me, most obviously raised the big questions I was concerned with. Then there were the people, in the last three stories, who just might be able to find some answers. The middle people were mainly the defeated. A very loose arrangement, I recognize, but it seemed important to do everything possible to give a collection of stories written over a period of ten years some sense of continuity and connection". Would you care to comment further about the process of shaping *Spit Delaney's Island*?

JH: Only to remind you that my shaping of the book was in the selecting and arranging of stories, not in the writing or revising of them. It simply became a matter of moving the chosen stories around so that their positions benefitted not only themselves but their neighbours—just an editorial job. I had no faith that people would read the stories in order. And reviewers gave me more credit than I think I deserve for the sense of unity the book has. The stories were *written*. It just seemed to me to make sense that they be shown off in the best way possible.

The first Spit story was written after the collection was accepted for publication. I liked it, so I added it in place of some other. Six months later, almost against my will, the second Spit story came along and I liked it too and decided to add it to the collection. Then thought, why not use them as bookends? Both the second Spit story and the collection itself had some other title.

The present title of the book was something I came up with afterwards—as a title appropriate to both the story and the group of stories. The choice of title, like the arrangement of stories, being all a part of that business of making a book—which has little to do with the writing of the stories.

TS: As you made the selections for *Spit Delaney's Island* and started to shape the book, did you give any thought to foreign or Canadian authors who had already succeeded in shaping a collection of short stories into a unified whole?

JH: I had no notion then—as I had with my next collection—of making a book which could be related to the obvious story-cycle books, like *A Bird in the House*, or *Winesburg, Ohio*, or *Dubliners*. It was reviewer response to *Spit* that caused me to go out and read books I'd only read in fragments—like *The Golden Apples* and *Sunshine Sketches of a Little Town* and *Dubliners*.

You see, I had no notion while I was writing the stories—and very little while I was arranging them for the book—that I was writing of a peculiar or particular region. Readers told me what I was doing. But to me, the world of "After the Season" was as different from the world of "Separating" as, for someone else, Toronto is from New Orleans. I sent them out thinking, this is as varied as the world can be, and back came the word: your stories all come out of a remarkably unified world. To the person from Port Alice meeting the person from Victoria, the notion that all of Vancouver Island is a single world is ludicrous. Why, they don't even talk the same.

TS: Does a sense of continuity and connection make a collection of stories better?

JH: Not necessarily better but more satisfying, I think.

TS: To the reader or the writer?

JH: To the reader. This is something that I think only my instincts were telling me when I was trying to create the book out of those many stories. But judging by responses through reviews, through correspondence, it seems to have given an awful lot of readers a sense of satisfaction to notice the coherence. Therefore it makes it a more satisfying, pleasurable book to read. I think that's probably justification enough.

From a personal point of view at the time, it was to give *me* that kind of satisfaction. It began as a random collection of stories. I sent Macmillan everything I'd published up to that point, which was about twenty stories, and out of that we made selections and out of the selections we made the coherence. No story was included or excluded on the grounds that it contributed to or detracted from some preconceived shape that the book should have. The stories were chosen first. Then I sat down and tried to make an order out of them.

TS: Does it follow that a novel is more satisfying than a unified book of short stories?

JH: No. A good novel is satisfying in one way, a coherent collection of short stories is satisfying in a different way, and a series of randomly collected short stories is satisfying in a third way. They achieve different goals.

TS: I suspect that a lot depends on each reader's individual aesthetic sense, on his or her demands for different degrees of unity and satisfaction with different kinds of unity.

JH: Certainly. If my concept of a book from the very beginning was totally unified, I would be writing a novel. I can't imagine writing a collection of related stories, although I know people have done it. I can't predict myself clearly enough to be able to do that [laughter]. I would head off in another direction that would spoil the collection altogether.

It's afterwards that the shape is noticed. With *The Barclay Family Theatre*, I had three-quarters of the stories in front of me before I realized what tied them together, where they overlapped, and why they must belong in the same book.

TS: Is a story cycle a more difficult undertaking than a miscellany of stories?

JH: Not necessarily more difficult but more challenging in that it adds one more demand on the writer, one more need from the book—perhaps a larger vision of the total effect the book should have.

TS: Once you had recognized the shape of what was to become *The Barclay Family Theatre*, how did you set about finishing the book?

JH: The last two stories to be written fitted so beautifully into the pattern that I can't remember ever consciously thinking, now I've got to write these two stories so that they fit into the pattern. I remember thinking, how wonderful, isn't that convenient and lucky! The stories, I think, come up to the surface when they're needed.

I went home from Ottawa at the end of 1979 perfectly prepared to be confronted with a story that had nothing to do with a collection at all and that I would write and do something else with. But it so happened that when I cleared the decks and looked at what I had, I realized there were two gaps in the book and both of them were sitting there waiting to be written.

TS: Which stories were these?

JH: The two new stories were "Mr. Pernouski's Dream" and "Ladies and Gentlemen, the Fabulous Barclay Sisters!".

TS: In preparing *The Barclay Family Theatre* for publication, what attitude did you take towards making revisions in stories that had been published previously in magazines, for the sake of adding to the impact of the collection as a whole?

JH: Frank O'Connor used to revise his stories over and over all his life. He felt a story was never finished until he died. Sean O'Faolain accused him of "forgery", claiming that you were never again the same person who wrote that story so you have no right to monkey with it. Personally I can't imagine myself wanting to make changes to a story once it's in book form—not because I consider it perfect but simply because it has taken on its own life without me and I would be as foreign a meddler as anyone else would be who wanted to make changes to my stories. Also, I never read them—except those I read aloud at public readings, and that's a different matter altogether. A reading is a performance and it might as well be someone else's story I'm reading. Though I do find myself editing while I'm reading aloud—that's more for the purposes of the moment and has little to do with the printed story.

Very little tailoring was necessary in the making of *The Barclay Family Theatre*. Only a couple of stories were written before I realized what was happening, that I was exploring the lives of the men in the lives of the seven Barclay sisters. It was no surprise. The Barclay family had been with me since *The Invention of the World*—Maggie Kyle's mother was one of the sisters, and you may remember that Grandpa Barclay was something of a hero to Wade Powers. Clay's mother in "The Concert Stages of Europe" was born a Barclay, and two of the women in "The Plague Children" are Barclay sisters—one of them, Clay's mother again. There was nothing strange in this. I was working out of the same community.

It was noticing this—and remembering the powerful influence my own exuberant and numerous aunts had on my early years—that made me wonder whatever had happened to the remaining sisters. They had all, fortunately, gone off into lives quite different from my own aunts'—though less happily, in some cases. I discovered I'd already written about one of them—Gladdy Roote, in "More Than Conquerors"—and about another in a different context—Mabel Weins in *The Resurrection of Joseph Bourne*. This discovery happened, incidentally, in Tokyo, where I discovered that Jacob Weins had come along with me to sort out his post-slide life and to complain that I hadn't treated him with enough understanding in the novel, and that Mabel Weins spoke with a voice that was obviously the voice of one of the Barclay sisters.

Everything fell into place. "Ladies and Gentlemen, the Fabulous Barclay Sisters!" was written last and should be read last. Because it goes back to the beginning of it all again, with Clay Desmond, the protagonist of the piano story, and later the frustrated novelist in Ireland.

TS: Would you give a few examples of the changes that you made, and discuss what you think these added to the meaning and the effect of *The Barclay Family Theatre*?

JH: By the time I've made these few changes, they seem so natural and right to me that I find it hard to believe that the original stories were any different from the revised. No changes were made for the purposes of the book—that is, I refused to allow my desire for a coherent collection to do damage to an individual story.

But writing a new story would show me something I hadn't noticed about an old story—that the novelist in "The Lepers' Squint" for instance, whose name is Philip Desmond, is obviously the same person as Barclay Desmond, the "Clay" of "The Concert Stages of Europe" and "Ladies and Gentlemen, the Fabulous Barclay Sisters!". He couldn't possibly be anyone else—yet for some reason as an adult he'd chosen to use what must have been his middle name all along. Nothing of the story was changed, but a connection was noticed and then illuminated simply by adding Barclay to his name when it's mentioned once—on the first page of his manuscript, I think.

When I reread "The Concert Stages of Europe" with the added knowledge of the Barclay family I gained from writing the other stories, I realized that this boy would obviously have approached his grandparents and his aunts for money and votes in his attempt to win that radio amateur hour. What we read in a story is what the writer has selected for us—for whatever his reasons. I simply selected one more scene and a few references to the aunts that had no reason for being there before ... only things that *must* have happened in the original story but didn't make it onto the page. If the added scene had made the slightest bit of difference to the outcome of the story, I would have had to conclude that it just couldn't have happened in the "real life" of this sequence—and not add it at all. No grafting allowed. Only showing a few things that were invisible before.

The changes I made to "The Plague Children" had nothing to do with the fact that it had become one of a group of connected stories—the connection was already there. What happened was, the fiction came alive, actually happened in my parents' community, almost as if I'd *made* it happen—some accused me of exactly that—and real life provided me with new information I couldn't bear to leave out of the story: details, anecdotes, that supported but didn't in any way alter the substance of the story.

One of the most exciting things about working on these stories was discovering the connections that existed between them without my conscious knowledge. Any other revisions you might find were simply a matter of polishing the style a little and had nothing to do with building a story collection.

TS: Would you comment on how you see the stories in *The Barclay Family Theatre* working as a whole?

JH: The seven Barclay sisters are the overriding presence throughout the book, although my attention is given to the sons, the husbands, and the lovers of them. The other thing that ties the stories together is the fact that they all involve invasions of one kind or another. These are Vancouver Island people, some of whom go out to invade the rest of the world and are in turn invaded, some of whom stay home and are invaded by outsiders.

It wasn't until the last story—"Ladies and Gentlemen, the Fabulous Barclay Sisters!", which is again first-person—that Clay Desmond, the boy who plays the piano in "The Concert Stages of Europe", through remembering the effect that his six crazy, melodramatic aunts had on his childhood, comes to understand why it was inevitable that he became a fiction writer. And it isn't until the last story that he remembers, also, that one of those aunts who liked to write plays about the neighbours, thinly disguised, when challenged with "Isn't that an invasion of privacy?" said, "All fiction is an invasion of one kind or another, or it fails".

TS: I'd like to switch our focus and ask you about your own reading and its influence on your writing. bp Nichol once noted that there is a wide gap between literature as it really exists—what people write and read—and literature as it is taught or studied—the academic tradition. You've already prepared a number of anthologies of literature for school use. If you had the opportunity to edit an anthology of your favourite short stories, what ones would you choose?

JH: Well, I could fill a good number of volumes with favourites. The first to come to mind, though, would be Flannery O'Connor's "Revelation" or the title story from *A Good Man Is Hard To Find*. There's no end to my admiration for her skill—though I share almost none of her vision of mankind. Frank O'Connor's "The Drunkard". Gabriel García Márquez's "Big Momma's Funeral". Alice Munro's "Dulse"—first published in *The New Yorker*—though there's any number of her stories I would want to reread and reread. Rudy Wiebe's "An Indication of Burning". John Cheever's "A Miscellany of Characters that Will Not Appear" and Eudora Welty's "Moon Lake".

This is ridiculous. Now I don't want to stop. Alistair MacLeod's "The Boat" and Faulkner's "Barn Burning". Patrick White's "At the Dump" and something by William Trevor. Something by V.S. Pritchett. Mavis Gallant's very funny story called "Speck's Idea". "The Leader of the People" in Steinbeck's *The Red Pony*. And on and on and on.

TS: In view of this avowed interest in other writers, how do you perceive critics' claims about assorted literary influences on your work?

JH: It puzzles me that so much is made of the fact that I've learned a few things from some South American novelists. Perhaps critics who mention this don't know that practically to a man those Latin Americans claimed to have learned it all from William Faulkner—who, as you know, was one of my heroes.

No one seems to have noticed that the biggest literary influence on my life and work—and the earliest influence as well—was the early Al Capp. After all, L'il Abner was the closest I ever saw the printed page coming to reflecting the world I lived in. I *knew* those people. I lived for Saturdays when I could pore for hours over those frames, and later when I met them or their cousins again in Faulkner and Flannery O'Connor and Reynolds Price I felt that somehow except for the accents they could have lived on Vancouver Island before the B.C. Ferries made it less of an island. That is no insult to anyone—I loved the people of Dogpatch.

If I recognized my neighbours and relatives in the South, I also recognized plenty of them in the world of Macondo and Piura—more than I recognize, frankly, in the world of fictitious southern Ontario, though I think Alice Munro's people may have sent their relatives out this way at some time. The coastline running past this island also runs past Asturias's home and García Márquez's home and Vargas Llosa's home.

Please understand this: to me ALL fiction is foreign fiction—except perhaps for the works of Bob Harlow and Roderick Haig-Brown and a few others—and South American fiction is no more or less foreign to me than Patrick White or John Nichols or Mordecai Richler. Because I grew up where I did it was inevitable that the writing even from other parts of Canada—a blank world to me until I was an adult—should seem foreign, or at least "other". By necessity, then, *any* literary influence would have to have been a foreign one. The alternative would have been to try to create a literary heritage out of trees and ocean and rain.

I don't know why I'm going on about this when it's really not important except that maybe I'm raising a question that may be fairly important to those writers who were born at this end of the country: what do you do when you start out with *no* literary heritage (not even a pretence at owning a borrowed one)? It seems to me you either make a virtue out of it and construct poems out of cougar tracks or you borrow a heritage from the native Indians who lived here before you or you decide to make all that excites you in the world—all cultures equally—your own to learn from as you please.

I do have the sense to know, however, that fiction grows out of place, not just other books. People elsewhere give me quite a bit of credit for imagination but anyone who lives on Vancouver Island will tell you I make up less than you think. Most would tell you they could do better. I remain careful, however—well I was careful, for instance, to make sure that nothing happened in *Bourne* that hadn't already happened on this island or isn't likely to happen, preferably seen with my own eyes. We've had tidal waves, which have washed up our inlets and left towns covered in mud and fish; we've had freighters—I remember a Japanese freighter hauling cars was washed up into the bay at Tofino and then left grounded there; I met the Peruvian seabird once in an airport bus; the little town of Port Alice is often in the process of sliding down the mountain when there's too much rain; several mayors on Vancouver Island like to dress up in costumes on occasions; Jacob Weins's cactus is no more ludicrous than the six or seven palm trees growing in Nanaimo (tourists don't know they're covered up for protection in the winter—with canvas tents). Reviewers and critics can have their fun calling it magic realism or imported South Americanism or whatever they want to but I know what I know. So do the many island residents who consider that I'm just recording the way things are.

Fiction as Invasion:

The Barclay Family Theatre

Ann Mandel

Each hourly newscast begins with the latest on the Argentine invasion of the Falklands, while I sit here thinking about the metaphor "fiction is invasion". What does it imply? Aggression? Hostility? Ideas about property, privacy, territorial imperatives and rights? The metaphor comes from the last page of Jack Hodgins' *The Barclay Family Theatre*, a collection of linked stories. The narrator of this story has just been named as a liar, from which it follows he might as well be a writer; not only can he now say anything he likes, he can "'write it down in a book, where people will assume it's the truth'" (298). Plotting a fictional version of a family event, he asks, "Another invasion of privacy?" (299) "Of course", he is told. "All fiction was an invasion of one kind or another, or it had no point" (299). Since invasion, as event and metaphor, figures prominently throughout the book, the statement invites consideration.

When the Argentinians first invaded the remote, insular Falklands, and Britain sent off its luxury-liner-cum-troopship, one heard a great deal about the fantastic, surreal, comic, anachronistic aspect of these

---

First published in *The Fiddlehead* 134 (1982). Reproduced, with revisions, by permission of Ann Mandel.

events. Now it appears that the ensuing hostilities have brought into question conventionally-held opinions about modern weaponry and warfare. When Jack Hodgins' first books appeared, focussing on (and invading?) insular fictional communities similar to those on Vancouver Island, critical attention first turned to the fantastic, magic, and generically peculiar elements in his work. With this, his fourth book, I think it is possible to see more clearly not only what literary conventions Hodgins works in, but in what sense the militant metaphor is appropriate, even central, to his fiction.

Hodgins has been called a "magic realist", a "fabulist", and a "regionalist". As with all labels, arguments can be made for and against these particular ones. The magic realism term, advanced especially by Geoff Hancock in the anthology *Magic Realism*, seems to me the most problematical. As borrowed from South American "el realismo magico" and used in relation to such story-tellers as García Márquez, Asturias, and Cortázar, it seems to fit. As drawn from modern art and connected to painters such as Magritte, de Chirico, Colville, and Pratt, it is surely wrong. The exuberance, humour, and exaggeration of a García Márquez, Hodgins, Kroetsch, or Rooke (all called magic realists by Hancock) have little to do with the controlled metaphysics of these painters. Indeed, many of the characteristics Hancock gives to magic realism more sensibly belong to "fabulist" or "fantastic" fiction as Borges defines it in "Tales of the Fantastic". The motifs Borges assigns to fantastic literature—double figures, confusions of reality and illusion, stories within stories, time travel, monstrous transformations—all appear in Hodgins' fiction, which, like fantastic literature, is rooted in an oral, popular culture. Hodgins himself has expressed discomfort with the regionalist label, fearing its suggestion of quaintness. But if one thinks of regional literature as involving (as I and others have argued[1]) a mental landscape with certain mythic patterns embedded in it, such as a search for home or self and the articulation of individual and collective memories rather than anything like environmental determinism—regionalism as close to both idyll and apocalypse—then the term has some pertinence to Hodgins' fiction.

Comment has tended, then, to emphasize Hodgins' writing in relation to modern and contemporary fiction. *The Barclay Family Theatre* confirms me in my feeling that Hodgins' affinities are rather with the old and generally conservative tradition of satire, and that the techniques of fantasy—plus the use of low similes, inflation and deflation, lists, catalogues, and anti-climax—serve him less as they do, say García Márquez, than as they do writers from Swift to Haliburton to Richler who use fantasy, humour, and linguistic extravagance to attack human folly, gullibility, pretension, and cowardice. *The Invention of the World* has a comic structure; it begins and ends with weddings. It opposes two societies, the better of which is established by the novel's end, and its many collisions are funny. But its main concerns are utopian dreams and their failure, fakery, the power of myths to delude, and the almost wilful way in which people allow themselves to be tricked, swindled, trapped. Salvation comes when individuals accept responsibility, marriage, community—the real as opposed to the miraculous. What *is* miraculous is what is natural.

The Invention of the World suggests that it is human nature to fool ourselves; it suggests too that we are always on the edge of going out of control, of slipping away from the rest of the world, of becoming insular. *The Resurrection of Joseph Bourne*, set in a truly remote community, Port Annie, perched at the sea's edge, also opposes illusion and reality, pro- and anti-progress factions, the fake and the genuine. Everyone in the town dreams of some kind of community, some kind of miraculous acceptance, but as in *Invention*, the really marvellous is simply what is human, imperfect. What matters is not the material world but the spiritual world felt through human community, *not* place. The town disappears; what remains is the eternal unseen.

Hodgins' vision in these books appears to be a kind of cross between Browning's and Swift's.[2] In *The Barclay Family Theatre*, Hodgins abandons fantasy as a technique, though not as a subject, and turns to a set of motifs (present to a degree in the other books) which are traditional to satire: clothes and body imagery; theatre lexis; and patterns of travel to, or invasion by, an alien culture. The question of vision itself is theme and technique. At what point does our necessarily imperfect (because human) vision become the squinty acceptance of a fiction, a deliberate narrowing of life? And can or does that narrow view have value?

The book's epigraph is spoken by a character from *The Invention of the World*, J.G. Barclay:

> I guess a man who's sent seven daughters out into the world has launched just about every kind of invasion you can imagine. Now let's close down this show and go home. There's cattle and cut hay and real life to be faced tomorrow.

Each of the eight stories concerns, directly or tangentially, one or more of the seven fabulous Barclay sisters, noted for their ability to scandalize, satirize, and victimize whole communities. All have married, some more than once; if weddings are central to *Invention*, marriages are important here—marriages long past any romantic illusion. Through marriage, Hodgins explores aspects of loneliness and community. Muses one husband, "After all these years of marriage, could he claim to know how much of her was real, how much disguise?" (189) Yet despite this estrangement—and despite double-chins, sagging paunches, and failing muscles—real affection can exist, and does, in some of the more compassionate moments in a book which more often shows how cruel people can be to each other.

Consciousness of failing or aberrant bodies indeed constitutes a major element of the stories. An adolescent body shoots out of control; frail Bella Barclay Robson's heart batters her helpless chest; Mr. Pernouski, the fattest man to ride the B.C. ferries, is trapped by his weight at the bottom of a sea cliff—he must effect his own resurrection. In "More Than Conquerors", Hodgins juxtaposes a young marriage being destroyed by hope for the bodily resurrection of a dead child with an old couple's crude but comforting acceptance of each other's aging selves. Hodgins uses body imagery to show how the flesh pulls down vanity and dreams, invades fantasy with its insistent reality, at the same time that the body, material, vital, is itself vulnerable to invasion. In "The Plague Children", a small community of middle and old-age hobby farmers is invaded by a horde of young magic mushroom pickers. The battle that follows between youthful arrogant opportunism and property protection is really a battle between life and the invasions of time, a fight no one gets out of alive. The body is an invaded island.

"The Sumo Revisions", the longest, most ambitious of the stories, interweaves sexual ambiguities and insecurities, athletic contests, theatrics, and questions about the reality of the seen world. The physical body seems the most real thing we can know, but a change of perspective, of culture, can make even that turn strange, a fraud or trick. Jacob Weins, ex-mayor of Port Annie, has been thrown into suicidal despair by the loss of his public role and his flamboyant costume collection. In Japan to recuperate, his ability to understand what he sees is assaulted by *kabuki* theatre where men play beautiful women who are disfigured and die on stage, by *sumo* wrestling where those huge bared bodies are easily misinterpreted, by invisible yet present emperors, by unrecognizable food, even by his own portrait. "'Dammit, he's made me a Jap . . . a Japanese!'" exclaims Weins, to which his guide, Hiroshi, replies: "'Perhaps to this old man all the rest of the world is populated by Japanese people who are hiding behind masks—only some have more successful masks than others'" (232). Surrounded by a confusion of public and private roles, Weins comes to understand something about the failings and possibilities of limited vision. Not a retiring man, he decides to rise from the waters of his private hell, re-enter public life, and take up once more his foolish, stagey, but now somehow forgiveable career as role-player.

The theatre imagery introduced by the book's title appears specifically in the titles of the first and last stories—"The Concert Stages of Europe" and "Ladies and Gentlemen, the Fabulous Barclay Sisters!"—and throughout in theatre, clothes, and costume imagery. Mr. Pernouski dresses up his girth and his hopes in red-and-white tartan jacket, white pants, and shoes. Eleanor Barclay views the world as a series of backdrops for her costumes. The plague children appear as exotically-garbed foreigners, invading not only the fields but also Dennis Macken's collection of forty-seven caps. Such imagery is a traditional way of revealing people's pretensions, hopes, self-consciousness, and defences—their masking of reality. The real for Hodgins, though, is not visible. As in Browning, the body is vision's medium. But as with Swift, the body is not the naked animal but the body clothed in experience. And not content with one serviceable coat, we pile garment on garment. Thinks Lily in *The Invention of the World*:

> there's no sense telling me just be natural because by the time a person's got to my age there's a pretty good chance there's no such thing as natural, or it's buried too deep to come out. Maybe that's what life is, forgetting what's natural, or maybe that's what life *isn't*. Maybe our natural life goes on without us while we slap on layer after layer of what we think is life but is only pretence. (261)

Yet Gulliver's conviction that clothes are a "false covering" is not the answer; that after all is madness. In her communally purgative striptease at the end of *Joseph Bourne*, Jenny, shedding most of her past, still stops short of shedding a final piece of lace, of finishing the dance, knowing that it's the unseen and imperfect that's important. One cannot recover a mythical "natural" innocence. Innocence, rather, means naïvety or gullibility. Eden can only be resurrected as Mr. Pernouski's Eden Realty Co. All the world *appears* as a stage.

Three of the stories in *The Barclay Family Theatre* involve travel to a strange culture: Bella, in "Invasions '79", dares the foreigners of and in Ottawa; Barclay Desmond looks for roots in Ireland; and Jacob Weins suffers Japan. Travel allows Hodgins another satirical technique, shifting perspectives and angles of vision so that trust in sense experience breaks down. The usual appears ridiculous; the self feels ridiculous. Unwanted revelations occur. Even worse for Bella than Ottawa is suddenly seeing her son's life in a new way: "He was leading her into territory more strange and frightening than any she'd been in before. It was cruel of him, to make her feel so helpless" (45). Such revelations are unexpected invasions. Yet revelations one does anticipate may not materialize. Looking at a portrait of himself, Carl Roote, hoping for enlightenment, sees nothing he recognizes or needs. Art, in these stories, is not necessarily an expansion of vision or a source of community. On the contrary, Desmond, trying to write his novel, reflects that some kinds of blindness can be a blessing. "What good is vision after all if it refuses to ignore the dark?" (179)

> Because hasn't he heard somewhere, that artists—painters—deliberately create frames for themselves to look through, to sharpen their vision by cutting off all the details which have no importance to their work? (179)

While acknowledging the need for celebration, he also thinks "That words, too, were invented perhaps to do the things that stones can do. And he has come here, after all, to build his walls" (180).

"The Lepers' Squint", with Desmond as refuser of the feast, is the least comical of the stories because least distanced from its characters. Though written in the third person, it stays close to Desmond's mind, while the first and last stories, though first person, are the most purely comic, distanced by a child's limited, puzzled perspective and the distance of the narrator from his youthful self. Throughout, Hodgins distances the reader by frequent appeals to our superior knowledge ("His specialty... was some old poem.... Its title went something like *Toil Less and Crusade*" [24]) and by preserving in us the same uncertainty about his characters' motives that they feel about each other's and their own. Some of the comic ideas work wonderfully well. The cardboard piano keyboard in the first story is the basis for some fine jokes. Occasionally Hodgins' style seems to develop tics. One of his stylistic markers has been the use of "Though...", "Still...", and "Not that..." clauses ("Though to tell the truth...", "Still, she made sure that...", "Not that he despised..."). Not that such clauses can't be effective, but in "More Than Conquerors" one finds an irritating six initial "Though..." sentences within a couple of pages. That story, too, contains some clumsy exposition and a remarkably awkward and obvious passage in which the arbutus tree is presented as a symbol of death and resurrection within nature. When I encountered the Hotel Arbutus on the last page, I winced.

Distance, heights and depths, cliffs and pools, chasms, descents, and resurrections: these are the directions of the stories, the view lines of Hodgins' vision. They are not random. His targets are not social but philosophic and intellectual: all those attachments to the material world which cut people off from hidden reality, all those aspects of fantasy which cut people off from each other. It is solipsism Hodgins attacks. Fiction is invasion of an islanded self, invasion by insight sharpened to a weapon. Paradoxically, such fine honing is itself a limitation, a mask, and a defence. Communality exists in tension with individual perception in much the same way that, in the concluding story, flair counterbalances reliable dullness, with Hodgins granting ambiguous value to both. Similarly, he seems to extend toward his characters the same grudging, limited, but at times delighted tolerance that the citizens of Waterville feel for the outrageous Barclay sisters whose techniques he shares.

Sooner or later the show has to close. Argentina launched its invasion at least in part to distract its citizens from a desperate internal economy. J.G. Barclay reminds the wedding revellers that, having launched his own seven distracting invasions, he must return to real life waiting at home. Certainly Hodgins' fictional invasions are diverting and funny; they are also impatient, even desperate reminders that responsibilities and larger invasions await just outside the book's protective covers.

Notes

[1] See, for example, Ann Mandel, "The Frontiers of Memory: Wallace Stegner's *Wolf Willow*, a Neglected History" and Eli Mandel, "Images of Prairie Man".

[2] I am thinking particularly of Browning's "Fra Lippo Lippi" and of Swift's *A Tale of a Tub* and *Gulliver's Travels*.

Works Cited

Borges, Jorge Luis. "Tales of the Fantastic". Ed. Robert Harlow. *Prism international* 8.1 (1968): 4-16.

Browning, Robert. "Fra Lippo Lippi". *Robert Browning: The Poems.* Ed. John Pettigrew. Supplemented and Completed by Thomas J. Collins. Vol. 1. New Haven, CT: Yale UP, 1981. 540-50. 2 vols.

Hancock, Geoff. "Magic Realism". *Magic Realism: An Anthology.* Ed. Geoff Hancock. Toronto: Aya, 1980. 7-15.

Hodgins, Jack. *The Barclay Family Theatre.* Toronto: Macmillan of Canada, 1981.

——. *The Invention of the World.* Toronto: Macmillan of Canada, 1977.

——. *The Resurrection of Joseph Bourne; or, A Word or Two on Those Port Annie Miracles.* Toronto: Macmillan of Canada, 1979.

Mandel, Ann. "The Frontiers of Memory: Wallace Stegner's *Wolf Willow*, a Neglected History". *Laurentian University Review* 8.1 (1975): 92-102.

Mandel, Eli. "Images of Prairie Man". *A Region of the Mind: Interpreting the Western Canadian Plains.* Ed. Richard Allen. Regina: Canadian Plains Studies Centre, U of Saskatchewan at Regina, 1973. 201-09. Rpt. in *Another Time.* By Eli Mandel. Erin, ON: Porcépic, 1977. 45-53.

Swift, Jonathan. *Gulliver's Travels. Jonathan Swift: A Selection of His Works.* Ed. Philip Pinkus. Toronto: Macmillan of Canada, 1965. 1-286.

——. *A Tale of a Tub. Jonathan Swift: A Selection of His Works.* Ed. Philip Pinkus. Toronto: Macmillan of Canada, 1965. 287-443.

Creatures of Clay:
The Barclay Family Theatre

Wayne Grady

> We address mankind, who are naturally blind, and decline with the fall of the leaf.
> Frail creatures of clay that endure for a day, whose estate is compounded of grief.
> In the shadows you grope, without wings, without hope, like dream-stuff and destined to die.
> —Aristophanes, *The Birds*, ll. 630-32

The Barclay family's roots go back, as we learned in *The Invention of the World*, to 1924, when old Jackson Barclay brought his wife, Kate, and their seven daughters from a dirt farm in Alberta to Waterville, in Vancouver Island's Comox Valley where Hodgins himself was born and "where nature gave you a little help" (141). Grandpa Barclay, displaying a talent that he seems to have passed on to his daughters, would "never miss a chance to tell a harmless joke on someone else, then hunch-up and give a big wink that pulled his whole face out of shape" (141). Some of the branches on the family tree are a bit tangled. One of the daughters—Christina, as we infer through close rereading—married a man named Maclean and gave birth to a girl named Maggie, the Maggie Kyle who is the central character of *Invention*. Another daughter, Lenora, married either a man named Miles, as we were told in "Other People's Troubles" in *Spit Delaney's Island* (where she is called "Lenore"), or a man named Desmond, as we see in "The Concert Stages of Europe" and "Ladies and Gentlemen, the Fabulous Barclay Sisters!", the first and last stories in *The Barclay Family Theatre.*

The rest of the family history is fairly clearly delineated in *The Barclay Family Theatre.* Bella Barclay married a man named Robson and had two children, James and Iris, both of whom now live in Ottawa ("Invasions '79"). Christina married again, this time to a real estate broker named Pernouski, and spends much of her time on buying trips for her import store ("Mr. Pernouski's Dream"). Gladdy married Carl Roote ("More Than Conquerors"). Mabel married Jacob Weins ("The Sumo Revisions"), the mayor of Port Annie in *The Resurrection of Joseph Bourne* until a giant mudslide put an end to his dreams of Port Annie as a Hollywood resort by putting an end to Port Annie itself. Frieda married Eddie Macken ("The Plague Children"). The Macken family is nearly as reputable as the Barclays: we remember Nora Macken from "The Trench Dwellers" in *Spit Delaney's Island,* who "used to tell how the Mackens first settled on the north slope of the valley more than fifty years ago when Black Alex, her father, brought the whole dozen of his children onto the Island in his touring car and started hacking a farm out of what had for centuries been pure timber land" (73).

Barclay Miles (called "Duke") is the sensitive and observant ten-year-old in "Other People's Troubles", the seventh story in *Spit Delaney's Island,* whose father is brought home from the bush with his nose flattened and one ear missing, a bandaged mummy whose grotesque appearance causes Duke's mother, "Lenore", to run off in terror to hide in the bedroom. The story is told from Duke's precocious point of view but in the third person, a device that lends an air of maturity and objectivity to the event that contrasts well with the boy's own newly comprehended involvement in the family. Duke appears in *The Barclay Family Theatre* as Barclay Philip Desmond (called "Clay"), the son of Lenora and her miraculously restored husband whose surname this time is Desmond.

"The Concert Stages of Europe", the opening story in *The Barclay Family Theatre,* is told in the first person by Clay Desmond. The principal concern of this story seems to be nothing more complicated than Clay's schemes to get out of taking piano lessons. Clay is neither blessed nor cursed, as Duke partly came to be, with Hodgins' own heightened awareness. There are, however, in "The Concert Stages of Europe", some undertones of a more serious intent: Clay, too, learns what it means to be a member of a family, to have other people's expectations—like their troubles—thrust upon him. During an otherwise unremarkable talent contest, when Richy Ryder of CJMT asks the otherwise unremarkable question, "'What are you going to be when you grow up?'", Clay answers, "'Nothing'" (20), giving voice to his parents' worst fears. His answer is a blend of cowardice and rebellion that strikes a deeper, more resonant chord than the undeniable humour, which is right out of W.O. Mitchell's *Jake and the Kid* stories.

Near the end of "The Concert Stages of Europe" Clay remarks that

> Being part of a family was too complicated. And right then I decided I'd be a loner. No family for me. Nobody whose hearts could be broken every time I opened my mouth. Nobody *expecting* anything of me. Nobody to get me all tangled up in knots trying to guess who means what and what is it that's really going on inside anyone else. No temptations to presume I knew what someone else was thinking or feeling or hoping for. (22)

Clay's naïve insight is, of course, negated by two things: the final story in the book and his own first-person, involved form of narration. In the final story, "Ladies and Gentlemen, the Fabulous Barclay Sisters!", we learn that Clay is the author of all the stories in *The Barclay Family Theatre*, and he couldn't be a bigger or more complicated part of the family than that. Despite his avowed dissociation from the Barclay clan quoted above, Clay gets himself into a somewhat embarrassing situation by emulating the shenanigans of his six fabulous aunts precisely because he *wants* to be a part of the family. When Eleanor remarks to him that "'Life at your place is so dull'", Clay begins to suspect that "if I continued to live in that household I'd become like [my parents], honoured and trusted and dull. Life would be much more fun if I lived in the Barclay house" (289).

Clay does not actually move into Grandpa Barclay's house (Jackson Barclay has by now diminished into a silent, nameless spectator of his daughters' incomprehensible fantasies), but he does engineer a fantasy of his own in an attempt to be as much like the sisters as possible. The attempt fails—and the Barclays scorn failure more than anything else—but Eleanor consoles him with the Barclay philosophy: "'If no one is going to believe you anyway, you may as well tell them lies from morning to night'" (298). The notion appeals to Clay, who has at last come to accept his Barclay blood. "'You can tell them any old thing that goes through your head'", continues Eleanor, "'Or write it down in a book, where people will assume it's the truth'" (298).

Just as the two stories about Spit Delaney are the first and last stories in *Spit Delaney's Island*, the two stories about the young Clay Desmond form the bookends for the six other stories in *The Barclay Family Theatre*—they provide a kind of moat, creating an island upon which the rest of the book takes place. These stories define the stories between them as a moat defines the space it encloses. The metaphor of the moat is borrowed from "The Sumo Revisions", in which Jacob Weins speculates on the life of the Emperor of Japan on his protective island in the middle of Tokyo. The moat as a circular line of defence against the outside world as well as a kind of prison wall that keeps its occupant shut off from the rest of society is a powerful thematic and structural symbol for Hodgins, and indeed for Canadian literature. And if we expand the metaphor to think of Vancouver Island as the Emperor's fantasy palace, and the Strait of Georgia as a moat, we can see why Hodgins has framed or defined his six central stories with these two retaining walls.

"All fiction", Eleanor concludes on the last page of the book, "was an invasion of one kind or another" (299), and Clay's book is certainly about fiction as well as about invasions. It is therefore fitting that the second story focusses on language and literature in dealing with some of the various forms of invasion. "Invasions '79" is about Bella, now widowed, visiting her son James in Ottawa where he is a professor of English literature specializing in Chaucer's *Troilus and Criseyde*. It is the only story in the book that does not take place on an island, unless Ottawa is seen as an island in Canada much as St. Petersburg was an island in nineteenth-century Russia. The analogy is not farfetched, for James has fallen in love with a girl from the Soviet embassy, and Bella has come to save him from the Reds that she imagines must be under his bed. She does save him, in a roundabout way, saves at least his skin. But it is his soul about which James worries, and Bella knows that "She hadn't the language for saving anyone's soul" (65).

In a world where fiction is an invasion, language is a weapon. But weapons can be used either for defence or by the aggressor (as Bella, watching the Soviet invasion of Afghanistan on television, realizes), and what James apparently needs is a more aggressive invasion than "timid Bella" (284) can muster. Iris, his sister, may have the answer: "'What he needs... is to have his mother come along and slap him down, knock some sense into his stupid head for a change'" (29). James *is* slapped down, but only indirectly by his mother. It is his Armenian poet, Marta, who finally adds poignancy to the four lines from *Troilus and Criseyde* (5.1054-57) that James has hung on his apartment wall (36):

> She seyde, "Allas! for now is clene ago
> My name of trouthe in love, for everemo!
> For I have falsed oon the gentileste
> That evere was, and oon the worthieste!"

It is no coincidence that James is a Chaucer scholar, for Hodgins' method is like Chaucer's, and *The Barclay Family Theatre* is organized rather like *The Canterbury Tales*—a frame-narrative that may in a sense be seen as the first collection of interrelated short stories in English. Like Chaucer, Hodgins assigns one story to each of his principal characters, including himself;[1] and, like Chaucer, Hodgins is both comic and instructive, though he stays well within the realm of gentle satire and declines to pick up Chaucer's famous rapier. The story that Hodgins, as the older Philip Desmond, gives himself is "The Lepers' Squint". Like "The Tale of Melibee" in *The Canterbury Tales*, "The Lepers' Squint" is significantly placed and quite unlike its companion pieces. As the fifth of eight stories, coming between the two novella-length stories "More Than Conquerors" and "The Sumo Revisions", it may be seen as a fulcrum balancing the stories of the flesh that precede it and the stories of the spirit that follow it.

"The Lepers' Squint" takes place in Ireland, a dark green island of myth and murk, and the story bears somewhat the same relationship to the rest of *The Barclay Family Theatre* as the account of Donal Keneally's folk-heroic origins in Ireland bears to the rest of *The Invention of the World*. Philip Desmond, with his wife Carrie (who *might* be the resurrected Carrie Payne from "More Than Conquerors") and their three children, has rented an old house in Bantry Bay, where Philip is attempting to write a novel—trying, in other words, to create a fabulous world within the charmed circle that all islands represent to Hodgins. As the mysterious beauty of this island—in the person of Mary Brennan, an Irish writer—takes over Desmond's imagination, he finds that he has to come to terms with himself, as a writer, before he can learn to transcend his limitations as a human being. Language, which earlier was a weapon for fending off or perpetuating invasions, becomes a wall between the writer and his world, but a wall in which there is a window through which the writer squints: the controlling metaphor here is the church whose name has provided Hodgins with the title for this story. Desmond recognizes that he has shut himself off like a leper from "celebrating something he'd come here to find" (180). However, he also realizes that this sacrifice is made in exchange for a greater artistic integrity—that walls with narrow holes do not in the end separate him from life, but give him the distance and the perspective (like the aperture of a camera rather than a cell window) needed to write his novel: "That words, too, were invented perhaps to do the things that stones can do. And he has come here, after all, to build his walls" (180).

A fortress also figures in "The Sumo Revisions", the sixth story. It is Hirohito's imperial palace in Tokyo, definitely designed to keep things out but, since the American occupation of Japan in 1946, at least partially intended to keep Hirohito in. With its surrounding moat and park it is literally an island within an island, a charmed circle that is doubly safe and, for Jacob Weins, doubly attractive: "He preferred, in fact, the opposite bank of the moat, the jungle of leafy trees where the Emperor apparently lived beneath one of those barely glimpsed roofs" (195). The Emperor, Weins knows, has rejected things of the spirit—he is "the only person in the world to have signed a paper declaring [himself] not a god" (195), though Weins seems unaware that Hirohito was forced to sign that paper by the Americans. Weins himself has similarly rejected things of the spirit for things of the flesh, as signified by his departure from the *kabuki* play to go to a *sumo* wrestling match. Not until Weins meets a former *sumo* wrestler who, like himself, is wasting away in retirement, does he realize that the thousand natural shocks that flesh is heir to leave the mind relatively free to explore the possibilities of the imagination. "The Sumo Revisions" ends with Weins imagining himself taking his seat in the House of Commons—the Canadian version of Hirohito's imperial palace—presumably having overcome the ignominy of being forced into retirement by an act of God. He has become, we are compelled to realize, hubristic and quite mad: for Weins, the walls of his fortress have no focussing aperture.

As in his first two novels, Hodgins' concerns in this collection are "invention" and "resurrection".[2] The Barclay Family Theatre itself, in which the sisters act out plays based on real events in Waterville, is a comic combination of the twin concerns; and in almost every story there is an artist who embodies the macrocosmic progression from birth to death, from things of the flesh to things of the spirit. The painter Eli Wainamoinen in "More Than Conquerors" says he believes that "every work of art was a violence itself, a cry, a hand-slap to wake the hysteric to reality" (111), which is exactly what Iris prescribed for James in "Invasions '79". It should also be remembered that Wainamoinen is a Finn, and in "The Concert Stages of Europe" Clay had declared that "If anyone had ever asked me what I did want to be when I grew up, in a way that meant they expected the truth, I'd have said quite simply that what I wanted was to be a Finn" (5-6). Wainomoinen is also old, close to death and concerned with matters of mortality and with ways to escape it: there is a failed Lazarus scene in the funeral parlour across the street on the night of Wainomoinen's first one-man show.

Accompanying the artist figures are a number of characters who either put on or take off disguises. By means of this motif Hodgins almost obsessively raises questions about illusion and reality that always seem to grow out of questions about life and death: Hodgins as Prospero. Jacob Weins, who has already attempted suicide, regularly used to dress up as Henry VIII or Cyrano de Bergerac when he was courting Mabel. Mabel herself used to dress up with her sisters for the Barclay theatre-in-the-garage. Even fat Mr. Pernouski's salesman get-up, "a red-and-white tartan jacket and white pants and shoes" that earned him the nickname "the Plaid Tank" (78), takes on the aspects of a disguise. But like the costumes of Jacob Weins, like Eli Wainomoinen's painting of Carl Roote in "More Than Conquerors", and like these eight linked stories, the purpose, for Hodgins, of Pernouski's elaborate disguise is not to create an illusory truth, but rather to *reveal* the true man that lies beneath its comic surface.

Notes

[1] After the Prioress finishes her brief tale of the Christian child slain by a group of Asian Jews, Chaucer begins his own tale of Sir Thopas, a rollicking, romantic tale reminiscent of that of the Knight. The Host cuts Chaucer off ("Namoore of this, for Goddes dignitie"), and Chaucer switches to his tale of Melibee, which he tells in prose rather than verse. The tale of Melibee may be seen as a turning-point in the pilgrimage from the city of man (the Tabard Inn in Southwerk) to their version of

St. Augustine's City of God (Canterbury). The tales before Chaucer's own are earth-bound, even earthy, or else deal with false religiosity. After the tale of Melibee, the tales become more and more concerned with spiritual matters.

[2] Although Hodgins thinks of "invention" as a parody of divine creation and artistic creation, and although "resurrection" means more to him than artistic transfiguration, it is illuminating to consider Hodgins' preoccupation with these ideas in the context of Northrop Frye's discussion of "creation" and "recreation" in his *Creation and Recreation* (3-11, 62-71, et passim).

WORKS CITED

Aristophanes. *The Birds. Two Classical Comedies: The Birds by Aristophanes The Brothers Menaechmus by Plautus*. Trans. and ed. Peter D. Arnott. New York: Appleton-Century-Crofts, 1958. 1-59.

Chaucer, Geoffrey. *The Canterbury Tales. The Works of Geoffrey Chaucer*. Ed. F.N. Robinson. 2nd ed. Boston: Houghton Mifflin, 1957. 1-265.

———. *Troilus and Criseyde. The Works of Geoffrey Chaucer*. Ed. F.N. Robinson. 2nd ed. Boston: Houghton Mifflin, 1957. 385-479.

Frye, Northrop. *Creation and Recreation*. Toronto: U of Toronto P, 1980.

Hodgins, Jack. *The Barclay Family Theatre*. Toronto: Macmillan of Canada, 1981.

———. *The Invention of the World*. Toronto: Macmillan of Canada, 1977.

———. *The Resurrection of Joseph Bourne; or, A Word or Two on Those Port Annie Miracles*. Toronto: Macmillan of Canada, 1979.

———. *Spit Delaney's Island: Selected Stories*. Toronto: Macmillan of Canada, 1976.

Mitchell, W.O. *Jake and the Kid*. 1961. Laurentian Library 21. Toronto: Macmillan of Canada, 1974.

More Shenanigans:
An Interview with Jack Hodgins (1990)

J.R. (Tim) Struthers

TS: Jeffrey Crane, the focal character in your novel *The Honorary Patron*, seeks to explain the views put forward by the early twentieth-century painter Kandinsky about the inner necessity and the spiritual nature of art. Of course, what these terms denote will change, sometimes radically, with each artist. But I was wondering if you would comment on your own sense of the inner necessity of, or within, or behind *The Honorary Patron* and your next novel, *Innocent Cities*?

JH: I think this is one of the most important aspects of all that a novelist brings to his material. You could take any plot or any collection of characters, you could take any raw story, and write 15,000 different novels. But each writer would have found something inside the material, or in the collection of characters, that made a connection with himself. When I'm looking around the world and responding to a million stories that are demanding to be told, out of the trunk of history—stories that haven't yet been fashioned into a modern novel—something has to choose this one instead of that one. And I suspect that on some instinctual level, on some level that I don't understand at all, perhaps coming out of my past or what's important to me, this story will stand out as demanding my attention while that story you can save for somebody else. Once I've committed myself to a story or a collection of people needing to be written about in my way, then the thing that it's going to become, the novel or short story or collection or whatever it's going to be, will have to come from my staring at the material until I somehow understand the connection between me and the material.

Consider *The Honorary Patron*, for instance. If I'm writing a story that seems to be about an older man who has decided his life is over, who has gone into early retirement and decided he's not going to do anything more because life is too complicated, and if I'm going to see what happens when I drag him back from staid, safe Europe and put him on Vancouver Island, then I've got to consider what kind of a story this is, what style, what language, I'm going to use, how much emphasis I'm going to put on different settings. With that particular novel, I began writing it as if I were writing a European novel. I deliberately shed my Vancouver Island idiom, I deliberately shed my more comfortable speaking voice, I deliberately shed all the things I had learned how to do while writing about Spit Delaney and Company, and I adopted another voice that somehow was a little more sophisticated, a little more controlled, a little bit more educated than any one I had used before. It seemed right for the beginning of that novel.

But as the novel progressed and the man moves from Zürich to Vancouver Island and gets involved in stock-car races and nudist beach parties, then the world seems to be falling apart around him, and somehow the language had to move in that direction as well. Through the novel I felt my own language changing along with his experience, so that the novel itself took on a kind of shape for me which reflected that sort of coming down from the sophisticated European society into the messy life of Vancouver Island and somehow bottoming out and perhaps rising a little to a kind of a synthesis, I suppose, at the end—because he does go back to Europe, though he's no longer the same man who lived in Europe before. What I had originally imagined was going to be a 120-page novella became what it became because it had to, because the language demanded it, the story demanded it, the characters demanded it, and, ultimately, whatever the theme might be demanded it as well.

The same thing happened with *Innocent Cities*. I stumbled upon a little story in history, some real people who existed in Victoria in the Victorian Age, who came from the state of Victoria in Australia. I learned of letters from this proper Victorian lady back to her younger sister in Australia, inviting her to come and be her husband's bed-partner. And the younger sister was on the next boat to Victoria! I knew that there was something here that I wanted to track down. What I discovered was a wonderful story of adultery and bigamy and deceit and treachery and perhaps murder that happened right under my nose, so to speak, one hundred years ago. And I asked, what have I got, do I modernize it, do I write a modern novel? I mean, this could happen now. And what do I know about the Victorian Age? But no, I couldn't wrench these people out of their Age. They were acting the way they acted because of where they lived and when they lived. So I had to go to them, I had to steep myself in research. Well, okay. I learn everything I can about the Victorian Age. I learn everything I can about the history of Victoria, especially in those particular years. I go to Australia and I go to the town they came from. And I read all about San Francisco, where one of the people lived. But that does not tell the story. That just gives me what I need to know to be able to handle the story.

And then I started thinking. What do I know about Victoria except that it is a city in which all of the buildings are a series of false faces put on top of false faces? The whole history of the city has been a process of growing tired of a certain face and putting on the most fashionable new face. You have false Tudor, and then you get tired of this and put false Spanish over top of the false Tudor. And then you get tired of that and put false something else over top of it. I thought, okay, this is a novel about deceit, this is a novel about a woman using every dirty trick in the book to get her husband back, even though he's happily married to somebody else, and ruining the lives of everybody in town. But at first glance she's one of the most attractive, dynamic characters imaginable. I realized that the novel had to be structured architecturally so that the process of reading it is the process of stripping off one false face after another. Once I knew that, then I knew the order in which the story was to be told.

It was not chronological at all. It was a matter of coming in at the point where the woman is the most noticeable, a mystery woman, and then moving backwards in time and then forwards in time as we learn things. The reader is constantly having to adjust his or her attitude towards my central character. So the architecture became the central metaphor. My central consciousness of the novel is a builder who wants to build the beautiful cities of the future but hasn't got a hope [laughter] living where he lives and in those times. And then the novel becomes an architectural thing which I am building. What it means in both those cases is that as the storyteller—and I can never afford to forget that's what I am—the storyteller is never unconscious, as far as possible, of the effect the order of the story is having upon the reader. If you write the same plot in a different order, you've written a different story. And the order in which you get the material that I'm giving you in this story is what the novel is.

I don't know if that answers your question but it certainly is what I thought about first. That was the inner necessity of the story. The stories just exist, and I have to find what it is that demands my attention rather than another writer's. What it was, in the case of *Innocent Cities*, was some love I have for architecture, some love I have for shapes, some experience I have of teaching mathematics. All those things came together and it seemed like a natural connection: this is my story, even though it originally had been uncovered by a historian, Terry Reksten. I'd heard her tell about it, and I had to go to her and ask if she was going to do anything more with it, and she gave me permission to do this. In effect she had done all she wanted to do with it, so it became mine. Once the story became mine, I had to study it and decide how to tell it.

TS: The phrases "inner necessity" and "spiritual nature" of art suggested to my mind some such word or notion as "value". And I began to reflect about the nature of value and then a little more specifically about the nature of literary value. I wondered if we would need to make some kind of adjustment once we moved from talking generally about value and one's sense of one's place in one's civilization and its multiform values to talking particularly about literary value. How would you come at that, at expressing a sense of value and more specifically a sense of what is most essential in terms of literary value?

JH: Well, I think first I have to come to terms with the fact that the writer's values are inescapable, that it is never necessary for a writer to say "These are the values I want to support somehow in my writing". Whether you like it or not, the way you see the world, the things that are important to you, the way you feel about other people will come through in every word that you write. As I tell my creative writing students, you won't hear me talk much about theme in this course because you can't escape it, you don't need to think about it, it will be an automatic result of how you see the world, the way you treat your characters, the material you choose in the first place. Your own particular values are going to be there in every step that you take along the way. The "literary" value will be much more complex than I can articulate or even, I suspect, imagine. But it will have something to do with the reader and the experience of reading. It might be the relationship between the reader and the characters, the feeling that the reader gets about fellow human beings from cavorting with these people for a while.

John Gardner has said that reading fiction is an opportunity to exercise our capacity for love. It's like practising up for real people [laughter]. He's assuming that if you are caring about fictional characters there's a tendency to carry that over into real life. Now that has been challenged, of course. But it is something that I would take quite seriously. I want my readers to feel certain ways about certain characters and I want my readers—not to pass judgement, necessarily, but—to possess attitudes towards characters' behaviour. This may be why I find it more comfortable to use a strong narrative voice, rather than to use first-person with one of my characters telling the story, although I've done that too, occasionally. I enjoy the responsibilities and opportunities of being the narrative voice that somehow has the ability or the power to guide the reader throughout the story, looking this way or looking that way. You cannot predict totally, of course, the effect of your words. But I think you have to take the responsibility for at least trying to.

TS: Would you see yourself as being more interested in patterns or in details?

JH: I wouldn't want to have to choose between them [laughter]. For me the details are the things that jump out and demand my attention and cause me to search for the story. This little detail tells me about a character. This little detail somehow makes the whole room come to life. Okay. I am gathering those details, I am presenting those details, but they are not very interesting to me by themselves until I start to see a pattern emerge. This happens at a later stage. When I'm writing a first draft, I don't think about these things at all. I'm just trying to get the story nailed down. But when I'm looking over my story, trying to figure out what I've done, then I start to see that for some reason or other the details that present themselves have certain things in common. I ask why, why am I secretly or privately obsessed with this?

And then of course that's when the fun begins, because that's when I start to understand what my own story is about, when I can discover the pattern, when I can begin to understand the pattern that has suggested itself somewhere other than in my surface concerns with getting the story told. Then I'm beginning to discover—for lack of a better term, I call it "the secret life of a story". I think a story worth telling has that kind of secret life which perhaps demanded your attention in the first place without you knowing why, and which will surface as you're writing it, or as you're rewriting it. So I wouldn't choose between them. I need the details, but I'm using them to look for the patterns.

TS: Would it be possible to say that the details serve as metaphors for the pattern?

JH: Yes. The details that stay. Not the details that get thrown out, which you would never see. But the ones that I have chosen to retain because they are the pattern in miniature, because they are pointing the way to the pattern.

TS: I've been thinking lately about the language of fiction and the language of criticism, and I've become exceptionally interested in looking at metaphor as perhaps being the form of language which would best allow the critic to overlap with what the writer is trying to do. Does that seem fair?

JH: Of course it seems fair. It seems perfectly logical. The kind of thing I just babbled about [laughter] concerning architectural imagery in *Innocent Cities*—well, that's a connecting point, it seems to me, for the critic. For the critic who wants, for whatever mysterious reasons I don't understand, to get inside that novel, it seems to me the logical entry place would be to recognize the pattern, to recognize that I'm using the architectural metaphor as my entry to the novel and then to see why and of course to judge whether it works or not. I think metaphor is something that the writer and the critic can have in common. That's, to me, the overlap.

TS: I'm just starting to work on this mentally in terms of understanding the short story form. But it seemed to me that one might be able to develop a series of metaphors for different kinds of stories and for different kinds of things that different sorts of stories attempt. Among the phrases or categories or possibilities that came to my mind were things like genesis stories, discovery stories, revelation stories.

JH: I think that's one of the things you sort through when you are faced with story. This is a narrative that demands to be told. So why are you attracted to it? Then, what are the things that are repeated? Then, what echoes does it suggest of other stories I have read? And then you think, of course this is a genesis story, of course this is a quest story. But I will hasten to say there's some mischievous part of me that doesn't want to be content with any of those. If I've got a genesis story on my hands, or if I've got an exodus story on my hands, I immediately start thinking, but that's not enough, what else is there? The sparks start to fly when I begin to see that, looked at from this certain angle, an exodus story can also be a quest story or whatever. You start having fun with genre-blending or type-blending—just bringing a fresh angle to it. Given these patterns that are already in the air around us, what can you bring to it that's unique and special and fresh? Well, you bring your own vision to it: from where I sit [laughter] in this little part of the world, when I look at that story I see it no longer as a genesis story, no longer as an exodus story, but as an exodus story that really is a Western in disguise or something like that—you understand what I mean. I'm not content with the inherited patterns. I want to monkey with them [laughter].

TS: I'd like to ask you about titles as well. How important are titles? What meanings or associations do they have for you? For example, *The Honorary Patron*. Was that a nod in the direction of Graham Greene's *The Honorary Consul*?

JH: No, it wasn't. The fact that it might have been mistaken for a nod was almost a reason to change the title. *The Honorary Patron* seemed an appropriate title from the very beginning. Having experienced the inaugural season of a theatre festival on Vancouver Island very similar to the one that Jeffrey Crane experiences, I was aware of the honorary patron of that particular event and thought of how strange this whole thing must look to a European, used to European culture, coming in and watching our shenanigans. Then I got intrigued with the whole idea of "honorary" versus "authentic". The metaphor implied in this became irresistible. So I became wedded to the title. It was not an intended literary analogy. It was purely descriptive, a way of introducing the metaphor.

TS: And with *Innocent Cities*?

JH: *Innocent Cities* took a long time to come because for a long time I felt that the "real" title was one I couldn't use, since somebody else had already used it—that is, Italo Calvino's *Invisible Cities*. I had other titles that I thought I was going to have to use because I couldn't use the one I really wanted. It was going to be this and it was going to be that. And I thought, I'm disappointed, but it'll do. After all, what does it matter in the long run? And then very close to the end I realized that it had to be *Innocent Cities*. It just leapt out at me from somewhere and, once I'd thought of it, there was no conceivable alternative. It worked from every angle I could think of.

What was interesting to me was that after I'd chosen that title, which seemed to me to fit with everything else in the novel, a European critic who is very familiar with my work commented that it was very oxymoronic—which hadn't occurred to me at all. But I thought, well of course to a European the notion of an innocent city would be totally bizarre, impossible. This is a very North American notion, that a city could ever have been innocent. The novel indicates that cities don't stay innocent for long, but the fact that they even wanted to be innocent is perhaps a North American notion. So already the title is beginning to tell me more than I realized it was saying.

TS: We all have our cities that we're trying to build and all have our cities that we're trying to move towards.

JH: [laughter] Yes. That's true. Fictional and otherwise.

TS: You have made some important moves geographically, and, I am sure, spiritually and emotionally, along with doing a fair amount of travelling on particular occasions. After a couple of years in Ottawa you chose to return to your native Vancouver Island and have now for several years been teaching creative writing at the University of Victoria. But you have continued to visit different places, just as you made earlier trips to Ireland and Japan. Among those various travels, what things stand out in your mind as vital components of the actual experiences? And have things come to your mind in retrospect as a result of travelling?

JH: This is a whole new topic that could take forever [laughter]. Patterns are still emerging. Meanings are still emerging. I've barely begun to sort them out. For instance, it's only now with the country falling apart that I've begun to understand how important it was that I lived in Ottawa for two years. I discovered what the world looked like from Ontario, which was very different from what it looked like back home. And even though I went back to Vancouver Island, I felt that I was somehow more of a Canadian from having lived in Ottawa—and perhaps understood my own part of the country a little better from the experience. So you never know when it's going to hit you what's useful in travel.

This latest adventure in Australia started out just as an opportunity to spend time with a friend, a novelist there, who'd invited me to come back. He happened to be going on a research trip and I said, sure, let's go. It seemed like a "boy's own adventure", a couple of middle-aged men setting off into the outback in an old unreliable pick-up truck. But by the time I was through a month of his company and exploring parts of Australia that few travellers ever see and meeting people out of a world totally foreign to me, I knew that *I* had been through quite an important journey in my life. I didn't know what it meant. I just knew that it was significant in some way.

And I thought, okay, I'm not going to worry about it, it may take me the rest of my life to figure out why I went home feeling that I'd been through a much more significant journey than any I'd ever taken. What does it mean? What is my relationship with this new place? Why am I not sure even that I want to continue living in that other country? What is it going to look like when I get back home? And how have I changed? I came home and started writing down the trip and almost immediately began to see patterns. Details first. Because I'm hoping somebody will read this book, I'm having to give the details first. Then I began to realize, I hadn't thought of this while I was watching it, I hadn't noticed that until it suddenly surfaced, why is this showing up now after I'm already home? And by the end I began to get some understanding of what the trip was really all about.

I'm still in the process of discovering that, so I'm not going to make any grand conclusion here. It seems to me that these journeys are opportunities to look at ourselves from a different angle, to look at our everyday world from a different world, and to discover the patterns we take with us. There's a sense when you set out on a journey that you're leaving everything behind. But of course we all know you're not leaving everything behind—you're taking yourself with you. But what you're taking with you, even if you're shedding almost everything else, is the things that you've been responding to, the patterns that you've been reacting to, wherever you've been. And sometimes by being in a foreign environment you will recognize things that you wouldn't even notice in your own territory where they blend into the landscape.

TS: Which writer were you travelling with?

JH: Roger McDonald. A novelist and poet. Author of the novel *1915* and other works. My wife, Dianne, and I met him and his wife, Rhyll McMaster, on their farm when I was there in '87 and we got along very well. He was struggling with a new novel and I was struggling with a new novel and we were commiserating. He was curious about what I did teaching creative writing. Eventually I suggested we continue the conversation in letters. So we started writing back and forth about our own work and the artistic problems we were having, making suggestions, and eventually he sent me his new novel, *Rough Wallaby*, in manuscript, to do with as I wished, and I did the same thing with *Innocent Cities*. The next thing I knew he was inviting me to come and have this sort of archetypical Australian walkabout—on four wheels [laughter].

TS: Another Australian writer whose work I was introduced to by Jack Hodgins via one of the epigraphs in *The Resurrection of Joseph Bourne* was David Malouf.

JH: Yes. A very fine writer. Somebody who is doing something different in every book that he brings out. Enormously sensitive to language and the experiences that language is creating in the reader's mind as you're reading the story and the importance of the depth in the language to suit the material you're dealing with. A superb writer. But quite aside from his fiction, I'm interested in the writing he has done on "home". He has written a lot about what it means as a metaphor to have grown up where he grew up—the house, your home, as your first environment.

TS: *12 Edmondstone Street*.

JH: *12 Edmondstone Street*, yes. And the notion of Brisbane architecture as significant to his way of seeing the world. That started me thinking about the kind of background I have, the kind of architecture I grew up with, discovering it has more in common with Australian architecture than it has with, say, Ottawa architecture. That notion became one of the themes of my journey, responding to a different architecture, responding to a different landscape, and relating it to landscape and architecture at home.

TS: Are there any other Australian writers that you might wish to mention?

JH: *Yes.* There are some very exciting novelists and short story writers. Amongst them are Rodney Hall, whose novel *Captivity Captive* is one of the most beautiful and frightening novels I've read in a long time, and one I wish *I* had written. Thea Astley, a terrific novelist and short story writer. Olga Masters, author of a collection of stories which is also a novel at the same time—Canadians tend to think that we invented the form. Olga Masters' novel or story collection, whatever it is, is called *A Long Time Dying*. A beautiful thing. She's marvellous. Let's see. Who are some of the most exciting writers? Kate Grenville is very good as well. Marion Halligan. Glenda Adams.

TS: What do you empathize with most in the writing that you read?

JH: I don't know that I can isolate anything. My first relationship is with language. The way the first paragraph is written, the voice that comes through that language. But if I were still responding only to voice on page six, maybe there's not much else here but style. It's the voice and the language that will get me into it, but it will be the relationship that I set up with the characters that will keep me in it. The people. Whether I care about them or am curious about them or am fascinated by them.

TS: Something that has interested me for a long time in your work has been the appreciation you have shown for writers of many centuries ago: Shakespeare, obviously, and also the Romantics. What do you think of as the inner necessity that propelled the Romantic Movement? How would you describe that?

JH: I'm not sure I can. No. It has been too long since I read the Romantics and what's coming to the surface now could be entirely distorted. I don't think I can comment on that.

TS: When a character of yours—Jeffrey Crane in *The Honorary Patron*—sees a girl holding a copy of *The Poetry of John Keats*...?

JH: [laughter] I really don't know. I've just gone blank here. No. I really think that question is too important to answer off the top of my head.

TS: Some people think that the Romantic Movement is dead.

JH: Oh, I don't think the Romantic Movement is dead. It has evolved. It has also been distorted. This is one of the reasons that I'm so leery of it. Because the Romantic Movement has come to represent some of the most unattractive possibilities in human nature: the selfishness, self-centredness, self-celebration, narcissism, the unrealistic tendency, all those other things that got associated with it. So you get these very bizarre theories—people expecting writers to be mad or they can't be "real" writers. I'm suspicious of all that. But I don't think that has got much to do with the inner necessity of the original Romantics: the idea of the search for truth and beauty and perfection.

TS: Once again there are false faces to be stripped away.

JH: Always. Always. The Romantics were very good at constructing false faces and somehow falling victim of their own mythology. It's a dangerous territory. I suspect that to some readers I'm probably a Romantic writer, but I don't identify with a lot of the things that I associate with the Romantic Movement. However, I think it lives—and I think it lives especially in the popular imagination.

TS: What are you looking forward to in the next few years?

JH: [laughter] Opportunity to write more books. I've got two books half-finished and demanding my attention. Opportunity to travel more, to go back to Australia many times. To continue enjoying my marriage, and our children. To continue teaching promising writers. Opportunity to do the things that I love doing.

TS: Delightful. Thank you very much.

Hodgins' Houses of Words:

The Honorary Patron and *Innocent Cities*

JoAnn McCaig

"To the designer, the *real* building remains in his head."
—Jack Hodgins, *Innocent Cities* (289)

I

Jack Hodgins is an artist who defies categorization. As Stephen Slemon and Ajay Heble have suggested, Hodgins is a post-colonialist who believes in deconstructing conventional literary structures. Heble points out that in general "Hodgins' novels seek to re-create and emphasize communal, rather than individual, experience" and that this communal emphasis links Hodgins to other Commonwealth writers "who reject the Eurocentric cult of the individual in favour of formulations that enable articulation of the values of their own cultural heritage" (679). On the other hand, as David L. Jeffrey and J.R. (Tim) Struthers have

---

An earlier version of the discussion here of *The Honorary Patron* first appeared in *Canadian Literature* 128 (1991). Reproduced by permission of JoAnn McCaig.

argued, Hodgins is an artist who upholds the view that art aspires to grace, harmony, and wholeness. Struthers perceives Hodgins as writing out of the tradition of biblical allegory and sees in his work a belief "in the eternal mysteries and ideal values whose immanence in the human spirit makes possible a resurrection of the world" (131). In short, Hodgins is concerned not only with what is but also with what could be. The tensions between these two impulses find structural expression in Hodgins' work in linear and circular elements that recur with remarkable regularity and consistency.

When asked about these structural elements in his fiction, Hodgins responded:

> These patterns which you're recognizing—I haven't deliberately planned it that way but they obviously recur—simply reflect my feeling about the necessity for renewal and for new beginnings. And again for escape from the prison of the past. The past equals for me the inherited mythologies with all the lies that go along with them.... And the need that each person has, to whatever degree he or she can, to step free from those chains and create himself or herself anew.[1]

The idea of the past as a prison carries through into Hodgins' perception of literary form as well: "I'm trying to invent my own structures that are applicable to the way I want the story to be read rather than just sort of plugging into an inherited view". As a post-colonialist, Hodgins deliberately subverts the inherited mythologies of literature through his own manipulations of literary form.

At the same time, Hodgins challenges the disbelief or nihilism of the modern novel in which, as a character reflects in *The Resurrection of Joseph Bourne*, "believers were always made to look like fools, with empty hands" (139). W.J. Keith writes of that novel, "Although 'the sense of an ending' broods over it in characteristic late twentieth-century fashion, the sense of a beginning is, refreshingly, more conspicuous" (105). Keith adds that "this positive stance contributes to a sense of rich completeness" (106). The positive quality of Hodgins' work is a deeply felt and consciously implemented stance, which is clearly seen in the structural and thematic tensions—and the ultimate balance—between duality and unity, fragmentation and order, despair and faith, the Old World and the New.

The circularity of Hodgins' narrative structures becomes a formal expression of this striving for unity. The dual plot lines of his first novel,

The Invention of the World, are resolved by full circle journeys; the myth of Keneally is returned to the place where it began and Maggie Kyle finds her new life after returning to her birthplace, then enacts her new vision on the site of Keneally's old colony. In Hodgins' second novel, *The Resurrection of Joseph Bourne*, the first cataclysm facilitates Bourne's death and resurrection; the second both destroys the community and reaffirms its indestructibility. In his third novel, *The Honorary Patron*, Hodgins subverts the downhill-slide structure of modern tragedy—his isolated twentieth-century rational man does find redemption. Here the motifs of drama and visual art evoke the contrary forces of fragmentation and unity, while in *Innocent Cities*, his fourth novel, language and architecture serve this purpose. *Innocent Cities* deploys various structural elements of the Victorian novel; however, the content, the action, and the characters constantly chafe against and question the very structure, the very literary conventions, in which they find themselves.

Hodgins' treatment of his characters also reflects and embodies his own position as a novelist. In his novels, characters search for the ageless truth hidden within the persistent lie of the old myth, and create a new myth for themselves out of that grain of truth. For the central characters in each of his novels, a confrontation with the past—with the old myth, the prison of the past, the inherited mythologies—brings new life and growth, a resurrection of sorts. In short, the quests of his characters parallel his own quest to make the novel anew.

II

Jeffrey Crane's story, in *The Honorary Patron*, did not require a dual plot structure connecting past and present as did *The Invention of the World*, because, according to the author, the cause-effect chain of *The Honorary Patron* was quite chronological, whereas causes and effects in the first novel were more complex psychologically, mythologically, and geographically. Neither is there, in *The Honorary Patron*, the gossipy narrative voice mimicking the responses of a dozen characters found in *The Resurrection of Joseph Bourne*. Though the community itself plays an important role, the focus is on the transformation of Jeffrey Crane himself, and the novel is seen through his consciousness alone. As Alberto Manguel has observed, while the story is told in the third person, it is "a third person that barely disguises the voice of Crane"—and, while the author's voice is evident, "we, the readers, know that it is Crane's version we are hearing" (14).

Hodgins has identified two imperatives which influenced the form of *The Honorary Patron*. First, he wanted to use as a structural model Thomas Mann's novella "Death in Venice", which takes the form of a steady downhill slide from the lofty heights of a life of the mind into sensual obsession and debasement. Secondly, he consciously strove to achieve a higher level of sophistication in his writing style. The first imperative is seen in his structuring of the novel while the second is apparent in his deployment of motifs. Both elements imply the tension between opposites seen elsewhere in Hodgins' work.

Though "Death in Venice" provided the original framework for *The Honorary Patron*, Hodgins found his early drafts unsatisfying. To this former high school teacher of English and mathematics, the geometrical shape of the work seemed wrong, possibly because the tragic mode is one which conflicts with Hodgins' positive view of life: "If I'm using the pattern of the tragedy, I'm always discontented with the inevitability of it", he says. Thus, Hodgins found it necessary to adapt a traditional structure, in this case the tragic pattern, to suit his own aesthetic and personal vision: " I'm subverting it somehow and having always to find new ways of organizing the material to suit the way I see the world instead of the way literature has tried to teach me to see the world".

In this respect, the connection drawn by Ronald Hatch between this novel and Graham Greene's *The Honorary Consul* is a useful one; both examine obsessive love and the vacuity of "honorary" status in life (39). But, more importantly, both subvert the tragic pattern of, say, Mann's "Death in Venice" or Lowry's *Under the Volcano*. Both undercut the notion that those who attempt to stand outside of life are vulnerable to obsessions which lead inexorably to doom. In the ironic reversal which characterizes Greene's novel, the condemned man is rescued while his rescuer is killed. In Hodgins' hands, it is the husband who dies and the (would-be) lover who survives. Interestingly, in both Greene's novel and Hodgins', the honorary personage is the survivor, whereas in Lowry's treatment of the theme, the inevitable death sentence of honorary status is carried out with chilling finality. Thus, Hodgins takes the inevitable downward diagonal line of the tragic pattern and *bends* it—through the use of his familiar device of bookends, described by Eleanor Wachtel as "a framework that contains the centrifugal forces" (9), and through narrative structures and motifs which imply circularity. The "circular and doubling structures" (57) noted by Linda Hutcheon in *The Invention of the World* are very much in evidence here.

Hodgins has described the structure of *The Honorary Patron* as "quite conventional. At least it begins in a European conventional style that gradually breaks down as the protagonist becomes more and more involved in Vancouver Island life, that is, in the chaos and disorder of life itself" (Delbaere 88-89). In *The Honorary Patron*, the linear, realistic structure breaks down when the action shifts to the New World, or revisits the past. The first such disruption coincides with Crane's arrival on the Island. The first section of the second part of the novel describes the opening ceremonies of the festival; the second flashes back to "The sky over Vienna" (40/47) three days earlier; the third details Crane's journey itself; and the fourth returns to the opening ceremonies, thus creating a bookends structure within a single part, a circle within the larger circle enclosed by the scenes in the restaurant overlooking the Lindenhof.

Another structural breakdown occurs in the opening section of the third part of the novel, which is given in the form of a letter to Franz. Hodgins confesses that, at one point, he attempted to impose the epistolary form upon the narration of Crane's entire relationship with Annamarie, but found that it did not work. However, Crane carries on an imagined conversation with his friend throughout, as in "A good wallow was what it had become, Franz" (265/327). Hodgins kept that early letter as a signpost of what he calls "that quirky disorientation of the narrative position" which occurs at the end of the novel, that is, the metafictional aspect which causes the reader, as Hodgins observes, to ask "whether everything did not take place in the professor's head" (Delbaere 89). In the letter to Franz, Crane expresses his uneasiness about the "absence of order" (90/109) in the town and he resolves "to keep from falling apart" (91/112). In short, these breakdowns in conventional form are structural expressions of the protagonist's own confusion and disorientation.

Hodgins' two earlier novels, *The Invention of the World* and *The Resurrection of Joseph Bourne*, attempt to reconcile the past and the present, the human and the divine, the individual and the community. *The Honorary Patron* attempts a similar reconciliation. Crane denies his own past and yet believes in the controlling power of history; he does not acknowledge his own higher aspirations because he is unable to conceive of that kind of hope. As in *The Invention of the World*, Hodgins' use of the circle here has three levels of meaning, each building on the other. First, the circle is seen as a trap, in the "*'Gemütlichkeit'*" (51/61), the self-satisfied stagnation of Crane's retirement. Secondly, the circle is a wheel, as represented in the motion of Crane's overseas journey and in his travels up and down the Island highway with the Shakespearean Hash troupe. Finally, a sense of reconciliation or wholeness is provided by the circular elements of bookends and the development of characterization.

Past and present are connected in Crane's disastrous relationships with two married women. Both relationships ultimately result in the death by suicide of the wronged husband, though Crane's implication in Bud Blackstone's death is more tenuous than in that of Edward Argent. The suggestion is that as long as Crane refuses to acknowledge the past, he is condemned to repeat his mistakes. The cycle of life itself is part of the novel's circularity, in that the plot centres on an aged man who returns to the town of his birth and boyhood. As in *The Invention of the World*, where Maggie returns to Hed, and Keneally (in ash form) returns to the stone circle, here Crane must go back to his birthplace in order to achieve self-renewal. With the bookends structure, Hodgins suggests that it is necessary to go back before one can move forward. In the first part of the novel, Crane is unwillingly reclaimed by the past in the person of Elizabeth Argent. In the last, he acknowledges his past, personified by Blackie, and perceives a more positive future, in which both Elizabeth and Anna-marie may play a role. By confronting his past, the central character is symbolically raised from the dead, is made new.

As noted, Hodgins' second imperative in writing this novel was to strive for a higher level of sophistication than was evident in his earlier works, which, he says, "I sometimes think of as hacked out with chain saws". An indication of this increased sophistication is the way in which he extends the structural metaphors of lines and circles into the central motifs of the novel: drama and art. Hodgins creates a structure in which Crane redeems his life by re-examining those two areas to which he had aspired in his youth. He will confront the past not only in geographical and human terms, but also in the symbolic forms of drama and art.

In his two previous novels, Hodgins employed structural linearity and juxtaposition to suggest the deconstruction of the old myths which facilitates the rise of the new. He used structural circularity to express the necessary *relationship* between the past and the present (the idea that the past can never be totally destroyed) and also the ideal of wholeness and unity. While these elements are certainly present in

The Honorary Patron, the complexity of this work adds another dimension. The deconstructive impulse—that related to shattering the old myths—is seen in the motif of drama. The unifying impulse—that related to the concept of grace, harmony, or wholeness—is worked out through the motif of visual art.

The process by which Crane renews himself is signposted as a drama from the very beginning. The first part of the novel moves at a stately pace, painstakingly setting the scene and establishing character. The many references to the "staginess" of the scene make it clear that this is Act I. The implication is that Crane is being unwillingly drawn back into the drama of his own life. Drama is part of the liberating force which will move him from the sidelines of life back onto centre stage.

The Old World/New World duality provides the context for Crane's personal drama. Not only has he stepped outside of life in a geographical sense by choosing to live in Switzerland, a politically neutral land-locked island which has "stepped outside" (41/48) of history and is as fastidiously clean and self-consciously picturesque as a movie set; he has also stepped outside of his own life by retiring his dreams, one by one. Crane's personal history is a litany of discarded aspirations, failed relationships, and compromises. His rejection of New World vitality in favour of Old World order has made him a "'*corpse*'" (246/304).

Crane acts out the process of redemption, his revision of the old myth, by stepping out of his prescribed roles as honorary patron and esteemed professor. The relationship with Anna-marie unfolds against the backdrops of Crane's personal past and the history of the Island itself. The first cracks in the foundation of his fantasy begin to appear when they confront Ingrid Eccleston, who says, "'If you've come here hoping to find the past still alive, forget it. It isn't'" (204/251). But for Crane, the past *is* alive, in Anna-marie, revealed to be the granddaughter of his rival, Edward Argent. In a way, his obsession with the young actress is an embrace of the past, in the sense of that blood relationship. But it is also a rejection of the past, in terms of Anna-marie's youth but also in terms of the way his obsession with her allows Crane to avoid confronting his real past, his unresolved relationship with Elizabeth. Fittingly, it is beside the Troilus and Cressida fireplace at the castle that Crane's romantic scenario falters. The love affair is doomed, for Anna-marie is false as Cressid.

Drama provides a process through which Crane deconstructs his Old World self and achieves self-renewal. In *The Honorary Patron*, the line between the Old World and the New World illuminates the relationship between the old myth and the new myth, between the past and the present. Crane's obsession with Anna-marie causes him to play the fool; the absurd man prowling the streets of Vancouver Island towns in pursuit of the girl is far more alive than the "'sententious bore'" (25/30) of Zürich. The vitality of the New World is the liberating force which drags Crane out of his cocoon to declaim Shakespeare in a parking lot, to roll up his trousers and effect the sea-rescue of Madame, to participate in a nude protest march, and to fall heedlessly, foolishly, in love. For Hodgins, the Island *is* the edge, the extremity, of the New World; it is a place where magical transformations can occur, where the self can be made new. Hodgins remarks to Stephen Godfrey that "Vancouver Island seems to attract the kind of people who want to believe there is more than one kind of reality" (C1).

This vitality has its negative aspects as well. Hodgins has a great deal of fun with the excesses of North American culture in this novel: the shopping malls, the cultural pretensions of the literati—"'An experiment with spinach and blue cheese!'" (93/114)—and Blackie's lakeside spread with its five-acre lawn studded with plastic lions, ceramic gnomes, and Bambis. A more serious negative aspect is raised when a terrorist bomb in an Old World airport is discovered to be the product of the New World entrepreneurial spirit.

The mythmaking process in a post-colonial culture is an important issue in *The Honorary Patron*. At a dinner party given by one of the benefactors of the Festival of the Arts, the mention of a historical drama based on a local figure sets off an argument, in which Crane questions the way history has been rewritten for the stage. He remembers George Dunbar as a villain, an exploiter, who had different rates of pay for "'men'", Chinese, and Indians: "'poor, worse, and almost slavery'" (105/130). Elizabeth counters that "'He was *interesting*, dammit! . . . He was good *drama*! What more could anyone want?'" (106/131) What Crane wants, apparently, is the truth, not "'History . . . replaced by fiction'" (106/131). "'History was never anything else,'" Elizabeth replies; "'You ought to know that. People choose the history they want. More to the point, they choose the history they need'" (106/131).

Crane believes in the past; for him, mere acknowledgement is not good enough. Elizabeth, on the other hand, understands the need to find a seed of truth in the inherited past, and to acknowledge it in order to enrich the present: "'We've nearly forgotten how to tell what to believe.

What about those old stories filled with pioneer giants—the wonderful romances and dreams and magical changes?'" (107/132) To her, the need to create a new mythology for the New World overrides any compulsion for historical accuracy. Like the Ojibwa elder in Robert Bringhurst's article who is asked by an anthropologist whether *all* stones are alive and answers, "No. But some of them are" (C1), Elizabeth understands that myths do not necessarily have to be true in order to be useful or meaningful.

In both personal and regional terms, the motif of drama performs the same function as the structurally linear elements of the novel: it allows expression of the deconstructive impulse, the idea that the myths of the inherited past need to be shattered in order to create a liberating new mythology. The motif of visual art, on the other hand, provides the unifying or circular element. The literary adaptation of a visual art form is one of the hallmarks of Jack Hodgins' fiction. In *The Honorary Patron*, the author uses expressionism as emblem in his exploration of the circular relationship between the past and the present and of the human aspiration to perfection or unity. Crane struggles to reconcile the bleak world-view of Vasily Kandinsky's abstractions with the passionate expressionism of Egon Schiele.

The motif is introduced in the first part of the novel, when the two main characters visit the Kunsthaus. For Crane, Kandinsky's fragmented, chaotic works comprise "some of the most astonishing work done in this century"; for Elizabeth, the exhibit is merely "'clever'" (23/27). Crane points out that the artist speaks for his time, setting out "to discover what must replace the landscapes and human figures and scenes of family life that earlier painters had used as their subjects without even suspecting they had no real substance at all" (24/29). In the second half of the section describing the reunion in Vienna, Franz and Crane visit another museum, and it is here that Crane betrays a trace of emotional life. He is deeply moved by Egon Schiele's *Die Familie*, partly because of the paradox that "the tension that existed within the work . . . achieved a sense of the collective life that was being celebrated" (46/55). This painting, which is reproduced on the dust jacket of the McClelland & Stewart first edition, is a haunting work which conveys both the loving circle of man, woman, and child and the tension of their separateness.

The Schiele/Kandinsky duality is a revealing one. While Kandinsky's work appeals to Crane on an intellectual level, Schiele's art moves him on the same unexamined plane which leads him to visit churches "for the pleasure of looking into the tranquil faces" (25/30) of the worshippers. He is only vaguely aware that he is pursuing some ultimate reality, some created world, which contradicts the death sentence pronounced by Einstein and Kandinsky.

The motif of abstraction versus expressionism comes full circle in the final part of the novel. While Kandinsky's stark canvases reflect the chaotic universe suggested by Einstein, Egon Schiele's tragic *Die Familie* speaks of human longing for wholeness as an unrealized, perhaps unrealizable, dream. Yet, paradoxically, the artist creates something approaching "the enduring, the true, the real" (24/29) out of the void—through his art. This mixture of starkness and hope comes together in the work of the New World artist Joe Hobson, with whom Crane plays a cat-and-mouse game of rejection and approach. In the climactic scene at Crane's crumbling childhood home (in which the black hole of the past threatens to swallow the assembled cast), a young man parachutes into the scene and explicates Hobson's art.

Back at the beginning of the novel, when Elizabeth is trying to convince Crane to act as Honorary Patron to his hometown Festival of the Arts, she urges him to confront his past by reminding him of the adventurer that he once was: "'You were a paratrooper once, you were *trained* to drop in on other people's countries, it shouldn't be this unthinkable deed you seem to want it to be'" (28/33). However, he reminds her that his training had to do with dropping behind *enemy* lines; clearly, he views the past as an enemy. For Crane, paratroop training marked the death of his dreams, when he was injured in a bad landing. When *"Der Engel vom Himmel"* (313/388) drops into the action, Hodgins draws several narrative and thematic threads together—in an open-ended way of course. In a Jack Hodgins novel, nothing can be neatly resolved, as the young man's T-shirt, which reads "STOP MAKING SENSE" (306/380), insists.

The angel reveals several things about Joe Hobson, the young artist whom Crane has snubbed. The angel says that Hobson was accustomed to exploring the mines (as Crane had done as a child), mines which Crane now describes as "what the world had forgotten or chosen to ignore" (317/392). Furthermore, Hobson painted what he saw there, tunnels "'Dark, and dirty—falling beams and dripping underground creeks'" (317/392), but he always added something unexpected. In fact, in one picture which the angel describes, Hobson seems to have imported Schiele's family to the Nanaimo coal mines: "'A naked family. Huddled together in the dark like they're waiting for someone to let them out'" (317/392).

In addition, Hobson was fascinated, like Kandinsky, with Einstein. Several of his paintings "'have the old guy's face just sort of peeking out, like he's trapped in the tunnel walls. You could miss it if you didn't look real hard'" (317/392-93). The angel goes on to explain that Hobson did this because it "'Seems he heard somewhere that when Einstein died he was working on something new—something that would sort of balance out what he scared everybody with before'" (317/393). Crane decides that "the resisting force he'd glimpsed, and hoped to find proof of . . . , depended upon the sort of courage and imagination this young artist seemed to have. Also, perhaps, this boy crouched in the back of the jeep. A supreme intelligence, you might dare to say, manifesting itself in the enterprises of the human soul, to keep things from flying apart" (317/393). The force which keeps things from flying apart is the impulse to unity.

On first reading, it seems an odd authorial choice to present such a key revelation at a double remove: Crane recounts the story to Franz, as it was told to him by the parachutist. One reason why Hodgins chose this indirect revelation instead of allowing his protagonist to see these paintings himself is that until Crane confronts his own past—Elizabeth, Blackie (and by implication, Edward Argent), as well as Crane's sister, Tess—he is not ready to receive the wisdom these works represent. When first invited to view the young man's art, Crane resisted, for "Of course he had retired from all that" (71/86). This method of indirection also allows the paratrooper to represent the "courage and imagination" (317/393) which Crane lost or misplaced in his own youth; thus, the paratrooper is a suitable bearer of the message. A third reason is that Hodgins is making a point, familiar from his other work, about the randomness of grace: all of Crane's seeking after absolute truth is vain, but wisdom can and does drop unexpectedly from the sky—and with typical Hodgins irreverence, it is neither particularly bright nor articulate, and is wearing a Talking Heads T-shirt. The "parachute angel" (305/379) adjusts the course of Crane's life by landing in the wrong place, much as Crane had set the course of his own life more than forty years earlier.

The circles, the bookends, the clashes and connections of Old World and New, all lead Jeffrey Crane (and thereby the reader) to an epiphany. And it is not a world-weary pronouncement of the impossibility of progress. For Hodgins, the full circle structure implies a sense of completeness, of harmony. At the same time, as Hodgins states, "It also leaves the future open" (Delbaere 89), as might be expected from his earlier novels. Hodgins concludes *The Honorary Patron* with an ironic comment on his own literary structures. When Franz urges the novel's protagonist to go on with his story, Crane replies, "'What you're *saying* is: not even a life devoted to History has destroyed your persistent hope for the occasional happy ending'" (322/399). This happy ending the honorary patron then provides. Here, the reader can sense a self-conscious poke at the author's admitted compulsion to discover "what it would take to bring that guy back to life", to subvert the inevitability of the tragic pattern and tell a tale of redemption, to bend the downward slanting line around into a circle. The structural and thematic tensions in his fiction suggest that Jack Hodgins is grappling with the postmodern dilemma: if we shatter the myths, refute the lie of history, and dispense with the old-fashioned concept of meaning, what is left? Clearly, Jack Hodgins believes that, even in the postmodern age, some sense of hope for the future must remain.

III

Innocent Cities, Hodgins' fourth novel, finds the author once again grappling with received notions of history, literary form, and language; but as usual a positive philosophical stance is very much in evidence. In this context, Stephen Slemon's differentiation between postmodernism and post-colonialism is useful. For Slemon, in "Modernism's Last Post", one of the ways in which the post-colonial is distinguished from the postmodern is in its position on the referentiality of language. Whereas postmodern writing *"necessarily* admits a provisionality to its truth-claims" (2), post-colonial writing maintains "a mimetic or referential purchase to textuality", one which allows for "the positive production of oppositional truth-claims" (5). The positive production of oppositional truth-claims underlies both the structures and the content of Hodgins' fiction and this quality, among others, allies him not with postmodernism, but with post-colonialism. His fourth novel, *Innocent Cities*, readily invites a post-colonial reading strategy.

Innocent Cities, as Hodgins explained to Peter Wilson, had its genesis in an archival document uncovered by Victoria historian Terry Reksten, from whom Hodgins was taking a course (D17). In this letter, sent from Victoria in the 1880s, a married woman asks her unmarried sister to leave Australia and come to Canada to take over certain wifely duties; in short, she invites her younger sister to sleep with her husband. Further research by Hodgins revealed that this woman had originally come to Victoria to reclaim her errant husband, and, in so doing, broke up the husband's new family—a wife and several adopted children. Hodgins was fascinated by this material, as he told Peter Wilson, "because it's so un-Victorian, so intriguingly juicy. You've got adultery and bigamy and deceit and mysterious deaths and fascinating characters" (D17). However, just as he used the historical Aquarian Foundation only as a starting point for his fictional Revelations Colony of Truth in *The Invention of the World*, in this case Hodgins took the original story only as a suggestion: "I'm a fiction writer, not a historian.... I began from scratch and invented brand new characters whose lives were roughly parallel" (D17).

The complex narrative which grows from the seed of this archival document can be summarized as follows. Kate McConnell Jordan arrives in Victoria to reclaim her husband, James Horncastle, proprietor of The Great Blue Heron Hotel. In so doing, she displaces Horncastle's new wife, the beneficent and earthy Norah, as well as her brood of adopted children. However, Kate's vengeance, her search for justice, brings her nothing but misery; she ends up paranoid, opium-addicted, and a virtual prisoner in her prized hotel. The novel's protagonist, Logan Sumner, is in love with Norah's eldest adopted child, Adelina. As a result of Kate's machinations, Sumner's romance with Adelina is destroyed—with the result that he is left vulnerable to the charms of Annie McConnell, Kate's younger sister, who was originally summoned from Australia to fulfil the concubine's role. However, Annie has an independent spirit and ultimately makes her own choices.

The structure of *Innocent Cities* closely parallels that of *The Invention of the World*, in that there are two narrative lines, one ascending, one descending, which cross at various points. The fortunes of the "good" characters, the protagonists—Maggie Kyle in *The Invention of the World* and Logan Sumner in *Innocent Cities*, both native Vancouver Islanders—are ascendant. Both of these characters begin in considerable confusion and difficulty, move through a process of debunking and revising old ways of thinking, then rise to a positive resolution in the end—in terms of romance as well as achieving a sense of identity, of belonging, within their own culture, place, and time. The "evil" characters, the antagonists—Keneally in *The Invention of the World* and Kate Jordan in *Innocent Cities*, both from the Old World, he Irish, she English—

experience increasing alienation, desperation, and a steep descent, both ending in defeat and (self-)destruction.

Narrative voice in *Innocent Cities* is fluid. One of the attractions for Hodgins of South American magic realism, as he explains in the interview by Geoff Hancock, is that

> The whole world gets in on those Latin American novels just as the whole world got in on a William Faulkner novel. This is such a contrast to the many novels that tend to be about one person's problems that ultimately weren't of much importance or interest to anybody but himself. (56)

An omniscient narrator opens and closes the text of *Innocent Cities*, and occasionally comments on the developing action. In the narrative itself, third person limited point of view is the norm, but point of view shifts between the two central characters. For example, the focus is on Sumner in part one, Kate in part two, then back to Sumner (to hear Horncastle's account of his bigamous affairs) in parts three and four. Narration may also begin in first person, with dialogue, but then switch to third person limited, as in Kate's account of her life in Australia and Horncastle's story of his days in San Francisco. The use of multiple points of view and omniscience is one way in which Hodgins rebels against the prevailing literary ideology of the British/North American modern novel, in which a first person or third person limited point of view is the norm.

In *Innocent Cities*, however, Hodgins' rebellion goes beyond voice. Whereas he addressed the problem of historical truth in *The Invention of the World*, in this novel his concern is more with the problem of language and form. One might ask why a 1990 novel is so concerned with Victorian literary form and Imperialist ideology. In *The Empire Writes Back*, Bill Ashcroft, Gareth Griffiths, and Helen Tiffin acknowledge the importance of the question "why the empire needs to write back to a centre once the imperial structure has been dismantled in political terms" (6-7). The answer is that "the weight of antiquity continues to dominate cultural production in much of the post-colonial world" (7). The most useful reading of *Innocent Cities* in my view, as it is in Ajay Heble's, is one informed by post-colonial approaches and ideas.

Just as Logan Sumner is bedevilled in his efforts to construct European palaces in this colonial enclave, so the storyteller, the West Coast writer, is bedevilled in his attempt to construct a Victorian melodrama out of a colonial story, a story in which characters' identities are fluid and appearances are as deceptive as the façades of buildings. Many of the characters in *Innocent Cities* live under assumed names; again and again, reference is made to previous discarded identities. Norah Horncastle is revealed as the former Mrs. Thompkins (124). Sheilagh Monahan of Ballarat is now Lizzie Sheepshank in Victoria and prefers not to be reminded of "her period of hard labour as a result of that 'lost-brooch misunderstanding' on the part of her employer" (231) back in Australia. Then there is Mrs. Olfried Thornycroft, "who had thought herself to be Mrs. Olfried Harrow until only recently, when her husband was discovered to be hiding his real identity as heir to the famous Salisbury Thornycroft family of embezzlers" (299).

Masquerades abound also; both buildings and people masquerade as something more refined and more European than they are. The Doric façade of The Great Blue Heron, for example, encloses and conceals the original heart of the hotel, the simple log structure where James Horncastle began serving drinks to thirsty miners decades before. The local bag lady, Mary One-Eye, masquerades as Queen Victoria. And following a royal visit, two Native women and Zachary Jack, Logan Sumner's Native assistant, perform a hilarious pantomime of British propriety. Ladies' fashions are described as masquerades also—and dismantling those particular false fronts becomes the life's work of Kate's alter ego, the "good" sister, Annie. In her delivery of "A Few Words on the Modern Woman" (302), Annie asks why Native women don't enslave themselves to "'the tortures and indignities'" (308) of Victorian fashion, and hypothesizes that the Native woman "'... has better sense. Perhaps she understands instinctively that today's woman, who is educated, enterprising, and ambitious, is beginning to insist that she is more than a doll to be weighed down with impossible draperies for admiration, and she is more than a mother and wife to be harnessed in clothing for work ...'" (309).

While architectural and social façades raise questions about the authenticity of colonial life, the most delightful and inventive metaphor for the author's and the protagonist's dilemma is "MR. SUMNER'S TROUBLESOME GRAVESTONE" ([1]). When Mr. Sumner's wife died, he erected a simple tombstone for her, inscribed with the words "LOVED FOREVER" (4). His own stone, placed next to hers, originally read "HUSBAND OF JULIA, INCONSOLABLE" (4). However, six months later, the still-grieving man ordered the stone carver to add the words "CURSING GOD, AND UNABLE TO FIND ANY MEANING IN LIFE" (4).

When Sumner's heart lightened some months later, another inscription was needed: "BUT PREPARED, ALWAYS, TO GIVE THANKS FOR NEW HOPE" (5). A year later, however, the "ALWAYS" was changed to "OFTEN", because "hope, like building-booms, can come and go" (5).

The tale of a tombstone which narrates the ups and downs of the hero's heart and fortunes runs through *Innocent Cities*; it is a suggestive image for this character and this novel. Words which are carved in stone are thought to be fixed, permanent, immutable as death—like the constraints of imperialist language and naming. Yet Sumner's stone is in a constant state of flux: as Kate remarks, it becomes "a monstrous cairn offering a running commentary on the shifting state of his soul!" (220) When Sumner's love affair with Adelina ends, he descends into near-madness, and uses his tombstone to create a fictional self:

> According to the stone, he has designed and built a magnificent variety of splendid buildings around town, including a glorious cathedral with a gleaming spire of white marble, with Byzantine archways and baroque domes, and with fifty-seven stained-glass windows brought from Italy, high on a certain hill overlooking the city, on a location which anyone can recognize as the site of Peterson's pig farm! (220)

When the city fathers ask him to explain this fantasy, Sumner replies that he is "merely recording his life as it would have been if these had only been more prosperous times" (220). But the subtext here is that, disappointed in romance, Sumner clings to and fantasizes Old World structures, trying in imagination if not in fact to impose them on his colonial world, just as he tried and failed to build a Victorian fantasy of romance and happy endings with Adelina.

The authors of *The Empire Writes Back* note that two of the hallmarks of post-colonial literature are the preoccupation with language and with place and displacement. According to post-colonial theory, "place, displacement, and a pervasive concern with the myths of identity and authenticity are a feature common to all post-colonial literatures in english" (Ashcroft et al. 9). Hodgins' pervasive concern with place and displacement is particularly well developed in the character of Logan Sumner, whereas the issue of language as "the medium through which a hierarchical structure of power is perpetuated, and the medium through which conceptions of 'truth', 'order', and 'reality' become established" (Ashcroft et al. 7) is explored through the character of Kate Jordan.

After being jilted by Adelina, Sumner experiences a sense of displacement, what Ashcroft, Griffiths, and Tiffin might describe as a "crisis of identity", along with a wish to pursue "the development or recovery of an effective identifying relationship between self and place" (9). When Sumner first meets Annie McConnell, he is preparing to leave Victoria for a tour of Europe because he feels "'unnecessary'" (279). Sumner says he has

> ". . . listened to thousands of voices convincing me that Home is somewhere else. They live here, all these people, but they all seem to have brought along a more beautiful, more cultured, more *interesting* home with them, which they never tire of talking about. Home is Surrey. Or Boston. Or Munich. It is as though the place of *my* birth were merely an empty stage, or a blank magic-lantern screen for them to project their own remembered homes upon. I've been invaded from too many directions to feel there is anything left for me." (279)

The connections between post-colonial architecture and language pervade this text, this house of words.[2] Just as Sumner's architecture is constricted by "'remembered homes'" (279), Hodgins' art is constricted by, or at least defined in relation to, a Eurocentric literary tradition.

Sumner eventually does get to Europe—for his honeymoon with Annie. At the end of the novel, he and Annie are happily married and are raising their own two daughters as well as Kate's neglected children. Their home, as Lady Riven-Blythe observes, is not constructed according to European standards:

> *He has built the most peculiar house, not at all in the fashions favoured by other successful businessmen, reminiscent of homes in Oxford or Edinburgh or San Francisco or Rome. This has more in common with the houses built by the Indians in their villages, its great roof kept up by a structure of posts and beams carved from giant trees.* (384)

Furthermore, according to Lady Riven-Blythe, "*The marriage is as unconventional as the house, by local standards*"—in that Annie continues to work for women's rights, "*to cross the continent speaking in theatres on the subject of female shackles*" (386) such as fashion, while Sumner remains at home with the children. Ultimately, once Sumner finds himself engaged in the rush and fulfilment of his new family life, the tombstone is destroyed, Sumner having found the stone "'unnecessary'" (383). Once again, Hodgins suggests that the old ideals and values, both literary and social, are necessarily and usefully questioned and re-visioned in the post-colonial world.

One of the many post-colonial elements in the novel is the powerful image of construction, of home, of the house. The authors of *The Empire Writes Back* assert that "the construction or demolition of houses or buildings in post-colonial locations is a recurring and evocative figure for the problematic of post-colonial identity" (28). In the case of *Innocent Cities*, as Hodgins explained to Peter Wilson, the architectural metaphor which structures the novel originated in the author's research, when he discovered that the architecture of Victoria has often consisted of putting false fronts over false fronts (D17). This concept is extremely suggestive, for it applies not only to architecture, but also to Victorian propriety and morality, gender ideology, and literary form itself. *Innocent Cities* is "Victorian" in several ways. Its temporal setting is the late Victorian period and its geographical settings include Victoria, British Columbia, Canada and Ballarat, Victoria, Australia. The novel is also outwardly "Victorian" in form: it retains such qualities as shifting points of view, the pitting of good versus evil, elaborate headings, epistolary narrative, retrospective narrative, the confiding and occasionally intrusive narrator. Yet it bristles with challenges to and subversions of its European antecedents. In *Innocent Cities*, Hodgins confronts the technical, moral, and cultural dilemma of building a fictional structure out of New World subject matter and Old World literary forms and language.

The relationship between architecture and language resonates throughout *Innocent Cities*, as Kathy Mezei observes (C20), but architecture, façades, and instruments of construction also define the novel's protagonist. Sumner dreams "of erecting magnificent structures which would be admired and photographed and later imitated by strangers who had come from all parts of the globe to see them" (18). The paradigms for Sumner's dream structures are Old World style opera houses, cathedrals, and grand hotels. Ironically, however, the method by which Sumner actually earns his living in the New World of his birth is by producing faux-Old World façades:

> Eventually, Sumner Construction became known for an expertise in a particular *spécialité*—giving to the buildings they renovated

> an appearance of having been just newly erected, by applying new and inexpensive façades over the old. Houses, shops, warehouses, even factories . . . could put on the style of any foreign architecture desired, in the manner of ladies' fashions, depending upon what books had been recently read, what photographs admired, what foreign travel just completed. . . . In the privacy of the workshop he and his carpenters spoke of "putting on m'lady's newest face". (18-19)

Furthermore, Sumner has the unusual personal tic of constantly measuring things—his hand, a lady's foot, the doorway in which he stands—as if he were constantly trying to get his bearings in the world.

It is not a large step to associate Sumner's dreams and dilemmas with those of the post-colonial novelist. For example, a work of fiction can certainly be seen as a construction, a house of words. Certain Eurocentric forms and designs are demanded of literary fiction, yet these forms, designs, and conventions often do not translate well to colonial experience. This is where façades come in, in two senses. To impose Old World structures on New World materials is to create a false front, a false story. On the other hand, to get away with subverting European forms and structures is a way of liberating the tale (and its teller). As Salman Rushdie said, ". . . the Empire writes back to the Centre . . . " (qtd. in Ashcroft et al. epigraph). Hodgins' subversions of Victorian literary conventions can be read, to borrow the words of Ashcroft, Griffiths, and Tiffin, as a "project of asserting difference from the imperial centre" (5).

In the introduction to his anthology *The West Coast Experience*, Hodgins likens the writers collected in that book to "Adams gone mad in Eden, naming everything in sight" (1). Interestingly, Hodgins develops this line and gives it to Kate McConnell Jordan Horncastle in *Innocent Cities*. In the course of her narrative to Logan Sumner, Kate describes her need to escape the jungle atmosphere of Australia:

> "Listen! It is the fault of that old lunatic Adam who started it all, I think, and all his lunatic offspring males who became explorers and geographers and dictionary-makers—all of them wanting, I'm sure of it, to nail everything down into some sort of rigid identity in order to perpetrate some awful fiction upon us. That whole ancient worn-down flattened-out continent wished to strangle the breath out of me with the arms of its endless forest of *names*!" (77)

The significance of naming, the linguistic attempt to fix meaning, is far-reaching in the novel. As Ajay Heble remarks, in *Innocent Cities* "the interaction between self and place is played out through an exploration of linguistic dislocation" (678). The power of patriarchal language to control meaning threatens Kate, fixes her in a gender role, leaves her disenfranchised, disempowered.

The relationship between feminist and post-colonial writing is worth noting here. Women "share with colonized races and peoples an intimate experience of the politics of oppression and repression, and like them they have been forced to articulate their experiences in the language of their oppressors" (Ashcroft et al. 174-75). Kate leaves the Antipodes to reclaim her errant husband, to escape her hated older sister, but also because of a wish "'to flee from a crowded, strangling jungle of words, of beautiful *names*, to live in a world of ordinary *things* again, a world of regulations and laws that created human order'" (85). The colonizing project of naming causes Kate to long for the securities of the old, familiar repressions. She hopes to find in Victoria, British Columbia, Canada an orderly, more English world than that of Ballarat, Victoria, Australia. However, despite her triumph in reclaiming her husband, the constrictions of language still entrap her.

Two key scenes in the novel, one in Australia, one in Canada, mirror each other and establish a complex connection between imperialist language and patriarchal oppression, placing Kate in a state of helpless terror of and rebellion against the roles available to her under patriarchy—sexual object, domestic slave, dutiful mother. In the first, Kate and her children are staying with Kate's much-envied sister, Lilian, who has married well and who lives on a huge estate near Brisbane. During the visit Lilian's husband, Paul, shows a sexual interest in Kate, under the guise of instructing her on the names of plants and wildlife on the estate:

> "Jarrah," he said. "Say it. Jarrah."
> "Karri," he said. He held his mouth a certain way, so that you could almost taste the word with him. You could almost taste him tasting the word. His lips, beneath the heavy grey moustache, were always moist. (73)

One day, in their wanderings, Paul and Kate discover the children playing in a hollow tree. The discovery terrifies Kate; to her, the tree is "a dark, round, soaring tunnel populated by the headless bodies of all their children, her own children and her sister's children, all those children to whom she was expected to devote her life" (74). Her helplessness elicits the overt sexual advances of her brother-in-law, which she resists, but Kate has bad dreams that night:

> She dreamt that she had become lost in the dark, roaring storm of Paul's laughter, a thrashing jungle where tubular vines all leaned into the blackened sky with their snakish arms around her children, carrying them up and away from her into the thrashing turbulence of the upper limbs. (75-76)

Kate escapes Paul's clutches shortly thereafter, but as her new life in Victoria crumbles, she once again encounters sexual threat, naming, and lost children at the site of a hollow tree. At the Agricultural Fair, shortly before James Horncastle's tragic (and silencing) accident, Kate notices that her children are missing. She, Annie, and Lizzie Sheepshank go off searching for them, Lizzie all the while *naming*:

> "Wild hawthorn, Annie. Scrub oak. Snowberries—like pearls on the branches, I always think, now that the leaves are going. Salal. Pine— white pine. Arbutus." (349)

Kate, a rather negligent mother, can't locate the source of her anxiety— but once again she finds herself in a hollow tree, this time the residence of the mysterious and threatening Hawks, a rejected suitor. And once again, the threat to her children is combined with sexual threat, as Hawks crudely tries to lure her into his bed:

> He would try to *talk* her up, as though the sounds and shapes of his words could serve as stairs to put your feet upon. One more man had built a universe out of words. His charred hollow tower was not wrapped in salvaged brand names like the Indian's barn, or inscribed with accounts of a fictitious career like Logan Sumner's tomb, or held upright like the Blue Heron by the sound of barroom tales, but the idea was much the same. (352)

Kate resists, and is oppressed by, these houses of words—but unlike Annie, who attacks them with political activism, or Norah Horncastle, who maintains a serene Christian faith, Kate has only her own selfishness and ambition, and her end is tragic.

Whereas the architectural metaphor defines the novel's protagonist, Logan Sumner, the issue of imperialist, patriarchal language defines the antagonist of the novel, Kate Jordan. As Kate's sanity crumbles, her facility to understand and use language dwindles. For example, she attempts to convince Horncastle to sign over the hotel to her, in order to protect it from his spendthrift ways and proclivity for gambling. When Horncastle refuses, and describes her machinations as "'a betrayal of all your vows'" (336), Kate is bewildered:

> She didn't know what he meant. Though her ears had clearly heard the familiar sounds, her head would not receive them. A cushion of fog forbade it. Had hotels and vows been named with her in mind? She heard them now as though they'd been invented for some category of people that excluded her. They were not her words. She was not sure that she *had* any words. (336)

Following Horncastle's stroke, in which he becomes "the speechless hostage... of his grim keepers in that silent hotel", it seems to Sumner that all of the family has been struck dumb, as though "some blow... had given them all a whack to the skull... leaving them unable to find, or use, or believe in a language that said what they wanted it to say" (374).

Zachary Jack, Logan Sumner's Native assistant, is a useful counterpart to Kate in the matter of language, demonstrating what Stephen Slemon, in "Magic Realism as Post-Colonial Discourse", describes as "a binary opposition within language that has its roots in the process of either transporting a language to a new land or imposing a foreign language on an indigenous population" (12). Zak is constantly in trouble for supposed linguistic crimes. Readers first encounter Zak in the jailhouse, where he has spent the night for uttering yet another "'criminal word'" (22), this time for naming the wife of a local citizen a "klootchman" or "squaw". Zak's problem is that the language he has been given by white culture is inadequate; he says, "'this tongue in my mouth don't belong to me'" (22). Zak is the abandoned child of a Nootka woman and a Scottish carpenter. He has lost his Native tongue since the disappearance of his mother: "'I don't remember my mother's language any more. A dozen words maybe. All the rest were slapped out of my head by that schoolteacher'" (327-28).

Zak's attempts to use English get him in trouble constantly. Toward the end of the novel, he lands in jail once again, this time for swearing at a policeman, and, as Sumner explains, "'He says he's going to stop talking at all, it's too dangerous using a language somebody else has given you'" (346). Like Kate, Zak is colonized by language. Unlike Kate, however, he retains his free spirit. Kate fears and hates the natural world—she shoots at the white cockatoos outside her Ballarat cottage because "'Nobody should be expected to live in a world where birds are the size of pigs that laugh in your face'" (52). Zak, on the other hand, is determined to emulate a bird's liberty by inventing a flying machine, the first passenger in which, incidentally, is a young pig.

The relationship between language and architecture is made manifest in a scene involving Sumner, Annie, Norah, and Zak at the White Birches Roadhouse, where Sumner Construction is applying yet another façade. Zak says, "'You get stripping these false faces away, you start to think that some day you'll find something you could call the real one'" (288-89). When Annie asks how one would recognize the real one, Sumner replies that "'To the designer, the *real* building remains in his head'" (289). As Geoff Hancock has said, one of Hodgins' early ambitions was to be an architect (51), and it is easy to see the analogy implied between the designer of buildings and the designer of literary works.

Annie clarifies this connection later in the scene, when she tells Sumner, "'You wished us to believe that to a designer a building represents something perfect. I understand that much. As a work of art may do'" (292). But Annie remains puzzled by Sumner. She says to Norah, "'He strips the false faces off other people's buildings, claiming that he's getting closer to the "truth". At the same time he erects a tombstone telling elaborate lies. Is there any hope of understanding him?'" (292) Once again, the analogy between Sumner and his post-colonial creator is hard to ignore. Hodgins questions and undermines old truths, old cultural and literary assumptions, yet at the same time uses his tall tales to create a new mythology for the New World. In *Innocent Cities*, as Aritha Van Herk points out, "Hodgins shows us the colonies at war and in love with Victorian imperialism, the colonies becoming themselves, their moments of transition between outpost and city" (C4).

In the interview by Geoff Hancock, Hodgins addresses the question of failed utopias in the colonial utopia that is the locale of his fictions. He ascribes these failures to

> People coming for the wrong reasons. People coming for a dream that is based on values that were doomed anywhere in the world and had

no hope at all of surviving, here or anywhere else. It's a fact that Vancouver Island seems to have attracted romantic idealists from the beginning. They have been defeated, not because their dreams weren't worth going after, but because they brought with them their old values. The materialistic trappings and the selfish pursuits. (64)

In *Innocent Cities,* Jack Hodgins creates a character who embodies the "old values" of "materialistic trappings" and "selfish pursuits" in Kate Jordan; in characters like Logan Sumner and Annie McConnell, however, Hodgins suggests with his characteristic optimism the possibility of the re-visioned and self-defined New World Man and Woman.

The novel closes with a kind of epilogue, told at a chronological and narrative distance, in which Sumner's Native-like architecture and his re-visioned family are described by an observer, the transatlantically torn Lady Riven-Blythe, whereas Kate's imprisonment and silence are described by Sumner. He and the narrator end the tale with a legendary story about how Horncastle's two widows, Kate and the ever-compassionate Norah, engage in a weekly ritual. Every Tuesday, in The Red Geranium, the two women sit across from each other at separate tables and have tea. They do not speak to each other. They have not spoken since Horncastle's death, years earlier. Yet, as the narrator reports, in the words of the proprietor of the café, "'one of them [Norah] is keeping the other one alive, and one of them [Kate] is allowing the other to try it. Don't ask me how! And both of them are trying . . . to build some kind of new language between them, to build something out of silence that isn't death'" (391). Thus, Hodgins concludes *Innocent Cities* with the suggestion that silence *is* death and insists on the necessity of building a language to describe experience, to express faith in human connection and community.

Hodgins' primary achievement in *Innocent Cities,* as in his other novels, is to challenge the restrictive structures of history, literary form, and language, while at the same time reaffirming the human striving for creative self-expression, for belonging, for the building of community. And just as the author's quest mirrors the quests of his characters to articulate and understand their place in the world, so the reader's role parallels the author's in building or creating a structure to describe experience outside the dominant culture.

A Note On The Texts

Page references to *The Honorary Patron* are given for the original hardcover edition as well as for the first paperback edition. Page references for the original hardcover edition and for the paperback edition of *Innocent Cities* are identical.

Notes

[1] Unless otherwise indicated, all remarks by Jack Hodgins quoted here are taken from a personal interview on 27 June 1988.

[2] I'm indebted to Aritha Van Herk for this phrase, which grows out of the title of her review of *Innocent Cities*, "A Crazy House of Fiction".

Works Cited

Ashcroft, Bill, Gareth Griffiths, and Helen Tiffin. *The Empire Writes Back: Theory and Practice in Post-Colonial Literatures.* London: Routledge, 1989.

Bringhurst, Robert. "Myths Create a World of Meaning". *The Globe and Mail* [Toronto] 7 May 1988: C1, C18.

Delbaere, Jeanne. "Jack Hodgins: Interview". *Kunapipi* 9.2 (1987): 84-89.

Godfrey, Stephen. "Hodgins Brings His Island into the Literary Limelight". *The Globe and Mail* [Toronto] 19 Sept. 1987: C1.

Greene, Graham. *The Honorary Consul.* 1973. London, Eng.: Penguin, 1974.

Hancock, Geoff. "Jack Hodgins". *Canadian Writers at Work: Interviews with Geoff Hancock.* Toronto: Oxford UP, 1987. 51-78.

Hatch, Ronald. "The Power of Love". Rev. of *The Honorary Patron*, by Jack Hodgins. *The Canadian Forum* Oct. 1987: 39-40.

Heble, Ajay. "HODGINS, JACK (1938-)". *Encyclopedia of Post-Colonial Literatures in English.* Ed. Eugene Benson and L.W. Conolly. Vol. 1. London: Routledge, 1994. 678-79. 2 vols.

Hodgins, Jack. *The Honorary Patron.* Toronto: McClelland & Stewart, 1987. M&S Paperbacks. Toronto: McClelland & Stewart, 1989.

———. *Innocent Cities.* Toronto: McClelland & Stewart, 1990. M&S Paperbacks. Toronto: McClelland & Stewart, 1991.

———. "Introduction". *The West Coast Experience*. Ed. Jack Hodgins. Toronto: Macmillan of Canada, 1976. 1-2.

———. *The Invention of the World*. Toronto: Macmillan of Canada, 1977.

———. *The Resurrection of Joseph Bourne; or, A Word or Two on Those Port Annie Miracles*. Toronto: Macmillan of Canada, 1979.

Hutcheon, Linda. "The Postmodernist Scribe: The Dynamic Stasis of Contemporary Canadian Writing". *The Canadian Postmodern: A Study of Contemporary English-Canadian Fiction*. Toronto: Oxford UP, 1988. 45-60.

Jeffrey, David L. "A Crust for the Critics". Rev. of *The Resurrection of Joseph Bourne*, by Jack Hodgins. *Canadian Literature* 84 (1980): 74-78.

Keith, W.J. Rev. of *The Resurrection of Joseph Bourne*, by Jack Hodgins. *The Fiddlehead* 124 (1980): 105-07.

Lowry, Malcolm. *Under the Volcano*. 1947. Penguin Modern Classics. Harmondsworth, Eng.: Penguin, 1963.

Manguel, Alberto. "Too Little Too Late". Rev. of *The Honorary Patron*, by Jack Hodgins. *Books in Canada* Aug.-Sept. 1987: 14.

Mann, Thomas. "Death in Venice". *Death in Venice and Seven Other Stories*. Trans. H.T. Lowe-Porter. New York: Vintage, 1963. 3-75.

Mezei, Kathy. "Lives and Lies". Rev. of *Innocent Cities*, by Jack Hodgins. *The Globe and Mail* [Toronto] 15 Sept. 1990: C20.

Slemon, Stephen. "Magic Realism as Post-Colonial Discourse". *Canadian Literature* 116 (1988): 9-24.

———. "Modernism's Last Post". *Past the Last Post: Theorizing Post-Colonialism and Post-Modernism*. Ed. Ian Adam and Helen Tiffin. Calgary: U of Calgary P, 1990. 1-11.

Struthers, J.R. (Tim). "Thinking about Eternity". Rev. of *The Resurrection of Joseph Bourne*, by Jack Hodgins. *Essays on Canadian Writing* 20 (1980-81): 126-33.

Van Herk, Aritha. "A Crazy House of Fiction". Rev. of *Innocent Cities*, by Jack Hodgins. *Calgary Herald* 24 Nov. 1990: C4.

Wachtel, Eleanor. "The Invention of Jack Hodgins". *Books in Canada* Aug.-Sept. 1987: 6-10.

Wilson, Peter. "Not-So-Innocent Colonial Times". *The Weekend Sun* [*The Vancouver Sun*] 3 Nov. 1990: D17.

The Stuff of Literature and the Stuff of Life: An Interview with Jack Hodgins (1995)

J.R. (Tim) Struthers

TS: *The Macken Charm* is a *Bildungsroman*—the story of the development or education of its hero and narrator, Rusty Macken, in the summer of 1956, before he heads off from Vancouver Island to the mainland to go to university. The novel focusses on a very brief time period, which you have succeeded in making feel *pregnant* with possibilities. At the time being described, at the time being remembered, the big question for seventeen-year-old Rusty is "Who was I going to be?"—yet it's interesting this is asked in the past tense, or remembered in the past tense, at a stage when he has presumably become something else, though we are given at most hints of what this could be.

But in addition to being the story of the development or education of its protagonist and narrator, Rusty Macken, *The Macken Charm* would appear to be a novel of education for others as well. After all, Rusty isn't the only one who asks questions. There's his outrageous Uncle Toby—a name that brings to my mind a character in Laurence Sterne's equally playful *Tristram Shandy*. And there's Uncle Toby's stunningly beautiful wife, Gloria, or Glory as she's usually called, whose funeral—"funferal" [laughter] as James Joyce put it in *Finnegans Wake*—opens the book and represents the central event of the book and sets the—I suppose one might call it tragicomic—tone of the book. Then there are the narrator's parents, whose portraits are for me the most deeply affecting part of the book. But at least as importantly there's the writer, for whom this book also represents a novel of education and who no doubt was led to ask different kinds of questions as he wrote it. And of course, and very importantly as well, there's the reader, for whom, in my case, Rusty's question "Who was I going to be?" is, in the process of reading the novel, transformed into other questions: for example, "How do I want to live my life?"

The Macken Charm is an extremely delicately, extremely subtly, extremely gracefully, and—I want to say *therefore*—deeply moving novel, so moving that I wasn't sure I'd have the courage or emotional strength to present myself in front of you to talk about it. What I'd like to start by asking you is can you recall how—with what scene or image or notion—this novel began to take shape in your imagination and how it grew?

JH: A number of elements have been haunting me for a long time, images that go right back to my childhood, and that have been demanding attention in some form and not getting it up to now. At some point I realized I had these things hanging around nagging, and I guess the idea of the funeral and the idea of using a seventeen-year-old protagonist/narrator in 1956 allowed me to come to terms with them.

Those images include an empty seaside hotel. My parents, like Rusty's, when they were first married, were given an empty hotel to live in. They spent the first year of their marriage in it—which sounds to me like a wonderful way of starting a marriage. I remember going back as a small child and playing in all those empty bedrooms and imagining all the people who had stayed there and imagining what it would be like to live in such a great contained playground where every room had its own kind of magic and its own view on the world and its own relationship to the other rooms. I played in those rooms with cousins. The place had taken on a kind of magic for me even then because of those mysterious hallways and the stripped-down beds and the great lovely dining room with the French doors overlooking the ocean. This structure burnt down in my childhood and of course is no longer there. A few years ago, while we were visiting my folks, we went up to the site—which was a piece of property that my parents had the opportunity to buy for almost no money at all shortly after they were married, but turned down. A piece of useless waterfront, who needs ten acres of waterfront? They chose a little stump ranch inland instead [laughter].

TS: My Mom recently revisited the five acres in the country outside London, Ontario, which she and my Dad had sold for I believe $7,000 in the late 1940s—just before I was born—and which is now being offered for sale at $350,000 [laughter].

JH: Well, anyway, we tramped over this piece of property, which had gone wild, and discovered an old rosebush and a few bricks. But everything else had been cleared away. It was just a neglected field of long grass.

TS: Did you remember that rosebush from your childhood?

JH: Well, I remembered that the hotel was sort of encased in—I'm not sure of this, but I think it was encased in—rosebushes that climbed all over the verandahs, like a fairy-tale building. This made me think of it as a wonderful location that I must somehow bring back to life. And once I'd got started, of course, I discovered symbolic implications in the empty rooms and the playing of different kinds of games in all of them—for somebody who regrets having to be just one person. Things took off from there.

That hotel has always been with me. I also remember playing in a wooden hull of a boat that had been dragged in nearby. Probably today parents wouldn't allow their children to play in it, but this was a wonderful playground. And of course at that time, I remember, comic books were full of people being tied up to pilings and to ships' hulls to wait for the tide to come in and drown them. It was a particularly delicious way of destroying people that cartoonists obviously found they could drag out over several weeks of Saturday morning coloured comics. So it was a wonderful place, a magical place, to play.

Another memory that haunted me was the death of—now, this was not of a close relative but—a woman, whom I didn't know but who was on the fringes of this huge family, by drowning, by drowning herself, in a tiny bit of creek water. As a small child I was fascinated by the notion that somebody could want to die so badly that she could do it in a shallow creek. What would bring someone to do this?

Again I didn't realize this was haunting me, but along came this other image, once I'd got started, of this old Model T Ford that used to go by our place with this giant riding in it who, everybody knew, had once accidentally killed his own son. Even as a small child I sensed that this must be the most horrible thing that could happen to anyone, and how could he still be alive and breathing and driving his car up and down the road? I hadn't anticipated that he would become as important as he did—he's not central to the novel, but his very minor role gradually increased to become almost a sub-plot.

I think it was Janet Frame, the New Zealand writer, who said we write about the things that haunt us. And that's certainly a very important part of why I write some of the things I write—to deal with them, to see how they fit, to find out whether they have had any other repercussions in my life or whether they're just magical memories.

TS: I think what's so important about this kind of book or so many of Alice Munro's stories is the kind of emotional depth that memory allows in the telling of the story.

JH: Yes. It's one of the reasons, I suspect, I did not write this novel when I was twenty-five. If you just talk about the externals of the novel you could say, oh, this is the kind of novel many people write first, the growing-up novel, the getting-away-from-home novel, the leaving-the-family-behind novel. I was never tempted to write that kind of novel at the beginning of my career.

TS: Munro's *Lives of Girls and Women*, which was completed just before she turned forty, was her way of dealing with that.

JH: I wasn't ready to do it then. It didn't even interest me at the time. I had other things on my agenda. I suspect I needed all those years to remember those images through a lot of other things that had happened since, including other images that I could relate to some of those early ones. So I think maybe it's only recently that I've had the experience, the maturity, the clear-sightedness, or whatever, to be able to deal with that.

TS: There's a wonderful piece of advice given by an older writer, loosely based on Morley Callaghan, to a younger writer, loosely based on Hugh Hood, in the story "Where the Myth Touches Us" from Hugh Hood's first book, *Flying a Red Kite*, where, as you may remember, the older writer urges the younger writer not to write up his few real stories too soon.

JH: It's something I'm grateful I didn't do. Possibly I tried. I suspect that when I was writing stories for Earle Birney at UBC they came out of some of these things—I was nineteen, how much did I understand, how much of the world had I experienced? I wasn't ready to write them. I couldn't see them clearly enough. I still believed, I guess, in the great world of literature—that the stories were out there somewhere in this other world and that my own background was not the stuff of literature. But now I feel that Rusty and Rusty's family and Rusty's world are inescapable. In various ways I am connected physically and emotionally and psychically and spiritually to all of these characters, and though putting some of them down on a piece of paper doesn't get rid of them in any way—I don't want to get rid of them—it does pull them together and help make sense of them for me. And I needed to be older before I could do it.

TS: I'm very interested in your use of the phrase "the stuff of literature" because when I was thinking of phrases that would help me focus my questions for this interview, phrases that would help me come to terms with the powerful response that I had to *The Macken Charm*, I found myself thinking of the potential tensions between, but in the case of this novel the wonderful overlap and intersection and marriage of, what I'd call "the stuff of literature" and "the stuff of life". Rusty's question "Who was I going to be?" is transformed for me, as a reader, in different ways. It's transformed into the question "How do I want to live my life?" but it's also, and perhaps most interestingly, transformed into some such question as "What are the ways of understanding?" And that is how this novel most profoundly touched and held me.

But I do want to ask about the stuff of literature. I want to ask about any special questions of technique that were raised for you in the writing of this book. And I also want to ask if there were any models that you had in mind, at least on the edge of your consciousness, of novels, possibly of short stories, that seemed successful in doing the kind of thing that you wanted to undertake here. There's a delightful passage in your book *A Passion for Narrative* where you begin with the comment "The critics call it *intertextuality*" [laughter] and then say, subversively, "You can think of literature as a conversation that covers the globe and spans all time", I think what I'm really asking is: what questions of technique were on your mind, or emerged in the writing of this book, as important challenges for you, and were there any other writers with whom you found yourself in conversation—unvoiced conversation—as you wrote the book?

JH: I think the initial impulse to structure was an external one—in contradiction to my firm belief that the structure must grow out of the internal needs of the story that you're writing, which of course this eventually did. But initially I wanted to see how tight and short a novel I could write, because I have again and again wanted to write one of those beautiful little 150-page novels that do everything so cleanly and clearly and quickly. Of course once I get started I discover that there are so many other people who want to get in on the story, and so many other things to say, and life is so complex that I just can't seem to do this kind of thing. Still, I knew I wanted a structure that would force me to be as economical as possible.

TS: And that's why I mentioned short stories—because I was wondering if there might have been any lessons that you learned writing short stories, and continuing to write short stories, that you brought over into the writing of this book.

JH: Yes. No question. I'm not sure I can be specific in naming influences because I'm still too close to it and I suspect that at some point I blotted out from memory whatever those were. What I was left with was a strong sense of what the pattern must be, and I tested it by trying it other ways. I backed the story up, started two weeks earlier, and discovered that I gained things by doing that but I lost things I could not afford to lose. I also had the choice of telling the entire story—which covers at least ten years—chronologically, as some novels do of course: when I was ten, this happened, when I was eleven, that happened. Just the relationship between Rusty and Glory from the day she arrived in 1946, the day of the earthquake, until the day of her funeral. But this never seriously tempted me because it felt loose, it felt sloppy. I had to start on the day of the funeral and I had to do the whole story within twenty-four, twenty-five hours.

One of the important things about structure is that it is what determines the reader's experience. As much as the language does, the order in which you link events and emotional responses within a story controls the reader's entire experience. I had the choice of putting the reader through an *intense* twenty-five hours or allowing the reader to sit back and relax over a ten-year period. Well, that automatically affects distance, intimacy, involvement, and emotional connection between the reader and the characters. And I wanted this story to be intense.

Even though it is a memory story, from somewhere in Rusty's future, I still wanted to have the immediacy of a story that might have been told the day after. Now Rusty wouldn't have had the ability to tell the story the day after, but I wanted him to be a middle-aged person who could remember being seventeen with that kind of intimacy. So it had to be the story of those twenty-five hours, which, of course, presented me with an *incredible* problem of somehow fitting in the last ten years, which were important to character understanding, not to mention the last two weeks, which were very important immediately to the plot—all, somehow, without making the story feel as if it had stopped to go back and fill in. It's one of the most common short story devices, of course, to begin as close as possible to the end and then, when you've got your reader interested, go back and fill in.

TS: As you do in "Separating", for example, the opening story of *Spit Delaney's Island*.

JH: Yes. What it depends upon, I suppose, to work, if it works, is that the opening must be so interesting to the reader that he or she is willing to go back and find out how we got here before getting to where we're going. Now, that short story device did not by itself appeal to me for this novel because, for something as long as that, what it would do is to get you interested only to say, okay, now we're going on this long journey—which wouldn't be all that different from doing the whole story chronologically. I somehow had to create the illusion that the clock is ticking through these twenty-four hours, twenty-five hours, even while you are re-experiencing the earlier weeks and the earlier years, which meant I somehow had to use flashbacks that were both flashbacks and not flashbacks—they were returning to earlier times and yet you weren't really returning to earlier times. For a long while this felt like an impossibility. I thought I'm not sure I can do this but I am going to try. And I tried many different ways, moving things around and reordering things and creating new kinds of transitions. It was through trial and error, mostly, that I discovered how the story needed to be told.

TS: How about intuition, a lifetime of reading, and nearly four decades of constant writing?

JH: And a million other things. Yes. It boils down to instinct or to sensitivity. It works because it works or it doesn't work because it doesn't work and you don't need to know the reason unless that's going to help you find a solution. If it doesn't work, get rid of it. And I knew this novel was far too important to me to be satisfied with something that almost works. I had to believe there was a way of making it flow forward even when I was going into the past. It meant a great deal of hard choices, selection, arrangement, throwing away, rearranging, just moving a paragraph from here to there and then re-experiencing it as the reader might, imagining what this would look like to the reader, until at some point I just felt, okay, this is a whole, this is a "thing".

It's impossible for the one doing it ever to know—unless maybe twenty years later—what the finished product looks like to the person who's coming to it fresh. But I wanted to get as close as I could to creating the feeling that this was how this book had to be written. When I read a wonderful novel by somebody I think is a terrific writer, the feeling I get is that it couldn't have been any other way, it's as if this book came as a gift, a package, and I wouldn't be surprised to discover that all the writer had to do was to sit down and record it. Now, you and I both know that this doesn't happen very often, if at all, and I don't expect it to happen to me, but I want somebody else to think, oh, that was probably an easy book to write because it just looks as if it came as a package.

TS: Is that a feeling you get from a book like, say, William Faulkner's *As I Lay Dying*?

JH: Yes. Of course it is. It's the kind of book about which I suppose critics could say, well, this is one of those novels where he sat over an overturned wheelbarrow and just whipped it off without ever really thinking very much about it.

TS: I was thinking of the fluidity and the openness, even a dream-like quality, of *As I Lay Dying*.

JH: Yes.

TS: Uncle Toby, the outrageous character whom the young Rusty admires and wants to be admired by, is described in terms that led me to think of the phrase "dream-merchant". Uncle Toby runs the sawmill and is described as preparing lumber that is literally and metaphorically the stuff that will allow other people to construct their dreams. And so, to develop the metaphor, I wonder about the notion of a novelist, like Faulkner in *As I Lay Dying* or like you here, as a dream-merchant.

JH: What is a novelist trying to do to the reader but to start a dream going? The novel is not happening on the page alone, and it is not happening in my head alone. The novel has to happen in the reader's head. When I'm reading something that I love, I'm not aware of the book. A dream is happening. Somebody else has started the dream and is controlling the dream, but I'm the one who is experiencing it. The real dream-merchant is the one who somehow grabs hold of somebody else and says I want you to dream this dream along with me. For Toby, it was, I want to give you a better house to live in. For Rusty, at that time, it was, I want to create those movies that you can go and sit in a dark room and experience.

TS: Was there in fact a 1915 film called *Under the Crescent*?

JH: There certainly was! I have a copy of the book!

TS: The photo-play by Nell Shipman.

JH: Well, today they would call it a novelization. Nell Shipman wrote the screenplay—and I think directed it, though I'm not sure. Then she wrote a novel version of it which was published with still photos from the movie and, at the front, a photograph of this beautiful woman who had written it. It was my mother's book. Because it's falling apart, I now keep it in a zip-lock bag. As a boy, I used to study it just as Rusty did. But I didn't remember it through the first fifteen drafts or whatever of this novel. At some point in my research I was trying to find out which Canadians had gone south to work in the movie industry so that I would know more of what Rusty was faced with. And I uncovered the name "Nell Shipman". I didn't remember that she was the woman who had written that book and made that movie. Nell Shipman entered the novel as just another Canadian who went south and made movies and then disappeared.

Then at some point I came across a pile of old books that had never quite got unpacked when we moved to Victoria. They were the kind of thing that just got stored. You didn't throw them away because they mattered to you, but you didn't need them either. And in this pile of books, which included things like *Lorna Doone* and *The Little Prince*, I came across *Under the Crescent* and thought, this is interesting, I guess I probably should have a look at this since I'm interested in movies at the moment. When I opened it up, the name "Nell Shipman" leapt out at me. My gosh, this is her, this is the same woman, I've known her all my life, I didn't know she came from Victoria! So obviously the book had to enter the novel as well, which led to Rusty's memory of reproducing that movie in the woodshed with his cousins. Like the burnt-down hotel, that book was lying around waiting for me to do something with it.

TS: So unpacking the attic pays all kinds of different dividends [laughter].

JH: You just never know what you may find. Not to make too much of it, but that's certainly an example of the kind of thing that novels are made of. You drag all these things around in your head until they demand to be talked about. And I just happened to be dragging a few boxes of neglected books as well. Of course, the novel did not grow solely out of memory and musings about images that have haunted me. There were the usual notebooks filled with my scribblings—glimpses of characters, bits of dialogue, questions, researched facts, descriptions of places, notes on books read, lists of possible names, newspaper stories, etc.—from which I selected those that lent themselves to the kind of novel I wanted to write, and those that triggered further insights, and especially those that suggested connections among the ideas and images I was thinking about.

TS: I described the way you have structured and focussed this novel as being *pregnant* with possibilities. I think I developed the metaphor of being pregnant from Rusty's own reference to wishing he had been conceived in all thirteen rooms of the second floor of the old hotel so that he could grow up and be all of the thirteen or more characters whose roles he had played in childhood games in those rooms—or so that he, as is suggested, could discover a vocation which somehow embraced all of those roles. Conception, of course, is a very important metaphor in Laurence Sterne's *Tristram Shandy*—Tristram doesn't even get born for a few hundred pages. But as for my sense of your novel, what I feel is that it's pregnant with possibilities of the future and of the past. *The Macken Charm* finishes beautifully, lyrically, yet doesn't end—and so I wanted to ask you where it's going. Is there going to be a sequel?

JH: This feeling that you're identifying here is something that must be resisted by the writer, because I think one of the marks of a good piece of work is that it suggests other lives and continuations and befores and afters and the sense that every single person in this novel could deserve a novel of his or her own. So when suggestions occurred to me during the writing that, hey, something else could come out of this, I resisted. I said to myself this book has to be written as if it's the only novel I will ever write, as if this could be my last novel—so that I'm not saving things for something else, so that I'm not tempted to cheat the reader in this one in order to feed another, later book. All the other dreams that might be triggered by this one in a reader's mind are the reader's and not mine. I've started them, they're between the lines—let the reader write those other novels. Even so, having got to the finishing stages of this one, where there was no question the novel was a completed whole, I began to realize that out of all the possibilities there were two that were still open to me and that not only were open to me but demanded my attention in the same way that Rusty's story had.

Now they did not turn out to be sequels in the ordinary sense. They turned out to be, or they are turning out to be, companion pieces, with similar roots geographically, with connections through personal relationships and through an exploration of certain related themes that feel as if they need further exploration. I don't want to talk about them while I'm still working with them, beyond saying that I find myself thinking and writing about Rusty's friend Sonny in middle age.

TS: Is there a specific year in the future when the novel focussing on Sonny is set? Have you chosen a year for it?

JH: At the moment it is vaguely in the early 90s. One of the next jobs I have to do is to be more specific, because Sonny is someone who is aware of what's going on in the world.

TS: And the other novel, the other companion piece, what are you exploring in it?

JH: I find myself interested in the origins of Rusty's and Sonny's community, when soldiers returning from the First World War were given by the Canadian government these pieces of land that were impossible to farm. This small bit of history presents me with another of those haunting things I have to deal with—the great forest fire of 1922 that swept through the settlement I later grew up in, but didn't destroy the little community that had already set down its roots.

TS: Is there a focal character for the novel set in 1922?

JH: Yes.

TS: And you've found . . .

JH: There is at least one character who is important to all three and I've just recently discovered that. I won't say any more because it could all change. If I say any more you'll start writing your own novels and then be disappointed when they're not what I write.

TS: It all sounds wonderful.

JH: Well, we'll see [laughter].

TS: Wonderful to live inside, I mean.

JH: It's a huge world and all these people still excite me, still fascinate me. What will come of it I have yet to discover, though in the meantime I'm as absorbed as I can be in new problems which are quite different from those I faced in writing *The Macken Charm*.

TS: So you have begun drafting the second and third novels?

JH: I have several drafts of the second one right up to the crisis, climax, whatever you want to call that end part where everything comes together. And I go back and take new runs at it, making changes every time. There's still something important I haven't yet discovered.

TS: And the third one? How far are you with it?

JH: For the third one, I've begun listening to the voices and recording the voices and I have a structure and a scheme that is so irresistible that I cannot avoid doing it. I don't want to talk about it because it's fragile and risky, and so different that I can't find a model for it, but everything about it demands that I try this.

TS: How wonderful.

JH: Well . . . [laughter].

TS: [laughter] How scary.

JH: It's scary but it's exciting as well. I need somebody to lock me in a room until I've done them both. But I also need to be out there with my antennae working because, well, like the Nell Shipman book, life keeps giving you gifts even once you're committed to something, or maybe especially when you're committed to something. You don't really know what gifts you need to keep until you know what you're doing, so I need to be open to all kinds of gifts that I haven't yet been given. This is what has been obsessing me. This is what will continue to obsess me. It hasn't anything to do with *The Macken Charm*. It has a lot to do with me and whatever else has been happening.

One of the exciting things in writing *The Macken Charm* that triggered a lot of this is the thrill of once again working in the idiom of my earliest years. Whenever it was that I found the voice for the novel—I can't remember when—it was like finding Spit Delaney, it was like finding all those characters in the Spit Delaney stories, it was, oh my gosh, I'm back in that skin again. I'm not suggesting it was easy but it was comfortable.

TS: Would there be any examples that would help you find a way towards answering the kinds of questions which you are now wrestling with as you realize you are writing not one book but three? Are there any examples, or are there any lessons that perhaps you have learned and maybe aren't even conscious of at this point but that you can imagine, if you think back, you might have learned from other works of this kind, works in which writers create a series of three novels, a trilogy?

JH: There are some warnings I take from them. There are some areas where I feel what others have done is not what I want to do. Generally speaking, I think of a trilogy as a story that takes three books to tell completely. Even though the books may be self-contained, you need part two to understand part one fully, etc.

TS: What would you be thinking of there? Faulkner's *The Hamlet, The Town*, and *The Mansion*?

JH: That kind of thing. *The Hamlet*, for me, is a wonderful novel on its own. But if you want the Snopes's story, you read all three books. On the other hand, since we're talking about Faulkner anyway, there are characters in Faulkner that wander in and out of a number of his works and for me they're all part of the same story yet the works are completely different and separate. So I take a number of warnings and a number of images or metaphors for myself here to remember. I *must* remember that each novel, even if I think of them as companion pieces, must be as individual as humans are. Whatever overlaps are possible must not affect the way I write the novel. I mustn't give in to the temptation to wink at the reader, to reward the reader who may have just read the other novel. I must always write Sonny's novel as Sonny's novel period, as if that's the only novel I will ever write, as if *The Macken Charm* has disappeared off the face of the earth and only the Sonny novel will survive. Not because I think that's superior to a traditional trilogy but because it is more consistent with whatever it is I'm trying to do here. I do feel very strongly that the continuations and the overlaps are an important part of a large pattern but only in the sense that all things are important as part of a large pattern in the world.

TS: What kind of example does Robertson Davies' Deptford Trilogy offer?

JH: The Deptford Trilogy, I think, is a superb example of each novel's ability to be itself, with its own voice and its own explorations and its own revelations. But, even so, that trilogy very brilliantly sets up in the first novel a need to read the other novels. And brilliant as that is, and rewarding as that is, that's just not what I'm trying to do. I don't even think of these as one, two, three. I think of them as triplets, not first child, second child, third child, but three equal partners in some larger scheme.

TS: Or a big altar-piece, a triptych, an immense painting?

JH: Yes. Or fragments of a mural, the rest of which you have to fill in yourself. The fact that I'm discovering some connections is exciting for me but I don't want that to be crucial to the reader.

TS: You speak of filling in the connections. One of the wonderful things for me in reading, as I experience fiction now, is when I feel I've been given an opening for both my memory and my imagination, that the writing of the novel is controlled but open enough to allow all of that.

JH: This is a reading experience which I treasure myself, and which happens when I'm reading things that matter the most to me—where I find myself filling in the gaps or pausing at the end of a chapter to dream my own next chapter or even an alternative novel. It can sometimes actually get in the way if I'm not careful but I assume that is because I'm reading as a novelist and as an appreciative reader. Certainly the writings I treasure create not only the dream that was intended but other dreams as well.

TS: I wonder if something like Italo Calvino's *If on a winter's night a traveller* might present some of those opportunities to you.

JH: Of course. That gives you, I can't remember how many, all these novels you could write yourself if you wanted to finish them off, and yet they are also their own novel.

TS: One of the questions *The Macken Charm* led me to ask was "How do I want to live my life?" The novel provides a range of examples by way of answer to this question. There's the inspiring but often desperate and often damaging vigour of the narrator's Uncle Toby: Toby's actions and reactions, his love of climbing to the tops of roofs and the tops of church steeples and, very late in the novel, even the top of a glacier—from which he's saved in an action that strikes me almost as a re-writing of a famous poem, "David", by your creative writing teacher Earle Birney.

JH: [laughter].

TS: But I won't ask you to comment on that. The novel, as I say, raises the question "How do I want to live my life?" and gives various examples of behaviour as possible answers to that. There's the inspiring but often desperate and often damaging vigour of Uncle Toby. There's the healing, saving vigour of family and of community, remembering, reconstructing, literally and metaphorically and you might even say allegorically resurrecting the old hotel spontaneously in the course of the wake that they have for Glory after she commits suicide.

But there's another question the novel raises, though it doesn't use these exact words, the question, which I've taken and rephrased from the Bible, "What are the ways to understanding?" And for me the answer to this, an answer which *The Macken Charm* beautifully exemplifies, is contained in a phrase that a man who was really a second father to me, a man named Fred Hammerton, used to repeat. He was the manager of a paint store and a fisherman and duck hunter and he loved to work with wood. And what he used to say to me was "Keep it light, son. Keep it light". He was a teacher, really. He wasn't selling paint when he was selling paint. He was teaching you about paint and about how to apply it and about how to live your life and about how to understand life and he'd take time with you to offer recommendations on how to go about learning all of this.

For a writer, keeping it light would involve handling structure and tone and individual sentences and phrases in such a way that they don't ever become intrusive. You need to keep the life of the work as mysterious as the wind or the sea. I can't help but think of the epigraph to W.O. Mitchell's *Who Has Seen the Wind*, which I believe was the first adult Canadian novel that I read, back in high school, where for my final three years I had an extraordinary English teacher named Art Fidler. And the epigraph read: "Who has seen the wind? / Neither you nor I: / But when the trees bow down their heads, / The wind is passing by". The phrase "Keep it light" reminds me of the wonderful description near the end of *The Macken Charm*, the description of Old Man Stokes playing the piano—not the first time a character has played a piano near the end of a novel of yours if I remember *The Invention of the World* correctly [laughter], but a lovely passage. Here it is:

> A few chords announced Stokes's intention. Then a run up the scale and back. A single clear note was struck repeatedly as though he were listening hard for a sound within the sound. My mother and Kitty

went back to slapping their brushes up and down the verandah of the hotel. Somewhere inside, hammering started again.

At first I couldn't tell what he played in the bed of that truck. Something clear and light, something that sounded like a single plaintive voice busy at narrative. A simple pretty melody sailed forward a while, then suddenly turned back on itself and became something else more frightening and complex before breaking free to soar again. It raised gooseflesh along my arms. He'd lifted this from the air: the song of wind in the rotting hull.

Keep it not necessarily comic but light. Let it edge into something perhaps a good deal more complicated—Rusty's secret attachment to Glory and his feelings of responsibility for her suicide come to mind, feelings of sorrow and of loneliness, "lamentation" is a word that you use a couple of times late in the text of the novel, for others and for ourselves—let it edge into something perhaps a good deal more complicated, then let it swirl back or soar. I can only imagine that to write fiction like this would involve extraordinary delicacy and a great deal of experience both writing and living, experience of literature and experience of life. I think it would involve a different kind of knowledge, literary knowledge imbued with human knowledge, without which, though a lot of critics and teachers of literature don't seem to understand this, literary knowledge is hollow, dead. The sort of lightness of feeling that Ethel Wilson creates when she describes the water-gliders in her novel *The Innocent Traveller*, or that you can hear in the tone of Earle Birney's novel *Turvey*, or that Roderick Haig-Brown conveys in his descriptions of fishing in *Fisherman's Spring, Fisherman's Summer, Fisherman's Fall*, and *Fisherman's Winter*, a quartet which I dip into at appropriate seasons of the year—it has become a ritual for me—because they give me pleasure and contentment.

What I'm saying here is that if *The Macken Charm* offers me an answer to the question "What are the ways to understanding?", I suppose the answer is this: that there's a knowledge of the textures of things—as a young man you built your own house outside of Lantzville, so you'd know what lumber feels like when it comes from the sawmill and after you've used a medium grade of sandpaper on it and after you've used a fine grade of sandpaper on it, and those are things that this man I mentioned to you, Fred Hammerton, knew too. If there's an answer, then, it's that there's a knowledge of the textures and smells of things (wood, for example—Uncle Toby operates a sawmill) and a knowledge of how people look and sound, call it knowledge of life, human knowledge, knowledge of the heart, that can't be excluded from the ways in which we as readers and teachers and critics fumble towards an understanding of literature. Is that what you hope for in a reader, discovering how to respond as much with the heart as with the mind?

JH: You've phrased the question so beautifully that I think the only appropriate answer is silence. I feel so inarticulate and clumsy and heavy-handed that I feel I have to work seven million times harder than anybody else in order to aim for the effect that you've just described, which to me is an ideal version to be sought after but not necessarily to be achieved. I would never know myself when or if I achieved it.

TS: It's not to be achieved by the writer alone. It takes a reader.

JH: It's a partnership. I think my job must be to work seven million times harder than I want the reader to work so that it will look as if I'm only triggering the responses and leaving the rest to you. Now that is so delicate and so difficult that I think it's impossible for me to know whenever I've achieved it. But it is my aim to leave the work to you, to leave the joy of filling in the gaps to you, to give you what you need to start things happening. And how do you ever know that about somebody else? There's a great deal of trust here. I have to earn the reader's trust, I have to create an atmosphere in which the reader and I are on the same wavelength, and then I have to set up the small things that trigger the big things. And this is perhaps like the water-skeeter going across the surface of the water with those light, light steps. But who knows what the effect of those light steps is on the water beneath or upon the observer? It's something that may have begun as a deliberate attempt to compensate for my own inarticulateness and clumsiness and tendency to say too much, but also out of a great admiration I have for those who can avoid overdoing it. This is something I'll have to continue trying to do.

I've been speaking in terms only of the reader's experience of the story and of the language, how I want to trigger all those things in as light a way as possible. But the other part, it's not just a literary experience, it is an experience of entering the lives of other people, of getting to know what it's like to be someone else, of gaining some insight into others, of identifying with, of empathizing with, of discovering something that others have to offer that we may not have stumbled on ourselves. And that is something I have to trust to be the result of the combination of all those things: the treading lightly, the creating of other people's dreams through the smallest of triggers, whatever it is I uncover in the characters, their feelings and their sense of one another, the extent to which I can create the illusion—no, it's not an illusion—to create the sense that the reader and the characters are not all that different from one another. I mean, this is a mirror—not simply a mirror—it's an image of the world we live in and there are all these stories walking around and all these people living their individual lives but in fact sharing more than we can ever guess.

I think one of the things that fiction does and must do and does best is allow us to overlap a little. I think Margaret Laurence spoke of humans overlapping. And John Gardner reminded us that one of the things that fiction does is allow us the opportunity to practise loving. The characters are imaginary but the relationship we set up with them is keeping that facility in good health. If we can experience that relationship with other people on the page, maybe we're better capable of experiencing it with other people on the street.

TS: Are your parents both still alive?

JH: Yes they are.

TS: I wanted to say that I can't imagine a better gift than the one you have been able to offer them with this book.

JH: Well, even though the novel is fictitious and all the aunts and uncles are composites and inventions, I didn't need to go far beyond my memory of my own parents in their forties to create the portrait of Rusty's folks. I was cheated out of the usual need to rebel. I recognized early that I had wonderful parents, but I hadn't always realized how important this would be to my life. To be attempting this very small snapshot, if you wish, that tries to capture a little bit of them—it would be presumptuous to think that I am capturing them, I'm not, but I am giving glimpses of them, at least as they appear to me, as people who have always had my admiration and love but for whom I also have an increasing amount of appreciation—and to be reliving their forties, from my point of view, as they are still experiencing another stage of their lives, was a very strange and moving experience.

TS: I think it's wonderful that you have been able to present them with the sort of long love letter that few of us have the chance to present or the talent to write and I wish to congratulate you on this book.

JH: Well, thank you very much.

A Checklist of Works by Jack Hodgins

J.R. (Tim) Struthers

A   Books (Novels, Short Fiction and Excerpts, Children's Book, Non-Fiction, Anthologies and Textbooks) and Manuscripts

NOVELS

A1   *The Invention of the World.* Toronto: Macmillan of Canada, 1977.
———. New York: Harcourt Brace Jovanovich, 1978.
———. Scarborough, ON: Macmillan-NAL, 1978.
———. Macmillan Paperbacks 16. Toronto: Macmillan of Canada, 1986.
———. Afterword by George McWhirter. The New Canadian Library. Toronto: McClelland & Stewart, 1994.

A2   *The Resurrection of Joseph Bourne; or, A Word or Two on Those Port Annie Miracles.* Toronto: Macmillan of Canada, 1979.
———. Scarborough, ON: Macmillan-NAL, 1980.
———. Macmillan Paperbacks 47. Toronto: Macmillan of Canada, 1990.

A3 *The Honorary Patron.* A Douglas Gibson Book. Toronto: McClelland & Stewart, 1987.
———. M&S Paperback. Toronto: McClelland & Stewart, 1989.

A4 *Innocent Cities.* A Douglas Gibson Book. Toronto: McClelland & Stewart, 1990.
———. St. Lucia, Queensland, Austral.: U of Queensland P, 1991.
———. M&S Paperback. Toronto: McClelland & Stewart, 1991.

A5 *The Macken Charm.* A Douglas Gibson Book. Toronto: McClelland & Stewart, 1995.
———. St. Leonards, New South Wales, Austral.: Allen & Unwin, 1995.

Short Fiction and Excerpts

A6 *Spit Delaney's Island: Selected Stories.* Toronto: Macmillan of Canada, 1976.
———. Laurentian Library 58. Toronto: Macmillan of Canada, 1977.
———. Macmillan Paperbacks 26. Toronto: Macmillan of Canada, 1987.
Spit Delaney's Island. Afterword by Robert Bringhurst. The New Canadian Library. Toronto: McClelland & Stewart, 1992.

A7 *The Barclay Family Theatre.* Toronto: Macmillan of Canada, 1981.
———. Laurentian Library 74. Toronto: Macmillan of Canada, 1983.
———. New Press Canadian Classics. Toronto: Stoddart, 1991.

A8 *Beginnings. Samplings from a Long Apprenticeship: Novels Which Were Imagined, Written, Re-written, Submitted, Rejected, Abandoned, and Supplanted.* Toronto: Grand Union, 1983.

Children's Book

A9 *Left Behind in Squabble Bay.* Illus. VictoR GAD. Toronto: McClelland & Stewart, 1988.

Non-Fiction

A10 *Over Forty in Broken Hill: Unusual Encounters Outback & Beyond.* St. Lucia, Queensland, Austral.: U of Queensland P, 1992.
Over 40 in Broken Hill: Unusual Encounters in the Australian Outback. A Douglas Gibson Book. Toronto: McClelland & Stewart, 1992.

A11 *A Passion for Narrative: A Guide for Writing Fiction.* A Douglas Gibson Book. Toronto: McClelland & Stewart, 1993.
——. New York: St. Martin's, 1994.

Anthologies and Textbooks

A12 *Voice and Vision.* Ed. Jack Hodgins and William H. New. Toronto: McClelland & Stewart, 1972.

A13 *The Frontier Experience.* Ed. Jack Hodgins. Themes in Canadian Literature. Toronto: Macmillan of Canada, 1975.

A14 *The West Coast Experience.* Ed. Jack Hodgins. Themes in Canadian Literature. Toronto: Macmillan of Canada, 1976.

A15 *Teaching Short Fiction; A Resource Book to* Transitions II: Short Fiction. By Jack Hodgins and Bruce Nesbitt. Vancouver: CommCept, 1978.

Manuscripts

A16 Jack Hodgins Papers
National Library of Canada
Ottawa, Ontario

Two accessions, the first including materials up to 1984 and the second including materials up to 1990, are located at the National Library of Canada. A finding aid for the first accession and a preliminary finding aid for the second accession are available. No restrictions on consultation.

B	Contributions to Periodicals and Books (Short Fiction and Excerpts, and Non-Fiction)

Note: When an item is reprinted in one of Hodgins' books, this fact is noted in the entry through one of the following abbreviations:

B / *Beginnings*
BFT / *The Barclay Family Theatre*
HP / *The Honorary Patron*
IC / *Innocent Cities*
IW / *The Invention of the World*
LB / *Left Behind in Squabble Bay*
MC / *The Macken Charm*
OF / *Over Forty in Broken Hill*
PN / *A Passion for Narrative*
RJB / *The Resurrection of Joseph Bourne*
SDI / *Spit Delaney's Island*

Short Fiction and Excerpts

B1	"Every Day of His Life". *Northwest Review* [Eugene, OR] 9.3 (1968): 108-20. *SDI*.

B2	"The God of Happiness". *Westerly* [Nedlands, Western Australia, Austral.] 4 (1968): 5-9.

B3	"Promise of Peace". *The North American Review* [Cedar Falls, IA] ns 6.4 (1969): 27-32.

B4	"Yesterday's Green Summer". *Descant* [Fort Worth, TX] 13.4 (1969): 39-47. *SDI* (revised—"Other People's Troubles").

B5	"A Matter of Necessity". *The Canadian Forum* Jan. 1970: 245-47.

B6   "The Graveyard Man". *Descant* [Fort Worth, TX] 15.4 (1971): 2-10.

B7   "Witness". *Alphabet* 18-19 (1971): 67-73.

B8   "After the Season". *Wascana Review* 6.2 (1972): 55-69. *SDI*.

B9   "Edna Pike, on the Day of the Prime Minister's Wedding". *Event: Journal of the Contemporary Arts* 2.1 ([1972]): 26-33.

B10 "Open Line". *The Antigonish Review* 9 (1972): 11-17.

B11 "Passing by the Dragon". *Island: Vancouver Island's Quarterly Review of Poetry and Fiction* [Nanaimo, BC] 2 ([1972]): [33-40].

B12 "Three Women of the Country". *Journal of Canadian Fiction* 1.3 (1972): 22-38. *SDI*.

B13 "By the River". *The Capilano Review* 1.3 (1973): 5-12. Rpt. in *Scope* [Durban, Natal, So. Afr.] 31 Mar. 1978: 105, 108-09, 111. Rpt. in *Canadian Number*. Ed. Rosemary Sullivan and Frank Davey. *The Literary Half-Yearly* 24.2 (1983): 178-85. *SDI*.

B14 "The Importance of Patsy McLean". *Journal of Canadian Fiction* 2.1 (1973): 5-7. *IW* (revised).

B15 "At the Foot of the Hill, Birdie's School". *The Canadian Fiction Magazine* 12 (1974): 81-94. *SDI*.

B16 "In the Museum of Evil". *Journal of Canadian Fiction* 3.1 (1974): 5-10.

B17 "Silverthorn". *Forum* [Houston, TX] 12.1 (1974): 24-26.

B18 "The Trench Dwellers". *The Capilano Review* 5 (1974): 11-24. *SDI*.

B19 "Great Blue Heron". *Prism international* 14.2 (1975): 38-43.

B20   "More Than Conquerors". *Journal of Canadian Fiction* 16 (1976): 49-88. *BFT* (revised).

B21   "The Religion of the Country". *Spit Delaney's Island: Selected Stories.* Toronto: Macmillan of Canada, 1976. 98-114.

B22   "Separating". *Spit Delaney's Island: Selected Stories.* Toronto: Macmillan of Canada, 1976. 3-23. Rpt. in *Scope* [Durban, Natal, So. Afr.] 27 Oct. 1978: 125-26, 129-32, 134-35.

B23   "Spit Delaney's Island". *Spit Delaney's Island: Selected Stories.* Toronto: Macmillan of Canada, 1976. 170-99.

B24   "A Conversation in the Kick-and-Kill: July". *Sound Heritage* [Victoria, BC] 6.3 (1977): 55-56, 59, 61, 63-64. *RJB* (revised).

B25   "The Lepers' Squint". *The Story So Far 5.* Ed. Douglas Barbour. Toronto: Coach House, 1978. 49-65. *BFT* (revised).

B26   "Spit Delaney's Nightmare". *Toronto Life* Jan. 1978: 41-44.

B27   "THE INVENTION OF THE WORLD". *Viva* Feb. 1978: 99-108. *IW.*

B28   "The Concert Stages of Europe". *Saturday Night* July-Aug. 1978: 36-38, 43-49. *BFT* (revised).

B29   "Miss Schussnigg's First Spring". *Peter Gzowski's Spring Tonic.* Ed. Peter Gzowski. Edmonton, AB: Hurtig, 1979. 54-56, 58.

B30   "The Plague Children". *Weekend Magazine* [*The Globe and Mail*] [Toronto] 4 Aug. 1979: 10-13. Rpt. in *Canadian Issue.* Ed. Katherine Govier. *Aquarius* [London, Eng.] 13-14 (1981-82): 29-41. *BFT* (revised).

B31   "Invasions '79". *The Barclay Family Theatre.* Toronto: Macmillan of Canada, 1981. 24-67.

B32 "Mr. Pernouski's Dream". *The Barclay Family Theatre*. Toronto: Macmillan of Canada, 1981. 68-100.

B33 "The Sumo Revisions". *The Barclay Family Theatre*. Toronto: Macmillan of Canada, 1981. 181-261. Rpt. (excerpt) as "Victims of the Masquerade." *Interface* [Edmonton, AB] Sept. 1981: 30-34.

B34 "Those Fabulous Barclay Sisters". *Toronto Life* Jan. 1981: 54-55, 89-95. *BFT* (revised—"Ladies and Gentlemen, the Fabulous Barclay Sisters!").

B35 "Change of Scenery". *Small Wonders: New Stories by Twelve Distinguished Canadian Writers*. Ed. Robert Weaver. Toronto: CBC Enterprises, 1982. 31-43. Rpt. in *The Canadian Forum* June-July 1982: 23-26.

B36 "The Day of the Stranger". *Chatelaine* Dec. 1982: 54-55, 78-80, 83, 86. *LB* (revised).

B37 "Faller Topolski's Arrival". *True North/Down Under* [Lantzville, BC] 1 (1983): 45-53.

B38 "The Crossing". *Vancouver Magazine* Feb. 1985: 34, 36-37, 44, 56-57. Rpt. (with author's commentary) in *Encounters and Explorations: Canadian Writers and European Critics*. Ed. Franz K. Stanzel and Waldemar Zacharasiewicz. Würzburg, W. Ger.: Königshausen and Neumann, 1986. 12-19.

B39 "Earthquake". *The Canadian Forum* Mar. 1986: 17, 19-22. Rpt. in *Kunapipi* 9.2 (1987): 90-98. *MC* (revised).

B40 "Loved Forever". *Books in Canada* Aug.-Sept. 1988: 13-15. *IC* (revised).

B41 "Excerpt from *Innocent Cities*". *Multiple Voices: Recent Canadian Fiction: Proceedings of the IVth International Symposium of the Brussels Centre for Canadian Studies 29 November 1 December 1989*. Ed. Jeanne Delbaere. Sydney, New South Wales, Austral.: Dangaroo, 1990. 247-58. *IC*.

B42 "Extract from *Innocent Cities*". *Kunapipi* 12.1 (1990): 114-17.

B43 "Balance". *Paris Transcontinental: A Magazine of Short Stories* 7 ([1993]): 97-109.

B44 "Galleries". *O Canada 2*. Ed. Cassandra Pybus. *Meanjin* [U of Melbourne, Parkville, Victoria, Austral.] 54 (1995): 246-58.

B45 "In the Forest of Discarded Pasts". *Paris Transcontinental: A Magazine of Short Stories* 11 ([1995]): 25-34. MC (revised).

B46 "Over Here". *Prism international* 33.3 (1995): 54-65.

Non-Fiction

B47 "A View of Absurdia". *BC English Teacher* 9.1 (1968): 28-30.

B48 ———, and William H. New. "Afterword". *Voice and Vision*. Ed. Jack Hodgins and William H. New. Toronto: McClelland & Stewart, 1972. 244.

B49 "Introduction: Deeper into the Forest". *The Frontier Experience*. Ed. Jack Hodgins. Themes in Canadian Literature. Toronto: Macmillan of Canada, 1975. 1-2.

B50 "Introduction". *The West Coast Experience*. Ed. Jack Hodgins. Themes in Canadian Literature. Toronto: Macmillan of Canada, 1976. 1-2.

B51 "An Experiment in Magic". *Transitions II: Short Fiction; A Source Book of Canadian Literature*. Ed. Edward Peck. Fwd. Geoff Hancock. Vancouver: CommCept, 1978. 237-39.

B52 Letter. *Toronto Life* Apr. 1978: 11.

B53 "Author's Commentary". *Stories Plus: Canadian Stories with Authors' Commentaries*. Ed. John Metcalf. Toronto: McGraw-Hill Ryerson, 1979. 121-23.

B54 "Bus Griffiths: A Legend All Unknowing; Logger, Fisherman, Cartoonist, Painter and Writer—He Creates the World He Loves Best in His Works". *Westworld* 6.4 (1980): 37-38, 41-44, 46.

B55 "External Despairs: From Japan to Norway, There's a Growing Interest Abroad in CanLit. Now If We Could Only Send Them Some Books...". *Books in Canada* Jan. 1980: 6-8.

B56 "Ottawa Cityscape". *Chatelaine* Feb. 1980: 39, 70.

B57 "Introduction". *Vancouver Island and the Gulf Islands*. By Menno Fieguth. Toronto: Oxford UP, 1981. [v-vii].

B58 "Golden Threads among the Grey". Rev. of *A Sleep Full of Dreams*, by Edna Alford. *Books in Canada* Jan. 1982: 13-14.

B59 ——, et al. "Ode to Joy: Joy Kogawa's Poetic Narrative about the Japanese Canadians During the Second World War Is the Best First Novel of 1981". *Books in Canada* Apr. 1982: 5.

B60 ——, et al. "Pride of the Sox: W.P. Kinsella's Lyrical Celebration of 'the Gentle, Flawless, Loving Game' of Baseball Is the Best First Novel of 1982". *Books in Canada* Apr. 1983: 8-9.

B61 "Vonnegut Makes Comical Ghost Irresistible". Rev. of *Galápagos*, by Kurt Vonnegut. *The Weekend Citizen* [*The Ottawa Citizen*] 14 Dec. 1985: C3.

B62 "[Author's Commentary on 'The Crossing']". *Encounters and Explorations: Canadian Writers and European Critics*. Ed. Franz K. Stanzel and Waldemar Zacharasiewicz. Würzburg, W. Ger.: Königshausen and Neumann, 1986. 10-11.

B63 "Home Is the Haunter: In Alistair MacLeod's Short Stories, in One Form or Another, the Past Always Forces Itself upon the Present". Rev. of *As Birds Bring Forth the Sun and Other Stories*, by Alistair MacLeod. *Books in Canada* Aug.-Sept. 1986: 12-13. Rpt. (abridged) in *Contemporary Literary Criticism: Excerpts from Criticism of the Works of Today's Novelists, Poets,*

Playwrights, Short Story Writers, Scriptwriters, and Other Creative Writers. Vol. 56. Ed. Roger Matuz. Detroit: Gale Research, 1989. 198-99.

B64 "One of the Masterpiece Novels of Our Time Scans European History". Rev. of *The Death of My Brother Abel*, by Gregor von Rezzori. *The Weekend Citizen* [*The Ottawa Citizen*] 2 Aug. 1986: C2.

B65 "Shipwreck as Told by a Master". Rev. of *The Story of a Shipwrecked Sailor*, by Gabriel García Márquez. *The Weekend Citizen* [*The Ottawa Citizen*] 9 Aug. 1986: C3.

B66 "From My Notebook, May 1987". *Overland* [Mount Eliza, Victoria, Austral.] 108 (1987): 69-72.

B67 "Waltzing along the Songlines to Creation". Rev. of *The Songlines*, by Bruce Chatwin. *The Ottawa Citizen* 29 Aug. 1987: C3.

B68 "Turning Ugliness into Beauty: Australian Author Lets His Imagination Create Fiction Out of a Triple-Murder Legend". Rev. of *Captivity Captive*, by Rodney Hall. *The Ottawa Citizen* 13 Feb. 1988: C3.

B69 "Fun with Oscar and Lucinda: Kind and Gentle Odd Couple Turned into Interesting 'Good' Characters for Once". Rev. of *Oscar and Lucinda*, by Peter Carey. *The Ottawa Citizen* 28 May 1988: C3.

B70 "Afterword". *Sunshine Sketches of a Little Town*. By Stephen Leacock. The New Canadian Library. Toronto: McClelland & Stewart, 1989. 187-91.

B71 "Leaving Home: A Memoir". *More Than Words Can Say: Personal Perspectives on Literacy*. Fwd. Knowlton Nash. Toronto: McClelland & Stewart, 1990. 104-13.

B72 "Down the Red Dirt Road...". *The Review* [*The Weekend Australian*] [Sydney, New South Wales, Austral.] 9-10 June 1990: 3-4.

B73 "Last Voyage of Hero: Tapestry of Raging Swipes through Violent History". Rev. of *The General in His Labyrinth*, by Gabriel García Márquez. *The Ottawa Citizen* 27 Oct. 1990: I3.

B74 "So This Is What It Means To Be Bogged". *Island* [Sandy Bay, Tasmania, Austral.] 50 (1992): 31-35. *OF*.

B75 "Breathing from Some Other World: On Writing the Spit Delaney Stories". *How Stories Mean*. Ed. John Metcalf and J.R. (Tim) Struthers. Erin, ON: Porcupine's Quill, 1993. 202-12. *PN* (revised).

B76 "*Over Forty in Broken Hill*: Two Excerpts". *Australian & New Zealand Studies in Canada* 9 (1993): 71-80. *OF*.

B77 "Some Thoughts on Writing Fiction: Brief Notes to Myself". *How Stories Mean*. Ed. John Metcalf and J.R. (Tim) Struthers. Erin, ON: Porcupine's Quill, 1993. 142-53. *PN* (revised).

B78 "This Ain't No Dude Ranch for Roughing-It-in-the-Bush Wannabes". *The Globe and Mail* [Toronto] 27 Feb. 1993: F9. Rpt. (revised) as "Psychic R&R at a Working Sheep Ranch in Queensland." *Los Angeles Times* 26 Sept. 1993: L1, L10.

B79 ——, et al. "Memorable Images: The Winner of the SmithBooks/Books in Canada First Novel Award Is John Steffler's *The Afterlife of George Cartwright*". *Books in Canada* Apr. 1993: 12-13.

B80 "Il Porcellino". *Writing Away: The PEN Travel Anthology*. Ed. Constance Rooke. Toronto: McClelland & Stewart, 1994. 98-108.

B81 "*Graduation:* The World Needs Your Dreams; Vancouver Island Writer Jack Hodgins Recalls the 'Deceptive Nature of Education'". *UBC Reports* [U of British Columbia, Vancouver, BC] 15 June 1995: 7.